Ebook ISBN 978-1-83889-349-1

Kindle ISBN 978-1-83889-348-4

Audio CD ISBN 978-1-83889-345-3

MP3 CD ISBN 978-1-80280-266-5

Digital audio download ISBN 978-1-83889-346-0

Boldwood Books Ltd
23 Bowerdean Street
London SW6 3TN
www.boldwoodbooks.com

WE BELONG TOGETHER

BETH MORAN

First published in Great Britain in 2021 by Boldwood Books Ltd.

Cover Design by Debbie Clement Design

Cover Photography: Shutterstock

A CIP catalogue record for this book is available from the British Library.

Paperback ISBN 978-1-83889-347-7

Large Print ISBN 978-1-80280-345-7

Hardback ISBN 978-1-80280-207-8

For Julia Childerhouse

As iron sharpens iron, so a friend sharpens a friend.

1

As I hurtled down the country lane, horrendously lost and half blind with panic due to fleeing for my life, sanity and quite possibly my soul, it was perhaps understandable that I didn't spot the sheep in time. A sudden crack of lightning through the rain-splattered windscreen revealed it to be about five metres closer than whatever the stopping distance was for apocalyptic tornado-like conditions.

Screeching in horror, I automatically wrenched the steering wheel to the right while jamming on the brakes, skidding into the opposite lane and praying that no one else would be stupid enough to be out here at five in the morning.

A few terrifying moments later, as I tried to remember how to undo the seatbelt, I swapped that prayer into hoping that someone would not only be heading my way, but carrying a tow rope and whatever else it would take to haul this hunk of junk back out of the ditch I'd ended up in.

I closed my eyes, dropping my head to rest against the steering wheel as I fought to steady my rasping breath, and tried to ignore the creaks of the wheels straddled between the grass verge on one side and the muddy bank on the other.

'Come on, Eleanor, get a grip,' I eventually croaked. 'You can't stay here for the rest of the night.'

Or could I? Huddling in the tiny seat, a loose spring poking into my backside, I contemplated whether the best thing to do was sit it out until the storm cleared and the sun came up.

A sudden *thud* against the passenger window startled me out of my stupor. I scrabbled about for the interior light switch, feeling a mix of dread and hope as I finally managed to pop open the seat belt and shuffled across to peer through the blurry window.

'Baaa!' The sheep – presumably the same one, I

didn't get that good a look at it the first time – knocked its nose against the window, giving me another jolt. Slumping back into the driver's seat, I resumed the head-against-the-steering-wheel-until-a-better-solution-miraculously-presents-itself position.

It was January. Four days earlier I had celebrated the new year, ripe with promise and potential, in a Welsh castle, surrounded by the rich, famous and genuinely fabulous. Wearing an outfit that came with the compliments of a hot new British designer, swigging sophisticated cocktails and sampling food created with the express purpose of impressing me, as the revellers chanted down to midnight I leaned over and kissed my gorgeous boyfriend, who whispered that this would be the Best Year Ever. And I had agreed with him. Now, half-buried in a ditch, the tatty remains of my life spilling across the back seat, thunder and lightning booming in my ears, fear and exhaustion rattling my bones, I changed my mind. Which made sense, seeing as nearly everything else he'd ever said to me had turned out to be a crock of lies.

But enough wallowing. If the sheep wasn't going to help, I'd better come up with another plan. I grabbed my phone from my bag and clicked to contacts.

Okay... who to call?

Not my parents. They were hundreds of miles away, and would be blissfully asleep for another hour at least.

Not Marcus, obviously, since he was a scumbag liar who I was never talking to again.

My thumb hovered over Lucy. As someone who worked for me, was it okay to wake her up this early in the morning and ask her to come to my rescue? Maybe, but considering that later today I'd be terminating her internship, it hardly seemed fair. Besides, she couldn't drive. What was she going to do, order an Uber to pick me up from 'shallow ditch, winding road, back of beyond, somewhere in the Midlands'?

Were you supposed to call the police under these circumstances? I twisted round to see if I could tell whether the back half of the car was sticking into the road. Thanks to the sizeable verge, I didn't think so. Could I call them anyway, or was that a waste of police time, given that there was no emergency? I wasn't hurt beyond several bumps and bruises, and a quick check of the car door confirmed that I was quite capable of exiting the vehicle without assistance.

And once I had to provide my name, let alone other details like why I was here in the first place, driving through the heart of a severe weather warning in what might possibly have once been a stolen vehicle in the middle of the night...

I didn't want to go there.

The perfect person to call was Charlie. While she was unlikely to be able to help, as the person who I was on my way to visit, she lived at least somewhere in the area and would surely know someone who could. Either way, she would turn the whole thing into a hilarious story by the end of the call, and have a bath running and a hot chocolate waiting for me when I finally made it to her farmhouse.

But I couldn't call Charlie, because the last phone number I'd had for her had stopped working over a year ago, around the same time she disappeared on social media for the hundredth time since I'd met her.

I opened the maps app to find out the name of the road I was on, in case I could persuade a local taxi firm or an all-night breakdown service to come and help. Bolstered by discovering that I was on Ferrington Lane, given that the village nestled into the border of Charlie's family farm was Ferrington, I began searching, managing to type in 'taxi' right before the screen went black.

And yes, while racing about my flat chucking random stuff into bags four hours earlier, I'd forgotten my charger.

This was not good news.

I slipped a few inches lower in the seat, shrinking my hands up into my coat sleeves and tugging the hood over my head.

A couple of tears may have trickled out – my face was too numb with cold to feel anything. At this point, I had two choices: clamber out, wade through the rapidly swelling ditch water, and wander about in the storm until either I found help, someone found me, or I died of exposure. Or I could wait it out until morning and spend the time trying to figure out what my next move was, or even better getting some sleep.

Resigned to option two, I gingerly climbed into the back and buried myself under a pile of clothes. The slight tilt of the car meant that I had to wedge myself in a half-sitting position so I didn't topple forwards into the footwell. The rain continued to hammer the car from every angle, even as the flashes of lightning grew fainter and the storm gradually blew into the distance. Eyes fixed on the deep darkness, I watched for the first glimpse of sunrise.

* * *

I was woken up sometime later by a glare of light accompanied by the sound of tapping on the window and a man's voice. 'Hello?'

Jerking upright, my stiff limbs sending jumpers flying, I hastily rubbed the sleep from my eyes. It took a few gormless seconds for me to remember where I was, what had happened, and who I was. Tugging my coat around mismatched pyjamas (I'd left in a hurry), I braced myself. The man opened the car door, the glow of the sunrise casting his face in shadow.

'Are you okay? Can you move, or are you hurt?'

'I'm okay.'

He leant in and offered a hand to help me

clamber out, steadying me as I navigated the gap between the back of the car and the sodden grass.

Ouch.

In answer to his second question, yes, I hurt. Almost everywhere. My numb fingers found a bump on the side of my forehead, coming away smudged with blood, and I vaguely remembered my head smacking against the window as I'd bounced into the ditch. The man released one elbow, and I staggered, my knees buckling until he grabbed it again, peering anxiously into my face.

'Are you all right to ride in my car? It's about thirty minutes to the hospital. If I call an ambulance it could take hours to get here.'

'No!' I shook my head, instantly regretting it as a bolt of pain ricocheted around my skull, but my voice was a hoarse whisper and I needed him to understand. 'I don't need to go to hospital. I'm just stiff and a bit sore.'

I straightened my body as far as possible to prove it, biting back a wince as I took a step away from his grip, managing to stop wobbling after a couple of seconds.

'I really think you ought to get checked out.'

I shook my head. 'No. Thank you.'

We stood there for a moment, surrounded by the stillness of the storm's aftermath. Murky fields stretched out beyond the verges on either side of the road, the horizon crowned with the scattered silhouettes of bare trees against a background of soft pink and gold, watery streaks of winter dawn. The man, who looked to be somewhere in his early thirties, glanced at the muddy Jeep parked a few metres away and then back to me.

'I can drop you at the surgery then. The nurse will be able to get you cleaned up.' He gestured at my head, frowning.

'Honestly, it's a few bumps and scrapes. What I really need is a hot shower and a change of clothes.' I did my best to put on a nice, normal smile. 'But my phone died last night so I can't get hold of anyone. Would you have time to give me a lift to Damson Farm? I got totally lost last night, so I don't even know what direction it's in.'

He folded his arms, the frown deepening.

'It's near Ferrington. Salters Lane?'

'I know where it is.'

Well, that was a start. Although he didn't appear very willing to take me there.

'Or, if you don't have time, could I quickly borrow your phone and call a taxi?' My weary legs wobbled again, causing me to suck in a sharp breath as pain shot up my back. I limped back a few steps and leant against the side of my car, which promptly slipped several inches further into the ditch.

'Come on.' The man had grabbed my arm just in time to stop me tumbling backwards into the empty space where the car had been. He started walking me over to his car, one arm around my waist as I rested my weight against his thick raincoat, too spent to argue.

'Oh, I need my stuff!' I only remembered this crucial information once I'd reached the Jeep and he'd helped boost me into the passenger seat. Before I could say anything else, he'd jogged back and fetched my shoulder bag. Finding the keys still in the ignition, he locked the car.

'No, my things from the back. And the boot.'

'I'll fetch them later.' He slid up into the seat next to me.

'I really need to change my clothes.' Or, more accurately, change into clothes that didn't create the impression I'd absconded from a care home.

'It's fine.'

'No, it really isn't fine!' He started the Jeep and began pulling away, leaving me beginning to wonder just who I'd willingly climbed into a vehicle with on a deserted road at no-witnesses o'clock. For all I knew he was part of this whole thing – *you idiot, Eleanor!* I swivelled my aching neck around to get proper look at him. Hmmm. Tufts of dark hair poking out from under his woolly hat. More than a smidgen of stubble covering a tough-looking jaw and mouth set in a firm line. Wary hazel eyes fixed on the road ahead. I didn't think his thick, curling eyelashes were relevant to this assessment, but the faint scar slashing from his eyebrow down to his earlobe was undeniably interesting. His hands were definitely working hands. Rough hands. Murderer's hands, ready to strangle a woman and leave her for dead in a dirty ditch, far enough away from her abandoned car not to arouse suspicion?

As if echoing my increasingly lurid thoughts, a thin wail erupted behind me. The driver simply sighed.

I inched my head further round to find a baby in a car seat. I didn't know a lot about babies, but from what I could make out of this one, face poking out from the giant orange ski-suit thing she was engulfed in, she was too small to walk, or talk. Her eyes closed as she took a deep breath and let out another wail, scrunching her tiny face up and waving stubby arms, hands hidden in the sleeves of the suit.

Without taking his eyes off the road, the man flicked a button, the pulsing tones of hardcore dance music filling the car.

'Really?' I couldn't help asking. Even I knew this was not standard lullaby fare. But within a matter of seconds, the baby had stopped crying, stuffed a suit cuff in her mouth and now stared at me with giant hazel eyes, as solemn and unnerving as her dad's.

And while the frenetic music pounded at my headache, I felt a prickle of excitement at the choice of tune. This was one of Charlie's favourites. A coincidence – or a sign?

I was about to find out. Before the first song had come to an end we had turned off the road and bumped our way down an unpaved track up to Damson Farm. I rested my head against the back of the seat and blew out a long sigh. The dashboard display told me it was 8.17 a.m. The odds were a three-way split that Charlie would either still be in bed, still be up from the night before, or be up and dressed and on her way out the door to catch a helicopter. Either way, I really hoped she'd be in. I was in desperate need of a bathroom, a cup of tea and somewhere I could rest my battered bones.

To my surprise, my rescuer not only got out of the Jeep, but unclipped the baby from her seat and walked with me towards the main house. The farmhouse was not quite how Charlie had described it. She'd told me stories of a place bursting with life and colour, chickens pecking about, semi-wild cats slinking round every corner and dogs greeting visitors with a wagging tail. This place felt deserted. Like a ghost farm. Faded, chipped paintwork on the door and shuttered windows. A dead clematis hanging off a rotting trellis beside the front door. The weather didn't help, admittedly, gloomy skies reflecting off the grey puddles pooling in the gravel yard, but there was nothing else. Not a pot plant or a hanging basket. Not a bird singing in the distance or a string of lights left over from Christmas. Just quite a few straggly weeds.

This did not look like the kind of place my best friend would live. For the first time, I felt a stab of anxiety that maybe she wouldn't be here.

But I shook that off, even as I limped across, concentrating so my trainers didn't slip on the wet slabs that formed a square in front of the door. Damson Farm had belonged to Charlie's family for generations. She belonged to the farm. If she'd moved on, she'd have told me. She always had before. But the tweak of hesitation was enough to allow the man to stride past me, open the door and step right in. After a moment dithering, my bladder compelled me to follow him, moving through a hallway and finding myself in the kitchen that Charlie had told me about so many times. Again, the picture she'd created of hustle and bustle, baking and cooking, the Aga always warm, the kettle always steaming, was a million miles away from this cluttered, soulless, decidedly grubby and sad-looking room.

The man dropped his car keys onto a pile of mess on a dresser. 'There's a bathroom across the hall.' He nodded towards the entrance hall, paved with the same dark red tiles as the kitchen. It was when I glanced back that I spotted the highchair. The empty baby bottles amongst the mound of dirty pots by the sink. The pram pushed up against one wall.

This was his house. His and the baby's house. So, where was Charlie?

My brain stuck there, unable to process the possibility of what a man and a baby in Charlie's house could mean. I ducked across into the bathroom and spent a hasty five minutes sorting myself out as best I could – which wasn't very much, given what I was working with. After an initial glance in the mirror I had to steel myself before I could face a closer inspection. I'd lost my hat at some point during the night, and my deep brown mahogany-on-a-good-day hair was now a matted mess. Huge greyish-purply rings surrounded each listless, bloodshot blue eye. The bump on my head was smeared with dried blood, speckles of which also covered the rest of my face. And if you could find a foundation to match this skin-tone it would have been called 'hint of corpse'.

Lovely. I splashed water on my face, dabbing gently at the blood stains with some toilet roll, and wondered why on earth this man had let me in his car, let alone his house.

I didn't wonder for long. My frazzled brain had far more important things to worry about right then. And to be honest, if he had turned out to be one of the bad guys, as long as he let me sit down and maybe have a hot drink before bludgeoning me to death, I couldn't summon up the energy to care.

I returned to the kitchen to find a steaming mug sitting on the table, opposite where he sat with a matching mug, the baby next to him in the highchair giving the impression of a very unorthodox interview panel. Hat and hood off, I could see they both had the same thick, tufty dark hair. I gingerly lowered myself into a seat, before taking a few sips of scalding, sugary tea while I fought through the fog to come up with something to say.

'Thanks again. I dread to think what would have happened if you'd not arrived when you did.'

The man shrugged. 'You'd have slept a bit longer until someone else came along.'

'But they wouldn't have lived at Damson Farm.' I paused, questioningly. 'I presume you do live here?'

He nodded.

'I'm kind of surprised you brought me here without asking any questions about who I am.'

'You weren't in a fit state to answer any questions.'

I took another gulp of tea, my hand barely able to lift the mug up to my mouth.

'So, now that you've warmed up and are sitting down, why are you here?'

'I'm a friend of Charlie's. Charlie Perry.'

His eyebrows raised slightly, before he quickly pulled his features back into neutral. 'She's not here.'

I felt a rush of relief that at least he knew who she was, that this was the right Damson Farm, that she hadn't made the whole thing up to cover up a boring childhood living in a three-bed detached house in the suburbs. 'Well, I guess that's not so surprising. Do you know when she'll be back, or have any contact details so I can let her know I'm here?'

'Given you're having to ask me that, you clearly aren't that good a friend.'

'The last number she gave me hasn't been working. I assumed she'd lost her phone again.'

'Look, no offence but Charlie made a lot of *friends*. If you're someone she met in a hostel somewhere, or worked in a bar with for a few weeks, then I'm sorry but she's not here. I can give you the number for a garage who'll tow your car to wherever you're headed next, and drop you there once you've finished your tea.' He bent down to pick up the crinkly fabric doll the baby had gleefully thrown onto the floor, then stood up, making it clear that I had finished my drink, whether I'd actually finished it or not.

It took nearly everything I'd got, but I heaved myself to my feet, too, gripping the chair with both hands.

'I know Charlie makes friends everywhere she goes, which is a stupid number of places. I know she drops everything and moves on after a random conversation or an out-of-date flyer catches her attention. I know that she disappears completely for months at a time and then turns up again as if she'd never been gone. I also know that this is the only place she's ever called home. I know this because she's invited me here tons of times during the twelve years we've been friends. The last time I heard from her she said she'd be staying here for at least a year, probably a lot longer. And this time I believe she meant it.'

He eyed me silently for a long moment, his hand reaching up to stroke the scar on the side of his face. 'Eleanor?'

'Yes! Yes, I'm Eleanor.'

'Okay.' He let out a long, slow sigh, and for the first time I noticed how tired and drawn he looked. His hazel eyes were utterly forlorn. 'I'm sorry to have to tell you this, like this, after you've clearly had a crap night. But Charlie died.'

What?

The words engulfed me in a torrent of devastation – shock and anguish crashing up through my stomach and lungs, my heart, until it hit my brain.

Breathless, distraught, I could only reply with a gaping mouth and shaking head before everything went blurry and then black.

2

I woke to find myself lying on a sofa, an older woman peering at me, one hand on my wrist. A mass of curly salt and pepper hair framed her head in a huge circle, and glasses dangled on a chain over her thick aran sweater.

'Ah! There you are!' She offered a brief smile. 'I hear you've had a bit of a night of it.'

I swivelled one eye to see the man loitering behind her, his expression tight.

'Do you know where you are?' the woman asked.

'Damson Farm?' I managed to mumble. *A living nightmare?*

'Excellent. I'm Doctor Ziva Solomon. Can you tell me your name?'

I closed my eyes, concentrating so I got the right one. 'Eleanor Sharpley.'

'Ah-ah, keep your eyes open. Look at me. Watch my finger. Very good. What day is it today, Eleanor?'

She asked me a few more questions along those lines – *keep looking at me!* – while simultaneously prodding about my person, before nodding briskly. 'Bumps and bruises, but nothing serious. I'd put the fainting down to exhaustion, shock and excessively low blood sugar. What do you reckon?'

I reckoned I'd feel much better if I was allowed to close my eyes and lie here in peace for a few weeks.

'I'm prescribing more sweet tea, some decent painkillers and a round of hot toast.' She placed a cool, wet cloth on my head and it felt like I'd died and gone to heaven...

Died... Someone's died. Charlie. Oh, Charlie.

My face crumpled, the pain in my forehead intensifying as the tears began to flow, my heart contracting with sorrow. Charlie had died and I hadn't even known. I'd assumed... just thought that... no one had told me... my *best friend* and she'd gone... I hadn't even been at her funeral, said goodbye...

Pelted by one realisation after another, I curled over and gripped the cushion beside me, wrapping myself around it as if that could protect me.

I sobbed, probably wailed a few times, dribbled snot and tears and goodness knows what else on the cushion. But I couldn't care less that I was in a strange house, with a strange man and his matching baby, pouring out unbridled emotion while crumpled on his sofa.

The doctor was there for a while, patting my shoulder and telling me how sorry she was. And then she was gone, and it was just the man, pulling up a low table and placing tea and toast on it, jiggling the baby on his hip and offering me a piece of kitchen roll.

A good while later, and by that point I could have failed the doctor's 'what day is it' test, my tears dribbled to a stop. I took a few slow breaths, wiped my face with the remains of the kitchen roll clutched in my hand, pushed my hair off my face and creaked to a sitting position.

I looked at the tea. The man stood up from where

he'd been sitting in an office chair. 'I'll make you a fresh one.'

I managed a weak smile as he nodded at the baby, curled up in one of those baby bouncers, head tilted to one side, chewing absentmindedly on her fist as she stared at me. 'Can you keep an eye on this one?'

Not waiting for me to reply, he grabbed the toast plate and disappeared. I took the time to appraise the room – too small to be the main living room in a house this big, it looked like a sort of nursery-study hybrid, with a desk underneath the large sash window opposite me, covered in papers, mugs and other mess. The wall to one side contained bookshelves stuffed with books, folders and other random items. The wall across from that had a changing table pushed up against it, on top of which was a mountain of tiny clothes, a packet of nappies, several of which were spilling out, wipes, bottles, a dummy and other baby related paraphernalia. The floor was relatively empty, but a pile of clutter in the space between the desk and the changing table implied that this was because everything had been shoved out of the way to create a path to the sofa. The walls were bare, the paintwork shabby. The grimy window was framed by a wonky blind. Looking up, a bare bulb swung amongst trails of cobwebs. This room was worse than the kitchen. Full of stuff, but empty of all warmth or beauty.

The man returned, placing a mug in my hand and fresh toast on the table.

'Thank you.'

He nodded.

'I'm so sorry for ruining your day like this.' Sorry, and embarrassed.

'And I'm sorry you had to hear such bad news straight after crashing your car.'

'If you could call that garage, I'll get out of your way as soon as possible.' I took a tentative bite of thick, buttery toast, resisting the urge to groan in relief.

'I already called. The car's... not *fine*... but shall we say, no worse than it was before rolling into the ditch. They'll drop it off later.'

'Thanks. You've been unnecessarily kind.'

He shrugged, burying his face in his own mug. 'Charlie would have done the same.'

'Probably.'

He looked up, the faint tug of a smile on his lips. 'And then cooked you a three-course dinner before inviting you to move in.'

'She'd have burned the dinner, though, left the kitchen a total wreck and ordered a pizza.'

He full-on smiled then. 'That sounds about right.'

I chewed slowly on another bite of toast, working up to my question. 'Um... can I ask what happened?'

'How she died?' He sighed, putting the mug down and deftly plucking the baby out of her chair and tucking her into his chest before continuing. For the first time I clicked that this could be Charlie's baby, but before I could ask, her dad spoke again. 'This is Hope. Charlie's daughter. She was born in June.'

A girl. Dressed in a green top and blue trousers, it had been impossible to be sure. I mean, she was incredibly cute, with thick hair and huge eyes, a tiny nose and round, rosy cheeks, but don't most babies look that pretty?

'Charlie had... struggled with being pregnant. And afterwards, she got worse. We discovered later it was post-partum psychosis. She was last seen by the old Ferrington Bridge. They found her a few days later.' He shrugged, face blank, but his voice had cracked on the words. 'We'll never know what happened, but I've reached the conclusion it doesn't make any difference.'

'I'm so sorry.' My voice hitched, but what else was there to say? I was sorry for him, desperately sorry for Charlie who had wrestled with what she called the 'evil brain-death demons' for most of her life, and at the time she had most needed to live, they had won. Sorry for the rest of us who had to live on without her. But sorry most of all for this beautiful little girl who would grow up without her mother.

Charlie had saved me, from myself, and now I felt awash with regret that when she'd needed someone to talk her down – when she most needed someone to believe in her, I'd been oblivious. Slurping champagne and stuffing myself with cuttlefish tortellini, swanning about in my free clothes and worrying about how many millions of people liked me. When I should have been worrying about one of the very tiny number of people who loved me.

The pain of grief, so much harder to bear than

my superficial scrapes, my aching head and stiff muscles, settled over me like a thick, black blanket.

And there it stayed.

* * *

I'd met Charlie at Birmingham University. Under different circumstances I'm sure we'd never have spoken – for no other reason than she wouldn't have noticed me. But we were both studying English, both had flats in the same accommodation block, and by the time we'd walked back from our first tutorial together, she'd basically decided we were friends.

She invited herself over to my room for a drink, stopping off at the student shop for me to buy a bottle of vodka and some Coke, when I admitted that all I had was teabags. I then had to admit I only had one mug and no glasses.

After rifling through my sparse wardrobe, inspecting the solitary photograph on my desk, she plonked herself down on the bed, poured a generous splash of vodka into the glasses she'd pilfered from the shared kitchen and made her pronouncement:

'Eleanor Sharpley, you are in dire need of my help.'

I didn't disagree.

'But that's perfect, because I think I need you, too. We're an ideal match.'

She held up her glass to chink mine, before taking a long gulp.

'Firstly, why don't you have any stuff? Your capsule wardrobe says, "highly organised, overly sensible person". But who comes to uni with one mug and no glasses? It's like you didn't even consider the possibility of having a friend over.'

'I had to bring whatever I could carry on the train.' And no, I genuinely never expected to have anyone over.

'No parents to drive you?' She leant back against the wall, sweeping long, silvery-platinum hair off her forehead.

'They don't have a car. I don't think they know how to drive. And they work all weekend. It never crossed their mind to come with me.' It hadn't really crossed mine either until I'd arrived the first day of freshers' week and seen the queue of cars, jolly parents humping crates and suitcases, boxes of food and duvets up the stairs. My mum had handed me a tenner and a tub of scones and got back to scrubbing the bannisters.

It wasn't that they didn't care, they just didn't get it. Me leaving home and becoming a student was a world they couldn't imagine, let alone understand. They were sort of proud of their only child, but they were also bemused I hadn't been content to stay on and help run the Tufted Duck bed and breakfast they owned on the edge of Lake Windermere.

'So, tell me one fact that sums up all I need to know about your life so far.'

I took my first tentative sip of vodka and Coke, blinking as the burn melted into a warm buzz in my belly. 'Up until last week, I shared a bedroom with my grandma.'

'No!'

'I had the top bunk.'

Charlie burst out laughing. 'Perfect! That's brilliant! It explains everything! Did you pack up her side of the wardrobe by mistake?' She leant over and nudged my arm, to soften the tease. 'I mean, don't get me wrong, I love you already, but you look like you brought your old school uniform.'

Um, that's because I did? It was the only jacket I owned, and I might need to look smart for an interview or something. I'd picked the school badge off, of course.

'So, what's your fact?' A couple more sips gave me the courage to return the question.

Charlie thought for a while, twirling a strand of hair around one finger. 'I ended up spending my first night here in the Aston Villa football team *executive area* in some nightclub. Only I lost my bag, with my phone and bank card in it. I've got about three days' worth of food, if I'm careful. If the farm still had a landline I could call home and ask my parents to send me some money, but nobody bothers memorising mobile numbers, do they?'

'Can't you go to the bank and sort something out?'

She shrugged. 'I can't remember which bank it is. I just used the app.'

'Okay. I think we can probably come up with something before you starve to death.'

'Awesome!' Charlie topped up our glasses for another toast.

And that about summed up the next three years of our lives, and a good few years after that. Charlie was my first real friend, and it turned out that despite her befriending everyone, I was hers, too. She careened through her first year, always breathless from rushing in late, if she managed to turn up at all. She joined half the clubs in the university, and left them all again. Sang in the musical one term, sprinted in the athletics club the next. Holidays and weekends were one adventure after another, whether that was a part-time job as a roadie for a rock band, or a day trip to London that evolved into a week in Paris. She lived for the moment, making the most of all the ones she could. Because, all too frequently, with shocking speed and devastating impact, the evil brain demons would come crashing in. She'd disappear for days, sometimes weeks, on one occasion two months at a time. Buried under her duvet, her colour extinguished by the darkness. Her eyes empty, words lifeless.

I would call her mum, who'd sometimes come and bundle her back to Damson Farm, the place where she'd always eventually find some peace again, and gradually her joy would return like the apple blossom in her orchard after a long, hard winter.

We swapped her clothes for my lecture notes. Party invitations for study sessions. Towards the end of the first year, she cajoled me out on my first date, followed by my first kiss with a lovely boy who I think only went along with it because he was besotted with Charlie. She spent one Easter and a few weeks the following summer working at the Tufted Duck, charming my parents and grandma along with all the guests, until she was caught in bed with a guest's seventeen-year-old son.

Before Charlie, I had been a girl who shared bunkbeds with her grandma.

With Charlie, I was a woman who saw life as brimming with endless possibility.

And without her? I would maybe one day try to be the person she believed me to be.

Once I'd stopped crying, put some decent clothes on and found myself somewhere to live, that is.

3

After our brief conversation, baby Hope started crying, so the man, whose name I should really have known by now, spent a while changing her nappy and giving her a bottle and walking up and down until she would settle, just long enough for him to put her back in the baby chair where she'd start bawling again.

'I think we'll try a walk,' he said, after the third attempt. 'She normally spends Fridays with my mum, and I'm supposed to be in a video call at three. She really needs to go to sleep.'

'What time is it now?'

'Two-thirty.'

'I could take her for a walk?'

He looked me up and down. 'I'll see if Ziva's still in the orchard. She won't mind.'

Before stuffing Hope back into her ski-suit and wheeling her out in the giant pushchair from the kitchen, he brought me an oversized rainbow jumper and silver leggings that I could tell with one glance belonged to Charlie, and offered me the use of the shower.

'Help yourself to more tea, and whatever food you can find. Apart from the bananas – they're Hope's.'

'Thank you. And I'm sorry again for wrecking your day.'

'Yeah. I'm sorry for upsetting you, too.'

And with that, I was all alone in the farmhouse of a man I'd only just met and whose name I didn't know, about to shower and change into someone else's clothes. 'Are you taking the mickey, here, Charlie?' I whispered into the silence. 'Landing me in one of your adventures?'

I might have heard the echo of a giggle wafting in from the kitchen, but by then I was crying again, so it was impossible to tell for sure.

My host found me much later, crashed out with my face stuck to the kitchen table. I woke with a start, followed by a yelp as my sore muscles protested at the movement.

'Has my car arrived?' I asked, once I'd accepted some painkillers and a glass of water, wincing with the pain of moving my head enough to swallow without spilling.

'Yes. But... you really aren't fit to drive.'

'I'm not going far. I'll be fine.' What else was I going to do?

'Ziva said you needed to be kept an eye on for at least the rest of the day.' He took a small plastic bowl from the pile on the draining board, peering at it before giving it a wipe with a tea-towel.

'There'll be people there to keep an eye on me.'

'Where?'

'What?'

'Where is this place, and who are the people there who can take care of you?'

'With all due respect,' and I owed him plenty of that, all things considered, 'that's not really your business.'

'I think you'd best stay the night here,' he sighed,

lifting a banana from a bowl on the table and starting to mash it up, Hope banging out her anticipation on the tray of the highchair.

'I can't stay here!' I mustered as much indignation as I could, given my current shambolic state. 'I don't want to stay here.'

'I don't massively want you to stay here, either. But you're Charlie's best friend. She invited you. I can't let you head off in that excuse for a car when we both know that you haven't a clue where you're going.'

'Er, have you considered that I might think driving a short distance in my recently garage-inspected car to a nearby Travelodge on the way to my parents' house is far safer than spending the night in the middle of nowhere with a strange man whose name I don't even know?'

'Daniel Perry.'

'Daniel?' I repeated, as another piece of the puzzle clicked into place. 'You're Charlie's brother.'

'Well, yes. Who did you think I was?'

'Hope's father.'

'I am Hope's father.' He took a seat next to her,

offering her one plastic spoon to wave about while he scooped banana onto the other one.

'What?' My brain was too tired to process this.

'I adopted her.'

'So... does she have a biological father?'

'Well, she's not a clone.' He bristled, clearly not comfortable with the conversation taking this direction. 'Charlie never said who it was. I don't think she ever told him.'

He didn't add: *if she even knew who it was.*

'And you adopted Hope?'

He shrugged, using the spoon to wipe up a blob of food on the baby's cheek like a pro. 'She'd been living here since she was born. I was hardly going to pack her off to social services.'

'What about your mum?' Charlie's mum, Billie, who I'd met the few times she'd picked Charlie up from university, and with whom I'd exchanged anxious (me) and resigned (her) conversations a few times since.

'She lives in Ferrington, now. She sold off most of the land and then married and moved out a couple of years after Dad died. She couldn't fit a baby into her cottage.' He paused, ran a finger absentmindedly down his scar. 'She hasn't been back to the farm since Charlie's funeral.'

'Wow.'

'Yeah.'

I wondered how Daniel had managed it. Juggling work, grieving for his sister, dealing with the aftermath of such tragedy as well as a baby. No wonder the house was a shambles.

'Charlie never mentioned that Billie remarried.'

'She didn't know until afterwards. Mum wanted a quiet wedding. No drama. Charlie wasn't in a good place around then.'

I did some mental calculations. Charlie's dad had suffered a fatal heart attack not long after we started renting a flat together in London, four years ago. I was twenty-six. So Billie married when we were twenty-eight. I'd moved to a new flat by then. Charlie had left two days before Christmas and I'd given up waiting for her to come back (or pay any rent). I remembered a message on Valentine's Day:

Wishing my 1 true love a beautiful V-day, hope U get to spend it with someone special.

I replied several times, messaging and calling to ask where she was and to let me know if she was okay. One reply arrived, a few days later:

Yh I'm cool met a guy who got me a waitress job, bit mad out here but fun.

That was the last time I heard from her until the final messages, sent just over a year ago:

BACK AT THE FARM. WHY AREN'T U HERE?? PLEEEEEEAAASE VISIT. STAYING FOR GOOD THIS TIME. LOTS OF NEWS, I'LL EXPLAIN WHEN UR HERE.

I'd sent a brief message explaining that I had work engagements booked out for several months ahead, but I'd see what I could do. She sent one last reply:

EL I NEED U! It's different this time. PROMISE. Please come whenever you can xxx

But I'd grown tired of Charlie's chaotic interruptions, hurtling back into my life, letting me down and disappearing again. Also, if I'm honest, because I'd become so caught up in my own life – which had morphed into something I'd never had foreseen – I never got around to it. Until now. When I needed her.

I don't know quite how or when but, without ever meaning to, at some point I had become a horrible, self-obsessed person.

'So you'll stay?' Daniel asked, snapping me back to the present day. I considered this for a moment. Forced myself to acknowledge my aching limbs, bruised chest, the fog still clogging up my thought processes. Then I tried to picture setting off in the car and hunting for somewhere to sleep before I conked out at the steering wheel. I imagined the look on my parents' faces when I showed up looking like this.

Damson Farm was shabby and dishevelled, and a little bit dirty, if I'm honest. But this was Charlie's home, and I wasn't ready to say goodbye to her yet. Something about this place had wrapped its arms around me and welcomed me in.

Peace.

I realised this later that evening, having managed a bowl of cheap tinned soup and more toast, before Daniel showed me to a bedroom where he'd left my bags neatly lined up against the metal bedframe.

For the first time in forever, despite everything having turned on its head, despite the hideous threats, the turmoil and confusion about my career, I felt cocooned in peace. Maybe because for the first time in forever, I didn't care about any of those things any more.

No wonder Charlie had loved it here.

It was only when I woke up the following lunchtime that I realised I'd never spoken to Lucy.

4

I have a secret identity, of sorts. More like a pen name, an alter ego? Except that for the past year this other me has adopted the physical face of my intern and friend, Lucy. It's a long story...

After graduation, I managed to get a job working on our local newspaper, the *Cumbria Chronicle*, earning a generous twenty pence an hour over minimum wage, making tea, running errands and completing all other tasks that nobody else either wanted or could be bothered to do. Other people who'd got themselves an English degree with a dream of becoming a journalist might have worked to make something of this opportunity – chased down stories, left anonymous articles on the editor's desk, hustled and strategised and begged if necessary for that one big break.

In my head, I was going to do all those things. Once I'd learnt a bit more, grown a little wiser. For now I was pootling along, helping out at the Tufted Duck to top up my income in order to afford luxuries like socks and petrol, and enjoying living in the most beautiful countryside in the UK.

And then Charlie came to visit, and everything changed overnight.

We had eaten out at a recently opened pub on the edge of the town. It was, to put it bluntly, outrageously terrible. The worst meal either of us had ever eaten, served by the most incompetent staff. And then they had the audacity to drop a card on the table asking for an 'honest review' on the Windermere Community Facebook group, in exchange for the chance to win a free meal.

Oh boy. The wannabe journalist in me was roused, fuelled by a nasty bottle of wine and my best friend. The review was most certainly honest:

Having lived in Birmingham, my friend and I have enjoyed our fair share of delicious curries. We've also had a couple that resemble cat sick. The Gourmet Gannet provides the novel experience of a curry that not only looks like vomit, it smells like it, too. At least, we presumed the lukewarm plate of watery yet gloopy slop – a true scientific marvel! – was the curry my friend had requested. The waiter had previously tried to force a steak on her, insisting that my vegetarian companion had ordered it. 'You must have got confused,' he kindly suggested, scarpering away leaving the steak on the table. No, good sir, you're the one confused if you think we're accepting a charred lump of burnt shoe instead of the food we asked for. Poor chap, the whole debacle shook him up so badly that when he brought the alleged curry, he fumbled his grip and tipped the accompanying plate of undercooked rice into my friend's lap. Which, no, was not cleaned up or replaced. Not that she wanted it to be, given that the scattered grains carried a distinctive whiff of rancid fish.

But on to my food, arriving a mere seventeen minutes after the curry. I was tempted to ask if we could have the steak back. How difficult is it to create an inedible burger? Well, the Gourmet Gannet certainly rose to the challenge. Again, this left me questioning everything I knew about the science of matter, being both rubbery, gristly and mushy all at the same time. At fifteen quid, I wasn't expecting Michelin star food. I was, however, hoping for something no worse than Ritzy's Saturday night burger van. You won't be surprised to hear that the chips were burnt on the outside, raw in the middle, and devoid of seasoning, or that the burger bun was both stale and soggy. I can't review the accompanying 'garden salad', because I didn't want to deprive the slug of his single lettuce leaf and shrivelled slice of cucumber. He seemed to be enjoying them far more than I would have.

When I asked for tomato ketchup in an

attempt to render the burger at least slightly edible, I was told, 'We're not that sort of establishment.' That makes sense, considering flavour of any sort seemed to be not their sort of thing. either. I won't bore you with the dirty cutlery or the sticky, dog-eared menus. Neither will I expound on the hairs stuck to the table, or the dead flies in the ladies' loo. I won't blather on about the diners next to us, whose beef and onion pie looked as though it had been dropped on the floor and scooped back up again, nor how when they complained the waiter told them that it 'won't make no difference to the taste'. Because that's their review to give, not mine.

But I will tell you that both my friend and I invented a game called 'grubby waiter bingo', including points for things like nose picking, crotch scratching and coughing on the food, and that both of us got a full house before the bill arrived. I tell you this, because it's not a matter of opinion, as the manager helpfully explained was the reason we disliked the food, but of protecting the health and happiness of the good citizens of Windermere. Gourmet? I don't think so. A Gannet running the kitchen? That might be an improvement.

To my utter amazement, and Charlie's utter delight, the review went bonkers. You could say viral, by Lake District standards. The *Cumbria Chronicle* editor called me into his office, not to fire me, as I'd expected, but to offer me a part-time job writing reviews for the paper, providing I continued with the humour.

Back when I'd tentatively applied to study English at university, with the faint, flimsy hope that maybe one day someone would pay me to write something, I would have been horrified at the thought of mocking and criticising people's livelihoods for a cheap laugh.

But in the three years since graduating I'd had seventeen rejections for the novel I'd submitted to agents and publishers. All attempts at getting a different job with a less tenuous link to writing had failed. I was broke, bored out of my brains and beyond tired of getting up at 5.30 to cook a dozen breakfasts before going to work.

And, more to the point, I was still sleeping in a room so tiny that even with bunkbeds, only one of us could move about in there at a time.

Something needed to change.

I tried to keep things kind, and fair, but the worse the reviews were, the more people loved them. Once a week I found somewhere different – maybe a backwater pub, or a flashy, up-itself brasserie. If the food was okay, I would say that, and then maybe throw in something amusing about a poor member of staff, or the décor. Perhaps how the menu struggled to cater for allergies. I would rope in someone else from the newspaper, or occasionally drag one of the Tufted Duck staff along on some made up pretext. Every few months, Charlie rocked into town and we'd blitz several places in one weekend. Often, I went alone, which led to me more than once being able to write about a slimy waiter's attempts to hit on me. In the two years I wrote for the *Chronicle*, I wrote overwhelmingly positive reviews. I worked hard to find fantastic places to feature as a counterweight to the few necessarily dreadful ones. The first great article was for a restaurant specifically set up to provide training and jobs to those with learning difficulties. The food there was outstanding. Following my review, they were able to open a second restaurant in Kendal. Another was a couple who had a buy-one-share-one scheme, providing a meal for a homeless person for every meal paid for, along with cookery and gardening classes for clients of local foodbanks. One bakery was just so delightful I couldn't find a single bad thing to say about it. A café run by a Somalian couple who'd arrived as asylum seekers a decade earlier was similar. I also gave a fabulous review for the breakfast at the Tufted Duck. Over the months, their popularity grew. Restaurant owners knew that a positive review would see an immediate increase in custom, and the token 'although I was somewhat disappointed by...' mention became like a local in-joke, whereby readers knew if the worst I could come up with was a dodgy ceiling tile in the toilets or a rude fellow diner, then the place was excellent. The power was overwhelmingly terrifying and addictive at the same time.

And then a national newspaper called.

Three weeks later I was living with Charlie in

Crystal Palace. I had a blog, Twitter account and Instagram set up and an actual company credit card. They also insisted on a name, rather than 'The Phantom Food Lover' as I'd been in Windermere. Nora Sharp was born, and she hit the ground running.

Within a year or so, Nora had branched out into events. I started getting invited to book launches and award ceremonies, slipping about undetected in my uninspiring outfits with my boring hair and make-up, pretending to be someone's assistant if anyone bothered to talk to me. My followers grew from the hundreds to the thousands, and within a couple of years had reached the tens of thousands. Despite increasing pressure from my editor to focus on the negatives, as again that received by far the most interest, I tried to maintain my balanced approach, keeping the 'although I was somewhat disappointed...' section short and as sweet as I could get away with. I even started a blog, as Eleanor Sharpley, writing unfailingly glowing reviews to counteract every negative one the paper printed. Yet despite my efforts, even going so far as to have Nora endorse it, no one was interested in reading it (apart from my parents and grandma, who thought this was my real job). In the meantime, Nora continued to thrive in direct correlation to how heavily my articles were edited to maximise the criticism and downplay the praise. My new editor asked me to launch the YouTube channel, right about the same time that Lucy contacted me asking to be my intern.

And that was when things really started getting crazy.

* * *

Having charged my phone overnight using the one yellowing socket in the room and a charger borrowed from Daniel, I quickly scrolled through the Nora Sharp social media accounts. Lucy had added a fairly innocuous tweet and Instagram post about Nora looking forward to a restaurant opening later that week. I checked my emails, but nothing urgent had come in since I'd last checked on Thursday evening.

I called Lucy. I wasn't about to let her go over the phone if I could help it, but I could at least schedule in a video chat for later on (once I'd changed into a decent top and fortified myself with some breakfast).

The call went straight to voicemail. I left a brief message telling her I'd gone away for a few days and asking her to call me as soon as possible, following up with a WhatsApp for good measure.

I also needed to speak to my editor, Miles Greenbank. I definitely needed some caffeine before that conversation, however, and my first attempt at getting out of bed made it clear that I needed painkillers before I could go and get a coffee.

It took me a long, drawn-out, agonising eternity, peppered with yelps of pain and more than a few tears before I was out of the tiny bed and on my trembling feet. Having made it this far, I thought it best to press on, shuffling the short distance to the door and across the hallway to the bathroom. Eyes scrunched to slits, I did what I needed to do while avoiding looking at the rust, the mould or the cobwebs, and hobbled back to bed. I was still figuring out how to climb back into the bed, when there was a soft tap on the door.

'Hello?'

'Hello,' I croaked back.

'Am I all right to come in?'

Considering the events of the past couple of days, this was not a time to start worrying about pride. Or appearances. Or how badly my breath stank, given that I'd not had the energy to bother brushing my teeth. Daniel came in carrying a tray bearing a mug of tea, a sandwich and another dose of pain medication. He paused, frowning at me slumped against the bed on one elbow, ratty hair falling over my face like a witless old crone, before dispensing with the tray and backing out of the room again.

Great. I made one more half-hearted attempt to hoist a knee up on top of the stupidly high bedframe, instead collapsing face-first onto the mattress. Perhaps I could stay here until I recovered enough to slither the rest of myself up to join my top half. Maybe just a short snooze...?

'Here.'

Oh! I twisted my face around to see Daniel placing a wooden stool about a foot high beside me on the faded rug. He busied himself faffing about and doing nothing with the tray so I could clamber into bed with a modicum of privacy.

'Thanks.'

'How are you feeling?' he asked, handing me a glass of water and two pills.

'Can I answer that once these have had a chance to kick in?'

'Is there anything else you need?' He glanced at the ceiling, the floor, the pile of bags against the dresser. This was a box room. The heavy, dark green curtains blocked most of the daylight from entering, and it suddenly felt like an exceedingly small space for two people who had only just met, one of whom was wearing the other's sister's pyjamas.

'I'm fine, thanks. I need to make a couple of work calls, and hopefully by then I'll feel strong enough to get out of your way.'

Daniel sighed, shaking his head slightly. 'I'm taking Hope to Mum's for a couple of hours, after she missed seeing her yesterday. There's some as yet unidentifiable meat in a sauce defrosting for dinner. Hopefully by then you'll feel strong enough to come downstairs and watch whatever crap we can find on TV. If not, that's fine. Here.' He pulled a piece of paper out of his jeans pocket. 'My number. In case you need anything, or get stuck halfway down the stairs or something.'

I nodded, this simple token of kindness causing my throat to seize up with fresh unshed tears. My body wasn't the only thing about me that had arrived at Damson Farm feeling bashed up and broken. Having lost so much in the past few days, and about to sever ties with my last thread of security, knowing I could stay here for a while and do nothing, have no pressure or expectations put upon me – not even coming down the stairs – was the best possible medicine. I drank almost all of my tea, managed three bites of sandwich and then scrolled through photos of Charlie on my phone until I sobbed myself back to sleep.

Calling Lucy, speaking to Miles, would have to wait.

5

For the next few days, I followed the same pattern. If I'm honest, by the Monday I was physically much improved. The stiffness and ache in my limbs and neck were easing, the bruises fading into tie-dyed green and yellow splashes decorating my head and chest. Realistically, if I took it slow, I could probably manage to drive the 180 miles or so to Windermere.

But as the physical pain retreated, it seemed to increasingly expose the deeper pain that lay beneath my bumps and scrapes. My chest squeezed with anguish whenever I thought about Charlie, my emotions wading through denial, shock, bitter regret and deep, deep sorrow.

My phone lay abandoned and out of charge where I'd dropped it somewhere under the bed. Lucy would have been dealing with the emails coming through, sorting any posts or invitations that needed responding to. Vaguely, somewhere in the back of my mind I knew that the longer it took me to tell her that I was letting her go, the longer I'd have to pay her for. I ignored the faint buzz of guilt about not calling her back. We were usually in contact at least once a day, sometimes ten times that many, and my ambiguous message was hardly sufficient to explain what was going on. I knew she'd be worried. But petty issues like my employee, my money, my preposterous job, my life in London, seemed like a hazy hallucination caused by the strong painkillers I was still scarfing in some vain effort at dulling my heartbreak.

Even the threat that had driven me to bolt in the middle of the night seemed unimportant, a thousand miles away.

And surely they'd never find me here, anyway?

Finding it impossible to care, or worry about any of it, instead I lay in bed, crying, sleeping, staring at the stains on the ceiling, picking at the meals Daniel brought me and sinking further and further down into a pit of self-loathing and shame.

I needed to snap out of it. Or at the very least find the gumption and the grit to begin to slowly heave myself out.

Fortunately, Daniel and Dr Ziva agreed.

On Thursday, nearly a week after I skidded into a ditch, Daniel woke me with a mug of tea and a chipped bowl of porridge. A while later he came and retrieved the empty mug and still full bowl but this time he was carrying Hope, and before he took the tray away he plonked her on the bed and left her there.

It was a single bed, probably as wide as it was high. Hope looked as surprised as I was as she sat up and goggled at me, automatically cramming one hand into her mouth.

'Hi,' I managed, sounding like some sort of child-eating troll before I cleared my throat and tried again. She tucked in her chin, eyeing me warily. I tried to think of something else to say.

'How's things? Enjoyed any good bananas lately?'

Okay, apparently not, because her enormous eyes filled up with tears, and her lip began wobbling precariously. *Oh, no. Oh, crap. Please don't start crying. There's been enough of that in this bed for the both of us lately, I promise.*

She looked just like Charlie when discovering that yet another man had deceived her, or she got fired, or when she felt the evil brain-death demons of darkness stirring.

'Please don't cry!' *That's better, try saying it out loud, Eleanor.* 'There, there. I know this room is distressingly ugly, and you've been dumped here with a slightly unhinged woman who hasn't showered in several days, but I'm sure your dad will be back to fetch you soon.'

Only he wasn't. And when, a couple of minutes later, I ran out of small talk and Hope broke into full-on screams, wide open mouth revealing two tiny teeth as she scrunched up her miniature fists and let rip, he still didn't come bursting in to save her. Galvanised by how the pitch of her cries seemed to jab right into the bruise on my forehead, I upped my game. Pulling faces, singing jumbled snatches of nursery rhymes and patting her head did no good at all. And when I tried to take hold of her hand (that always made me feel better) she reacted with an instantaneous increase in both pitch and volume, while simultaneously diving for the edge of the bed.

Crap!

I instinctively jerked forwards and grabbed her around the tummy, pulling her up close as I sat back against the headboard. That seemed to help. The wails faded to a warble, and her body visibly softened as we adjusted ourselves to find a comfortable position.

'There we go, then. Is that better?' I mumbled more meaningless platitudes, leaning my cheek against her downy head as we gently rocked from side to side. After a while, Hope's sobs became sniffles which then dissolved into disconcertingly loud hiccups. She smeared a load of snotty dribble across her face and then batted her hand about, daubing it across my shoulder and pyjama sleeve. Letting out a long sigh, she then slowly tipped her head forwards, conking her chin on her chest as she fell asleep.

After a brief panic while I checked that she was still breathing, I settled back and closed my eyes in solidarity, listening to the sound of our twin breaths. Her heavy warmth nestling against my cracked heart was probably the best cuddle of my life so far. I know she was only a baby, and potentially not that great a judge of character yet, but I felt honoured – astounded even – that Hope trusted me enough to sink into a snuffly oblivion in my lap.

Her father, however, who had all the wisdom and common sense of an adult, also trusted me, it seemed. Not only had he left Hope here in the first place, he sent me a text casually letting me know that he'd 'popped out for a couple of hours, back around 12' and that there was a bottle of milk in the fridge.

It took everything I'd got. All the tattered shreds of courage and determination that had probably not been that courageous or determined to begin with, but from some previously untapped reserves, as midday rolled around, Daniel returned to find me sitting at the kitchen table chopping an onion, Hope burbling in her chair. Showered, hair brushed and *dressed in clothes suitable for leaving the house.*

'Okay, so I can't bear another sandwich and tin of watery soup. Having searched every cranny in your kitchen, and what I presume is meant to be a pantry, the best I can come up with is an omelette.'

'Great.' Daniel went to give his daughter a kiss.

'Did you have a nice morning, Hope?' He stopped then, and looked around. 'You've cleaned up.'

I shrugged. 'I've made a start. Hope helped.' I nodded to where she was banging a clean sponge onto the table.

It had been an exhausting start. After taking an absurd amount of time figuring out how to extricate Hope and me from my bed without waking her up, I'd gently placed her in the cot I found in what must be Daniel's room, and taken it from there (Daniel's room, unsurprisingly, followed the *shabby unchic* décor of the rest of the farmhouse, it was a health and safety hazard just kicking my way through the debris on the floor to reach the cot). By the time she'd woken up, I was clean and dry and had put my bedding and pyjamas in the washing machine and sorted through the rest of my stuff. I fed her the bottle, following the instructions Daniel had left on the kitchen countertop about how to warm it up first, then I stuck her in the baby chair and took a survey of the surroundings.

I thought about the sparkling kitchen in the Tufted Duck and shuddered at the comparison. I had reached a point in my life where I'd little idea of who

I really was, apart from someone I didn't like very much, but one thing I did know was that before all the madness started, I was a woman who knew how to get on my hands and knees and clean.

So that's what I did for the next hour and a half. I demolished the mountain of greasy pots in the Belfast sink, first scrubbing until I revealed the beautiful white porcelain beneath the grime. I wiped every crumb and unidentifiable sticky stain from the oak worktops, moving the microwave, toaster and everything else onto the tiled floor before I was satisfied. I then cleaned them all before placing them back again. Next, I wiped the cupboard doors, which turned out to be a pale cream instead of the yellowy-beige they'd been before.

At that point, I ran out of hot water and energy, so I gave up and started looking for some lunch.

'I don't think I can do any more today, but tomorrow I'll tackle the fridge and the oven. That is, if it's okay for me to stay on for another couple of days.' I picked up the knife and focused on chopping the rest of the onion. 'I kind of feel like this is something I can do for Charlie. Does that make sense?'

'If you feel like sorting the rest of the house then you can stay as long as you like.'

I finished chopping and put the knife down. Daniel was leaning against one of the newly cleaned and tidied worktops. He wore a white shirt with the top button undone, and suit trousers. They both needed a good iron. I again took in the tired creases around his eyes and mouth, the hair long overdue a decent cut, and the weary sag to his shoulders. It was abundantly clear that Daniel didn't have any kind of help around the house. He was a single dad with some sort of job that required smart shirts, and in between nappy-changing and bath-time and meetings, he had the burden of preventing his family's 250-year-old farm from falling apart.

This house had centuries of peace and goodwill soaked into the rafters and oozing from every crack and crevice, but its owner was clearly struggling to find any peace of his own.

And I knew that I could help. That I could really do something positive and worthwhile, for the first time in longer than I wanted to admit. And not only could I prove useful here, not only did Daniel and Damson Farm need me, but I understood, in a moment of clarity that I really could have done with about ten years ago, that I needed this just as much. Skulking back to hide at the Tufted Duck was not the answer. I couldn't bear having to explain to my family why I'd chucked in my glittering career in the big city. And what if whoever was out to ruin my life, and had done a fairly good job of it so far, was able to trace me back to the B & B? Looking over my own shoulder twenty-four hours a day was bad enough. Putting my parents and grandma in danger wasn't even an option.

I felt a bittersweet stab between my ribs as I thought about what Charlie would say at the prospect of me staying at the farmhouse, helping out her brother and spending more time snuggling with her daughter. And that was all the answer I needed.

'Okay. I think I can adjust my schedule to include returning this house to its former glory.'

'Oh, you have a spare year or two?' Daniel raised his eyebrows at me. I attempted a wry, nonchalant smile that broke into a full-on laugh.

'Yes. As it happens. I do.'

At least I would have, once I'd sorted out a few things...

* * *

Riding on the momentum of a stunningly successful morning, I called Lucy. She'd called me twice, and sent numerous increasingly anxious texts asking what was going on. I left another message apologising for the lack of contact, explaining that I'd been dealing with a personal situation, and asking her to call me back as soon as possible. I then called my editor.

'Nora! What can I do for you, darling?'

'Stop calling me darling, given that I'm your most highly bankable writer, not some strumpet on the side.' See? Nora was fierce.

Miles wasn't fazed. He was used to her. 'Writer and *friend*, I hope. But fair enough, I'll re-edit. Wouldn't want to end up portrayed as the sleazy boss in your autobiography one day. How can I be of service to you, Ms Sharp?'

'Miles, you know how much I appreciate everything you've done for me. The support and guidance, not to mention the incredible opportunity in the first place.'

'Your success is my success, Nora. You know that.

You fly, and I'm riding on your tail feathers. The paper wouldn't be the same without you.'

'Yes. Well. It's going to be without me. I'm calling to hand in my resignation.'

'You *are* kidding me.'

Miles then spent the next ten minutes interrogating me about why, and who had lured me away, and if it was TV then we could probably work something out, and if it was more money then how much would convince me to stay and so on and so on. It was rather flattering, actually. I expected a half-hearted sorry-you're-leaving and a token gesture of a pay rise. I replied with some random waffle about taking the reviews as far as I could, being famous for being nasty was wearing thin and it was time to try something new...

'Well. I'd never have guessed all that from this week's submission. It seemed as though Nora had got her old fire back. Only, one editorial note, and please hear me on this, but while upping the bitch-factor is super, and precisely what we wanted, I don't want it at the expense of great writing. Anyone can be mean but it takes wit and charm to get away with it. Felt like this one lost that rather.'

'Um. I didn't submit anything for this week. I was going to come on to that.' I had my whole car accident, friend died, personal emergency excuses all ready.

'Well, somebody certainly submitted something. Let me see... Ah, here it is. Appetito, just off Baker Street. You had the lobster thingummy.'

No. I didn't. I was lying in a creaky old bed stewing in my own self-pity. I fudged a non-committal reply, promised to let Miles know when I was back in London so he could arrange a proper send-off ('I'd love to read a review of your leaving bash!') and agreed that I would submit two more reviews to see the month out, then that would be that. I also promised, several times, that if I ever did write an autobiography I'd be nice about him and not mention the incident with the newsreader's son on the yacht.

I also had several months' worth of non-newspaper events and engagements scheduled in my diary. Fortunately, Nora Sharp rarely confirmed her attendance in advance, so there were only one or two that I needed to cancel and apologise to. Not that they would make a fuss if I pulled out. This was the fickle world of celebrity, after all.

I called Lucy again but it went through to voicemail.

Ten seconds later, a message from her pinged through:

Sorry am in a meeting. Is everything OK? All under control here, no need to rush back, but I've been SO WORRIED about you!

I replied straightaway:

I'm fine, but you submitted an Appetito review? Without talking to me about it 1st??

Yes! I didn't know what was going on and you'd missed the deadline. I didn't want you to get in trouble with Miles so wrote something just in case. You weren't replying to my messages and I didn't know what else to do. I'm so relieved you're ok!! xxx

While I was thinking about how to reply, she messaged again:

What happened? Is there anything I can do to help?

I'm happy to keep things ticking over, but it'd be helpful to know how long you might be away xxx

I tried calling her again, but it went straight to voicemail. Lucy was of the generation where phone calls were for emergencies only, but I drew the line at firing someone via a text, if I could help it.

Lucy, I really need to talk to you properly about this. Please call me as soon as you can.

No reply.

I felt another stab of guilt. Lucy had been clearly worried about me – and about what my sudden disappearance would mean for her own job. Deciding to write and submit a review off her own back showed how stressed she must have been. I'd handled this horribly, and it was completely unfair to leave Lucy feeling responsible for writing reviews on top of managing everything else. By failing to speak to her properly, I'd inadvertently forced her to become Nora Sharp – even if as far as she knew, it was only temporary. I had to tell her that I'd resigned from the paper, and I wasn't coming back, so she could speak to Miles and decide whether she wanted to keep Nora going, or whether we were going to formally lay her to rest.

Would a voicemail do?

If she didn't call me back soon, it would have to.

If nothing else, I needed to warn her about the stalker who'd crawled back out of the shadows. She had nothing to hide when it came to being Nora, she'd be able to talk to the police about it, let the newspaper know. Get it sorted once and for all.

I'd wait one more day for her to call me, then decide what to do.

* * *

Lucy had recently graduated when she contacted me. She'd studied marketing and journalism, and was looking for an internship. I was impressed with how succinctly she expressed her respect for my work, and the areas in which she hoped she could prove useful. Given that I still felt like a lost child bumbling about in a maze of adulting, I was very tempted to consider her offer. Except that I wasn't sure what I was meant to be doing half the time. I was hardly in a position to be mentoring or managing anyone else.

And then came the meeting with Miles and his marketing people, and the request for me to up my social media game, get with the times and stop hiding behind my mysterious persona.

'People demand personal, these days, Nora,' a PR manager, Duncan, drawled at me, flipping a greasy black fringe out of his eyes.

'Eleanor,' I muttered.

'They want to know everything about you. What you wear, how you stay in shape, who you're hanging out with. They want to *see* everything. Chilled back yoga before Sunday brunch, treating yourself to a boxset binge on a rare night in. Suited and booted for a meeting with your PR manager.' He paused to snort a few times at his own hilarity. I was, in line with the rest of the office, dressed down in jeans, a stupidly expensive T-shirt some up-and-coming fashion student had sent me, and a pair of mustard Converse.

'That's not really everything about me though, is it? That's only my personal appearance.'

'Right! Precisely! Like I said, up close and personal is what people are looking for. Gone is the age of the untouchable celebrity. Your fans won't care about your opinion if they don't know the real Nora.'

'How can people know the real Nora when she isn't actually real?' I asked. 'And I'm not interested in being a celebrity.' Not much, anyway. 'I'm a professional journalist, albeit one operating at the lighter end of the news spectrum. People have appreciated my articles for years without seeing me slobbing in front of the TV with a tube of Pringles.'

'I don't think that would be a good moment to capture,' Duncan grimaced. 'While your image is thankfully more about attention-grabbing than attractive, maybe swap the Pringles for a banana-flour muffin, given you're supposed to be a foodie?'

'*Supposed to be?*'

I turned to Miles in the hope that he'd add some much-needed rationality. 'How am I going to carry out my job if people know who I am? Half the places I go wouldn't give me a table. The other half would be on their best behaviour, which kind of defeats the purpose. If Nora Sharp walks into an event, it'll ruin it for most of the people there. No one'll be able to relax if they think I'm eavesdropping from the corner.'

'That being said, I have to listen to the experts,' Miles said, shuffling a few papers on his desk. 'You know that all print media is being forced to adapt in order to survive. It'll be a chance to freshen up the image, experiment with Nora's future direction. Most food reviewers aren't anonymous and they still get tables because no restaurant manager believes their food to be anything short of spectacular. And you being there will get any event buzzing. Once everyone's had a few drinks they'll be even more likely to spill the gossip knowing that someone's actually listening to them.'

'Kathy will set up the YouTube channel, talk you through the details and offer tips on sprucing up your image.' Duncan swivelled round to address Kathy, who'd spent the whole meeting slurping on her celery-infused water and staring out the window at the recycling bins below.

'We were thinking, what, a less civilian hairstyle? Perhaps a bright colour to distract from your face. I'm feeling teal, indigo, possibly apricot, with a chop less middle-aged-mum-at-the-bingo and more "don't mess me with me, I am a queen".'

Kathy deigned to glance across at me. 'That hair tone is upsetting. I didn't think they sold such dismal shades outside Eastern Europe.'

'This is my natural hair colour!'

Kathy widened her eyes, shoved her drink spout back in her mouth, and turned back to the window.

Panic started pumping through my system as Duncan droned on about eyebrows and cosmetic enhancements, underwear to provide a 'more natural silhouette'. Apparently my 34D breasts were totally last decade.

Looks aside, I wasn't overly proud. I knew my style tended towards too-busy-to-bother, and I was fine with that, like most women I would much rather be judged on what came out of my mouth and what I wrote than on how plumped my lips were. I knew that most people would judge me on who I was, not the lack of flaws on my filtered face.

But that was the problem, wasn't it? Because who I would be, in this instance, was Nora Sharp, and she was gradually being shaped by the media machine into a nit-picking dragon with a wedge of bitter lemon where her heart should be. In between all the positive, thoughtful, constructive reviews, Nora Sharp made her fame and fortune from the random sentences that were ripped out of context and then twisted into a cruel meme. If you searched for Nora Sharp online, the 'sharpest quotes ever' compilations and social media threads all created an image of a woman who relished other people's mistakes and failures, and enjoyed nothing more than getting thousands of other people to laugh at them along with her.

Nora Sharp had no right to expect any peeks into her personal life to be received with grace, or critiqued with kindness.

But there was worse.

Was I ready for my family to find out that Nora Sharp was in fact their beloved daughter, or the good citizens of Windermere and the staff at the Tufted Duck to discover that I was the person responsible for the failure of Emma from *The Great British Bake Off*'s new restaurant venture?

Nora Sharp had morphed into a monster, and at the end of the day I was the only one who could stop her. I could pretend my reluctance to reveal myself was shyness as much as I liked, but that's not what the real problem was.

I had promised myself that one of these days, when I'd finally got a publisher for the new novel I never got around to finishing, or my Eleanor Sharpley blog somehow ended up paying all my bills, I would stop. Once I'd gained enough of a reputation to be able to move into other areas of journalism, like those fluffy magazine interviews about a soap opera star's three-month wedding anniversary. Once I'd written the real food, rustic cookbook I dreamed about when sampling yet more unidentifiable gastro-gubbins.

I would stop. Kill Nora off once and for all.

But I needed a back-up plan, or at the very least a back-up bank balance to see me into the next venture.

I wasn't ready.

And then I remembered the email from Lucy, the enthusiastic wannabe-intern, prepared to help me out however she'd be most useful. I wondered what colour hair she had. Whether she'd be up for a revamp?

Two weeks later Lucy joined Team Nora. It

turned out she was sticking with the mahogany hair, almost the exact same shade as mine, but according to Kathy, on Lucy it was a tone that spoke of ageless glamour, not aged grandma. But all other aspects of Nora's brand got a reboot with Lucy more than happy to act out my YouTube scripts, as well as taking over Nora's social media accounts.

I hadn't realised how lonely life as a self-employed mudslinger had been until I had someone to share it with, and it was such absolute bliss that I convinced myself to overlook how Lucy played on the image of Nasty Nora. I traded in my unease for the joy of having someone to stand in the corner with at parties. To crack open a bottle of wine and eagerly discuss what invites to accept, decline or wait and see if we felt like turning up on the day. To have a *friend*, even if she was paid to be one. As momentum built, we started noticing the nods in her direction when we attended events and soon, to all intents and purposes, Nora became split between the two of us: I wrote, she swanned about in the eye-wateringly expensive clothes that people sent Nora. I contemplated going back to doing the restaurant reviews alone, in order to ensure anonymity, but then

Lucy adopted a wig and a smile so bright that no one would mistake her for Nora Sharp.

As an intern I didn't pay her much, but she got plenty of nights out and more clothes, bags and kitchen implements than even the two of us could make use of (so we often sold them on and split the difference). I also provided a generous allowance for her to maintain the requested 'spruced-up' image.

So, she got all the attention, I got to keep writing. A perfect partnership.

And then the messages started arriving.

And things started to fall apart...

6

I knew I had to start sorting things out so first I contacted my landlord and terminated my lease. I should call Miles and explain that Lucy wrote the latest article, and that she'd probably be happy to keep going if he asked her. I should call my parents and tell them I planned to stay at Charlie's farmhouse for a while. And once I'd done all that, I should probably think about what the hell I was going to do with the rest of my life.

Instead, I did something that felt even more revolutionary. I donned my coat, hat and the sturdiest boots I could find in my bags. I opened the front door, breathed in a huge, crisp lungful of January air and stepped into the winter sunshine.

Without allowing myself to think too hard about it, I strolled across the gravel yard to a gate leading into some sort of garden beyond. Ensuring the gate was closed behind me, I followed a track into a field of scrubby grass peppered with short, twisty-looking trees, their bare branches like bony fingers stretching out against the sharp chill. I had to duck my head a few times, to avoid some of the thickest boughs, keeping one eye up while the other watched for the tendrils of bramble snaking across the earth and the clumps of nettles. My hunch that this was some sort of orchard was confirmed when I stepped in a rotten apple, and suddenly started spotting them every-where. Apples, and what appeared to have been plums – or more likely damsons, I supposed.

I flicked through my memories for mentions of an orchard in Charlie's many conversations about the farm, soon recollecting stories about picnics under the trees, how her job had been to carefully wrap the picked fruit in newspaper, layering it in crates to store during the winter. Maybe she'd strung up a hammock and used to read here?

However, like the rest of the farm, this was nothing like her stories. While winter may have been partly responsible for the orchard being so austere, devoid of any life save the sleeping trees, the silence here seemed deeper than merely the seasonal lull. Like a long-forgotten enchanted wood, with the echoes of past pleasures frozen in time. I half expected to stumble across a statue of Mr Tumnus hiding in amongst the trunks. Only, instead what I found as I wound through the undergrowth, boots squelching into the mud, was the bees.

Or, more precisely, two figures covered from head to toe in beekeeping gear. Either that or there'd been a serious radioactive leak no one had bothered to mention.

No – definitely bees. I quickly spied a row of hives lined up a couple of metres from the far fence, and to my horror, one of the safe and securely dressed beekeepers was in the process of lifting the lid off one of them. I couldn't decide whether to move closer so that they spotted me in time, or turn and flee. I assumed bees could catch me up in seconds, so I plumped for yelling and waving my arms instead.

'Hello!'

Great. They clearly couldn't hear me while enveloped in their nice, safe, sting-preventing suits. I darted a few steps closer, pausing a few metres away as I dodged the handful of bees now buzzing around. 'Hello!' I cried, louder this time, before swiftly retreating again.

Both figures jerked their heads towards me, the one holding the lid scanning around before finding me lurking beside a clump of brown bracken, as if that could protect me from a swarm of angry insects. They hurriedly placed the lid back on the hive, before both of the beekeepers pulled back their hoods.

I recognised the person by the hive as the doctor, Ziva.

'Why, hello, stranger,' she beamed, before a bee to her left caught her attention. She pointed her finger at it. 'Come on, then, Derek, back into the warm you go. And you, Damian! Stop bothering our visitor and get inside!' She waited a moment, scanning around for any other escapees. 'There you are, Dylan, don't think I didn't see you there, hovering about! And you, Douglas, Dougie and Dougal!

Queen Delilah will be worrying about you! In you go!'

And to my amazement, most of them did buzz their way back to a small hole in the hive box and disappear back inside.

'Well, then.' Ziva stuck gloved hands on her hips. 'You're looking much improved! This is Eleanor, who I told you about,' she informed the other woman, who was much younger, with a cloud of dark, corkscrew curls. Behind her huge tortoise-shell glasses I could see Ziva's kind brown eyes, which along with her slender frame led me to guess correctly that they were mother and daughter.

'Eleanor, this is Becky, my youngest. She's helping me heft the hives.'

'Right. Hi.'

'Having recently chucked in a highly successful career in pharmaceutical sales on a whim and a prayer, she's otherwise rattling around the village getting up to mischief wherever she can find it.'

'Mum!' Becky groaned. 'I'm thirty-three, not thirteen.'

'Either way, you need something to occupy that

vivacious brain of yours. Maybe making a new friend would be the first step.'

'Ungh.' Becky smacked one glove over her face. 'I'm so sorry about my mother. The way she talks, you'd think *I* was the embarrassing one.'

We both stood there, feeling the self-consciousness of two girls on the first day of school wondering if they'd found a friend.

'Well, Becky? Why don't you tell her about the bees?'

Becky pushed her glasses up her nose. 'Don't be ridiculous, mother. No normal person is interested in hearing about the bees. Especially in this weather. Eleanor, I'm so sorry, please don't let us keep you.'

'Oh, don't be such an apiary snoot!' Ziva exclaimed, as if bewildered at the very thought I might not be wandering through life bursting with bee questions. 'I'm sure there are plenty of things she'd like to know, aren't there?'

'Um, yes. Of course...'

'Well? Ask away, dear! Oh, for goodness' sake, David, it's not warm enough to be out and about yet!'

Ummmm... 'Do you give all the bees names?'

Becky broke into a grin, her handsome features

suddenly adjusting to fit her face perfectly. 'These are all the D boys, because they're in hive D, with Queen Delilah.'

'Right.' Well, that made perfect sense now.

'Are you collecting honey?'

'Nah, not this time of year. We're hefting the hives, like Mum said. Checking the boys still have enough food to last until spring. The D boys are a bit light, so we're going to treat them to a slab of fondant icing as a top-up. Do you want to stay and watch?'

'No!' I replied, forcefully enough to replace Becky's grin with a look of surprise. 'I mean, I would, another time, but I'm a bit nervous of getting stung. I wouldn't want to do the wrong thing and make them angry.'

By *a bit nervous* I meant *extremely anxious*, but I didn't want to seem rude and upset the D boys.

'I'll let you get on. But, um, Becky, I mean, if you wanted and if you've not got much on at the moment, then, well, I'll be staying at the farm for a little while longer so if you were at a loose end one afternoon then you could, well...' *For goodness' sake, Eleanor!* I sounded like I was asking her out on a date. Why were words so much easier when you could write them down? 'Anyway, what I mean to say is feel free to come over for a cup of tea anytime. Or coffee, if you don't like tea. Or water. A drink! Any drink... well, obviously not *any* drink...'

Phew. I could feel myself sinking deeper into the mud.

'A cup of tea would be lovely! Thanks so much for asking! I will do that. Probably a day when Mum's busy so she doesn't tag along and spoil it.'

Ziva had the gall to look affronted. 'As if. I have my own friends, thank you very much.'

'What, Damian and Duke and Demetrius?' Becky smirked, making it impossible not to smile back.

'Do be quiet, poor Eleanor will be thinking we're completely batty, and when you come knocking for that drink she'll pretend to be out and then where will you be? Back to being a Noreen No Mates!'

'Well, I'd better get on and leave you to it,' I interrupted, my face having grown so stiff with the cold I sounded like I'd just had dental surgery. 'Really nice to meet you, Becky.'

I turned and hurried away before they could open the hive again.

* * *

'I met Ziva and her daughter today,' I told Daniel, later that evening after he'd put Hope to bed, then picked up a pizza from the takeaway in the village. We were eating at the kitchen table, which felt slightly awkwardly on the brink of date-like, but the only other option was me on the sofa in the study while he sat at his desk, and that was weirder. I'd had a peek in the other downstairs rooms while Hope had been in the bath – in addition to the shower room there was a spacious living room, formal dining room and rickety conservatory. There was also a utility room off the kitchen, with a door leading to the cellar. The bones of the house were stunning. The problem was they lay beneath layers of dust, grime, chipped paint, peeling wallpaper, general neglect and universal ugliness. What a total waste. I couldn't help thinking that Charlie would be distraught, even as she'd understand and offer her brother nothing but sympathy and encouragement. Or maybe she'd send a trusted friend along to help, and she only had one of those.

'Becky?' Daniel nodded around his mouthful of

pizza. 'Ziva mentioned she'd left her job, was around a lot more. You know, in passing, once or twice,' he added, eyes sparkling. 'Just in case I was interested.'

Oho! 'And are you?' I asked coyly, hiding behind a sip of raspberry lemonade.

'I am not. Everyone knows that Becky Adams has been in love with the same man since primary school. And it's not me.'

'So who is it, then? Does he know?' Now this *was* interesting. And if everyone knew, it wasn't even gossiping.

'Luke Winter. He's heard the banter, but doesn't really believe it. Brushes it off as a childhood crush. Becky's intimidatingly successful, has spent the past few years jetting around the world with her job. She was one of the popular kids at school. Popular because she worked hard to make sure that people genuinely liked her, not because they were scared of her not liking them. She was always looking out for everyone, especially those who didn't quite fit in. She could throw a wicked spin ball, too.'

'Sounds like Luke doesn't know what he's missing.' I helped myself to another slice of garlic bread. Nora Sharp would have given this grease-riddled feast a 0.5 out of ten, pronouncing that the rats wouldn't bother scavenging it out of the bin. Eleanor Sharpley, after a day of positively frenetic activity compared to the recent slump-fest, declared it perfectly delicious.

Daniel shrugged. 'He works as a tradesman, has never lived anywhere but Ferrington. Spends every Friday night with a pie and a pint at the Boatman and isn't interested in anything different. Rumour has it he won six figures on the lottery a couple of years ago and apart from buying a couple of tools and a new fishing rod, he gave the whole lot away. He's not exactly... your typical ladies' man. But he was the first person I called when Charlie went missing, and he was the last one to stop looking. It's obvious to everyone but Luke why Becky's smitten.'

'Why doesn't Ziva steamroller them together?'

'Oh, because Luke grew up on the New Side of the river.' Daniel offered me the last piece of pizza. I wrestled with being polite, but instead picked up a knife and indicated that we'd share it.

'What does where he grew up have to do with anything?' I asked, deliciously stuffed to the brim.

Was *the New Side of the river* some sort of local double entendre?

'Round here, which side of the Maddon you grew up on means *everything*.'

'So, what side are we?' I asked, baffled, but before Daniel could answer the whiffles and squeaks that had been intermittently emanating from the baby monitor crescendoed into poignant cries, and Daniel went to investigate, leaving me wondering if every baby that cried in the night sounded like their world had come crashing down, or just those who'd lost their mother.

7

The next day, Hope came to visit me at eight. Daniel knocked and waited for me to get up and answer the bedroom door this time. 'I thought I might go for a quick run before I drop Hope at Mum's, if you don't mind watching her?'

I wouldn't mind watching you. That thought, unbidden, got smacked back down into the secret depths where it belonged. Daniel suited the fitness look, and a man holding a baby while dressed in running shorts and a hoody seemed somehow extra appealing. But that would be a mixed-up, complicated place to head towards, even if I hadn't just come out of a relationship. Or was hiding my secret, shameful identity. Or was on the run from a vengeful stalker.

I took Hope from him, busying myself with kissing her fluffy head and saying hello while he disappeared down the stairs.

Later that morning, I remembered that I'd been meaning to ask Daniel about the bees.

'Is the orchard still part of the farm, or did it get sold off with the rest?' I asked as he tried to coax Hope into eating her toast rather than squash it into her ear.

'Yeah. We still have the orchard, and the meadow on the far side that borders the river. But it's fallen fallow the past few years, if I'm honest.' He gave up with Hope's breakfast, shoving the last jammy soldier into his own mouth instead. 'Ziva does a bit of pruning, stops the weeds from taking over, but leaving it to run wild has been great for her bees.'

'Is she there a lot?'

'She comes most weeks, depending on the time of year. More often in the busier bee season. It's only a twenty-minute walk from the edge of Ferrington, where she lives. In the quieter times, like now, that's when she does a bit of gardening. It's an excuse to get away from the village for a while. She's been re-tired six years but still can't walk down Old Main Street without several people asking her to have a quick look at their rash, or diagnose their cousin's cat.'

'I bet the orchard's beautiful in spring.'

Daniel smiled, lifting Hope out of her chair and glancing around for her coat. 'And in the late summer, when the trees are in fruit. And the autumn, of course.'

'I'm sorry I won't be here to see it.'

'Well, that's totally up to you,' Daniel shrugged, grabbing his keys and Hope's bag as he prepared to take her to his mum, Billie's. 'I've said you can stay here as long as you like. Would be a shame to miss the leaves changing colour.' He threw me a glance then that sent a prickle of electricity zipping up my spine. Did Daniel want me to stay? That look suggested that if he did, it might be as more than a cleaner, cook and babysitter.

'Charlie would have loved you to have seen it,' he added, voice softening. And at the same time as I realised that of course that warmth in his eyes was for Charlie, an accompanying shard of guilt and misery wedged itself firmly in my windpipe, preventing me from replying.

* * *

I spent most of that day cleaning the rest of the kitchen. Okay, that's not quite true. I spent some of the day cleaning and sorting. The rest I spent stressing out, worrying, lolling on the sofa day-dreaming, obsessively checking my phone in case I'd missed a call from Lucy, snoozing, grieving and ordering myself to go back to the kitchen and do some more cleaning.

It was a busy day. I virtually fell asleep face-first in the pie I'd cooked for dinner. Daniel, if anything, looked more tired than I felt.

'The kitchen looks amazing,' he said, once Hope had been picked up from Billie's and tucked into her cot for the night. I had to agree with him, but it was ninety percent down to the gorgeous farmhouse kitchen, and only ten percent down to me having cleaned and polished and tidied the whole thing, including some finishing touches like lining up a row of pretty, mismatched jugs and vases on the high shelf running along one wall. I'd also removed the grubby blinds from the two large windows – what was the point of having blinds when the view was nothing but an overgrown lawn and the fields and woods beyond? I'd taken the piles of random papers, tools, packets of lightbulbs and batteries and other unsightly mess crammed on the dresser and stuffed it into the cupboards instead, taking out the beautiful set of crockery, dusting it down so that the daisy pattern shone, and displaying it on the dresser shelves. Having cleaned the rest of the room, it now looked like a kitchen rather than a disused garage.

'And this tastes amazing!' Daniel added, nodding his approval. 'Where did you get the pie from?'

'I made it,' I admitted, somewhat abashed. I was a food critic who had grown up in a B & B. I knew how to cook, even if I'd hardly needed to bother in recent years. 'I found some frozen meat in the freezer, chucked in some floppy vegetables lurking in the pantry, not much else to it.'

We ate in silence for a while, me too weary to bother talking, Daniel apparently lost in thought.

'Your parents ran a hotel or something, didn't they?'

'A B & B. The Tufted Duck. In the Lake District.'

'I remember Charlie worked there for a while. She loved it. Said out of all the hundreds of places she'd worked, it was her favourite. She said it was more than a home from home, because homes can be hard work, and this place was a sanctuary, somewhere she could just be.'

'Well, that might explain why my parents kept having to fire her, then.' I laughed, even as my throat had swollen with the beautiful words. For me, the Tufted Duck *had* meant never-ending hard work, and being bossed about, and feeling like a perpetual child. But I could see how for Charlie, whose life was an exhausting torrent of chaos, the decades-old routines and simple, straightforward order to how we did things would have offered her some peace.

'Speaking of hard work, what is it you do all day, with your meetings and white shirts and all those spreadsheets?'

Daniel rolled his bloodshot eyes, stabbing at another piece of beef. 'It's boring and complicated and you look on the brink of nodding off as it is.'

'I'm interested! You can at least give me the general gist.'

'I'm a transmissions and distribution forecasting manager for East Midlands Energy.'

'Okay. Wow.' I nodded as if impressed and/or interested.

Daniel wasn't fooled. 'Don't wow! It's even more boring than it sounds.'

'If it's so boring, then why do you do it?'

'I'm not really in a position to be considering a career change. More importantly I can do most of it from home in evenings and nap-times, and it pays enough to keep things going. That takes precedent over thrills and spills these days.'

'Well, I suppose someone has to be a trans-forecasting... I'm sorry, I've forgotten it already.'

'We can't all work in the glamorous world of food critics.' Daniel looked at me pointedly.

'Um. What?' My last mouthful of potato became wedged in my throat, as the rest of the meal threatened to rise up and join it.

'I had a nosy at your website. It's good.'

I was too busy freaking out to appreciate the warm glow in his eyes as he said this, although somewhere below the building panic I did feel a squeeze in response to his deep, soft voice.

'I have to admit, I was sceptical as to how anyone could make a living out of it. But I can see why advertisers would want to be associated with yours.' He smiled. I tried to smile back, but my face was numb with horror. Outside of a select few at the newspaper, I'd thought Charlie, Lucy and my ex-boyfriend Marcus were the only people who knew what I did for a living. If one or two extras knew, I could live with it, but if Daniel knew, I couldn't keep living with him. This was meant to be a fresh start, a place where I could be me again, a me I actually liked. I didn't want people to think I was capable of being the horrible person Nora had evolved into.

'That one you wrote on the dementia patients from Sri Lanka, and how cooking food from their heritage helped them. I have to admit that coincided with a speck of dust blowing into my eye.'

Oh. Oh! The relief unseized my windpipe, and I sucked in a huge gasping breath.

'Don't look so surprised.' Daniel topped up my water glass. 'It was really good.'

I shook my head, as if dismissing his compliment. 'I didn't think anyone read that blog.'

He looked puzzled. 'I thought that was your job.'

'Um, yes. It is. Partly. I do other pieces as well, re-porting on current events. Things like that. They're much more popular.'

'Well, either way, I'm sure it beats spreadsheets.'

'It does. Well. It did.' I took another deep breath. 'I'm not sure it's me any more. So I'm taking a break to consider my options. That's one reason why I was coming to see Charlie.' I smiled, ruefully. 'She'd have had loads of ideas.'

Daniel nodded in agreement. 'All of them even more glamorous than flouncing about in fancy restaurants.'

'I think she once mentioned working on a fishing trawler? The pay was terrible but you got herring for breakfast.'

Then we were both laughing, and then I was crying again, and Daniel reached across the table and took hold of my hand, in a nice, older-brother-of-my-best-friend type of way, and that made me cry even more, because I really liked it here. I was starting to *really* like this man too, but now, with one throwaway lie-by-omission, I'd erected a firm barrier between us. As safe as this place might feel, as much as how Charlie inviting me here had been about regifting what the Tufted Duck had been to her – a sanctuary, somewhere I could simply be me – it was now the opposite of that. A place where, once again, I had to hide, and lie, and keep my shameful secret squashed away in the dark.

There was no one left alive who knew the truth and still loved me. The one person who'd claimed he did had turned out to be a big, fat fake. How could I expect Daniel to know the kind of things I'd written and tweeted and posted about people and still like me? Let alone want me here?

Was Nora Sharp going to haunt me for the rest of my life?

8

I'd met Marcus last June at the opening of a new 'nutritional experience' in Shoreditch. Crammed into a venue which could have once been the shoebox for the ergonomically designed trainers the manager-owner had sent me as an inducement to attend, it made room for three tables, a 'rejuvenation zone', containing yoga mats, kettle bells and stretchy rope things, and the 'rejuicination zone', which to my professional eye looked like a bog-standard takeaway counter.

Lucy hadn't come, seeing as she hated anything sports related. I'd intended to pop in for a quick taste of the menu samples, a slurp or two of their beet latte and cheese tea, which I fully anticipated would taste like liquidised toe-fluff, and as in-depth a conversation with the owner as I could manage without arousing suspicion. I hadn't worn the trainers, as that would be a dead giveaway, but had splashed out on the kind of outfit I thought women who attended nutritional experiences at nine o'clock on a Monday evening would probably wear: black and silver leggings, a sleeveless running top artfully cutaway to reveal my sports bra, and Lucy's smartest trainers.

I sidled in and began ambling around, feigning studious interest in the information posters and nodding appreciatively as the owner made his rambling speech about optimal performance and micronutrient replenishment, repeatedly interrupting himself by punching the air and shouting, 'Fit don't quit!'

'Nora Sharp, I presume?' Someone whispered in my ear, causing me to clutch my biodegradable juice carton so hard that the juice spurted out of the top and left a fluorescent green stain on the trainers.

'I don't know what you're talking about.' I flicked my hair and smiled sweetly. Glancing to my left, I saw a man with a huge shock of prematurely grey hair framing dazzling blue eyes and a mischievous grin.

'Come off it. No serious fitness freak would be caught dead in those trainers. And, no offence, but you've not got the physique of a woman who considers carbs to be nutritional cyanide.'

'Maybe I carb-cycle!' I tittered, still trying to act as un-Nora like as possible, while simultaneously resisting the urge to squirt my drink in his face.

'No. You've got the look of a woman who knows how to actually enjoy food. A real woman, not a haggard cyborg held together with stringy tendons and overly sculpted muscle.' He lowered his voice to a whisper. 'I mean, look at them.' He nodded at a pair of women standing nearby, who I had to admit did appear semi-bionic beneath their tiny bralettes and cycling shorts.

'Are you always this rude about people's appearances?' I hissed, while simultaneously feeling my shoulders de-hunch. I had felt more than a little overwhelmed by the rest of the guests, and it was a relief to know not everyone here was horrified by my clear lack of fitness finesse, or 'fitnesse', as Nora Sharp would call it in her review.

'Compared to you, Nora, I'm an absolute gentleman.' He winked, waiting a few seconds before adding, 'I don't mean it about the women, I'm just jealous and intimidated and wanted to crack your legendary iron shell.'

At that point, the speech was over, the crowd broke into a smattering of applause, more cheers of, 'Fit don't quit!' and, in my case, a whoosh of relief.

'Want to get out of here? Go and get some chips or something?'

Misinterpreting my hesitation as something other than nervousness and disbelief at a real-life man asking me to hang out with him, he held out one hand. 'Marcus Donahue-Black. I'm only here because the owner is my cousin. I hate exercise and I love doughnuts. And I apologise for my demeaning comments. I use humour as a safety net when I'm out of my comfort zone, and I was trying to impress you by being mean. I also apologise for assuming that you in any way resemble your online persona. I can immediately see that you are far kinder and more lovely than the memes would suggest. Can we start again?'

Given how lonely and tired I was of pretending to be someone else, the thought of eating chips with someone who seemed to understand my predicament after just one brief interaction made it an offer impossible to resist.

A handful of dates later, Marcus was my boyfriend. He was someone else who could come to meals and events with me, and it turned out he moved in the kind of circles where he was often already invited, so I could go as his date and no one would be any the wiser.

He lived in a swanky chrome and white apartment near the river on the Southbank, although we spent far more time out and about than in either of our homes. His job seemed to involve a lot of networking, and long lunches, and offering to connect people with other people who knew people, but he was fun, and we had a good time, and if the conversation remained on the lighter side, the relief at being with someone else who knew the truth about me was priceless. He'd throw me secret winks at opportune moments, make cheeky comments about the food we were eating – 'What do you think of the crab, darling?' – and it created an intimacy between us that I'd been craving without realising it. I could almost be myself with Marcus, as long as that was London Eleanor – a few shades classier, more content and more confident than I really felt – and with him, like with Charlie, I believed I could be my best self. Or at least a better one.

I'd glided along in the bliss of considering myself a girlfriend, one of a pair, half of a whole, and had quite begun to convince myself that I loved this uncomplicated man. I even mentioned him to my parents, and started thinking about bringing him home to the Tufted Duck (although I'd have to ask for a guest room, given that Grandma was still snoring strong in my bedroom at ninety-three). I spent time with his friends, on boats, and in country houses and at D-list celebrity weddings. And if these new friends seemed to spend more time passed out, scrapping over someone's so-called partner or crying in the toilets than they did enjoying themselves, well, who was I to judge? I felt honoured to be included.

And then, New Year's Day, while we were eating breakfast only hours after that beautiful evening in the castle, Marcus's phone bleeped with a message while he was chatting to a new contact on the other side of the dining room, his phone left sitting on the table between us.

It was a photograph.

In the time it took me to figure it out, several more popped up. To be honest, they would have made me feel sick even if they hadn't featured my boyfriend. A woman was also in the photos, but it was impossible to make out her face. A written message soon followed:

Best night of my life. Hope to do it again soon xx

Marcus knew a lot of women. They often messaged him. A certain level of flirting and schmoozing, he had assured me, was part of his job. I hadn't realised that naked gymnastics counted as flirting. The contact was saved in his phone as 'FireStarter'.

I said nothing, downing my coffee in one mouthful, grabbing the as yet untouched cinnamon swirl from his plate and hotfooting it out of there. The psychological advantage garnered from standing at reception already checking out when he finally noticed my absence and came looking, gave me the courage to speak.

'Who's FireStarter?'

The slightly confused smile dropped off his face for a second, before he remembered that appearing to be confused might be the best way to play it. 'Excuse me, darling?'

Ugh. I was too tired and angry and humiliated to faff about. There were times when being able to channel an alter ego superbitch came in handy. 'She's just sent you a pictorial recap of the other night.'

'You were snooping on my phone?' He stepped closer, ducking his head in an attempt to avoid a scene.

I took a step back. 'You left it on the table. No snooping required.'

His eyes narrowed. 'Can we talk about this somewhere else, please? Several of my associates are here.'

'No. Who is she?'

'No one,' he snapped, rolling his eyes in contempt.

'No one? No one, as in, you don't even know the name of the woman you cheated on me with?'

'Oh, come off it, Eleanor,' he muttered. 'What are you talking about, cheating? Please don't start getting all possessive on me, it doesn't suit you.'

'What?' I was the one to look confused, now. 'What else do you call it if you sleep with someone behind your girlfriend's back?'

'I call it perfectly acceptable, if they aren't exclusive.'

'You specifically asked me to be exclusive! In August, before I went on the Italian Nonna's food retreat!'

'Well,' he shrugged, glancing about the reception foyer, because it was apparently far more important that he maintained his reputation with his associates than with me. 'You didn't ask me back.'

So, I broke up with my non-exclusive boyfriend. Thankfully, he'd proven himself to be a total arse, so I wasn't too heartbroken about it. Just a little bit lonely – Marcus had made me feel like a grown-up, who knew what she was doing, and had a semblance of a future up ahead. He'd validated my job, laughing off my concerns with comments like, 'Lighten up, darling – you write humorous food reviews, you aren't testifying in court.' He made *me* feel a tiny bit less like an arse. Or, at least stopped me having so much time to worry about it.

But all that newfound empty time, the time that mattered, in between the fluff and the frippery of my increasingly ghastly job, was now time spent gradually facing up to the fact that I couldn't keep going any more. The further Nora slipped down this one-way slope to Bitchiness Abyss, the more I loathed what I did. And it wasn't 'only a job', it was my life, and if I had even the slightest modicum of self-worth, I had to acknowledge that how I spent my one precious life mattered.

Here's a useful tip when deciding whether your chosen career is destroying you one torturous meme at a time: if you are too ashamed to allow your family to read the words you write, then for goodness' sake, *what the hell are you thinking?*

I was free now though, wasn't I? Here in the strong, ancient embrace of Damson Farm? Tucked away in between the gently rolling East Midland hills, amongst the bees and the sheep, the lights of Ferrington glinting through the orchard? After all,

I'd had no more messages from the stalker since I'd left. Sure, I'd blocked them, but if they were that determined they'd have simply got another number.

Surely that must mean I was safe.

Mustn't it?

9

I decided to address that question by ensuring I was too busy and worn out to think about it any more. I finally gave in and left Lucy a message, explaining how I'd been doing a lot of thinking and had decided to resign, which of course then meant that unfortunately I would have to let her go. I told her I'd provide her with a stellar reference for Miles if she wanted to carry on as Nora, how much I valued her, and hoped we'd stay in touch blah, blah, blah. I also added that I'd had some disturbing messages. Although they had clearly been aimed at me, and they'd stopped now, I strongly urged her to put everything Nora-related on pause until I could fill her in.

For the rest of the weekend I worked on the study, sorting and dusting and scrubbing away layers of neglect. I folded Hope's giant heap of clothes into neat piles and rearranged her changing table so there was actually space to change her on it. Daniel helped me swap the furniture about, so that Hope had a space to sit near the window, and he could charge his tech without wires trailing across the room waiting to be tripped over.

I also cooked, and took Hope for a walk around the nearby lanes while Daniel caught up on some work. Then, finding him conked out on the study sofa, we baked cookies with the last of the flour and sugar. In the evenings, we ate dinner once Hope was asleep, lingering over a decaffeinated coffee until the ripe old party hour of nine o'clock, when Daniel would either go to bed or head back to his desk.

Sunday afternoon, Billie phoned Daniel and asked if she could speak to me, so we cried and talked and breathed through a couple of awkward silences.

'I'm sorry you weren't told,' Billie told me, voice

trembling. 'Things hadn't been... you know, things were never good between us, and then she didn't cope very well with me moving on. So we'd not seen each other for a long time, beyond the odd hello. I hadn't realised you'd stayed in touch. Although I wouldn't have known how to contact you even if I'd thought about it. And. Well. We were so over-whelmed with it all. Hope, the farm, the police. Given the circumstances, we kept things small. There'd been enough fuss.'

Given what circumstances? I wanted to ask. Charlie would not have wanted a small, quiet funeral, no matter what the circumstances of her death. She'd have wanted funny stories and noisy toasts and masses of food and drink, all finished off with a sin-galong. A send-off that people would have talked about for years afterwards. I felt a stab of anger that I had missed my opportunity to ensure she had a fu-neral befitting her. But then, it seemed like she'd changed in the year or so before she died. Who was I to say what this older, wiser, sober Charlie would have wanted? Who was I to comment on how a grieving mother, a bereft brother should say goodbye?

* * *

Monday morning, Daniel had a meeting in central London with important energy bigwigs, and needed to leave early to catch a train from Newark. 'I would have made my excuses and dialled in, but if you don't mind watching Hope again, it would make my boss very happy if I showed up in person.'

'Of course, no problem. But can you leave me some very clear and minutely detailed instructions?'

Waking just after 6.30, I slipped out of bed in the hope of squeezing in a coffee and maybe even a shower before my housemate's summons. At the first creak of the floorboard, a thin wail informed me that I was kidding myself. Daniel had taped a spreadsheet to the end of her cot. He might as well have written it in computer code.

Two hours later, Hope had been fed, changed and changed again. I, on the other hand, had only managed to consume a glass of water and the mushed up remains of her banana. For some reason, Hope thought she was the one with something to cry about.

An hour after that, watching the clock like a

crack sniper scrutinises their target, only while weeping slightly and with far less steady hands, I gave up trying to placate her screams and decided to distract myself with some further farmhouse exploring.

I peeked into three additional bedrooms on the first floor. Each contained a bed, a solid looking wardrobe and maybe a chest of drawers or a pair of matching bedside tables. The walls were covered in tatty wallpaper similar to the rest of the house, with threadbare carpets in indistinguishable shades, and yet more oppressive curtains. One of them must have been Daniel's childhood bedroom – there were football trophies decorating one shelf, the others filled with children's books and a wonky globe. There was also a tiny box room lined with shelving full of bedding and other odds and ends like broken lampshades and cracked leather suitcases. And then, behind the final door, I found another staircase. Balancing carefully as I carried Hope up the steep steps, we found an attic split into another bathroom, a large storage space tucked under the eaves, and what I instantly knew was Charlie's room. Stretching half the length of the house, the room included three gabled windows and a sloping roof on either side.

Rather than a carpet, brightly coloured rugs lay on top of faded floorboards. Three of the walls were covered in white wallpaper dotted with unicorns, while the wall opposite the windows was a deep yellow.

Her bed was utterly Charlie: a gold bedframe with a pale pink canopy, still made up with pink and gold speckled bedding. There were open wardrobes and shelving filling half of one wall, haphazardly stuffed with clothes, shoes and other accessories as if trying to make it impossible to find what she wanted quickly. A dressing table was covered in make-up, jewellery and other knick-knacks, and the rest of the room – a huge armchair, the bookcase, the floor – was simply filled with Charlie. Stuffed toys, souvenirs from her travels, pretty notepads and art equipment. Stacks of books and yet more shoes. A string of fairy lights in the shape of flamingos draped across one wall, mobiles and windchimes dangled from the higher points of the ceiling.

There were still old bottles of toiletries scattered about the tiny shower room. Musty, mildewed towels squatted in one corner, and a brightly coloured robe hung on the back of the door.

There was a photograph on the little table beside her pillow: Charlie in her pyjamas, in this bed, a newborn baby in her arms. I recognised the blanket Hope was swaddled in as the now worn piece of cloth that she snuggled in her cot. But I barely recognised the woman who held her: I had never met this Charlie. She looked... serene. Like she had finally found the answer. Like those brain-death demons of darkness had been vanquished forever by the tiny, beautiful promise in her arms.

Oh, Charlie.

I had never understood that heartbreak was a physical pain that genuinely felt as though something vital had splintered inside your ribs, leaving shards jamming into the soft flesh deep inside.

I lay on the bed on one side, Hope safely tucked up against me, buried my head into the sweet, subtle scent of my friend, and wished and ached for all that had not been, and now could never be.

Unfortunately, seven-month-old babies don't have much patience for moments of unbridled desolation. Once the wiggling became accompanied by whimpers, we got up to explore the contents of the room. Hope opted to make a thorough investigation of a plastic sandal while I tackled some notebooks.

I found it near the back of the second one. So far, I'd skimmed through poetry and scattered jottings that ranged from joyful exuberance through wistful musings to bleak, all-consuming anguish that skittered chills up my spine.

But here, I found hope for a future. Dreams and plans. My heart cracked all over again as I read pages and pages of Charlie's ideas to turn the farmhouse into a retreat. A *sanctuary*. A place for artists and writers, bakers and crafters. Overworked health workers who spent all day every day taking care of others at the expense of themselves. Businesspeople, frayed and frazzled and so stuck in their never-ending treadmill of achievement that they couldn't remember what was really important.

A chance for people to reconnect with the earth again. To slow down to nature's steady pace. To stop thinking and start *sensing*: to smell the damp wood after a storm, the fragrance of the blossom in spring. To listen to the sound of life thriving in every corner, every crevice – the birds, the bees, the rustling of the leaves. To taste – tomatoes plucked that morning, bursting with goodness. Herbs grown on the patio sprinkled over pasta rolled out the old-fashioned way. And, of course, to touch – hands buried in the textures of the garden, seeking treasure in the peaty vegetable beds. The kiss of sunshine on tired skin. The glorious exuberance of icy wind in their hair.

And to stop, and look. To soak up a world unobstructed by concrete and tarmac. Rolling hills stretching out across the horizon. A myriad of stars undimmed by city lights.

I was flabbergasted. I had no idea Charlie had this in her.

She had added sketches of the rooms, as well as listed the gatherings she would hold in the orchard and the field beyond that ran down to the river. Examples of menus, and plans for secret nooks she would create in the garden for people to sit and ponder. There were designs for a vegetable patch, and a fire pit beside a tiny stage area at the top of the meadow, space to dance as well as relax.

Charlie had invented a tiny heaven on earth.

She had peppered the pages with mentions of me: 'Ask El about prices', 'Check with El if this could work', 'EL I NEED YOU!', 'How much could El invest?? – would need to draw up contract so proper business partners.'

She'd finished off the last page of the notebook with this:

A place to feed your senses, your stomach, your creativity and your soul. To recharge, reconnect and reimagine. To wander and to wonder. To remember who you are, and that who you are matters.

I wanted to go to this place so badly my feet were twitching to get on up and get there.

And as I read, and thought, and wandered through my friend's imagination, Hope gnawing on her fist, eyes transfixed on the crystal mobile gently spinning above her, I began to wonder.

Could I create this place? Could I do it, without Charlie?

I could cook and clean, and probably manage some basic decorating. I knew how to serve people, take bookings, and complete most of the admin that came with running a hotel – and what I didn't know, I could ask my parents. Daniel could teach me how to grow things. I'd been to enough events to know how to create an atmosphere. And what if Nora ended her career by writing about how coming here had transformed her, been her grand epiphany?

My heart began to accelerate. It was like seeing the first streak of pale light washing across the horizon. Now, I had something worth working for. Worth living for.

I could do this.

I would do it for Charlie, as my legacy to her. And for Daniel, and for Hope. And for me. And every other lost and lonely, stress-riddled, worn-out, washed-up person who needed it, too.

10

After cobbling together a basic lunch for us both out of a giant jacket potato and some cheese and salad, we went shopping. Ferrington had two small supermarkets according to my online search, one on Old Main Street, and one on the New Side of the river, imaginatively called New Main Street. I could have made a longer trip to a proper supermarket, but I wanted to have a look around the village – and although Daniel had left me full instructions about how the pram converted into a car seat, a walk seemed enough of an expedition for now.

It was a twenty-minute stroll through the orchard, across the field and along a short footpath beside the river until we reached the first row of cottages that led us into the village. The day was mild for January, although the sky was overcast and the shadows gloomy, and pushing Hope ensured my cheeks retained a warm glow. It was easy to spot the shop, and I was grateful I hadn't risked driving as every space was full along the narrow street leading up to it.

The village was, shall we say, not as picturesque as I'd been expecting. There were some older, cottagey type houses along Old Main Street, but the row of shops was a 1950s eyesore, and looked as though the only fresh paint it had received since then was graffiti. Along with the Ferrington mini-market was a hairdresser featuring faded posters of women showcasing their eighties' perms, the pizza place that Daniel had been to the other day, a Greggs and an off-licence which also advertised 'cheapest vapes on the Old Side'. The only vapes on the Old Side, I would imagine. There was the Old Boat House pub that advertised a riverside garden and local sausages, and a miners' social club that looked like a cheaper version of the pub. Opposite all this was the dinkiest, quaintest old-fashioned church I'd ever seen.

So maybe not quite picture postcard, but at least there was no air pollution, hardly any litter, and I could hear ducks quacking along the riverbank.

I went straight into the shop, loading up as much as I felt able to hang off the back of the pushchair – a fairly even mix of cleaning supplies and food. The selection was basic, to say the least, and they had completely run out of bananas.

Not to worry. We had a good hour or so before it started to get dark, and that gave us an excuse to cross the river to try the shops on the New Side.

Or not, as it turned out. The bridge, which stood in between the pub and the shops, was blocked off with concrete barriers, low enough for me to see that the stone structure had completely collapsed in the centre, leaving a gap of several metres where the Maddon flowed thick and grey beneath it.

I checked the maps on my phone, but couldn't spot another bridge anywhere in the village. A woman was scurrying up the road towards me, head down, woolly hat pulled low and chin tucked into her scarf.

'Excuse me?'

She jerked briefly to a stop, shaking her head at

the pavement before hurrying past and into the off-licence. The rest of the street was deserted, so, quickly deciding to dismiss her strange response as perhaps mistaking me for a chugger, I followed her in.

Wow. It was like stepping into a nightclub, more like the kind of place I'd expect to find back in London than a rural village in the East Midlands. All the shop fixtures – the display cases, floor and counter, plus the walls and ceiling – were black. Backlighting caused the rows of spirits to glow in varying luminescent shades. In the centre of the room a glitter ball spun, pinpricks of light whirling around it. Techno music pumped from enormous speakers hung in the far corners, and behind the counter a man dressed all in black bounced his base-ball-capped head slightly out of time to the beat.

'All right?' he asked the woman who'd entered before me, without breaking his stride. He looked about the same age as my dad, with a long, bleached ponytail dangling beneath the cap and a pair of headphones the size of grapefruit around his neck.

She leant her head so close to him that I couldn't hear her reply, but he bent under the counter and fetched her a packet of cigarettes. Realising that it would look more than a little strange to be standing in this shop without buying anything, particularly with a baby, even if she was transfixed by the light show, I grabbed a bottle of wine. Sidling up as if queuing to pay, I tried to act as though it was a total coincidence me being here, rather than following the woman in immediately after she'd made it clear she didn't want to talk to me.

'So,' I said, going for bright and breezy but ending up more along the lines of potentially-inebriated-while-in-charge-of-a-baby. 'Lovely day. I mean, for this time of year. Well. Not really a lovely day, but at least it isn't raining! I mean, that storm the other day – phew!'

While I was jabbering on, the woman had paid for her cigarettes and turned to go, head still ducked like an armed robber avoiding the CCTV. I took a slight step to the right to block her path, and before she could object gabbled, 'Anyway, so the bridge seems to be blocked off. What's the best way to get across the river?'

The woman froze, eyes swivelling from side to

side as if she was preparing to brandish a weapon and demand the contents of the till.

'I just needed some cigarettes!' she blurted. 'The Co-op's run out of Jase's brand and I didn't have time to go anywhere else. I'm not sticking around.'

'Wait, are you...?' the man asked, his eyebrows shooting up into his cap. 'I mean, I'm an open-minded fella. The bank doesn't discriminate against the source of my poundage, after all. But I thought you must be from Middlebeck or summat. We don't serve traitors and scabs or their scabby women in 'ere.' He shook his head in disgust. 'Better get back where you belong before I offer you a refund on them cigs.'

'I know, I'm sorry. I'm leaving now!' And with that, she pushed past me and fled. Utterly baffled, I dumped the wine on the nearest shelf and reversed the pushchair back out the door as fast as I could drag it.

'You one o' them too, are you?' the shop assistant called after me. 'Didn't you see the sign in the window? No kids and no New Siders.'

By the time I'd manoeuvred the pushchair through the heavy door, the woman was scuttling back down Old Main Street. I ran after her, Hope's wheels skidding on the damp pavement.

'Hello!' I called. 'Hey! Can you please stop for a moment!'

To my surprise she did, although that turned out to be because her car was parked there. I upped my speed and reached her just as she wrenched the door open. 'Please! I'm not out to have a go at you. If it makes you feel better, that guy just refused to serve me,' I gasped.

She paused, her curvaceous frame half in and half out of the car. 'You're from the New Side, too?' she asked, glancing around furtively. 'And you came here with a *baby*?'

'No,' I replied, then added quickly as the look of alarm reappeared and she made to slam the door shut. 'I'm not from any side! I'm from Windermere, and London, and I'm currently staying at Damson Farm.'

'So, what do you want?' she asked, clearly eager to get away.

'I want to get across the river so I can buy Hope some bananas. The mini-market's run out and besides milk it's her main food group.'

'You can't get across from the village. Have to go back to the main road. It's miles away, though. It'll take hours to walk there and back. And there's no pavement for most of it.' She looked up and down, sizing us up while still half in and half out of the seat. 'Stick her in the back, I'll take you.'

'I thought you were short on time. In the shop you said that you didn't have time to go anywhere else...'

She rolled her eyes. 'Course I had time. I was bored and fancied a mission. Plus, don't tell anyone in the village I said this – like, literally, don't or they'll lob a brick through my window or slash my tyres or something – but who in their right mind can be doing with a stupid old feud anyway? And the pleasure I get from knowing Jase is smoking cigs from the Old Side is worth the risk. He'd choke on them if he knew.' She cackled, eyes glinting, and I started to wonder if a lift was a bad idea. But then she looked me directly in the eyes and said, 'Trust me, he deserves it. I'm Alice, by the way.' Her dark eyes were so lovely that I felt like I *could* trust her, so together we clicked the car seat part of Hope's pram into the back of her Fiesta, loaded the frame into the boot and then I took my first voyage into the New Side.

'So, I don't know anything about this whole Old and New Side thing,' I said as we sped out into the open countryside. 'It seems a big deal, though.'

Alice grimaced. 'It is a big deal. Or at least it was. See, Ferrington was a mining town. Apart from Old Main Street, New Road and a couple of the smaller side streets, every house in the village was built for the miners back in the fifties. Ferrington was just a bridge and a boathouse surrounded by a few farms before the mine opened. The pit is who we are. But in the strikes, back in eighty-four, the village was split. The Old Side of the river went on strike, and it was brutal. Some families starved. All of them froze. If it wasn't for the help of the farms, who stayed neutral, whole families would have died. But the New Side, they wouldn't strike. Said they needed to keep working to support their elderly parents, put shoes on their kids' feet. And the worst part of it is, the entrance to the mine is on the Old Side, so every morning the New Siders had to cross the village to get to the picket line. It was their right to work, to keep earning a living, but the Old Side didn't see it that way, so they thought it was their duty to stop them.'

'And the only way to the mine was across the bridge.'

Alice nodded, slowing down to pull a sharp turn onto a dual carriageway. 'They blockaded it, day after day. The New Siders had to push through, getting spat on and kicked and shoved. Plenty of times men ended up floating in the river, from both sides. New Side started using boats, but then one of them was tampered with, and an old guy died. As the Old Siders got hungrier and colder and angrier and more disheartened, the worse it got because they blamed the New Side scabs. It soon reached the point where you didn't dare cross the bridge for any reason. Young women were getting hassled, people knocked off their bikes. Fights breaking out in the miners' club, windows smashed and worse. And then, a year or so after the strikes were all over, we demolished the bridge. And that was the last time the whole village did anything together. Now, we're two villages who happen to share a name. There's a campaign to officially change to New Ferrington and Old Ferrington, but these things take time, and the powers-that-be don't understand it so they aren't exactly hurrying things along.'

'Wow.' I let all this sink in as we began to re-enter the village, on the other side of the river this time. Someone had scrawled 'NEW' in black spray paint on the Ferrington sign.

'So, are both sides back working in the mine now?' I asked.

'You're joking?' Alice glanced at me. 'You really aren't from round here, are you? The mine closed in ninety-four. Over thirty-five years since the strikes, twenty-five since the mine shut for good, and we are still just an ex-mining town, because we don't know how to be anything else, and we don't have anything else to be.'

Well, I could relate to that...

'When the mine shut, it broke us. I mean, don't get me wrong, there are towns and villages all over who faced the same. No jobs, no purpose, defined by a miserable past, with no hope of a future. I'd not let anyone else hear me say it, but it's not as though mining is all that. Dangerous, dirty, knackering work with crap pay. But it's like even people my age, who weren't born when the strike happened, we've grown up feeling wronged, like we're the bottom of the slag heap, abandoned and left to rot. Maybe the anger will fizzle out, die with the mining generation. But I think it's more likely we'll still be angry – no jobs, no money, no help – just no one will remember how we ended up here.'

And I'd thought my life was depressing...

We pulled up then at the Co-op. The road mirrored Old Main Street almost perfectly. There was a Gregg's and a hairdresser, only the off-licence was a betting shop and instead of Pepper's Pizza, it was the Ferrington Fish and Chippy. Opposite the Old Boat House stood the Water Boatman pub, and instead of a replica old church, a white Methodist chapel squatted.

Alice waited in the car while I nipped in for the bananas, and this time I noticed the glances from other customers as I whizzed round, choosing the self-checkout to avoid an interrogation by the glowering older woman behind the till.

'So, were your family miners?' I asked as she drove us back to the farm, fascinated by this woeful tale of a village split in two.

'My dad was nineteen. He kept working because

he wanted to marry my mum. His dad mined too, of course. My uncle had three kids, one with cystic fibrosis, so he kept working. Mum's dad had retired with bad lungs, so that was another reason for Dad to keep earning, to help her family out. It wasn't that they didn't sympathise, or get why people did strike, but they never believed it would work. And turned out they were right.'

'So in the end the strikers did it all for nothing?'

'Yep.'

'And Jase, is he your husband?'

Alice shrugged. 'We moved in together a few months ago. To be honest, it was a rush decision and if he doesn't pull his finger out soon I'll be reconsidering. Only problem is, working in the Water Boatman doesn't make nearly enough to get my own place, and however much I love her, and everyone who knows me knows I do, I can't face going back to sharing a bedroom with my Nana.'

'You what?'

And right there I had made myself a new friend.

11

I arrived back at the farmhouse just after five. Alice had dropped me off at the end of the lane, leaving us to enjoy the last few minutes of daylight as I bumped Hope's pushchair the short distance up to the yard. Daniel's Jeep was parked in its usual place, and the cosy glow of lights from the hallway welcomed us back. Unclipping Hope and shrugging her out of the orange snowsuit, I expected Daniel to appear any second – or at least to call hello. Instead, I found him in the study. He was stretched out across the sofa, top two shirt buttons open to reveal a smattering of chest hair, one shoe kicked off, the other still dangling precariously from the end of his foot. One arm splayed out into open space, he looked as though he'd fallen asleep mid-air. His features had softened in sleep, the pucker between his brows smoothed out and his mouth carrying the hint of a smile. I could see Charlie there, only, perhaps Charlie on a bad day. His complexion was stark against unruly dark hair, the shadows from the sidelamp emphasising hollows beneath his cheekbones. He looked like a man with seven months' worth of sleep to catch up on.

It was nearly nine by the time he appeared, skidding into the kitchen in his socks, hair gloriously dishevelled, one side of his shirt hanging out.

'Eleanor! Hi!' His scrunched-up eyes darted around the kitchen.

'She's out for the count,' I replied, unable to keep from smiling.

'She's okay? Everything went okay? Has she had her milk, and bedtime porridge?' he gabbled, eyes still searching for evidence.

'Yep.'

'You didn't give her a bath? Because she'd be fine with a clean nappy and change into a sleepsuit.'

'She had a bath. We splashed and sang and

squirted her blue whale. It was a very lovely time. And then a story, milk and she settled straight down.'

He stared at me, this new information flitting across his face like data on a computer screen. 'Why... why didn't you wake me?'

'You looked like you needed the sleep.'

'But you've had her all day.'

'It was fine. We enjoyed it. Here.' I fetched a bowl and scooped out a ladleful of minestrone from the pot simmering on the stove. 'This is what real soup tastes like. And there's fresh bread on the table.'

After a few seconds of him staring at me, I placed the bowl on the table and pulled out his usual chair, before coming to sit down opposite.

'Wine?' I asked indicating my half-finished glass.

'I'll get myself a beer in a moment,' he said, slowly, picking up a spoon and eyeing the soup as though he didn't know where to start.

I got up and went to the fridge, twisting off the top of a beer and placing it in front of him.

'I can fetch my own beer.' He looked up, frown firmly back between his eyebrows.

'I'm aware of that.' I shrugged.

'You've done more than enough for me today.'

I took a nonchalant sip of wine. 'I don't understand why you sound angry about that.'

That was a teensy fib. I did understand, but I wanted him to acknowledge it.

'I'm not angry. I'm just... uncomfortable. I didn't need you to bath Hope and put her to bed. You should have woken me up. And now you've made soup and baked bread and you're handing me beer. I really appreciate you watching her, but I don't need you to step in and start mothering me. We can manage fine. We have been – we *are* – coping fine. If I was a woman, no one would think twice about whether I could balance a job and a baby and then cook myself dinner at the end of the day. Single women do it all the time. Why is it that because I'm a man, because I'm not Hope's biological dad, people assume I can't do this, that I need help?'

'Daniel, it's quite clear that you can do this. Even if it is grinding you into a total wreck. Although plenty of single parents have cleaners. And childcare! I didn't help because you needed me to, I put Hope to sleep because it was one of the loveliest things I've got to do in months. Years, probably. I love cooking. And I didn't bake the bread, I got it from the

Co-op. They sell fresh food over on the New Side, did you know that?'

'What, you went to New Side?' Daniel took a long swig of his beer to alleviate the shock.

'Yes. And we survived.'

'You took *Hope* to New Side?' His voice had risen a few notches. Another swig.

'I thought you were neutral in the Feud of Ferrington.'

He shrugged. 'No one's really neutral.'

'Well, I am.' I gave him a pointed look. 'Anyway, what I was saying is, I loved helping. But there's more to this. I've been freeloading off you for over a week now, eating your food and using up your hot water. I think we need to talk about what happens next.'

He put down his spoon and looked at me steadily. 'I said you're welcome to stay as long as you want.'

'That's ridiculous. You don't even know me.'

'I know that you left London in the middle of the night and drove through a storm to get here with nothing but a few jumbled bags of clothes, even though you'd not heard from Charlie in well over a year. So, whatever the reason for that might have been, unless it might follow you here, or if there's any possibility I might end up in trouble for harbouring a criminal... Apart from that...' He paused to glance at me then, and to my shame, I simply nodded. 'You can stay here as long as you need to.'

'Thank you.' I swiped at the tears now spilling over onto my cheeks, and Daniel gave a small smile to show that he knew how much I meant it. 'But if I'm going to stay then we need to work something out. Rent. Bills. Food.' I offered a figure that seemed reasonable, and to my surprise, he nodded his agreement.

'Fine. But if you're going to continue acting like my housekeeper and Hope's impromptu nanny, then I need to pay you.' He quirked one eyebrow before, predictably, offering me almost twice the amount I'd offered to pay in rent.

'No.' I shook my head.

'If you're going to insist on me paying you mate's rates, then I'm going to charge you mate's rates.'

'How about we call it even? It's exactly what Charlie would have done.'

Daniel finished off his drink while he thought about that.

I took a fortifying breath. 'Or... I have another proposition for you. Another idea of Charlie's...'

And then I got out the notebook, and it was a good job Daniel took that extended nap because by the time we finished talking it was hardly worth going to bed.

12

I had a lot of reasons for leaving London, resigning from my job and abandoning all of my stuff bar the bare essentials. I'd been gathering the courage to move on for a few weeks, as the growing rumble of discontent gradually gained volume every time I sat down to write, but then a parcel arrived on my doorstep, and the rumble became a blaring siren, drowning out all other thoughts.

Every woman with a public profile gets trolled. I suppose every man probably does, too, but I wonder if fewer of those messages involve graphic details about what the recipient should do with their body, or what the troll is going to do to said body. So, as my followers grew, and the trolls reproduced like rabid rabbits, of course I received a regular bombardment of nasty comments. Lucy and I accepted these as par for the course, deleting, blocking, and reporting as appropriate. That isn't to say that they didn't affect me. Many of them inspired nothing more than an eye roll. Some of them had Lucy and me laughing at their brilliant ingenuity. Far too many of them simply made me feel grubby and ashamed.

Delete. Block. Report.

It was part of my job, and one I grew far better at learning to handle like an emotionless robot. They didn't want to hurt me, they wanted to hurt Nora Sharp. Who didn't exist. Who wasn't, actually, me.

And then, just over a year ago, someone using the account name NoraShark sent a DM to Nora's Instagram account containing a link to a local news article about a Moroccan restaurant on the edge of Holborn. I had reviewed this restaurant. The food was great, and I made that clear in the review. The family who ran it clearly loved what they did. However, the main reason I had gone was to check out their new, heavily promoted live music evenings. The singer was dreadful, so of course a passing comment that people should go for the food rather than the entertainment ended up edited into a headline about serving earplugs alongside the starters.

This new article described how the singer, Layla Alami, who happened to be the daughter of the café owners, had been performing in public for the first time since completing chemotherapy. But of course nobody bothered to find that out until a video of Layla had gone viral, and the restaurant had become a local punchline. The so-called journalist who was supposed to be reviewing the evening certainly hadn't, because her focus had been on the food and the service. The customers stopped coming, and the owners hadn't the heart to continue.

They followed up the link with another message:

You did this. I hope you're proud of yourself for destroying a good family who did nothing but work hard and try to provide a decent life for their children. A beautiful girl is broken. She blames herself. Nobody else does. We blame you.

Despite what Miles and Lucy said, repeatedly, I blamed me, too.

We blocked the account, but over the next few weeks, more messages arrived, usually one every couple of days. The accounts changed every time: NoraShark1, NoraShark2 and so on. The messages ranged from the fairly mild, 'How can you carry on like normal when other people's lives have been wrecked?' to the disconcerting, 'One day you will know what it is like to feel the pain that you have caused others and when that happens my family can finally rest.'

The final message, sent from NoraShark32, when Lucy and I were both on the brink of contacting the police, said this:

I will find out who you are and then it will begin.

Lucy had found the children of the couple who ran the restaurant on Facebook. The Alami family seemed to be huge, with a community of aunts, uncles, cousins and various other relatives all in continual contact, despite living on three different continents. More online investigating revealed no clues about which family member might be sending the messages. Once they stopped, to be quickly replaced with more trolls eager to tell Nora how much they hated her, we breathed a sigh of relief and put it behind us.

Except... I couldn't help thinking about Layla Alami, who blamed herself, and her family. The knowledge that I had inadvertently caused such a horrible chain of events was impossible to forget. I sometimes lay awake at night wondering if there was a way to make it up to them. Hoping that, unlike me, they had genuinely been able to move on.

It was months later, in November, when Nora received a message from NoraShark33:

I know who you are.

An arpeggio of unease scrabbled up my back and gripped onto my throat. Lucy blocked them. I spent the whole night staring at the ceiling and praying it wasn't true.

A week later, from NoraShark34:

I know who you are and I know where you live.

No worse than a hundred other messages I'd had that year, but I deleted it with trembling hands.

Three more followed in the run up to Christmas:

Are you going to share your secret, or shall I do it for you?

Which one is the real you? The hateful bitch who destroys lives or the dreary coward who hides behind her?

Did you enjoy your goat's cheese pizza? If you did, will you tell everyone you hated it anyway?

That one sent me running for the bathroom, stomach heaving. I had ordered pizza the night before at an Italian restaurant a few streets away from Marcus's flat. It was the first time I allowed the proposition that this person was telling the truth to actually settle, instead of batting it away as the usual empty drivel.

Christmas Eve, NoraShark38 sent a picture of the dress I'd worn to a party the evening before. So that was a relaxing few days spent at the Tufted Duck, smiling and pretending everything was merry and bright as I flipped mince-pie pancakes while battling semi-hysteria.

I wondered about speaking to the police, but what could I say? The messages contained no explicit threats, they were sinister, but exposing my real identity was my problem, not a matter for the law.

December twenty-ninth, the day I got back from Windermere:

Nice trip home?

The next day:

Maybe now you're back it's time to discuss your plans for the new year.

All these messages were, of course, squashed in between countless others, ranging from gushing invitations to parties through to yet more of the usual violent vitriol. These felt different, though. And after that last one, a tendril of fear coiled around my lungs, constricting every breath. Only once Marcus had picked me up and we were safely over the

Severn Bridge and well on the way to our New Year's Eve party could I suck in enough oxygen to think straight. With Marcus's solid presence beside me, in the warm glow of the beautiful castle, surrounded by people who dealt with this sort of crap all the time, I was able to regain my perspective. Someone out there really hated me, but I could hardly blame them.

After arriving back in London a single woman, I let Lucy deal with the social media side of things while I cried, wallowed and tried to yank myself together and finally come up with a plan to move forwards with my life.

And then, late Thursday afternoon, I got a message to my personal email account. The sender was NoraShark@hotmail.com:

Not such a Happy New Year? Maybe it's time for Nora to RIP.

For once, I completely agreed. Outside of using it for things like Amazon purchases and my energy bills, about ten people knew that email address. In a flood of panic, I decided it was time for a break. I nearly bought a train ticket home, but then I imagined this person following me onto the train, finding out where my parents lived. What if they booked themselves into the Tufted Duck? Plus, how could I explain any of this to them? I needed to go somewhere far more difficult to trace, and I needed the flexibility and privacy of my own transport.

I needed to be with someone who knew who Nora was, and who'd listen to the whole story, hug me while I cried, have me laughing about the whole sorry mess and then come up with an outrageous plan to help me make it right.

I did a hasty search for used car dealers, diving into a taxi with my face encased in a scarf, hat pulled down low, and returning a couple of hours later with the only car I could afford to buy in cash.

I spent the rest of the evening pacing up and down, stuffing in Pringles and trying to form coherent thoughts that allowed me to rationalise what was going on. It was probably easy for someone with basic hacking skills to find out my email address, once they knew who I was. They still hadn't threatened me, not really.

They just wanted to torment me, it would seem.

I tried to calm down, collect my wits. I went through all my social media accounts, but Lucy had kept on top of things and there was nothing new that seemed to link to the stalker, or any of the Alami family. I tried to search the family's Facebook accounts again, but they were mostly set to private, and the few I could access were completely innocuous.

First thing in the morning I would pack up and head to Nottinghamshire, trusting and hoping that Charlie had meant it when she'd insisted that this time she'd be home for good. I put my doubts to one side and pretended to try to go to sleep.

When the first message pinged through to my WhatsApp, I nearly fell out of bed. Before I'd untangled myself from the duvet and fumbled for my phone on the bedside table, another one had arrived. Six more followed in quick succession. I read them perched on the edge of the bed, the only light the glow from the attachments as I opened each one with the apprehension and speed of a bomb-disposal expert snipping the red wire on a homemade device. The dread and dismay grew with each one. Most of the messages were a mix of news clippings, formal notifications and photographs clearly showing six different restaurants that had gone out of business in the past year. I recognised the name of each one because I'd reviewed them. Three of them were terrible and would have failed with or without me. Three more were okay, nothing special, and given how few new restaurants survived they wouldn't have succeeded without taking my carefully worded criticism on the chin and making some serious changes. My review could potentially have been their saviour.

The final news clipping was an obituary. Layla Alami's cancer had returned, and this time the chemotherapy could not save her.

You did this, message number eight starkly informed me. *You stole her will to fight.*

More messages, then:

How can you live knowing she has died?

Do you enjoy spending the blood money?

I told you to stop but you ignored me. Now it's too late…

Now it begins.

The flat intercom buzzed, and I let rip with a scream. I automatically threw my phone across the bed, heart thumping, the rest of me like one giant spasm of fear. Chest jerking with each heaving breath, I scrabbled off the bed and to the window, pulling back the blind with a quaking finger. I couldn't make out enough of the main entrance to see whether anyone lurked in the shadows there, but the rest of the street appeared to be empty.

Another message pinged.

Bloody hell. Should I call 999? I grabbed my phone and saw, to my utter terror, a photograph of the flat entrance. Not the main entrance, but the door into my actual flat, only a few metres down the corridor. In front of the door was a box, wrapped in brown paper and tied up with a red bow.

I waited an agonising fifteen minutes before creeping down the corridor, staring through the spy-hole, heart still veering dangerously close to super-sonic, trying in vain to quieten my sobs and rampant breathing long enough to hear whether anyone was still out there. I could leave it until the morning. Call Lucy and ask her to come over so we can look at it together.

While agreeing with myself wholeheartedly on this wise and rational decision, another part of me whipped the door open, snatched the box and slammed it shut again, clicking the locks into place before sliding down to join the delivery on the welcome mat.

'Crap, Eleanor, what did you do that for?' I whispered.

Now I was going to have to open it, wasn't I?

Slowly, gingerly, I unwrapped the box.

Inside, encased in plastic packaging, was, if my food-industry expert eyes were not mistaken, a heart.

A lamb's heart, at a guess.

Raw, obviously. Bloody and squelchy.

There was a typed note in the box:

A gift, seeing as yours appears to be missing. We will discuss your future plans in person soon.

Minutes later, having thrown an assorted pile of random items into the nearest bags I could find, I paused to take a photo of the heart, the box and its wrapping and then dumped it in the outside bin on my way the heck outta there.

13

Waking up the next morning, it took me a moment to remember why the usual feeling of *ugh* had been replaced with a flutter of anticipation: oh yes! I was going to make Charlie's dream come true and transform a ramshackle, rickety farm into an exquisite getaway venue. I was going to atone for at least some of the awfulness that I'd contributed to the world by spending the foreseeable future helping restore and build people up instead of smashing them down. Hope would have a beautiful place to live, and Daniel might even be able to take a day off once in a while. I'd cook, and clean, and for the first time enjoy the far more challenging and noble craft of being a creator, not a critic.

I couldn't undo what I'd done, but here at Damson Farm, I had the tiny twinkle of hope that I could at least, from this point forth do better. Time for my fresh start to commence.

I spent the day planning, plotting, poking my nose in the other bedrooms and making a list of what would need to be dumped, upcycled or stay as it was, and researching similar venues on the internet.

Then Lucy messaged:

I forgive you for firing me via a voicemail because I know something must be really up for you to walk away from Nora without even talking to me about it 1st, but honestly, WTF!?!?! I thought we were a team, not to mention friends! I can't believe that after every-thing you care so little about Nora, or me. I can't do that. I won't put Nora 'ON PAUSE' and I won't give up on her. I've spoken to Miles, and he isn't going to, ei-ther. I wish you all the best with whatever the hell it is you're doing, but, like I said: WTF!!!

I tapped out a quick reply, begging her to take the threats seriously and contact me, and then, with no small sense of trepidation, I looked at Nora's media accounts. Wow. Lucy had not been slow in adopting her new role. There were various images of her here, there and everywhere, entwined with random semi-celebrities and according to her captions having the time of her life:

#NewNora and #LetsGetThisPartySharp-ed and other gibberish about how from now on she was taking no crap and loving herself as she deserved, and not going to waste her shot.

I also quickly discovered that she'd changed all the passwords so I could no longer access any of the accounts. 'Well, Lucy,' I muttered while simultaneously deleting all the accounts from my phone and laptop. 'She's all yours from now on.' I didn't bother reminding her that at some point Nora Sharp probably ought to mention something about food.

I whipped up a tray of caramel brownies and raised a mug of peppermint tea in a toast of farewell to a friendship, a career and an imaginary woman who had been both the making and the breaking of me.

* * *

As usual, once Hope was in bed gently snoozing down the baby monitor, Daniel and I convened for dinner at the kitchen table.

'So, are you still set on turning my family home into a rescue home for stray city-slickers?' he asked, after we'd loaded our plates with butternut squash lasagne and squares of crispy focaccia.

'Only if you want me to,' I replied. 'It's totally up to you if I save your family home from crumbling into ruins while simultaneously creating Charlie's legacy, and securing a future for Hope. I'm easy either way.'

He let out a bark of laughter. 'I get the feeling you've never been easy about anything. I was half expecting to emerge from my study and find our first guests settling into minty cocktails and sourdough canapés.'

'Oooh, sourdough canapés. I'll add that to the list.'

Daniel stopped eating, serious now. 'Eleanor, this is a huge undertaking. A massive commitment. You can't decide this overnight.'

'How long did it take you to decide to keep Hope?'

He frowned, shaking his head. 'That's completely different!'

'Well, it is and it isn't. Sometimes someone or something needs taking care of. Needs someone else to say I'm going to make this work. And if it happens to be something you have the skills, experience and the time to do, why would you need a whole night to decide?'

'What about the money and resources? I don't have a lot I can invest in this. All the will in the world won't be enough to even get started.'

'I know we need to, like, do a million spreadsheets and look at costings and projections and expenditure and business plans, but I grew up doing this. I won't spend a penny on the retreat until you're happy we can see it through. But in the meantime, I have some savings. Not masses, but enough for paint, some new bedding and towels, toiletries, some other bits and bobs. I know what's worth spending on now and what can wait. To start with, why not let me just get the place looking nice again, a lovely place for Hope – and you – to live in?

Then you can decide about opening it up to other people.'

Daniel rubbed his scar. 'Can I be honest?'

'There's no point us talking about this if you can't.'

'Okay.' He took a sip of water. 'I'm concerned that you're doing this out of some sort of tribute to Charlie. Because you feel like you let her down by not responding to her invitations sooner. This is making it up to her. That's the last thing she'd want. She'd want you to be living your dream, not hers.'

I shook my head, vigorously. But he hadn't finished.

'Also, you can't start a project like this as some sort of therapy. Then, once you feel better move on, leaving me with it. I work with spreadsheets, not bed sheets.'

My instinct was to instantly brush off his concerns as preposterous, insulting. But this was his home, his life, and I owed him the respect of at least addressing his fears, so I took my time before I replied.

'I'm not a quitter. I stayed in a job that was wrong for me for years, because I'd been raised to be so responsible that I'd stick with something even if it half-killed me.'

'You hated your blog?'

'No! Not that job... Anyway. Hospitality is in my blood. I know what this will take. And, while we're being honest, where do you think Charlie got all those romantic ideas about providing a warm welcome to a weary traveller?'

'Um... Pinterest?' He winked, his open eye fixed right on mine. I disguised how it caused my stomach to backflip by pulling a face at him.

'I've been lost, for a long time now. The first day I hobbled in here, bashed up and beside myself, I could still feel the peace oozing out of these walls. This place is a priceless treasure, buried underneath the grot of neglect and... and heartbreak. It would be an honour, the best thing I've ever done, to do this. If you don't want it, can't face the disruption or the mess or the strangers, then I'll close the notebook and move on. But don't not do it because you think I'm following a whim, or a guilty conscience. Honestly, I think if you say no then I'm just going to start looking for some other falling down farmhouse and buy that instead.'

Daniel looked at me for a long moment. I tried not to worry about what he really saw. 'Okay.'

I think my whole face was beaming.

'To the first step!' Daniel clarified. 'Sorting out the place to make it nice for Hope. Then we can re-think what to do next.'

I held up my glass in a toast. 'The first step.'

Daniel shook his head as he raised his glass, but his eyes were smiling.

The logical place to start was the main living room. A large, L-shaped room with wooden French doors at one end, and enough seating for at least ten people, if you didn't mind threadbare, sagging arm-chairs or a couple of dubious looking stains. As well as the seating, there were built in floor-to-ceiling shelves either side of a fireplace with a paint-chipped mantlepiece, various mismatched side tables, a scuffed bureau and a TV cabinet containing an old video player and even older TV.

The clutter wasn't terrible, it was more the gen-eral air of tired neglect, reinforced by cobwebs in every corner and dust so thick it felt almost greasy.

Daniel had given me free rein to do what I liked with it all, as long as I didn't get rid of the photographs, books and any other personal items I happened upon. I spent a day sorting the ornaments and other smaller items into stay, go or upcycle. I dusted what felt like hundreds of books, resisting the temptation to sit and read the whole lot while putting a few to one side for later. The moth-eaten curtains were unsalvageable, but after a good wash some of the sofa covers came up okay. The following day, Hope and I visited a discount interior warehouse and picked up a load of brightly coloured cushions and matching throws, along with new lampshades, drawer handles and plain cream curtains to avoid detracting from the incredible view beyond the window. By Friday, I had scrubbed away the filth, swept up the insect carcasses, and to my delight when Daniel helped me roll up the grubby carpet, we discovered solid oak floorboards underneath. I nipped back to the warehouse and splashed out on a couple of rugs.

Saturday and Sunday, we painted the walls a soft, buttery yellow, and then came the fun bit – putting everything back again. I used the furniture to create two separate areas, one focused on the fire, the other around the French doors. I finished off with fresh flowers in a pair of stunning vases I'd found in the kitchen, along with a few candles, plus I replaced the faded oil paintings of shire horses and farm implements with photographs of the family and what appeared to be an old map of the farmland that I found in the bureau. The overall effect was bright, tranquil and scrumptiously cosy. Given time, and a bigger budget, I'd replace the fireplace with a log burner, and repaint some of the furniture, get the sofas professionally re-covered. But for step one, Daniel and I had to agree, while celebrating with takeaway pizza and a couple of beers, it was not half bad.

* * *

Monday, I decided to stick to paperwork and planning while my muscles recovered. I had just sat down at the kitchen table with a panini when a discordant clanging sound rang out so loudly that Hope dropped her bread stick.

'Eleanor, can you get that?' Daniel shouted through from the study. 'I'm three calculations away from a coffee break.'

'I don't know!' I called back. 'What *is* it?'

'Front doorbell!'

'You have a doorbell?' I raised my eyebrows at Hope, who simply stared back expectantly. 'You have a front door?'

It took another minute to wrench back the bolt and unjam the lock on the front door, which up until that point I'd presumed to be purely ornamental. Moving a cardboard box and an umbrella stand out of the way, I managed to heave the door open with an ear-splitting creak.

'Oh, hi!' I huffed, breathless from the exertion. It was Becky, Dr Ziva's daughter who I'd met in the orchard.

'Hi.' Becky gave an awkward wave. 'Sorry, I didn't mean for you to go to all that trouble. Should I have used a different door?'

'No, it's fine!' I opened the door wider. 'Sorry to keep you standing about waiting in the freezing cold.'

'No problem!' It looked like it might have been a problem. Becky was wearing navy leggings, mud-encrusted boots and a huge brown fleece. Even with a stripy bobble hat perched on top of her curls, she looked frozen stiff.

We looked at each other expectantly for a few moments, as if not sure whose turn it was to speak next. 'When we met in the orchard, you said to pop round, if I was at a loose end?' Becky said, eventually. 'To be honest, I'm at a loose end most of the time at the moment, but I wanted to leave it long enough to avoid seeming like I currently have no life. Or friends.'

'Right, yes, of course! Come in.' I stood back to let her in.

'Oh no, I didn't mean now, I wouldn't just turn up and expect you to drop what you're doing. Only I haven't got your number, so I thought we could either swap numbers, or arrange a time when you're free, and I'll come back then.'

I stood back to let her in. 'I'm free now. Please, come in. I'll put the kettle on.'

'Are you sure?' Becky's nose wrinkled up.

'You're not the only one who currently has no life. Or friends.' I turned and strode as confidently as I could down the corridor.

Becky followed me into the kitchen. 'Wow, this is nice! Looking a lot better than last time I came here. Which was years ago, to be fair.' She went to coo over

Hope, now smearing the soggy remains of her bread-stick across the tray of her highchair, while I made us a pot of tea.

After a few minutes of stilted small talk, Becky put her mug down. 'I'm sorry, but I can't not say anything.'

'Um... about what?'

'That's your lunch, isn't it?' She nodded at the now cold panini. 'I was going to pretend I hadn't noticed, but one of the reasons I gave up my job was because I'm fed up with putting on a polite face and pretending all the time. And now you think it's rude to eat your sandwich in front of me, when I'm the one who was rude for turning up here out of the blue and interrupting your lunch.'

'Um... it's fine.'

'Please, eat your sandwich.'

Deciding that was probably the least awkward thing to do at that point, I took a token nibble.

'Okay, so while I seem to be on an honesty roll, I'm going to take a risk and lay it out there.'

I reminded myself that Daniel thought Becky was a nice, normal person, and tried not to visibly brace myself.

'I like you, Eleanor. I know this is a bit primary school, but I've spent too many years schmoozing and charming people and I'm done with being fake. I sort of felt like we clicked. Friends at first sight. Is it too weird for me to ask if you'd like to skip all the faffing about and just be friends? Friends who can say, yeah, come in, but make your own cuppa because I'm in the middle of a panini. Without the need to be polite or worry about what the other one's thinking?'

I took a long, slow breath. Not because I wasn't sure what to say – because I wanted to savour the moment. I was done with being fake, too. And I wanted to eat my panini.

'That would be lovely.'

My business plan shoved to one side, we spent the next couple of hours doing the general getting to know you thing. I explained how I knew Charlie, and the tentative plans for the farmhouse, both of us weeping as we shared our memories of someone who had been a friend to both of us. I did skim over my previous job situation, but that was because we were 'done with being fake', and Nora Sharp was nothing to do with the real me. Becky filled me in on her old job, and how she left because she couldn't bear the loneliness any more.

'I pretended I felt lonely because I travelled around so much, but the truth is I was a big, fat fraud who couldn't trust the drivelling hogwash that came out of her own mouth. How could anyone get close to me, when there was no real me any more?'

I nearly told her, then. I would have told her, only Hope started crying because she was long overdue a nap, and by the time I'd settled her the moment had passed.

'So, you and Daniel,' Becky pronounced. I waited for her to expand, but no, that was it.

'What about me and my friend's brother who is also my landlord?' I asked, eventually, just to stop her from smirking.

'Your landlord who rescued you from the side of the road, invited you to move in and also happens to be both single, a really nice person and have a devastatingly sexy scar?' She shrugged. 'Just wondering how you were getting on. The two of you. All those cosy nights in together.'

'Sounds like you should be the one cosying up

with him if you think he's that great,' I retorted back, in a vain attempt to pretend I didn't agree.

She flapped one hand in dismissal. 'Nah. He's not my type.'

I resisted the urge to ask if pie and pint loving tradesmen were her type.

'So, how about you? Any sparks flying over the breakfast table? Are you like, spending your evenings hanging out together or what?'

'Wow. This really is a no-holds-barred, right from the get-go friendship, isn't it?'

Becky grinned. 'Don't worry, I've no one to gossip to. Well, apart from Mum, and I'm not about to feed that beast.'

I coughed. Straightened my mug on its coaster and cleared my throat again. 'Daniel is clearly a really nice guy. And yes, while we have spent some time together in between him working and looking after Hope, it would be far too complicated for me to entertain any notions of a spark. I love it here, and want to make a go of Charlie's dream. Developing feelings for her brother, who is, as you said, my live-in-landlord, would be a catastrophic move. So, in answer to your question, we're friends.' I smiled. 'Although I haven't officially asked him.'

'Okay, so to clarify, you fancy the pants off him but don't know if he feels the same way and don't want to make a fool of yourself?'

Before I could clarify her clarification by fudging something about how yes, of course I fancied him but I was hiding a horrible, shameful secret identity so couldn't do anything about it even if he hadn't been Charlie's brother, my landlord and possible future business partner, another clang rang out.

'What the hell?' Becky made as if about to duck under the table.

'It's the doorbell.'

'Wow. Sounds more like an intruder alarm.'

Which, it turned out, it might as well have been. Damson Farm was about to be invaded.

14

This time, Daniel got to the door before me. Due to my innate journalistic nosiness, I lurked a few feet behind him in the hallway to see who it was.

'Ah, hello there!' A man's voice boomed. 'Are we all right to leave our bags here?'

Then, as Daniel stood there looking a mixture of bewildered and incensed, the man wangled his way past him into the house, immediately followed by two women.

'This is so not what we were expecting!' One of them, dressed in what I knew to be a £2,000 coat, because I'd been given the exact same one in a different shade, muttered at the other, who scanned the hallway and stairs while unwinding a giant scarf from around her neck.

'Well, in here's not as bad,' the scarf unwinder replied, grudgingly. 'I mean, at least it's authentic.'

'Where do you want us?' the man asked, who'd come to a stop by the kitchen door.

'Um, how about back outside on the front step while we establish who you are and what you're doing here?' Daniel said, creaking the door open as wide as it would go.

'Heh, heh! Very funny,' the man chortled. 'It's the Stephe Winbrook party. Two doubles and a single. The other two will be arriving in an hour or so, they've got lost somewhere between back and beyond.'

'I think you might be the ones lost, actually,' Daniel replied, clearly losing patience. At that point, his phone rang from the study, and he quickly caught my eye. 'I have to take that. Can you deal with this, please?' He'd reached his study before finishing the sentence, firmly closing the door behind him.

'I'm really sorry, but you must have the wrong place.' Despite me knowing that this was true, I couldn't help automatically taking the £2,000 coat when the woman held it out to me. You can take the girl out of hospitality...

'Damson Farm?' the man asked. 'It's taken us hours to get here. This had better be the right place!'

'Uh, yes, this is Damson Farm. But can I ask why you're here?'

'We were invited! Booked the dates with Charlie yonks ago. She guaranteed a special advance rate for a midweek booking. Just the one night, like I said, three rooms. Perhaps you'd better check the system?'

My heart began knocking against my chest. Again, the hospitality in my blood kicked in. I smoothed down my jumper and stuck on my best smile. 'Certainly, if you'd like to wait through here, I'll do that right away. Did you say the booking was under Steve Winbrook?'

'I most certainly did not! *Steve!*' He let out a guffaw of laughter. '*Steve!*' The women tittered along with him, shaking their heads at my preposterous mistake. 'It's *Stephe*. Rhymes with beef. Short for Stephen. With a ph. If you ask Charlie, she'll re-member me.' He winked, and then winked again in case I'd missed it the first time.

I whipped open the living room door, hurrying in

to scoop up a stray beer bottle left over from the night before, and straightening a couple of cushions. 'Please, make yourselves comfortable.'

'I already have.' He gave me a deft full-body scan and winked again.

'Right, sir.' I couldn't force myself to say *Stephe*. 'I'll be back shortly.'

I hurried into the kitchen to check the non-existent system for a non-existent booking, instead grabbing my hair in both hands and frantically whispering a summary of the situation to Becky.

'Well, you'll just have to explain what happened.' She shrugged. 'I'll do it, if you want.'

I ducked back through to the living room. One woman was perched on the same sofa as Stephe, mumbling into her phone, the other had her head in a cupboard. 'Excuse me, you said you paid an advance rate? Can I please double check what that was?'

Stephe pulled his phone out and scrolled through it. 'Two for the doubles, one-five for the single. That's all meals and activities included. I did double check the offer on the website.'

There's a website?

'Right, £200, and £150. I'll be right back.'

'No, sweetheart!' Stephe called after me. 'Two *thousand*.'

Crap.

'We can't afford to refund them £5,000!' I whisper-screeched at Becky.

'Are you even liable?' Becky was cool as a cucumber. In fact, from the glint in her eye I suspected she might be enjoying herself. 'If someone who sold you a service has died, surely that's tough cheese? Isn't that what holiday insurance is for?'

'What if that means Hope is now liable?' I paced up and down, trying to get my head to stop spinning and start thinking. I had a sneaking suspicion that Charlie had taken thousands of pounds off these people, on the back of copious wild promises, without even considering the financial processes involved in setting up a business. If one of those snotty women got wind of this, who knows what the fallout would be? A bad review might be the least of our problems.

'I think I'm going to have to go ahead and let them stay.'

'*What?*' Becky squealed. No doubt about it, she was loving this.

'I can pull this off.' I nodded my head, mentally ticking through a checklist of the basics. 'We've got the bedrooms, I can rustle up some food, pour drinks. Figure out the rest as I go along. I can, can't I? I mean, I'm not sure I've got any other option at this point...'

Clang.

'That'll be the remaining guests, then.' I had to try and get the twinge of hysteria out of my voice.

I re-straightened my jumper, plastered the smile back on and went to greet them.

I was three steps down the hallway when Hope started crying.

So, Daniel emerged from his conference call to find five strangers lounging on his sofas, drinking tea out of his great-grandmother's best china and eating freshly baked scones with the last of his jam and the cream I'd been saving for a pasta dish.

Becky and I were upstairs frantically chucking clutter into the tiny box room and making up the beds using a mishmash of bedding that we were hoping to pull off as quaint rather than 1980s Argos.

'We're going to have to put someone in Charlie's room,' I said, when he came and found us.

'No.' He scooped Hope off the bedroom floor.

'They've booked two doubles! The only alternative is to squeeze another single in with this one and push them together. But then we'd have to swap this wardrobe for something smaller, and we simply don't have time to start humping furniture around.'

'There is another alternative.' Daniel looked resolute. 'You can tell them we've had an unexpected problem with the drains. Rebook for a later date.'

'We can't do that now, they've come from London! And they haven't exactly been impressed so far, they'll demand a refund rather than trek back up here.'

'Also, if you put all five of them on this floor, that's three rooms sharing one bathroom.' Becky deftly stuffed a pillow into its case. 'You can't charge two grand for a shared bathroom. A chipped, mouldy bathroom.'

'Crap!' I sank onto the bed, which protested with a loud creak. What was I thinking?

I was thinking five and a half thousand pounds!

We were going to have to keep bumbling on through.

'They could have your room?' I said, peeping at Daniel through my eyelashes. 'Then they can use your en suite.'

'They could not!'

'It's either that or Charlie's, or we send them away with a refund. Which do you prefer?'

Daniel huffed, puffed and stared at the faded carpet for a few seconds while blinking hard, before resting his head against Hope's fluff of hair. 'I'll start clearing my stuff out. Hope and I will sleep in the study. We can use Charlie's bathroom.'

I very quickly realised that we needed reinforcements. As well as sorting the bedrooms, clearing out and scouring the bathrooms, we needed to empty the dining room, and then find the time to prepare the three-course meal I presumed they were expecting.

I called the one other person I knew in Ferrington, praying she'd not have to work that evening, and would also for some inexplicable reason be up for getting involved in an unfolding disaster.

'Course I'll help!' Alice laughed. 'It beats another

night on the sofa listening to Jase playing Call of Duty. What do you need?'

* * *

My new friends were a revelation.

After showing the guests to their rooms, with an extreme apology about the lack of a bathroom for the single room (the drains excuse came in handy after all) and a promise of a slight discount, I used the guise of the glitch in the booking system to subtly discover precisely what Charlie had promised them.

A locally sourced, organic three-course dinner and breakfast I could manage.

The activities were a whole other matter. The Tufted Duck had not prepared me for what the third woman to arrive described as 'the lifestyle reconfiguration sessions'.

A bit of googling led Daniel to DamsonFarm.com and a basic stock template website that gave scant details beyond the address and some vague marketing waffle. Charlie had cleverly created the impression of exclusivity and up-scale secrecy, rather

than a half-baked shambles that hadn't made it beyond her notebook. So, at least our guests had no
preconceived notion about what lifestyle reconfiguration might look like in reality.

Becky had the best idea of the day so far: 'I think
we need to start with alcohol.'

Once Alice arrived, Becky swapped her fleece for
a smart pea-coat Daniel dug out of somewhere and
took everyone outside for some local mulled-cider
tasting. Local, as in Alice had picked it up at the local
Co-op. Mulled, as in I'd thrown in varying amounts
of cinnamon, cloves and orange juice and then
warmed up the three different brands of cider and
decanted them into rustic-looking pitchers I'd found
in the pantry.

As Alice and I raced back and forth emptying the
dining room, scrubbing the bits that showed and debating whether to go with crockery that almost
matched, or to embrace the situation with as random
a set as we could put together, Becky held court on
the patio outside, lit up by a couple of lanterns
Daniel found in the garage and the new living room
candles. As the group huddled amongst the weeds
around a hastily repurposed side-table, she spouted

forth the kind of spontaneous nonsense that had won her salesperson of the year six years in a row.

Pausing to duck her head back inside, Becky accurately assessed the situation as nowhere near ready and announced to the group that they would now be able to take a tour of the orchard and see the apple trees for themselves.

'What, this cider was made from apples grown here, on this farm?' I heard the endless-scarf woman ask, as I opened the dining room window to try to let the stench of mildew out.

'You can't seriously expect us to go trooping round the filthy countryside in the pitch dark?' the second man, Simon, said, his voice dripping with derision.

'Oh, come on man, where's your spirit of adventure?' Stephe chortled. 'We can trust Becky, she's an expert, after all!'

'Oh my goodness, Simon, are you in need of a top-up, let me rectify that for you immediately!' Becky trilled, sloshing another ladle of cider into his mug. 'Come on, someone grab that other lantern and please, do listen out for the ghost of the Damson Damsel. Don't forget to bring your drinks with you!'

I don't know what she did with them, but when they returned nearly an hour later, stiff with cold, designer boots encrusted with mud, cheeks aglow, they seemed in a far better mood than when they'd left.

'Right, then, dinner will be served at seven-thirty. Take your time freshening up. We'll see you in the living room for pre-drinks when you're ready.'

'Forty minutes?' I whispered. 'To prepare a three-course meal from scratch?'

Becky gaped at me. 'You haven't started cooking?'

'We've been cleaning, tidying, trying to find five wine glasses that aren't chipped and enough towels without holes in and a million other things that needed doing. Alice's been decanting shower gel and shampoo into old jam jars and making fancy labels out of chopped up birthday cards.'

'Well, we'd better get cooking, then, hadn't we?'

I grabbed her arm before she marched into the kitchen. 'This is amazing, Becky. We've been friends for less than five hours and I completely love you already, but you don't have to stay. Alice works in the pub, she's going to act as server for me.'

Becky glanced over at Alice, her brow furrowed.

'I've never seen you in the pub,' she said, all trace of perky saleswoman Becky vanished.

Alice nodded, stopping ironing a napkin to stick her hands on her hips. 'I've never seen you in the Boatman.'

Becky inhaled with a gasp. 'Eleanor, you probably don't know about all this yet, but she's a New Sider.'

'I know all about the feud that happened before either of you were born, I know that Alice is from the New Side, because she gave me a lift to the Co-op. What I'm not sure about is what that's got to do with my current predicament.' I went back to furiously slicing the potatoes for dauphinoise.

'Well... what will people think?'

'What people? I really don't think Stephe and Saskia are going to be particularly bothered.' I handed her a chunk of cheese and a grater. I really didn't have time for this. 'Alice doesn't care, do you?'

Alice, back to ironing, looked up, a glint in her eyes. 'I won't tell if you don't.'

'Ooh.' Becky's eyes darted from side to side as she contemplated this seemingly mind-blowing information, that two women from opposite sides of the same village could spend an evening in a kitchen together. 'Like a covert operation?'

Alice squirted a puff of steam from the iron into the air, as if making a point. 'Precisely.'

'I've been to thirty-seven different countries in the past six years, and got up to all sorts of things I hope my mother never finds out about. This is quite possibly the most exciting one yet.' She stopped mid-grate. 'Please don't tell my mum, though, Eleanor. She's giving me enough grief as it is. Or anyone else! I know it's stupid and I shouldn't care what people think. I know the whole New Siders being treacherous, sneaky bottom-feeders is probably a load of nonsense these days, but... well. No offence, Alice.'

'None taken,' Alice drawled. 'Why would I want anyone to know I'm hanging out with what *they* consider to be a smug, self-important snob? My lips are sealed.'

Becky's mouth fell open.

'Although I do have a bit of a blabber mouth from time to time. I mean, we New Siders can't be trusted, can we? I do hope I don't accidentally mention to Luke Winter on Friday when he calls in for his pie and pint that you're open to hanging out with

New Siders these days. I'll try really, really hard to keep my mouth shut, then.'

Becky turned a startling shade of beetroot, almost losing the tip of one finger as the grater slipped.

'Well, I mean, sometimes these things can't be helped,' she muttered, her voice about three octaves higher than usual. She tapped the grater to loosen any cheese stuck to the sides. 'I guess that's the risk you take in trusting a New Sider.'

'Okay, if we can draw the Ferrington politics to a close, we've got a sea bass with Prosecco Dauphinoise and seasonal vegetables and a locally sourced honey and damson tart to get sorted in, ooh, twenty-two minutes and counting.'

The kitchen door burst open, and Stephe and Saskia stumbled in. 'Did someone mention Prosecco?'

* * *

It was challenging work getting back into the swing of hosting paying guests. Five was hardly a demanding number, but it can only take one or two requests to turn a straightforward dinner into a stress-soaked slog.

No, we weren't aware that one of the guests was a vegan (apparently the cream tea earlier was an exception, because they'd had a hard week and deserved a treat). Yes, we could probably rustle up some second helpings (especially when that gave us more time to get dessert sorted). No, none of us 'gorgeous gals' were going to squeeze a chair in beside Stephe and tell him all about ourselves.

What we did have was Becky's party games.

'How's it going?' Daniel asked, wandering into the kitchen once he'd finally managed to settle Hope down, despite the ruckus.

'The food went down well. Mostly. One of them only ate green beans, but I get the impression that's all she ever eats.'

'What's next?' He picked up a slice of leftover tart and took a bite, eyes widening with appreciation. I resisted the urge to fan my face with the tea-towel. The adrenaline buzz made everything seem heightened, including Daniel's manly presence, loitering about taking up half the kitchen. I was feeling flushed with success, all dishevelled and triumphant, and it was teeteringly close to reckless.

'They've been asking what the after-dinner activity is.'

'So, what have you come up with?'

I nodded my head towards the living room. 'Becky is about to start, if you want to see for yourself.'

'I'd love to, but due to unforeseen circumstances I've not got my report done for the morning. Looks like it'll be a long night for both of us.'

He disappeared back into the study, and I slipped into the living room. The guests were all seated around Becky, posed dramatically to one side of the crackling fireplace. Her atrocious fleece was unzipped to reveal an even worse flowery jumper, but no one seemed to notice the unprofessional attire.

'Damson Farm is a place to dehustle and dehassle, to get away from all those crappy responsibilities and never-ending pressures. This, my friends, is a place where deadlines are dead, to-do is taboo. The only responsibility you have is to be you. The you you always wanted to be. Wild and free. Bold and beautiful. Here, you are an artist, a creator, an origi-nal. Your best you.' Becky paused.

The only sound was Saskia sobbing gently into a tissue while Simon muttered, 'Give me a break! Or at the very least a decent whisky.'

'But before you reclaim the real you, we need to lose the boring, money-bags, image-conscious you. So, who's ready?'

Alice, Becky and I were washing down the last of the tart with a pot of tea when Daniel strode into the kitchen. 'People are galloping up and down the stairs. Something that sounded distinctly like screaming came from the direction of the conserva-tory. If I didn't know better, I'd think they were playing hide and seek.'

Becky grinned. 'One more round and then we'll calm them down with sleeping lions.'

He shook his head as if mystified, grabbed the final corner of tart and whisked back out.

15

I managed a full two hours of sleep. Becky finished off the 'entertainment' with hot chocolate and buttery crumpets and I finished clearing up. The guests retired just before midnight, with the promise of a packed day of activities to come. I then sped ten miles to the nearest twenty-four-hour supermarket and loaded up a trolley with food and drink. I also chucked in some patterned notebooks with matching pens and about twelve different magazines. Arriving back at the farm around two, I spent an hour planning the next day, followed by another hour having an imaginary conversation with Charlie about how on earth I'd ended up running her lifestyle reconfiguration retreat. If anyone needed a life-style reconfiguration, surely that was me?

When the guests bumbled downstairs for breakfast at eight, I had kicked into action mode. The breakfast table was laid, a fire crackled in the grate and the kitchen was a bastion of organised efficiency. I was wearing a sleek charcoal dress that was the essence of respectable hotelier. After her disturbed night in the study, Hope was crotchety and disgruntled, but Daniel had taken her out for a walk before a work call at ten.

Chock-full of creamy cinnamon oat-milk porridge, smoky homemade beans on rye toast and a dozen eggs (the green-bean eater enjoyed a bowl of berries while the 'vegan' snarfed up the spare portion of eggs), the guests gathered in the living room for the first activity.

I took another emergency trip to Charlie's bathroom (the only one available to me at that point) to stare hard at myself in the mirror, channel something of my previous badass persona from the page to my actual personality, and grit my teeth until I was at almost no risk of bursting into tears, and then headed downstairs.

'Right, who's up for some vision crafting?'

'Vision what-ing?' Simon asked, glancing up from his phone.

'Ooh, yes,' green-bean-and-berries said. 'Is there a prize for the best one? Do we get a grade?' Her eyes went round with excitement. 'Or a certificate?'

'Absolutely not,' I replied, hastily continuing after her face plummeted. 'As you've already heard, Damson Farm is about you being you. It's your vision, your craft. How can any of us judge or critique, or *grade* someone at being their best selves?' I waved my hands around, trying to remember how Becky managed it the evening before. 'Here, we don't even judge ourselves!'

'So, to repeat, what exactly are we going to be doing?' Simon asked, not even bothering to look up this time.

'We are going to be considering four questions that are vital in the quest to reconfigure our lifestyles to become our best selves. Who we were. Who we wanted to be. Who we ended up being, and who we want to become. Some of you here have spent the past ten years running yourselves into the ground chasing what you're supposed to want. Meanwhile, your dreams are asking, "What happened to opening that café in the Alps? Where are the dogs we were going to rescue? You promised me we were going to learn the cello, try an open-mic poetry night, sit in the garden with a book and do absolutely nothing all day."'

'So. Once again.' Simon offered me a hard stare. 'What crap are we going to be wasting our time on this morning?'

'Um, cutting out pictures and taking the other craft stuff and sticking it on these plant pots. Then you're going to plant a seed, take it home and watch it grow, surrounded by your new vision.'

'Ooh, that's actually really symbolic,' Saskia said. 'I love cutting and sticking! It was my best subject at school.'

'I'm missing a board meeting for this,' Simon droned, raising his eyebrows at Stephe.

'Come on, old chap, we're here now. Might as well get your money's worth,' Stephe said.

'Oh, just one more thing,' I added, grabbing a bowl off the mantlepiece and holding it out. 'It's a no-phone activity.'

Simon sighed. 'Well, there'd better be some decent booze.'

By lunchtime, the dining room table was a snowstorm of paper snippets, soil and pipe-cleaners. Hope had thoroughly enjoyed sitting in her highchair helping Simon create his vision pot, which had ended up covered in pictures of penguins, white glitter glue and hundreds of tiny foam snowflakes.

'I just, you know, always loved penguins,' he explained, chin wobbling. 'Growing up, my bedroom was covered in posters of them. I adopted a pair of emperor penguins at the zoo, and they'd send me updates. I'd write back, and go and see them twice a year, and I swear they knew it was me. Peter and Penelope. Then, I dunno, exams and uni and work and before I knew it, we'd completely lost touch. Did you know,' he paused for a monstrous sniff, 'gentoo penguins mate for life. The male penguin finds a nice nest site, picks his woman, takes his turn when it comes to looking after the chick. A proper dad. A proper family. That's all I wanted!'

Simon wrapped his hands around the plant pot, tears threatening in his eyes.

Of course that was the moment Daniel poked his

head round the door. 'I'm on my lunchbreak, so I can take Hope.'

He walked around the table, picked up his daughter, plucked a pink feather out of her hair and a snowflake off her cheek and left without any comment on the mess everywhere.

To my monumental relief, the doorbell rang to announce my crew had arrived. I showed Becky into the dining room, with an apologetic shrug, and hustled Alice into the kitchen to start prepping an organic, locally supermarket sourced, Damson Farm lifestyle-reconfiguring version of a kids' party buffet.

I had never felt so exhausted. By the time they left, our guests had trooped back to the orchard to cover the basics of beekeeping with Becky, spent an hour baking honey bread, then lain on cushions on the living room floor and relearnt how to breathe before eating an afternoon tea incorporating the honey bread. While doing this, they had so often snivelled and grabbed each other's hands in moments of revelation about how their life in central London resembled a hive, that by the time they left it felt strange *not* to have constant chatter playing on a loop in the background.

Hard work I can manage. Emotional breakdowns and deeply personal outbursts I was not equipped to handle.

I dread to think what Nora Sharp would have made of it all. To my utter relief, for reasons I might begin to untangle once I'd had a decent night's sleep and a glass of wine, the guests had seemed to love it – Simon even commented on how the décor in the bedrooms and the decrepit bathrooms had been the perfect metaphor for his crumbling, neglected real self.

Even better, the ridiculously large tip meant I could pay my team. Becky refused it at first, until we agreed that she'd spend it on a secret Old Side, New Side and No Side night out, somewhere in Nottingham where no one would spot us.

'That was the most fun I've had in ages,' Becky said, opening the sole remaining bottle of Prosecco.

'That's what you call it?' Daniel asked, who had joined us for a late dinner of leftovers.

'Compared to farting on about pharmaceuticals

to people who mostly just want you to go away and let them get on with saving lives, it was fantastic!'

'Fun or not, it was a bloomin' success!' Alice said. 'Two thousand pounds each for that!'

'Charlie would have absolutely loved it,' I added. 'Seeing her dream come to life, even if it was completely last minute, chuck-it-all-together and hope for the best...' I had to stop talking and close my eyes.

'To Charlie,' Becky said, holding her glass up.

'To Charlie.' We all chinked our glasses in a toast, and for a brief moment it felt as though she was almost sitting here beside us.

'So, when's the next one?' Becky asked, after following our reflective pause with a long drink.

'Um, never?' I said, my eyes on Daniel.

He looked at me steadily across the table. 'Giving up on your dream so quickly? On *Charlie's* dream? Is that what your vision pot says?'

'You would really be up for doing it again?'

Daniel thought about this. When he was thinking a crease appeared between his eyebrows that a stupid, self-sabotaging part of me wanted to stroke until it softened away.

'With proper planning, some *reconfiguration* of

the farmhouse, sensible activities that people actually want to do... I don't think anything's happened in the past two days to make me change my mind.' The hint of a smile creased at the corners of his mouth. 'You sort of blew me away, to be honest.'

A flush of bashful pleasure cascaded up my neck and face like a scarlet tidal wave. Becky waggled her eyebrows at me.

'All three of you did. You were brilliant. We couldn't have done it without you.'

Ah, right. Of course. *All* of us blew him away.

'What d'you mean, "we"?' Alice asked, tossing her hair over one shoulder. 'I think your contribution consisted of grumbling, hiding in your study and eating the last of the honey bread.'

On that note, we called it a night.

16

Saturday evening, we got a taxi to a smart hotel with a cosy bar and a fancy cocktail menu in order to spend Becky's wages. I dug through the mishmash of clothes that I'd brought from my previous life, settling on a pair of jeans and a grey cashmere jumper that cost close to an overnight stay at Damson Farm. Alice had donned a floaty, embroidered dress that showed off her curves, and Becky had worn her usual leggings and a fleece.

'Oh no! You look really nice!' she groaned, once we'd shrugged off our coats and prepared to settle on a pair of sofas near the fireplace. 'Ugh. I knew I'd get it wrong. It was this or a starchy suit that needs tights. And when I handed in my notice I swore I'd never wear tights or court shoes again, unless I was in actual court.'

'You look...' I couldn't say she looked fine. She looked a scruffy mess. Alice grinned, waiting to see what I came up with. 'Comfortable. Which is surely the most important thing.'

'Where do you get all these amazing clothes from, anyway?' Becky asked, once we'd ordered our drinks.

'I needed them for my last job,' I mumbled, concentrating on taking a slurp of my Bellini. 'So, have you all recovered from the retreat fiasco? I still can't believe they went along with musical statues!'

'And what was that?' Alice asked, leaning across the low table.

'What was what?' I replied, all breezy as I inspected the menu. 'Ooh, these nachos look good. Anyone up for a sharing platter?'

'What was your last job?' She leaned even further forwards. 'Where did you live? How did you end up here?'

I looked at my two new friends, at their open,

lovely faces, and I could feel the truth clawing at my throat to get out.

But then I imagined how those faces would drop – with disgust, disappointment, dislike. How they'd pretend to understand, nod their heads and smile politely, but they'd realise the kind of person I really was, which was not their kind of person, no matter what side she came from.

And I was so damn lonely. I needed these two.

'Um, I was a freelance writer. I had a blog, did some features for newspapers. A bit of ghostwriting.' Strictly all true.

'Sounds like the kind of job you can do in pyjamas, not cashmere sweaters,' Becky asked, pushing her glasses up her nose.

'I had to meet clients. For the ghostwriting. I needed to present a successful image. And, you know, rich celebrities, they'd pass on their cast-offs. I hardly ever had to pay for anything.'

'Sounds cushy!' Alice said. 'Why'd you ditch it and come here?'

'Oh, you know.'

No, they didn't know why anyone would give up

the seemingly glamorous job of writing and move to a falling down farmhouse.

'I grew tired of it. Pretending my words were someone else's. I grew up in the Lakes, and big city life was starting to get to me. A bit like Stephe and co, just because something sounds like living the dream, doesn't make it *your* dream.' I wasn't sure they were convinced.

'Bad break-up?' Alice asked.

I pulled a face. This I could roll with. 'He was a lying, cheating sack of crap.'

'Well, why didn't you say so?' Alice rolled her eyes. 'Grew tired of swanking about with celebrities in free clothes!'

We of course had a good laugh about the retreat, going over our strokes of apparent genius along with the moments of utter cringe.

'So, what's next?' Becky asked. 'How are you going to get Damson Farm up and running for real?'

I shook my head. 'I'm not sure. All I was meant to be doing was sprucing up the farm before we decided what to do next. But amongst the lack of sleep, the preposterous activities and the stress of knowing we were one tiny misstep from a calamity the whole time, I sort of loved it.'

'I *totally* loved it!' Becky declared. 'Although, to be fair, it wasn't my money on the line.' She took another sip of her gin fizz then, before placing it carefully on the table. 'If you were looking for a business partner, however, I'd be up for it.'

I was speechless.

'I've got a fair amount of savings lying about just waiting for the right investment. I'm bored, lonely and I think I could bring something of value.' She paused to tuck a corkscrew curl behind her ear. 'I think we could work well together, as long as we draw up a proper agreement, make sure expectations and assumptions are all clear from the start.'

I swallowed. Blinked a few times. Shook my head in wonder.

'I mean, if you want to go it alone, I totally understand, absolutely no offence taken or feelings hurt. You don't even have to explain, beyond a "thanks, but no thanks". I'll still come and help you out as and when, obviously.'

I cleared my throat in a vain attempt to dislodge the chunk of emotions. Blinked a few more times.

'That sounds incredible.'

Becky's blank face broke out into her beaming smile again, bright enough to chase away any twinges of trepidation about whether before she invested in our future together, I should perhaps divulge my past.

New start. New life. New Eleanor.

The past was irrelevant, here, wasn't it?

'Well,' Alice chipped in, once I'd dried my eyes and blown my nose. 'Last I checked I've about thirty-five quid in the bank, but if you need a team member you can pay, instead of them giving you money, I'm all in.'

'Hurrah, our first employee!' I chinked Alice's glass with my now empty one.

'Who will be hired on a sub-contracted basis, and is therefore not an actual employee who requires national insurance payments!' Becky added, in an exact mirror of my celebratory tone, adding her glass to the mix.

And there you have it, Old Siders, New Siders, No Siders – Team Damson was born.

* * *

Every day the next week, Becky came to the farm. She'd known Daniel forever, and they quickly developed an easy camaraderie that helped settle my nerves about the whole thing. Becky hired a solicitor friend to help us plough through the legal side of our new venture, and it made sense to add Daniel as a director, given that we were using his property. We spent a couple of hours each morning working on the reams of admin, switching to cleaning, painting and sorting in the afternoon. Dotted amongst all this was time spent conducting what Becky deemed the most vital element to any successful business partnership: building trust and establishing a rapport, otherwise known as eating biscuits, savouring long lunches consisting of 'test menus' and 'test cakes', all accompanied by a steady stream of conversation.

Sometimes Daniel joined us, spooning mushed up carrot into Hope while making the odd suggestion or reeling us back in to reality when our ideas started straying beyond innovative and into downright silly.

I tried to pretend I didn't love those meetings best of all, but it was growing increasingly difficult. I knew this, because I was also struggling to remember why my growing feelings for Daniel were such a bad idea. He was a good guy. He was honest and forthright, the complete opposite of Marcus. A perfect example of the kind of person I was trying to become. He was a heart-squeezingly devoted dad. We laughed at the same things, were able to talk for ages or, more often, not bother talking at all. Most importantly, I felt completely comfortable with him – apart from those times he looked at me a second too long, or stood beside me to peer into the pan I was stirring, and I caught a whiff of his scent, and shivers ran up my spine that were far from comfortable.

I was rapidly starting to want to know everything about this man. I loved every second spent discovering who he was, who he had been – and, in the spirit of the lifestyle regeneration retreat, who he wanted to be. But the deeper we went, the more I wanted him to like me, the more important it became to keep the colossal shadow in my past hidden. Because the more I knew him, the more I knew that he wouldn't like what he found there. I was stuck, and it was distinctly *un*comfortable.

I also suspected that at times he could sense that

I was keeping something from him. Only, unlike Becky and Alice, he was patient, and gentle about it. At a loss of what else to do, I decided to simply enjoy his patience and his gentleness for as long as he'd let me.

17

One of the most important changes we needed to address was the bathrooms. Daniel had agreed that he would move into Charlie's room once we'd found the courage to sort through all her things and then redecorate. The storage space next to it could be adapted into a bedroom for Hope at some point, too. We spent a good while going over our options for the first floor, eventually agreeing to see if it was possible to convert the box room into a bathroom that could then have interconnecting doors to the two smaller bedrooms. It wasn't ideal, but as Becky kept reminding me, this was a retreat house, not a hotel or even a B & B, and we wouldn't be charging anything close to £2,000.

That gave us four bedrooms, with space for up to eight guests. If we managed to make a success of it ('What do you mean, "if"?' Becky retorted), then there were a couple of falling down outbuildings that were begging for a renovation. One thing at a time, however, as Daniel kept reminding us. Or, to be more realistic, about 300 things at any one time.

But we were getting them done. Damson Farm was being transformed.

I contacted Luke Winter and asked if he could provide a quote for completing the bedroom and bathroom plans. Two weeks into our new project, he came over to take a look and see what he could do.

Becky let him in, while I hovered in the background eagerly awaiting her life-long unrequited love.

'Becky.' He nodded, face unsmiling but what I hoped was the hint of warmth in his eyes.

'Um, hi Luke!'

Oh my goodness. Becky was close to spontaneous combustion.

Which might have explained why she then simply stood there, clinging onto the door, not saying anything else or making space for him to come in.

'Hi Luke!' I offered, over her shoulder, hoping that would be enough to kick-start her into doing something. Nope. I eventually resorted to firmly tugging her back out of the way. 'Come in. I'm Eleanor.'

'Yes.' He nodded. Of course he already knew that, along with everyone else wondering about what was going on up at the farm.

'Shall we get straight to it?'

Another nod.

'Becky, did you want to show Luke the first floor while I put the kettle on?'

'Um.' Becky glanced back at me, face afire, eyes golf balls of panic.

'Tea or coffee?' I asked Luke.

'Either.'

'Great. How do you have it?'

'However it comes.'

Wow. If he was this unfussy about his girlfriends, Becky would have no problem.

Becky was still frozen. Luke stood a couple of metres away, gripping a toolbox with both hands while examining a brown patch on the ceiling.

I decided to leave them to figure it out.

One way or another, they made it up the stairs. I found Becky standing on the landing, eyes transfixed on Luke as he measured a wall in the box room, his T-shirt riding high enough to reveal a strip of smooth, tanned skin.

I handed her a mug of tea, which, when Luke turned around to take the other drink, she then slopped all over herself. I resisted the urge to comment on how she'd made the effort to wear a pair of nice jeans and a snazzy blouse, instead taking the mug off her and shooing her into the bathroom. She was still in there when Luke left, with the promise of a quote to follow.

'You can come out of hiding now!' I called, my voice bubbling with laughter. She waited another minute before strolling out of the bathroom as if she'd been in there for a mere minute, rather than nearly twenty.

'I'll make myself a fresh drink, then we can get this landing carpet up, see what's underneath.'

As if. I followed her downstairs and as soon as we were in the kitchen, Daniel came and joined us, poking his nose into Hope's pram to check she was still sleeping.

'So, how'd it go?' he asked, grinning.

'Luke thinks it's totally doable. He'll send us a quote in a couple of days, but probably won't have time to do the work for a few weeks.'

'And?' He nodded at Becky, who had her back to us, watching the kettle as if a non-watched pot never boils, rather than the other way around.

'She tipped tea all over herself and then hid in the bathroom until he left.'

'Seriously, Becky? You can charm a load of obnoxious strangers into playing musical statues, and you can't handle being in the same room as Luke Winter, the most easy-going man on earth?' He shook his head. 'You've got it bad.'

Becky handed him a mug of tea. 'I've met a thousand Stephes at a hundred different events. Their flash and swagger don't intimidate me one bit. But a decent, kind, hardworking and honest man? Luke sees straight through all that sales-pitch BS, he's not interested. When I told him I got all As in my GCSEs he nodded politely before turning around and asking Monica Patchett if she'd like help finding her lost kitten. He's not impressed by any of the things I'm impressive at. All he's interested in is a person's personality, and I'm not sure I've got a real one of those left. Luke Winter would want a woman of *goodly character*. Not one who made a living conning medical professionals into buying life-saving drugs at rip-off prices.'

'How about one who walked away from all that?' I suggested. 'One who had the strength to admit that wasn't who she wanted to be, and who sacrificed a successful career to start over with nothing?'

'I have a lot more than nothing,' Becky groaned. 'The problem is I feel like *I'm* a nothing.'

I pulled out a chair for her to sit down on. 'Believe me, I get it.' Boy, did I get it. 'But don't insult me and Daniel by saying you're nothing. You're our friend, and someone we think worthy enough to partner up with in building our dream. Do you think Daniel would trust his family home to a nothing?'

'Okay,' she sniffed. 'But there's a long way between not-a-nothing and a woman Luke would consider crossing over to the Old Side for.'

'Oh, for goodness' sake! This isn't Romeo and Juliet! If Luke is such a good and decent person, he won't care about an old feud.'

'It makes it complicated, though. Old Siders are barred from the Boatman, Luke's local. It takes forever to detour around to his side. Let alone the constant grief from family and neighbours and everyone else. They wouldn't even serve him in the chippy if they thought he was sharing his fish special with me. What if we wanted to get married one day? We'd have to elope to avoid it becoming a mass showdown.'

I looked to Daniel for some rationality but he just shrugged. 'Old wounds run deep. It's not just Old Side and New Side to them. Ziva's father-in-law died during the strike. He was so malnourished and run-down that when flu turned into pneumonia, he couldn't fight it off.'

'Luke's great-uncle had a breakdown and left his wife and kids after the Old Side burned his bakery to the ground,' Becky added. 'This isn't some silly old feud to us. It's family, and neighbours. Lives changed forever, and every single one of them for the worse.'

'Yes, but isn't forgiveness and reconciliation the

only way to bring healing to those who've lost so much? There's a whole new generation who had nothing to do with it. And every Ferrington miner, whatever their side, from what I've heard, they all just tried to do what was best for their families. Surely continuing the feud means that no one wins.'

Becky twisted her mug round in her hands a few times as she thought about that. 'Yeah. Maybe. Probably most of the younger residents would agree it's time to start letting go. But easier said than done, to tell a man he has to forgive the people who watched his brother drown. To ask a woman, hey, isn't it time you got over having to let your children go hungry?'

'What if instead of focusing on what happened then, people had something new to concentrate on? Something that was good for the whole village, that would bring them together? Let each side see that the other side is simply other families, going about their business, trying to live their lives?'

'I can't imagine what.' Becky looked at Daniel.

He shrugged. 'Well, if Northern Ireland could reach a peaceful agreement, it doesn't seem crazy to think Ferrington could manage it.'

'Daniel, you're a genius!' I said, an idea exploding

in my head. 'Didn't they have a peace bridge some-where?' I whipped out my phone and did a quick search. 'Yes! Joining the unionist and nationalist sides of the River Foyle. Ferrington needs a peace bridge, and by getting everyone involved, we can bring the two sides together so once it's built, they'll actually use it!'

'That's never going to work.' Becky shook her head. 'No one will use it.'

'Maybe Luke Winter will when he comes to pick you up for your first date.'

At the mention of Luke, Becky's cheek flushed pink and she couldn't hide the smile tugging at her mouth.

'I get this is radical thinking to most Ferrings.'

'Try potentially life-threatening,' Daniel said.

'But I'm going to do some proper research, look into successful reconciliation projects, find out what worked, put together an unbeatable plan and then I'm going to build a damn bridge from your front door to Luke's and you can both thank me in your wedding speech. Now, didn't we have a carpet to rip up?'

* * *

In the end, before starting my End the Ferrington Feud project, we had some more recent history to confront. That Friday I had taken a day off from renovations to babysit Hope. I took her to see Ziva and the bees in the orchard, then walked to the river, where we stopped and watched the February sunlight flickering off the water and I pictured the precise spot where a bridge might go. With me looking after her on the Friday, Grandma Billie agreed to have her for the whole day on Saturday. Daniel had an important task to complete, and it was best done without a baby to witness the emotions it would inevitably conjure up. We did ask Billie if she wanted to join us, but she politely declined.

I gave Daniel a head-start up the stairs to Charlie's room. It wasn't the first time he'd been up here in recent weeks – as well as using the bathroom during the retreat, he'd fetched clothes for me on the first day I'd arrived – but entering your sister's room to fetch something and preparing to pack up her belongings for good are two very different things. I'd cried already that morning, and I hadn't even got up the stairs yet.

Knocking tentatively on her bedroom door, I found him sitting up against the bed, feet flat on the floor, hands resting on his knees.

'Hi.' I moved a pile of clothes from her dressing table chair and sat down. He didn't reply.

'We could do this another time, or not do it at all. Have another look at the plans and come up with something else.'

He frowned, shaking his head. 'No. It's the only logical option.'

'This is your family home, though. And Charlie's. If you're not ready...'

'I'm ready.'

'With all due respect, you don't look very ready.'

He looked up at me, then, and to my surprise he was smiling. 'I was just waiting for you, because I've no idea what half of this crap is, and even less of an idea about what to do with it all or where to start.'

My shoulders dropped several inches with relief. I opened the carrier bag in my hand and pulled out a roll of bin bags. 'Three piles: keep, recycle or charity shop, and throw away.'

Then I burst out crying. Because, it turned out, I was the one nowhere near ready to divide my best friend's life into bin bags.

We managed it, however, with a whole load more tears, some rueful smiles, deep belly-laughs and many, many stories exchanged. We had each known a different side to Charlie. Daniel knew Charlie as a little girl, before the brain demons hit. He'd known her in her peaceful place, surrounded by family, where she had no need to impress or put up any front. I knew the other Charlie – the adventurous, spontaneous, sociable Charlie. The woman who loved to get lost in a crowd, who thrived on the new and the waiting-to-be-discovered. Who wanted to cram in as much of life as she could, while she could, and bring as many people along for the ride as possible.

We also both knew the other Charlie, of course. But we weren't thinking about her today. Today was as good a celebration as we could manage of the real Charlie, not the one imprisoned for weeks at a time by illness, lost in a bleak fog of despair.

Once everything had been bagged or boxed up, we spent another hour trooping up and down two flights of stairs, filling up both cars before Daniel drove to the local recycling centre, and I dropped off a load of clothes, bedding and other useful items at Ferrington church, where they had a pick-up point for a clothing bank charity.

We then reconvened for takeaway pizza at the kitchen table. I'd suggested fish and chips, but Daniel wasn't in the mood to take a detour to reach the New Side, which, as I pointed out, was all the more reason for building a new bridge to save everyone the bother.

By unspoken agreement, we didn't talk about Charlie, instead moving on to lighter topics. Daniel told me more about growing up in a village, and honestly if anyone else had told me I'm not sure I'd have believed them. 'English country dancing' for PE? Cross-country that literally involved running, unsupervised, through the country, including a farm where the owner frequently brandished a gun at them? A self-appointed Ferring Sheriff who pa-trolled the Old Side, confiscating kids' scooters and locking 'stray' cats in her shed?

Daniel was equally intrigued by growing up in a bed and breakfast. Especially the kind of weird and wonderful characters who frequented the Tufted Duck, including the Henderson-Browns, who religiously came and stayed for a fortnight every summer, complained about everything from the shape of the fried eggs to the shade of towels, accepted their annual five per cent discount as compensation and immediately rebooked for the following year.

'This is the first time Hope's stayed over at Mum's for months,' Daniel said, changing the subject once the pizza boxes were empty. 'It's a bit disconcerting, not listening out for the baby monitor.'

'A wasted opportunity, then?' I asked. 'You could have got up to all sorts. Had a wild night out, got hammered, rolled in at irresponsible o'clock. You could have had a house party!'

He grimaced. 'No thank you, to all of the above. What I'm most looking forward to is an undisturbed night and no squawking wake-up call in the morning. I'm going to stay in bed and enjoy a lazy Sunday morning by myself.'

'Fair enough.' I sat back, blowing gently on my coffee to cool it down while trying *very* hard not to imagine a Sunday morning in bed with Daniel.

'Would you rather I left you to your solitude, then? Made myself scarce for the night?'

'No.' Daniel looked at me, steadily, and the air in the kitchen went completely still. Either that or my lungs had simply forgotten how to work, too distracted by the depths of potential in his gaze.

'Okay,' I managed to squeak, before immediately burying my head in my drink.

I was suddenly very aware that Daniel and I were alone in the farmhouse for the whole night. It was stupid. It wasn't as though Hope chaperoned our behaviour the rest of the time. But without her, it felt... it felt like I was falling for this man. That if circumstances were different, I'd be hoping he'd suggest we go through to the living room, and he'd come and sit next to me on the sofa, and then, well... without any chance of an interruption...

Thankfully, before I could follow that train of thought any further, Daniel drained the last of his coffee and stood up, stretching.

'Anyway, it's been a long day. I think I'm going to head up. Don't worry about the mess, I'll sort it in the morning.' He dumped his mug in the sink, pausing halfway to the door. 'Thanks for your help today. You being there turned what would have been an unbearable day into something... precious. Beautiful. And. Well. You seem to do a lot of that. I'm glad you were there. Are here.'

I nodded, unable to reply. And with a quick goodnight, he left me to spend the rest of the night clutching those words to my chest.

I was glad I was here, too.

18

I spent the next few days mulling over the feud issue. Was there any way I could try to get involved in this situation without coming across as horrendously offensive? The only positive outcome then being that both sides finally had something to unite them – their outrage at me, the patronising Out-Sider. I joined the community Facebook groups for both sides under different profiles (both fake), scrolling back through reams of posts to see what kind of problems the divide had caused (trying to resist the urge to get sucked into conversations about lost phones, found cats, Sally Jones' kids on the Co-op roof, or, one particular saga that went on for months:

'If Macca B don't stop leaving those fat balls on the rec where my dog can get at them it'll be HIS balls dangling from the bird feeder'.)

I scoured the websites for every village activity I could find, walked along Old Main Street to look at the posters on the miners' club noticeboard, then drove to the New Side to do the same at the Methodist chapel. Trying to find something that could cross the Maddon river, a common thread that I could tug on.

It kept coming back to the same thing: a bridge would be in everyone's interest. Reuniting the village would enable them to pool resources, save money and provide a desperately needed boost to local businesses. More importantly, rather than Ferrington's identity being forged around the worst time in its long history, a bridge would create an opportunity to celebrate something new and positive.

By the weekend, I'd found enough evidence to cobble together at least the bare bones of an argument. Becky was visiting her brother for a long weekend, and Daniel was juggling Hope alongside a work deadline, so I turned to my friend from the New Side.

Alice was working a double shift that Saturday, so I decided to treat myself to a late lunch, wandering into the Water Boatman just after two. About half of the tables were occupied, and another cluster of customers were gathered around a screen showing a football match.

Every single person turned to watch as I sidled up to the bar, glancing about for Alice, who was unloading a tray of empty glasses. She looked up at me and winked, nodding to a bar stool.

'All right, Eleanor?' she called, about three times louder than was necessary.

There was a general rumbling from the other customers. Scuttling to the stool I clambered on and kept my eyes firmly fixed on the row of bottles in front of me, but could still sense every eye in the room boring a hole into my back.

'Who's this, then?' one man asked, leaning on the other end of the bar. 'Ain't seen you in the Boatman before.'

'Oh, leave it out, Stigsy!' Alice shook her head, taking a wad of notes and about a pint of loose change from the man she'd just served. 'She's an Out-Sider. Only moved here a few weeks ago.'

'Moved where?' Stigsy said, leaning forwards to inspect me with a leer, as though he could find an address label, or catch a whiff of Old Side takeaway pizza.

'Damson Farm!' Alice folded her arms and stuck her chin up. 'Like I said, neutral.'

Stigsy sniffed. A few of the other men stepped closer, and a woman seated at a table in the corner with a set of dominoes called out, 'You know the rumours, Alice. Maybe Damson weren't so neutral as all that!'

'Yeah!' various people in the crowd agreed.

Oh my goodness.

What the hell had I walked into? I'd thought it was rural Nottinghamshire, not the Wild West.

'Shame on you, Carole-Ann Matthews!' Alice yelled above the growing murmurings. 'If we're talking rumours, what about your Dylan going to Ziva Solomon about his manky elbow because he couldn't be bothered to see Dr Porter over at Brooksby, eh?'

Carole-Ann turned scarlet, suddenly finding her dominoes deeply engrossing.

Alice picked up a tea-towel and began slowly

drying a pint glass, somehow making the gesture appear ominously threatening.

'And you, Dennis?' she asked, her voice soft with menace. 'You want to talk about the rumours regarding your little Tuesday night rendezvous? John Stoat, do I even need to mention the words MOT?' She scanned the room, eyes narrowed. I don't know about the rest of the crowd, but every hair on the back of my neck stood up.

'That was an emergency!' An older man with tattoos covering his bald head blurted, before grabbing his bottle of cider and flinging himself out the door.

'Now,' Alice carried on. 'If anyone of you want another drink today, or any other day I'm in charge of this bar, you'd better sit down, shut up, and make sure you don't pass within three metres of my friend here unless it's to extend a warm, New Sider welcome.'

The only sound in the whole room was my heart, approaching warp-speed as it rattled against my ribs.

'Well, a friend of Alice is a friend of ours, isn't that right, fellas?' A man wearing a tie and formal jacket over the top of his Mansfield Town football shirt said. 'Nice to meet you, love.'

'Cheers, Kev,' Alice nodded, the rest of the pub echoing his comments with rumbles of assent as they turned back to the screen and picked up their pints again.

I pressed one hand to my wheezing chest. 'And you arranged to meet me here why, exactly?'

Alice handed me a glass of white wine, eyes glinting. 'Nothing to get your knickers in a knot about. These lot know where the balance of power lies.'

'And you didn't think to warn me?'

'Nothing to warn you about!' She waved her hands at the now settled room. 'Besides, I thought it would be good practice for them, having a new face turn up. Prise open their narrow minds a fraction. Isn't that what you wanted to talk to me about?'

I took a long slow sip of wine, eyes closed as I regained my composure. 'I'm driving, obviously, I can't actually drink this.'

'Drink away. It's on the house. Ray over there starts his Uber shift in a couple of hours. He'll drop you back, no worries.'

I was very worried, actually. Although, the more wine that settled in my stomach, the more I remembered that this totally proved my whole point, that the village was in dire need of someone to come up with a brilliant idea to end all this nonsense once and for all.

Alice wasn't so sure.

'You want to *what?*' she whispered, leaning across the bar, eyes darting.

'Just an initial meeting, so we can get the ball rolling.'

'Did you see what happened here, less than an hour ago?'

'I did.' I stifled a hiccup. 'And I also saw that people actually need both sides. And they know it. The doctors, MOTs, they're just the tip of the iceberg. I've been looking into conflict resolution in small communities, and what we need is one person to stand up and speak out. The key is making sure that it's the right person – someone people listen to, and respect. Someone with standing, who wields power. Once you—'

'Blummin' 'eck, Eleanor, do not even joke about that being me!'

'Once this *very specific and wise and lovely person* starts advocating for reconciliation, all those other people who secretly want it too, who know full well that it's in the interests of everyone, once that person speaks up, other people have the courage to join them.'

'No.' She leant back, whipped her towel over her shoulder and went to serve more drinks.

Okay, stealth attack it was then.

* * *

After briefly contemplating walking home, wading across the river where it wound around the edge of the farm, I decided to save that escapade for warmer times, instead calling Daniel and offering him a cinnamon apple crumble in exchange for a lift home.

While I waited for him to arrive, I posted an event on each of the Ferrington Facebook groups. I'd been invited to enough events over the past few years to understand what motivated people to turn up to them. The difficulty in this case had been finding a suitable location. While admiring the impressive range of fruit ciders behind the Boatman bar, I'd had an idea that hit every base with one genius stroke, if I did say so myself.

Cider tasting in the orchard barn! Damson wine!

Damson and apple pies! Cakes! Tarts! Crumbles!
Jams and chutneys!

Next Sunday evening, a time that my rigorous research into Ferrington goings-on revealed had absolutely nothing going on whatsoever. Even the
takeaway vendors were shut. Both pubs were open,
but they were always open, and neither of them were
offering free drinks.

Underneath the giant font pronouncing THREE
FREE SAMPLES PER PERSON, I added, in much
smaller font, that there would be a 'short talk from a
local about Ferrington's glorious farming history'.
There. Now, no one could boo me when I gave a presentation that would of course mention Ferrington's
pre-mining history, before perhaps then dropping a
hint or two about how this could inform a potentially
glorious future.

In order to cover all bases, I adapted the posts
into real A4 posters, and printed out a pile of copies
while Daniel was bathing Hope, ready to pin to every
spare lamp post and available noticeboard the
next day.

All I had to do now was use my nationally ac-
claimed writing skills to pen a speech so convincing

in its brilliance that everyone who heard it would be too enthralled to either shout me down, run me out of town or wallop me over the head with a bottle of cider. And, immediately after that we could get on with raising the funds to build the Ferrington peace bridge.

You're welcome.

19

On Tuesday, after a morning sanding the hall floor, which Hope decided was alternately hilarious and terrifying, I realised with a jolt that it was review day. I couldn't resist peeking at Nora Sharp's social media accounts, just to check Lucy was safe and well, of course. Safe, well and loving every minute of it, it would appear: #GoingGlobal #FlyingHigh #Better-ThanEver. I then stuffed Hope into her snowsuit and we walked to the shops to buy bananas, a large slab of chocolate and, while I was there, I thought I might as well chuck in a newspaper.

The latest review was for an exclusive spa resort off the coast of Italy. I spent a few minutes scanning images and wondering why I'd never thought of #GoingGlobal, and then I read the actual review and decided that wreaking havoc and destruction in one country had been more than enough. Nora Sharp was an ill-placed comma away from getting sued. Or fired.

'Anything interesting?' Daniel asked, suddenly looming over my shoulder as I hunched at the kitchen table.

'Not really.' I twisted myself round to face him, plastering on a casual smile as I splayed myself across the open pages. 'Just, you know, thought I'd see what was going on back in London.'

'Missing the big city?' Twin worry lines appeared at the top of his nose.

'No!' I replied, letting out a derisive laugh verging on a cackle. I took a moment to breathe. 'I'm really not. I love it here. If anything, I'm looking to congratulate myself on making my best decision in years.'

I'd straightened up in my efforts to appear honest – which shouldn't have been that difficult, considering I was telling the truth. Daniel leaned closer, and while momentarily distracted by the proximity of his broad shoulder, accompanied by his now all-too-familiar scent and delicious warmth...

While I may have been closing my eyes and enjoying a shiver of loveliness, Daniel spied the review.

'Ugh!' he snorted, causing my eyes to snap back open. 'I can't stand that woman. What kind of moral vacuum must she have crawled out of to be able to not only live with herself, but act like she's *proud* of making a career from being unpleasant? I can't understand why anyone would give her the time of day, let alone read that poison.'

I flipped over the page, and tried to ignore the secret that thrashed in my guts.

* * *

A couple of days later, firmly refocused on the future, I persuaded Becky to help me clear out a space in the barn that stood closest to the orchard. After swinging open the double doors and shining Daniel's farmer-sized torch into the far corners, we agreed that a more professional opinion was required before venturing inside.

'I've already called Luke,' Daniel said, once we

retreated back into the warmth of the farmhouse to ask Daniel. 'He'll pop by in an hour or so.'

'It's your barn,' Becky squeaked. 'You're a fourth-generation farmer! Surely you don't need Luke to check it out for you!'

He grinned. 'I'm a transmissions and distribution forecasting manager, and I wouldn't risk setting foot in that barn without Luke's go-ahead. Whatever you two are planning, I doubt it's worth endangering lives over.'

According to my research, using the barn was going to save lives, not endanger them, but I wasn't about to argue against a visit from Luke.

While we waited for him to arrive, Becky distracted herself from the urge to hide in the cellar by prodding me further about the event.

'I think it's a lovely idea, could be a great evening, and those are in short supply around here, but what exactly is the point? Usually these things are done to raise money for something. This is free.'

I shrugged. 'I thought it might be a nice way to get to know some people, and try out some ideas for the retreat, test some new recipes. If the space works, we could think about hiring it out as a venue for parties, or weddings. Even corporate events.'

'Wow.' She raised her eyebrows. 'You've moved way beyond a retreat already.'

'The event space is just an idea. Really, I wanted to put on a free party in the hope I might make a couple more friends.'

'Or check out the local talent?'

'Yes! That's a good idea. We'll be needing more help once we—'

I realised by the look on her face that she was talking about a different sort of talent.

'Well, maybe Luke will come along, so you can be the ones checking each other out across the cider barrels.'

'Oh my goodness!' Becky burst out laughing. 'Can you imagine him turning up to an Old Side event. He'd be lynched!' Her laugh grew to what I considered to be completely out of proportion to the supposed joke. 'Or... or imagine if you'd decided to carry out some sneaky scheme to get both sides together, and then a load of people turned up from across the river! It'd be a full-on riot!' She snorted a few times, trying to get her next words out. 'You'd have to flee the country! Daniel could never show his face in the village again. I mean, the reality would *not* be funny, but the idea of you thinking it might work is hilarious.'

'I don't think you give the people of Ferrington anywhere near enough credit,' I huffed, ignoring a prickle of apprehension. 'You and Alice didn't take much convincing to work together. And when I was in the pub last week, Alice pointed out loads of people who'd sneaked over to the Old Side for one reason or another. I think this feud has become far more show than substance, only no one's brave enough to say it.'

Becky looked at me then, all trace of amusement vanished. 'Eleanor, promise you won't do something stupid. At least not without talking to me about it first.'

Before I could garble a jumbled lie (or confess the truth), Luke appeared.

After a rigorous inspection, he declared the barn to be solid enough. 'It's mostly surface damage, nothing that'll put anyone at risk. Although that ivy could be the only thing holding the back wall together, so be careful with that.'

'I don't suppose you'd have time to help us empty it?' I asked. 'I'd pay you for your time, of course.'

Luke flicked his gaze across to Becky, loitering a few metres away in the shadow of an oak tree.

'We'd *both* really appreciate the help, even if it's just half an hour.'

'I heard you make cakes.'

I smiled. 'I'm sure I could rustle something up. Why don't you two get started and I'll put the kettle on?'

I returned with tea and a decent chunk of carrot cake to see Luke and Becky lifting either end of a rusty water trough as they carried it out of the barn. Becky's face was glowing with exertion, her curls springing out beneath her bobble hat, and she looked positively gorgeous. I made a concerted effort to spend the next hour hefting the items small enough to carry by myself, leaving the larger ones for the two of them. It was working – Becky was keeping her composure, and even managed to stutter a coherent answer when Luke asked how the bees were doing.

'I could bring a couple of jars of honey over, if you wanted any,' she said, fiddling with her hat.

Luke raised one eyebrow in reply.

'I mean, I could bring them here! So you can pick them up when you come to install the bathroom.'

He gave a curt nod. 'Thanks.'

'Ever thought of moving out of the village, Luke?' I asked, dumping a crate of screws in the growing pile outside the barn doors.

He moved back inside to grab an old-fashioned roller lawnmower. 'Got no reason to move.'

'Well, then, Becky could drop her honey round to your house without it being a problem.'

Becky glared at me, mouth hanging open, making frantic tiny slashing motions across her neck.

'It's not a problem for me now.' He strolled past, swinging the mower as if it was made of cotton wool, not iron.

'It's a problem for Becky, given the response she might get from your neighbours.'

He paused, mower perched on his shoulder. Becky looked as though she might faint, whether from the topic of conversation or how rugged and manly he looked, I wasn't sure. Probably both. 'As tasty as Ziva's honey is, I'm not sure it's worth me moving house for, given that we've agreed Becky'll drop some at the farm.'

I resisted the urge to explain that honey was not quite the point.

Luke removed his gloves, pulled off his beanie hat to run a hand over his buzz-cut hair, then tugged it back on again. 'Time I headed off.'

'Well, thanks for all your help. Do you want me to pay now, or will you email an invoice?'

He took three strides over to where the remains of the cake sat on a crate, grabbed the lot and took a giant bite. 'Consider it paid!' he called, words distorted by a full mouth. Then he shot Becky a wink, jumped in his van and left her swooning in the spray from his wet tyres.

I spent that night twisting myself up in the duvet, imagining the various ways that the Ferrington mob might react to my idea. Then remembering how Becky had guffawed at the very thought of me inviting both sides to my stupid cider tasting, and spiralling into panic.

I lugged myself down for breakfast as soon as I heard Hope wake up, opting for coffee and a square of apple cake. My housemates were already enjoying their eggy soldiers.

After a fortifying gulp of coffee, I decided to go for it. I needed to be open about what I was planning. Given the risk – albeit surely a small one – of anything kicking off, Daniel had the right to know in advance, given that it was his farm.

'So... one of the reasons I'm clearing out the barn is because I'm planning a low-key type thing.'

Daniel looked up at me from under his brow.

'This Sunday evening.'

He waited, a blob of egg dripping off the end of his sourdough soldier.

'Like, with, cider tasting and food samples and, um, a short presentation.'

Daniel nodded, stuffing in the soldier in one bite. 'I was wondering when you were going to tell me about it.'

'You know already?'

One corner of his mouth tweaked up. 'I might not go on social media, but I do go into the village from time to time. Even if it wasn't plastered up and down

Old Main Street, this is a village. I couldn't take three steps without someone asking if I was really giving away free alcohol in my barn.' He took a spoon and scooped out the last piece of Hope's egg for her. 'I'm presuming it's some sort of publicity thing. Not that I'm sure how many of the random Ferrings who'll respond to the offer of free booze are the sort of clientele prepared to pay hundreds for a lifestyle re-configuration retreat.' He handed Hope her last piece of toast. 'You might get some future cake orders, though.'

'It's not totally for publicity.'

'Oh?' He looked at me, the creases sharpening across his brow. 'The short talk from a local?' He sat back, eyes widening as he pressed a finger against his scar. 'I'm not the local, am I?'

'No!' I gripped my hands together, took a deep breath. 'I am.'

'*You?* You're giving a talk about Ferrington's farming history?'

'Um, sort of?'

And then, because I couldn't bear to keep another secret from this man, who made me feel like it might be worth being myself – plus, I was genuinely starting to worry that I might be about to incite a mass brawl on his property – I told him precisely what I was planning on talking about.

'Okay.'

'That's all you're going to say? You aren't going to tell me I'm crazy or that I'm going to be responsible for instigating the Great War of Ferrington? Or at least that it's a total waste of time and effort.'

He smiled. 'How can trying to do a good thing be a waste of time? And as much as people might enjoy perpetuating the feud, very few of them would resort to violence, these days. Most likely people'll simply turn around as soon as they get there and realise both sides are invited. Some might decide to stay and heckle, start some aggro, but I'll deal with that. And you never know, one or two might even listen to what you have to say. In which case, it's a start. One tiny step closer to your peace bridge.'

Right then and there, I fell in love with Daniel Perry.

'Maybe keep the cider samples small ones, though. At least until you've finished your talk.'

20

Becky and I spent the weekend getting things ready. Did I feel guilty, duping my business partner and new best friend into helping me scrub the worst of the dirt off the walls, climb a ladder to swap the cobwebs in the rafters for strings of fairy lights and set up picnic tables, lanterns, a couple of patio heaters and other various bits and bobs we needed, all under false pretences?

Not as bad as I did when she donated two dozen jars of honey and a pallet of apples that Ziva had scrumped from the orchard the previous autumn. There wasn't anywhere near enough to make cider, even if I had had the couple of weeks needed to brew some, but Hope and I spent most of Saturday whipping up cakes, pies and tiny individual pastries for sampling, supplemented by plums from a Nottingham wholesaler. I wangled a discount from a local non-profit organisation producing traditional cider from wild orchards and then spent the rest of my budget on a crate of damson wine, along with tiny, compostable plastic cups for tasting, and a load of cheap cheese and crackers to go with the chutney samples.

Every time the anxiety started revving up again, I reminded myself of Charlie, and what she would have thought about it. I was certain that had she been here, she'd have been standing right beside me at the kitchen table, sleeves rolled up and face glowing.

The event was scheduled for 7 p.m. until 9. At 6.55, I added the last platter of cinnamon apple turnovers to the trestle tables lining one side of the barn. The lights were on, the heaters were blasting, and Becky and I were dressed in claret-coloured dresses to match the fruit themed décor (sprigs of dried flowers stuffed in milk bottles tied with red twine, red and green striped table runners, and strings of paper apples and plums draped from the rafters. Becky had even created a Damson Farm logo, thin, dark red text winding around a damson tree, which she'd blown up onto a massive poster and stuck on the back wall).

At one minute past seven, Ziva arrived, arm in arm with Becky's dad, closely followed by four of their friends. At two minutes past, Alice texted to say that she was on her way. At three minutes past, I was hiding behind the barn, bent over with my hands on my knees while trying not to throw up.

What the hell had I done?

Then I heard feet scrunching in the gravel behind me and a strong, warm hand gripped my elbow.

'Come on,' Daniel said, his breath warm against my neck. 'Becky's wondering where you are.'

'I just need a minute,' I said, breathing slowly to avoid retching in front of him.

'No, you need to get back to your event. Any second now someone from the New Side is going to turn up and you need to be there to provide the voice of reason.'

'Can't you do that?'

'This is your night, Eleanor. I'm not about to steal

your glory.' He twizzled me around to face him, taking one look at my stricken expression before pulling me into the warmth of his soft jacket, my face buried against his shoulder, his arms gently wrapped around me. 'You'll be fine. I've got your back. If it comes to it, Becky, Ziva, Alice, Luke... your back's not that big.' He gave it a friendly pat, as if to prove it. 'We can cover it.'

'Why didn't you tell me this was a terrible idea, and ban me from using your barn?' I mumbled into his shoulder, wishing I could simply stay there.

'Because it's not.' I could feel him smiling against my hair. How could one moment be so full of horror and so deliciously lovely all at the same time?

'If it was a good idea, someone else would have tried it. No one else is stupid enough to invite the whole village to a joint event, as if all that's needed is a teensy cup of cider and a piece of plum cake and everyone will live happily ever after.'

'Maybe that's because no one else is brave enough.' He paused. 'My sister invited the whole class to her birthday party, every year without fail.'

'Did they all come? From both sides?' I felt another painful wave of longing for my friend.

'No. To my parents' relief. But she kept on trying, anyway.'

The headlights of another car lit up the darkness beyond the edge of the barn.

'Come on, you're freezing. And as much as I believe in you, I've left my daughter in what might be about to turn into a bloodbath.'

I made a groan of protest.

'Eleanor, you started this. Imagine if it actually works. Imagine if at least some of the people who come, decide to stay and mend some bridges. Wouldn't that make it all worth it?'

The thing with Daniel was, when he spoke, something in me couldn't resist believing him.

He pulled away, and I allowed him to steer me by the shoulders, back around the corner and over to where a gaggle of people waited near the barn doors. A rush of adrenaline zipped around my nervous system. Fear-based, mainly. But also, mixed in there was a tiny bit of excitement. The faces were beaming as they were greeted by Becky, who handed each person three cardboard tokens, each of which could be swapped for a sample of cider or damson wine.

'Where've you been?' she asked, teeth gritted behind her smile. 'People are waiting for samples.'

'Sorry, I needed to sort something.'

'All sorted?' she asked, not fooled for a second.

I nodded, giving her arm a squeeze of reassurance as I nipped past her into the barn. Around twenty people were milling about in coats and scarves, either chatting with each other or looking hungrily at the tables. I hurried over to stand behind the drinks table, hoping Alice would arrive soon so she could start offering the food around. Seeing me taking up position, a queue quickly formed, tokens gripped in anticipation.

'Hello, everyone!' I took a deep breath, switched into hospitality mode, and got to work.

It took fifteen minutes before someone spoke the words I'd been dreading. The room had filled to around fifty people. Alice had arrived, bedecked in a red strapless cocktail dress and matching ankle boots, and was soon swishing around the barn brandishing trays. Daniel, wearing Hope in a sling, was playing Lord of the Manor, mingling his way through the clusters of villagers, nodding and smiling and stopping to make smalltalk. Once, he glanced over and caught my eye, giving an encouraging flick of an eyebrow, as if to say, 'See, it's going awesomely!' and my heart dissolved into mush.

'Um, excuse me?' An older woman interrupted, her face scrunched up in bewilderment and disgust. For a second I thought it must have been the cider. Then she pointed a gnarly finger at the middle-aged couple wandering towards us. 'They're from Bannock Lane.'

'Are they?' I asked, voice taut due to every muscle in my body having constricted at once.

'Yes.' She nodded vigorously, finger still extended like she was about to inflict a witch's curse on the approaching offenders.

'Would you like another sample, or I'd really recommend the tea loaf, if you want a little break between tastings.'

'Did you not hear me, child?' she replied, raising her voice, as she turned to face the intruders full on. 'That's Sue and Geoff Johnson! They're *New Siders*!'

Okay. Here we go.

Every single person in the room, bar Alice, froze. Daniel, bless him, tried to enquire after someone's sister, but he might as well have directed his question at the slice of pie they were holding.

The couple, suddenly realising they were in enemy territory, faltered about three metres from the table.

'Please,' I called out. 'Come and try the Sherwood Perry. It's got a hint of spice that is perfect on a chilly night.'

'Did you not hear what Angela said?' another woman scoffed, before turning to the couple. 'Have you no shame? Trying to sneak into an Old Side event! Ugh – one sniff of free booze and those New Siders are out on the scrounge.'

The crowd broke out into murmurs and scuffles. To my alarm, about half of them seemed to take a step forward, forming a wide circle enclosing the Johnsons.

'How dare you!' Geoff Johnson retorted, gripping his wife's arm. 'There were posters up and down New Main Street. And on the chapel noticeboard. This is a New Side event. You lot are the ones gatecrashing. Isn't that right, Paulie?'

A younger man, holding a cracker in one trembling hand, a piece of cake in another, turned pale, mouth gaping like a fish.

'What, are you one of them, too?' Yet another

man shook his head, face twisted in contempt. 'Greedy pack of freeloaders, the lot of them.'

Becky, standing on the opposite side of the room to me, carrying a tray of empty sample cups, gave me a wide-eyed stare, slowly shaking her head in disbelief, shrugging her shoulders in a gesture that said, 'You started this, now do something!'

'Um, excuse me, everyone!' I ducked out from behind the table and scurried over to where I'd cobbled together a makeshift stage out of old pallets. Daniel handed me the portable microphone he'd borrowed from a mate who ran a mobile disco, and I tried to stop shaking enough to keep it from repeatedly bashing against my face.

'Hello. Hi.' This was about as far beyond my comfort zone as it is possible to get. I'd spent years hiding from people who might take exception to me. Now I was staring into a packed barn of murderous glares, while raised twelve inches off the ground, just to make sure the people at the back could glower with an unobstructed view.

'So. I'm Eleanor, I've been living at Damson Farm for a few weeks now, and, well... I think Ferrington is fantastic.'

'Which side?' someone snarled.

'Both.' I paused to swallow, hoping it might bring my voice back down an octave or two. 'Both. I'm an Out-Sider, as you all know. I've no reason not to enjoy a lemonade in the Boatman any more or less than a double pepperoni from Pepper's Pizza. When the mini-market was out of bananas, I went to the Co-op instead.'

'Why not go to the Co-op in the first place, then?' Geoff Johnson interrupted. 'They always have excellent stock management.'

'Because it takes over half an hour to drive there!' I said, swiftly covering my nervous exasperation with a rictus grin. 'Surely, there are loads of you Old Siders who love a tasty portion of fish and chips now and again? Or New Siders who fancy enjoying a Sunday Roast in the Old Boat House.'

'Over my dead body!' The crowd began to chunter. A bead of sweat slid down my back.

'More like over hers!' a girl who looked about twenty sneered, 'She's the one invited both sides!'

'Is there a point to this?' someone else hollered, and to my shock I realised it was Alice. She grimaced at me from the back of the crowd, making frantic 'hurry up!' gestures.

Right. Yes. In a moment of utter recklessness, I forgot my Old Ferrington speech, took a deep breath, adjusted my slippery grip on the microphone, and got to the point.

'Forty-seven per cent of you on the New Side have to wait over two weeks for a doctor's appointment. The Old Side have a new GP which means as of two months ago, they're undersubscribed. Primary school children on the Old Side have to travel forty minutes on the school bus each way, because there's no bridge any more, instead of enjoying the health benefits of a short walk. The cost of the bus could pay for a whole extra teaching assistant. That means both sides miss out.'

I ploughed on for another few minutes, ignoring the heckles as I carefully stated the facts and figures, clearly highlighting all the ways that Ferrington lost out – financially, socially, convenience-wise, due to the bridge. 'Magda Riley has an advert up in the Co-op wanting a dog walker.'

'That's right, I do!' a woman in her forties called, waving her hand proudly. 'Since I started my new job

I don't have time to give my Doughnut a decent run in the morning.'

'Well, you might be interested to know that Poppy Pilkington has a poster in the mini-market volunteering to walk dogs for free because her mum's allergic so she can't have one!'

'It's not my fault!' a woman I presumed to be Poppy's mum said. 'I break out in hives all over!'

'My point being, this feud is helping no one!'

'It's all right for you to say!' one man called out. 'You weren't there!'

'With all due respect,' I replied, 'neither were you.'

There was a collective hiss of breath, followed by a stunned silence. I hoiked up my tights, and stepped into the breach.

'These awful, painful, tragic events happened before a quarter of the village were even born. And for the rest of you, the sad truth is that those younger residents are moving away from here in busloads. Who'd want to stay in a village ripped apart by past conflict?' I wanted to call it for what it was: bigotry, prejudice. But I thought about those one or two that might actually be listening to what I had to say, so I bit the words back.

'What if that generation, and those who come after them, know Ferrington as the place that for over a thousand years was the top crossing place on the Maddon? That before the bridge, the ferrymen ensured vital goods were able to reach the towns and villages across the region? James Black once transported twenty-seven sheep in his boat in one crossing. Roundheads used it to escape the advancing Royalists in the civil war. Some even argue that Ferrington Bridge is the real location for Robin Hood's infamous battle with Little John. What if your children grow up to be proud of this village, and all that it's achieved? Rather than believing it's a washed-up ghost village, only surviving on the bitter remains of anger?

'No one, this town included, deserves to be known for its lowest, ugliest moment. Why don't we remember Ferrington for its finest? I propose that we build a new bridge. A peace bridge. Signifying reconciliation, and forgiveness. A brighter future, that honours and remembers the past, but won't be defined by one chunk of it. You don't have to be an ex-mining town, known for what you're not. Let's decide who we *are,* and who we want to be, and let *that* be what counts.'

I paused to take another breath, my heart pounding. Daniel, Becky and Alice started clapping.

No one else joined them.

'I think we've all decided what *you* are!' Sue Johnson, the New Sider who'd started all this, had the audacity to shout.

'Yeah, and it's not one of us!'

'How dare you call us washed-up!' someone else cried. 'A ghost town? Living in the past? Those New Siders are just as much a load of treacherous bottom-feeders as they ever were!'

'Yeah! Bottom-feeders who belong on the bottom of the Maddon!' The older woman with the pointy finger then tossed her drink in my direction (it landed several metres short, splattering her own coat), and hobbled out, deliberately shoving into Geoff as she passed him. Within a matter of moments, a stream of villagers, Old and New, trooped after her.

In the end, only Ziva and her husband, Becky and Alice, Daniel and five other people remained.

Three of them looked to be in their twenties, the other two were Geoff and Sue.

'For what it's worth, we appreciate what you were trying to do,' Sue said, her arm tucked into Geoff's. 'But you had no place, tricking us all into coming here and not being up front and honest about it. Even if you were right, with all that stuff about money and pooling resources, and yeah, maybe it is time to lay the past to rest, give the next generation a chance. But this was not the way to go about it.'

And with that, the Johnsons turned and left too.

I retrieved a crumpled tissue from my pocket and wiped my forehead.

'Um,' one of the remaining guests cleared their throat. 'We didn't get our last two samples.'

'Here,' Daniel handed each of them a bottle of cider. 'Thanks for coming.'

'Er, I don't think so!' Alice said, snatching a bottle back from one of them. 'She was the one said they should throw Eleanor in the river!' She waved the bottle threateningly. 'Now get out of here!'

'Well, that could have gone a lot worse.' Daniel stepped up and bumped my side with his elbow.

'You think?'

'The barn's still standing, no one got hurt. They dispersed in an orderly fashion without the police needing to be called. I'd say that's a major win.'

'Might want to check your tyres aren't slashed, though...' Alice said.

'I don't know,' Becky mused. 'I'm really surprised by how well they all listened. I genuinely thought when you climbed onto those pallets that you might be leaving in an ambulance.'

'Well, I tried, anyway. And at least people seemed to like the food.'

'You got seventy-three people from both sides of the river together, in one place, enjoying themselves,' Ziva added.

'Yeah, for a whole fifteen minutes.' I sliced off a piece of Wensleydale and went to take a bite before realising that I couldn't stomach it.

'Fifteen minutes more than anyone else has managed!' Ziva took the cheese and stuck it in her mouth. 'At the very least, you gave us all a great deal to think about. And whatever they may have said, however fiercely they marched out, they'll have gone home thinking about it. I know this to be true, because I'll be one of them. Some of them will have to admit, however reluctantly, that you were right. And next time a New Sider needs the doctor, or an Old Sider drags her child out of bed at some unearthly hour to catch the school bus, they'll remember what you said. Now, we'll be off. I suggest you use the remains of the damson wine to celebrate an evening that Ferrington will be gossiping about for years to come. Becky will stay and help you clear up.'

'Is that doctor's orders?' Becky asked.

'It is.'

I thought she may have been about to protest, but at that moment Luke Winter appeared in the barn door. 'Am I too late? I thought it finished at nine?' He pulled up short when he saw Becky's parents, but to his credit he recovered admirably. 'Dr Solomon. Mr Adams.'

'Yes, in you go,' John Adams said. 'Everyone's welcome at Damson Farm this evening, and I think you're in time for the after-party.'

In the end, it was far too cold to stay in the barn without the mass of bodies to supplement the heaters. Instead, we packed up the remains of the food and drink and decamped to the farmhouse kitchen.

'How's Jase doing?' Luke asked Alice, once we'd filled our glasses with the remains of the wine. 'I've not seen him at football much this season.'

Alice, sitting opposite him, pulled a face. 'That's because he'd rather sit at home and play fake football on his X-Box. I wouldn't mind so much, but it means I have to watch telly on my phone, and if I want to read I need to go in the bedroom to get away from the noise.' She took a sip of wine. 'That's not true. I'd still mind. I might as well be invisible when he's gaming. And since he lost his job he's *always* gaming.'

'No luck finding anything else?' Becky asked.

She shook her head in disgust. 'Luck's got nothing to do with it. He's not even applied for anything yet. Still *considering his options*. Which is fair enough, only after four months considering, he's so far opted to remain seated on the sofa doing eff all.'

'Sounds like you need to have a conversation about it,' Becky said. 'You don't want to end up being taken for a mug.'

Alice shrugged. 'I don't want to end up one of those controlling, naggy girlfriends either, and there's worse things he could be addicted to. Let's face it, apart from that he's way out of my league. I've spent a lot of time considering *my* options lately, and for now Jase seems my best bet.'

I wanted to ask Alice why she thought a man who ignored her most of the time was out of her league. But by the way she flicked her hair over one shoulder, plastered on a grin and pointedly asked Becky if she'd been seeing anyone lately, I knew it was more important that I respected her closing the conversation.

Becky responded by choking on her mouthful of coffee.

'Do you know what,' she said, once she'd stopped spluttering, 'I really need to go. Busy day tomorrow.'

'So that's a "no" then?' Alice asked, for some reason refusing to let it drop.

'Yes, it's a no.' Becky yanked her long wool coat off her chair and over her shoulders, one sleeve whipping Luke, sitting next to her, in the eye.

'Do you need a lift home, Luke?' Alice asked.

'You're driving?' Luke asked back, blotting one

eye with his jumper sleeve, scanning her wine glass with the other.

'Becky is.'

'I don't think this evening is the best time for Becky to be venturing into the New Side,' Daniel frowned.

'Luke'll be with her!' Alice said.

'Right, I'm off then,' Becky interrupted. 'Um, Luke, if you need a lift then I'm sure it will be fine, if I maybe just keep my headlights off or something. I don't suppose anyone knows my number plate...'

Luke looked up at her, a polite smile on his face. 'I've brought my bike, but thanks for the offer.'

'Maybe another time?' Alice asked, face round with glee. 'Either of you free next weekend?'

'Oh, shut up!' Becky squawked, her bag thwacking Alice round the head as she raced out. Luke waited until her car had left the farmyard before making a swift exit.

'A bit too much?' Alice asked, after arranging her taxi.

'Yes!' Daniel and I answered in perfect sync, causing Alice to flicker her eyes between the two of us, another smile dancing at the edge of her lips.

21

After waking up the next morning, I spent a glorious hour thinking how lucky I was to be able to lie here in bed, watching the clouds float by the window. I was due to look after Hope later that morning, and I probably should think about clearing up the barn at some point, but it had been a hectic few days, and for now I was enjoying a cosy duvet, the first flicker of spring in the air and my ambling thoughts.

Until a text message pinged through to my phone, charging on the bedside table.

An unknown number.

The message was short, and to the point:

Running away doesn't solve anything.

As I sat there, lungs frozen, a second appeared:

Do you think you can get away with what you've done?

My heart skittered inside my chest, as a rising flood of panic sent my head reeling. I could barely focus on the third message:

I don't.

I dropped the phone onto the bed as if it had morphed into a venomous spider. At some point my body must have clicked into action, because when Daniel burst in moments later, I was quaking in the far corner of the room, hands clutching the collar of my pyjamas.

'What's happened?' he asked, voice sharp with alarm as he scanned the room.

It took another few moments for me to compose myself enough to speak. 'Nothing!'

'That yell didn't sound like nothing.'

'A... a spider. On the bed. It shocked me, that's all.' I tried to laugh.

He focused on the bed, frowning. 'Do you want me to chuck it outside?'

'No! No. It's fine. I can deal with spiders. It gave me a shock, that's all.' I rubbed my face with both hands, embarrassment supplanting the fear.

My phone pinged again, from somewhere in the rumples of the duvet. I resisted the urge to grab it before Daniel might see the message, even as my heart near exploded.

He shook his head, one hand gripping the back of his neck.

'For a split second there, I thought someone from last night had broken in,' Daniel managed a shaky smile, dropping his hand back down.

'You really think that's a possibility?' I asked, jerking my head towards the window.

'No.' He smiled for real then. It was ridiculous how even with the dread of the new messages, that smile felt like the first kiss of spring sunshine.

I grew gradually more aware that Daniel and I were standing in my not-especially large bedroom, both of us wearing our nightclothes.

Ping.

'I'd better get that.' My voice had dropped to a whisper. I so did not want to get it.

'Yeah.' Daniel ruffled his hair. Was it my imagination on overdrive, or was he flustered? 'I was hoping to jump in the shower while Hope was settled.' He disappeared around the door frame, only to reappear a second later, just long enough to say, 'Good luck with the spider.'

The latest ping turned out to be Becky, apologising for bailing on us so quickly the night before, and asking if I needed any help clearing up. I declined. Spending a good few hours clearing up the cider-tasting mess might help take my mind off both the far bigger mess that seemed to have followed me here, and the potentially even bigger one I would be landing myself in shortly if I didn't get a grip on my amorous feelings.

Perhaps unsurprisingly, clearing up the barn, spending a fruitless couple of hours flicking through wallpaper online, taking Hope for a long walk in the opposite direction to the village, all utterly failed to stop me churning over the latest messages in my mind. Over and over and over they went until I was ready to chuck my phone in the Maddon.

My initial instinct was to block the number. But then they'd only get a new one. If I let this number keep messaging me then when the police investigated my gruesome murder, they'd have all the evidence in one conversation. Plus, I'd tried ignoring them – running away – and it hadn't worked. As I tramped along the country lanes and footpaths, Hope strapped to my chest, one thought repeatedly sifted to the surface: I would rather know than constantly wonder about it. If things reached the point where I felt genuinely in danger – if, *please no*, they gave even the slightest indication that they knew where I was – I would speak to the police. I would definitely speak to Daniel. And then I would have to decide whether to face them, flip things around and try to contact the Alami family, or pack my bags and find somewhere else to hide.

The following day, Tuesday morning, I'd heard nothing more. I drove into Mansfield and bought a new phone, updating my Ferrington contacts and my family with my new number and then putting my old phone in my bedside drawer with the promise to myself that I'd only check it once a day. A promise I managed to keep for an impressive hour and fifty-seven minutes.

'You need to stop worrying about what they might do to you,' Daniel told me, as we tucked into a late dinner of pumpkin gnocchi on Friday evening, once Hope had settled in her cot.

'What?' I dropped my fork, splashing creamy sauce on my jumper, which made feigning cheerful confusion at his comment rather pointless. I did gather my wits quickly enough to realise that the *they* he was talking about wasn't the *they* I was worrying about.

'When I took Hope for her nine-month check-up today, people mentioned it, but I don't think anyone's gunning for you.'

'What did they say?'

Daniel pushed a couple of pieces of gnocchi around his plate.

'Come on. Whatever it is, I promise you I'll have heard worse.'

'They aren't so much angry, as, well... that's not true. People are angry. But at this stage it's no more than chuntering over village gossip. The receptionist probably summed it up best.'

I braced myself.

'She called you a deluded, impertinent pip-squeak and asked me to make sure you stop meddling in matters you know nothing about.'

'So, I can probably show my face in the village without risking a stint in the stocks?'

'In the Old Side, sure,' Daniel shrugged, his eyes glinting. 'I can't vouch for those snivelling, whiny New Siders.'

It being a Friday, and us being wild and crazy young things, we decided to find a boxset on the TV. Carrying our drinks into the living room, we picked an old BBC detective series, and settled back to watch. I don't know if it was because we were sharing a bottle of wine, but Daniel had sat next to me on the sofa. Positioned directly in the middle of his cushion, feet propped on the coffee table, I was nevertheless finding it increasingly challenging to concentrate.

About half an hour in, he picked up the remote and pressed pause. 'You're still fretting.'

'I'm not! Honestly, I meant it when I said I've faced far worse. Part of writing articles means people not only decide they hate you, they get pathetic amounts of pleasure from repeatedly telling you that.'

'Eleanor, you can't sit still. It's like sharing a sofa with a termite nest.'

'Sorry.'

'Don't be sorry, tell me what's up.'

Daniel's face softened in the glow of the table lamp. His arm twitched a few inches towards me, and my breath caught as I wondered whether he wanted to reach for my hand. I longed to lean my head against him, bury my face in his jumper and tell him everything, but instead I leant back, summoned up a self-deprecating smile and rolled my eyes.

'Sorry. I think it was "pipsqueak" that got to me.'

His eyes roamed my face, searching for the truth. I wished with a desperate ache that he could read my mind, even as I feared it.

Nothing could happen between us. It was a futile, miserable hope that the zaps of electricity were something he felt, too, when I was hiding so much. I could no longer pretend that my past life was irrelevant. But he'd made it clear how he felt about Nora

Sharp, and imagining him feeling those things about me was more than I could bear.

To never know Daniel as more than a friend, I could live with. To lose that friendship would break me.

I took the remote out of his hand, ignoring the flutter of attraction when my fingers skimmed his palm. Pressing play, I wiggled further back into the sofa and picked up my wine. 'I'm fine.'

* * *

It was a long night, spent twisting myself up in my duvet. After checking my old phone for the zillionth time, sure that this time I really had heard a notification ping through, I turned it off. I still heard the imaginary pings, but at least the remaining dregs of my rational self could now ignore them.

That wasn't the only thing keeping my brain whirring. My restless thoughts constantly roamed back to Daniel. To his eyes, his smile, every time he'd ever spoken to me or looked at me or happened to walk down the hallway at the same time...

To where he lay, wearing scruffy lounge pants

and a rumpled T-shirt, because even in March the farmhouse was still freezing at night, only a few metres away across the landing.

Most of all, I wondered whether he was thinking about me.

Nights like this, I ached for Charlie.

Hauling myself out of bed while it was still dark, I washed down a fortifying bowl of porridge with extra-strong coffee, stuck my hair in a ponytail, donned my scruffiest clothes, collected the necessary tools and climbed up to the top floor.

Since clearing Charlie's old room, it had sat there empty of everything but the bare furniture. Some of it would stay – I planned to repurpose an old chest of drawers and a bookcase to put in the side room for Hope, along with her changing table from the study, and the rest would go in the barn in case we wanted to use it somewhere else later on.

But first, the unicorn wallpaper needed to go. I checked the steamer had reached boiling point, grabbed a scraper and got cracking.

I took a brief lunch break to watch Hope while Daniel went for a run. I felt him eyeing me, sensed the trace of concern and questions behind his veneer of normality. Daniel was ready to listen the moment I was prepared to talk.

Re-emerging from the clouds of steam much later, I showered and changed into a sloppy pair of lounge pants and went to rustle up something for dinner. Daniel was sitting at the kitchen table with a newspaper.

'I cooked a rice thing.'

'Oh?' Surprised, I lifted the lid on a pot gently bubbling on the stove, dipping my head to investigate. 'It smells fabulous.'

'After working flat out since before dawn I'd imagine beans on toast would smell equally as delicious.'

'No, I love chorizo and prawns together. And is that feta?' I straightened up. 'For a straight down the line cheddar guy, this is impressive.'

He kept his eyes on the newspaper, pretending not to be bothered, but his eyes crinkled up at the corners. 'Well, your fancy metropolitan cooking ideas seem to have inspired me. And I presume Hope and I are going to benefit from all that bumping and scraping up on the top floor. This is the least I owe you.'

I fetched bowls from the dresser and ladled out two glistening mounds of deliciousness.

'Well, I can't start the master bedroom until you're out of there, so that makes the top floor next on the list.'

He filled glasses with flavoured water and handed me a fork. 'I'd have been happy to leave it undecorated, particularly considering everything else that needs doing.'

'You can't relax properly while surrounded by thirty-year old unicorn wallpaper, covered in Blu Tack stains and blobs of make-up! And Hope deserves a beautiful bedroom.' I paused, squeezing the sudden rush of tears back behind my eyeballs. 'I needed to feel close to her, today. Even if I was removing her wallpaper, I think she'd have approved.'

Daniel looked at me, his own eyes glistening. 'She'd have been so thrilled.'

I nodded in acknowledgement, unable to say anything more.

'This is really good!' I finally managed, a few forkfuls later. 'I might add the recipe to the retreat folder.'

'Why, thank you for the compliment, but it's a top-secret recipe.'

'I'm not sure it's *that* good.'

'Maybe not, but due to being unable to remember what I chucked in there, even I don't know the secret.' He put his fork down, turning serious. 'I am really grateful. I would have come and helped, only Hope's been grizzly all day. Bringing her up there would only have been frustrating for both of us.'

'I'm not sure a baby should be in all that hot steam anyway. And I thought we'd agreed that we're both equally grateful, so don't need to go on about it any more?'

'Yeah.' He pulled a rueful smile. 'You know. Still working through a few self-sufficiency issues.'

Daniel had given me a new start – a home, a purpose, and the chance to spend time with Charlie's beautiful baby, who made me laugh even harder than her mother had.

We were not equally grateful.

22

Sunday, I finished the last of the wallpaper-stripping and then took Hope out while Daniel got on with some work. After dillying and dallying about whether it was time to brave a stroll down Old Main Street, I decided to start by heading to the orchard. I could then choose whether to keep going along the river, and see where we ended up.

After the recent sunshine, the sky hung heavy with ominous rainclouds. Once Hope was in the sling, Daniel stepped closer to adjust her hood. He glanced up, meeting my eyes, and there it was again. That fizzle that started deep in my stomach and whooshed up through my body, sending my heart spinning.

'Have fun. Enjoy the river.'

'You too! Enjoy the spreadsheets.'

Such a snapshot moment of domestic bliss, if Daniel had leant closer and given me a goodbye peck, it would have felt perfectly natural. I dashed out the door before the flush on my cheeks gave me away. Definitely time for a brisk, breezy walk, with the added risk of encountering some verbal abuse at the end of it.

I found Ziva checking out the boy bees and their queens. Thankfully, she had the courtesy to take a break from poking about in a beehive while a baby was in the vicinity.

'Recovered from last week's excitement?' she asked, taking her beekeeping hood off and making the obligatory coos and smiles at Hope before perching on a nearby tree stump.

I shuddered. 'I'm completely mortified. That speech will be echoing in my ears for years to come.'

'It was an excellent speech!' Ziva declared. 'Clear, engaging, well delivered. You had us all transfixed. What more can you ask for?'

'Not being booed, heckled or having someone throw a drink at me before everyone storms out in disgust?'

'Well, there is that.' She waved a hand in dismissal. 'Bah. They'll have virtually forgotten about it in a week or two. One thing to know about the Feud of Ferrington: these days it is largely bark and no bite. All talk and no trouser, as my father would say.'

'How old were you when you moved here? Did you have family who worked in the mines?'

'I was only a child when we moved here, but my father was a GP, like me. It took a while for the village to accept him, but once they'd embraced him as one of their own he gave his heart to this place, looking after the people of Ferrington and the surrounding farms for over thirty years. He died in 1979. A heart attack. Which I can't help thinking was perhaps a blessing. He'd have been devastated to have witnessed what happened.'

'Becky mentioned that you lost your father-in-law during the strike. Does that mean you'd be against any sort of reconciliation?'

Ziva sat and thought about that for such a long time, I began to think she was deliberately ignoring me. Then she shook her head as if coming back to the present, and rested her chin in both hands.

'It was a very difficult time for our family. When John, Becky's dad, lost his father, it was heart-breaking. His mother never recovered. They were so angry, and so very sad. And some of his best friends – the boys he'd grown up with, worked in the mine with for decades – they didn't even come to his funeral. They've all passed on now, of course. And their children, grandchildren – should they be held accountable for what happened back then? Maybe, some of them. Some have said and done things since which were very, very painful. But does there come a time when these things must be forgiven? Of course.

'I meant it about your speech. It has disturbed me, in the best possible sense. One thing in particular has lodged in my heart and doesn't want to leave: how long are we going to be defined by what we are not? That's what got me thinking of my father. He was so proud to be welcomed as a Ferring. Like I said, it would have broken him to see what happened. Maybe I'm not the only one disturbed. Maybe now is the time for some honest dialogue. Some searching questions. To allow these old wounds to begin to heal. But I'm not sure you're the one to do it.'

'Could you be the one to do it?'

Ziva pulled a wry smile, pulling herself to her feet with an 'oomph'. 'Maybe twenty years ago. I may still appear to be full of vigour, but I'm not far off an old woman. And I have to think about John. While he may be open to change, his Israeli wife being the one to spearhead it would be another matter.' She reached out, her face animated again as she took hold of Hope's gloved hand. 'Now, I must let you get on with your walk, and you must let me get back to the F boys! What will Felix and Finlay think if I keep them waiting?'

We each turned our separate ways, her back to the boys, Hope and I to the river. I had so much to think about, my body felt stuffed with so many different emotions, jostling about demanding attention, I kept on walking, and walking, pounding out the questions and the frustration as we crossed the muddy meadow, strode along the side of the Maddon, all the way to Old Main Street.

Gathering my courage about me, I even braved a stroll around the mini-market. One man gave me the dead-eye from the end of an aisle, shaking his head in contempt when I ignored the evil stare. The young girl behind the check-out widened her eyes when she saw me approaching, but after a brief hesitation she ran my pack of bagels and bananas through the till, and even managed a tiny smidgen of a smile when I looked her in the eye, said thank you and wished her a nice rest of the day.

The proprietor of the disco-off-licence and cheapest vapes on the Old Side lingered in his doorway as I walked past.

'Yer barred!' he sneered, once I had clearly passed him. 'The baby 'n' all!'

Part of me wanted to swing around and demand to know why. The other, wiser me knew that he was dying for me to ask so that he could reel off all the reasons he'd come up with. Instead, I stuck my chin in the air and walked right on home.

Daniel emerged from his study once we arrived back at the farm. 'You need to call this number.' He handed me a piece of paper with a phone number scribbled on it.

'Why? Who is it?' I asked, dread filling me instantly.

He smiled. 'Nothing to look so worried about. Trust me. You want to call them.'

Maybe so, but I decided I needed a mug of tea and a piece of flapjack first.

'Hello? This is Eleanor Sharpley. I got a message asking me to call you?'

'Eleanor from Damson Farm?'

'Um, yes.' I supposed I was.

'Oh wow! Amazing! Thank you *so much* for getting back to me, like so totally quickly? I know you must be completely *inundated*, which is why it's such a total *quest* to track you down? Oh my gols, I still like, can't even believe it? Oh, hang on, there's Tamarind. Hey, Tammers! You'll never guess who it is! Like, totally? It's her, now, on the phone. Eleanor! No – can you believe it, *she* called *me*! I know! I know! ... I *know*!'

'Um, did you want something?' I asked, because the caller might know, but I certainly didn't.

'Well, I know this is like probably a total hashtag

fail already, but we'd be so happy just to go on the waiting list, if you ever have a cancellation – I mean, not likely, right? But stranger things have happened. So, could we put our names down? For like, four of us?'

'Your names down?'

'I know! I know! I'm cringing at myself even asking, but it took us *so long* to find the number of your assistant chappie, and you can't have bookings indefinitely, like they must come to an end at some point? So, whenever that date is, put us down. The full retreat.'

'The full retreat?' Slow, I know, but my brain was still catching up with my ears.

'Yeah, like the lifestyle reconfiguration one? Saskia said it totally changed her world! Like, that's why she resigned from Hardman and Hanes and re-branded as an apple guru? Whatever she did, we want that one.'

'Right.' *So wrong it's right?* 'First of all, let me take some details, then I'll figure out when we can squeeze you in.'

'*Yes*! I'm *totally* down for squeezing!'

Five minutes later, I had a party of four booked in

for a night on the May Bank Holiday weekend. I could hardly claim eight weeks wasn't enough time to prep for a lifestyle regeneration retreat, given that for the previous one I'd had about eight minutes.

I had some work to do.

* * *

Although the exclusivity of the retreat appeared to be its main appeal, we didn't want to be so exclusive that every potential customer needed detective skills to find us. Becky and I spent our mornings decorating the top floor, the afternoons creating a website that we hoped came across as mysterious and need-to-know rather than vague. We fiddled about with some numbers and costings, but with so much still to work out, we ended up simply adding something about how each retreat was custom-made, and to contact one of our retreat curators for a bespoke quote.

There was so much potential to waffle on about restoring well-being and cultivating emotional breathing space, spouting piffle that promised everything while refraining to specify what anyone would actually be doing in practice. We could have ramped prices through the roof and sniggered our way to a hefty profit. But that was not what we were here for. Becky and I were done with making money from spouting piffle. We wanted Damson Farm to welcome everyone who needed it. Those who thought they couldn't spare the time or the money most of all.

I worked with Charlie's notebook open beside me, and I sought to honour her dream in every word I wrote.

I was, however, realising that despite being a B & B girl born and bred, there was a lot that I didn't know about the ins and outs of the business. More to the point, while I knew *how* my parents ran the Tufted Duck, I didn't know *why* they chose to organise and plan and fry the bacon the way that they did. I'd be an idiot not to find out as much as I could as soon as I could.

I gave them a call that Wednesday afternoon, hoping to squeeze in a conversation during the relative lull between cleaning up from one weekend rush and getting ready for the next.

I hadn't spoken to them in a few weeks. My parents loved me, and I loved them, but neither of them had a mobile phone, and pinning them down for a conversation was not an easy task.

'Hi, Grandma.'

'Hello? Eleanor, is that you?'

'Yes. How are you doing?'

'Well, fine of course.'

'Are Mum or Dad around?'

'Who?'

'Wendy and Colin. Can you put one of them on the phone?'

'Colin has gone out.'

'What about Wendy?'

'What about her?'

'Can you tell her that Eleanor's on the phone and wants to talk to her, please?'

'She's upstairs, doing the family rooms.'

'Okay, but can you go and ask her to come and talk to me?'

'When do you want to talk to her?'

'Now, Grandma. Can you go and fetch her now, please?'

'Right.'

She hung up.

After leaving three messages on the answer

phone, and sending an email to the bookings line, I decided there was only one thing for it.

'I'm going to visit my parents for a couple of days,' I told Daniel that evening as we ate dinner. 'I've got loads of questions about how they run the Tufted Duck, and getting them on the phone is impossible.'

'When's the last time you saw them?' he asked.

'I stayed for a weekend last May, but they were full, so too busy to talk much past "Table three want scrambled eggs".' I shrugged. 'Then again, they're always busy. I can't remember them ever taking a holiday.'

'They never visited you in London?'

'I'm not sure they've been further south than Blackpool.'

'Is that what it's going to be like for us, once Damson Farm is open for business?' He stood up and collected my now empty plate.

'Most definitely not. We can't run a place to rest and recharge if we never take any time to practice what we preach.' I got up to help him with clearing up. 'Although you're hardly one to talk. You barely take a day off, let alone a holiday.'

'I took a month's leave when Charlie died.' He gave a rueful smile.

'That wasn't a holiday.' I flicked on the kettle. 'Maybe I should take Hope with me, give you a couple of days off?' I stopped then, as an even better thought occurred to me. 'Except then you'd probably end up working even longer hours without Hope to interrupt you. You should come!'

'What?' Daniel turned to face me, but he didn't look horrified.

'Come to the Tufted Duck. Best breakfast in the Lakes. I'm only going for two nights.'

'Are you asking me so you don't have to drive your death-machine?'

'No! I'm asking because it would be lovely for you to see the place that inspired Charlie to come up with her plans for here. And you could do with the fresh mountain air and soul-stirring views. Wouldn't it be amazing to spend two whole days without going in your study? No spreadsheets, no conference calls, the only forecasting required being whether to take a coat and what toppings you want on your breakfast pancakes?'

Daniel smiled. 'Sold.'

Becky was ecstatic about the idea of Daniel and I going on a 'mini-break'.

'It's a research trip!' I reminded her, for the fifteenth time. 'I'm going to be gathering information, grilling my parents and mostly holed up in the office while Daniel and Hope go and have fun.'

'Yeah, I completely believe you,' she smirked, dipping her brush back into the pot of cornflower paint we were using for Hope's new bedroom.

'We're staying with my parents! And my grandma!'

'Meeting the family. How very sweet.'

At that point I may have accidentally flicked blue paint in her hair.

23

In order to avoid the weekend crowds, we set off early Monday evening. Our plan was that Hope would sleep in the back of Daniel's car, but after an hour or so of fretful dozing she was well and truly fed up with the car seat.

'She's never been this long in a car before.' Daniel grimaced as he turned up the drum and bass playlist.

'Has she ever been further than Ferrington before?' I asked, swivelling round to waggle her stuffed giraffe in time to the music.

Daniel gripped the steering wheel harder.

'Please tell me you've taken her *somewhere* other than muddy fields and a bonkers village.'

'She's not even one yet!'

I waited, slightly aghast. I thought my parents were bad, but at least they took me to the beach every now and then. We even went to a castle once.

'She's been to the supermarket.'

'Wow, a real adventure.'

'And the hospital.'

'Another lovely memory to treasure, I'm sure.'

'To visit her mum.'

'Oh.' I turned back around, dropping Giraffe into the pile of road-trip necessities filling up the footwell. *Oh.*

A revamped 1970s floor-filler reverberated through the car as the glow of the sunset bathed everything with nature's own disco lights. I found a teething ring in my bag, which Hope chewed down on eagerly. The bittersweet memory of Charlie filled the space between us.

'Sorry. I know you've had other priorities than family fun days out in the past few months.'

Daniel sighed. 'No. You're right. It's not fair on Hope to have a dad who's too busy to do anything beyond getting her through each day. It's hardly what her mum would have wanted. I need to sort something so she can be properly looked after in the week, and then I'm free to give her my full attention at the weekends.'

'Either that or you give up your job and work with me and Becky, at hours to suit you.'

Daniel grinned. 'I don't think I'm quite cut out to be a lifestyle guru.'

'You can change beds and set tables. Plus, I've got so many plans for the garden that'll be a full-time job in itself.'

'I'm going to be cleaner and caretaker, then?'

I shrugged. 'There's accounting and admin, too, if you really can't live without spreadsheets. But I bet Hope would love to help her daddy bring the farm back to life.'

'If only it were that simple, I'd resign tomorrow. As idyllic as it sounds, the farm's not going to pay my bills or provide for Hope's future.'

'Your outgoings are practically nothing. Your biggest expenditure is a Friday night pizza. Let's see how this weekend goes, see what my parents have to say, and when we get back we can look at the numbers.'

'Maybe.'

'There's no maybe about how you and Hope will suffer if you don't start taking more days off.'

'Okay, well, your lecture has been sufficiently boring to send her back to sleep, so can we change the subject now?'

We did. We changed the subject more times than I can remember – meandering through childhood memories, dream destinations and whether halloumi is really all it's cracked up to be or simply cheese that squeaks.

As the shadows crept across the dashboard, Daniel's playlist softened into easy-listening classics and Hope snoozed gently behind us, I wondered if I'd ever spoken at such length and in such depth to anyone before. Charlie had spent a lot of time with me, but so often I had deferred to her opinions and ideas – not because she chose to dominate, but because I chose to tag along in her shadow. Becky was starting to get to know me, and we had chatted about everything from the evolution of feminism to what on earth Alice was still doing with Jase – which, to some extent, I supposed were the same topic.

But with Daniel, it was different. A whole new

level of getting to know someone, and letting them know me.

Except not all of me, of course.

Every time I talked about places I'd been or people I'd hung out with, my role at the newspaper, let alone how I'd ended up there, I had to censor my stories. Who was I kidding? I had to outright lie.

It was well after ten when I directed Daniel down the gravelly lane that led to the Tufted Duck. The only lights were the lamps bobbing on the boats in the marina to one side of us, and the cosy glow from the lanterns my parents had strung up along the porch up ahead.

We swerved around the side of the house to the staff car park at the rear. I gently scooped a rosy-cheeked, sleep-addled Hope out of the car while Daniel grabbed what bags he could manage.

'Are you sure they're expecting us?' Daniel whispered as I led him through the garden that was advertised as 'a stone's throw from the lake', which might be true if an Olympic athlete was the one launching the stone. 'It looks deserted.'

I smiled. 'It's nearly 10.30. The Tufted Duck clientele will all be safely tucked up in bed by now. This isn't the kind of establishment to encourage late-night carousing.'

At that moment, the kitchen door flew open and we were confronted with the silhouette of an elderly woman wearing a flannel nightgown and a head-scarf, brandishing an umbrella that looked to be nearly as long as she was tall.

'Who goes there?' she warbled, pointing the umbrella at us through the dark. 'Stop or I'll shoot!'

'It's fine!' I called, hastily passing Hope to Daniel before hurrying over, taking the end of the makeshift weapon and attempting to point it somewhere other than my face. 'It's me, Eleanor.'

'A likely story!' she growled, managing to jerk the umbrella away and make a thrusting jab at my stomach. Thankfully, her strength was about as effectual as her speed, and I had plenty of time to side-step the attack and move close enough into the kitchen light for her to see my face.

'Look, Grandma, it's me.' I placed one hand on her shoulder and smiled.

Squinting up at me, she took a moment to decide whether to believe her own eyes before grudgingly lowering the umbrella. 'You're late. Wendy and Colin are in bed.'

'Not any more, we aren't!' My mother stepped out from the doorway, cinching the cord of her quilted dressing gown tighter.

'What on earth is all this ruckus?' Dad asked, his bushy eyebrows bristling. 'This is a reputable establishment!'

'This woman stole my umbrella!' Grandma said, her face shining with glee as she pointed both index fingers at me.

'Hi, Mum. Dad.' I leaned past Grandma and gave them a wave. After a brief flash of surprise, they nodded in return, which was about as warm a welcome as a non-residential guest of the Tufted Duck would get. The older they grew, the more similar my parents looked. With only an inch between them in height, by day they lived in a uniform of plaid shirts and jeans so old they were fashionable again, and by night it was furry pyjamas and brown dressing gowns. Now both approaching seventy, their matching salt and pepper hair was kept short. Hands worn rough from all that cleaning, faces permanently tanned from all the gardening. Laughter lines were scarce, but years of worry were etched in permanent wrinkles. Solid, practical, predictable. Right then, it was precisely what I needed.

'Well, what are you doing turning up here at this time and scaring your grandmother and most of the guests half to death?' Mum retorted, ushering Grandma back inside.

'I did tell you in my message that we'd be arriving after ten,' I said, following them in.

'We?' Dad asked, eyebrows beetling in consternation as he waited for Daniel to pass him before closing the door.

'Yes!' I blew out a sigh of exasperation. 'I left two messages on the answerphone. Didn't you get them?'

Mum and Dad exchanged blank glances before turning to look at Grandma. 'Have you been pressing buttons on the phone again, Mother?' Mum asked, sternly.

'Well, how else am I supposed to listen to the messages?' she replied, shaking her head in bemusement. 'I've been answering that phone since before you were born. I think I know how it works.'

'So you didn't know I was coming?' I asked. 'This is ridiculous. I've called several times and emailed over the past few weeks. What if there'd been an emergency?'

'Well, has there been?' Dad asked, glancing around as if it might have snuck into his kitchen.

'No.' *Sort of. But that was back in January and I knew better than to try to drag you into that sorry mess.*

'What's the problem, then?'

I didn't add what I really wanted to say: *What if I wanted to just talk to my parents? Tell you how I was? Ask for advice or even find out how you were doing?*

'I hope there is no problem,' I replied. 'Because we've driven all the way from Nottinghamshire and were expecting a comfortable bed followed by an in-famous Tufted Duck breakfast.'

'Do you have a confirmation number or booking reference?' Mum asked, her eyes darting.

'Clearly not! I didn't think I needed an eight-digit number to visit my family home!' I couldn't bear to look at Daniel, the man who had welcomed a strange, bedraggled woman into his farm and given her a room and a hot meal. Plus a whole new life.

'Well, this is most inconvenient! We don't do walk-ins at this time of night. And besides, it's the

Weighbridge Walkers' annual Windermere Walking Week.'

'Mum, I am not a walk-in! I'm at the very least a customer whose booking you misplaced, and hopefully even more significantly than that I'm your daughter!'

'Well, this man isn't a relative.' She looked at Daniel and then jumped her eyes back to me. 'Is he? *Are they?*' she added, jerking her chin towards Hope.

'This is Daniel, Charlie's brother, and Hope, his daughter. And they'd like a room and a cot, please.'

'Well, I simply don't know...' The dressing gown got another tug. Dad said nothing, deciding instead to take Grandma back to bed.

'They can have the Mallard room,' Grandma called over her shoulder, in a flash of lucidity that put my suspicions about her previous nonsense in a whole new light. 'That walker cancelled at the last minute, remember, after tripping over their walking stick.'

I breathed a sigh of relief. 'Well, that's fine then, isn't it? If we can grab a hot drink then I'll get the room sorted.'

'Fine,' Mum frowned. 'As long as you're happy to share a double. I didn't want to presume.'

I felt a wave of embarrassment, quickly followed by an even warmer wave of something else at the thought of Daniel and I spending the night curled up in bed together.

'No! We won't be sharing a room.' I turned to Daniel and pulled my most apologetic face. He raised his eyebrows, the smile dancing at the corners of his mouth shooting my temperature even higher. 'Daniel is my landlord. I work for him, helping with childcare and housekeeping.' *Keep reminding yourself of that, Eleanor.*

'It's fine, Eleanor. We've become very open-minded in recent years in order to maintain our customer base. We don't ask those types of questions any more.'

'I should hope not! However, it won't be an issue because, as I've just said, we need *separate rooms.*'

'But we've only got one room!'

'Well, I presume you've not rented out my old top bunk to a Weighbridge Walker. I know they love it here, but even our regulars have to draw the line at Grandma's snoring.'

Mum looked shifty again. 'I haven't rented out your old bed, no.'

'Well, that's fine then, isn't it?'

'But we did move it into the Osprey room to create a second family suite. Your Grandma has a plain single now.'

'Okay. Fine.' It was, it was totally fine that I'd come home for the first time in nearly a year and there was no room at the inn. 'I'll grab a blanket and find myself a sofa.'

She folded her arms. 'You can't do that! It's against Tufted Duck policy. All guests must vacate the communal rooms by 11 p.m. No sleeping outside of assigned bedrooms.'

'I'm not a guest!'

She shook her head, jaw set. 'No sleeping outside of assigned rooms. Not even for family. Not even for *Charlie's* family.' Her voice cracked, and she sniffed sharply.

I closed my eyes, tried not to picture me and Daniel sharing a bed, counted to about two and then opened them again. 'Okay. I'll ensure I remain within the policy. Please go back to bed, Mum, we'll sort something out.'

She harrumphed and left us to it.

'I'd be happy to sleep—' Daniel started.

'Don't!' I held up one hand in protest. 'Please, don't let's talk about it until we've had a drink and something warm and fattening to eat first.'

Two mugs of hot chocolate and reheated slices of blackberry and apple pie later, we went upstairs to find that my parents had made up the Mallard bed and assembled a travel cot that took up most of the floor space.

'I'm so sorry about this,' I said, resisting the urge to bury my face in a frilly cushion. 'My parents live in their own world and sometimes I forget how bizarre it is compared to the rest of us.'

'How do they stay in business if they never answer the phone?' Daniel checked Hope's nappy and then tucked her gently under the pink blankets, where she let out a big sigh and scrunched up into a sleepy ball.

'Most of the guests rebook in person before they leave.'

He nodded to where a copy of the hotel policy had been propped up against one of the pillows. Underlined in red ink were choice sentences detailing no sleeping outside of a designated bedroom. No remaining overnight in any of the communal areas. No persons to occupy cars overnight. No sleeping or loitering in the grounds beyond 11 p.m.

'Looks as though you're sleeping in here tonight.'

I rolled my eyes. 'I can sleep on a sofa and then sneak back in here before they wake up. What's the worst that can happen if I breach the policy?'

Daniel smiled. 'You tell me.' He paused before adding, 'I did think you were here to ask your parents a favour, though, get some inside info on running a successful getaway venue.'

I thought about that, in between feeling embarrassed and awkward all over again.

'I don't mind if you stay.' He smiled again. 'It's a bit weird but I think we're good enough friends now to handle it.'

'Are you sure?' I was not at all sure that I could handle sleeping in the same bed as Daniel Perry. What if I rolled over in my sleep and wrapped my arm around his chest or something? What if Grandma's snoring was hereditary, and I snorted and snuffled all night?

'What would Charlie say?'

'She'd think it utterly ridiculous that we were even debating the issue.'

'I'll let you have first dibs in the bathroom.'

* * *

Daniel was the first to crack. I couldn't blame him. That had probably been the longest I'd ever stayed in one position without so much as twitching.

'Okay, so I've been thinking.'

I know. I could hear your brain whirring.

'We could both keep lying here pretending not to be wide awake, or we could give up and do something less stressful instead. That way, one of us might actually end up getting some sleep tonight.'

Daniel's voice was soft and deep in the darkness. Twisting my head slightly, I could just about make out the outline of his face, looking up at the ceiling. My heart thumped faster beneath the bra, T-shirt and jumper I'd worn, in a vain hope that increasing the layers between us would somehow lessen the impact of being in such close proximity.

He turned to look at me, expression swathed in

shadow, and every inch of my flesh broke out in goosebumps.

I couldn't breathe.

'Or you keep pretending and I'll carry on wittering until I've bored both of us unconscious? Okay, I can roll with that.'

I couldn't imagine anything I'd rather do right then than lie here and listen to Daniel's gentle murmurs through the dark. Except, perhaps, wriggle close enough to feel the warmth of his breath, lean forwards and...

'Gnnnnnn!' Our roommate let out an anguished groan before inhaling her lungs to maximum capacity and letting rip with precisely how she felt about waking up in the middle of the night in a strange cot, with a strange blanket, strange potpourri smells and strange shadows dancing on the walls.

There was an ungainly scramble while I tried to tuck myself out of the way so that Daniel, on the side furthest from the cot, could clamber over to grab Hope before the entire B & B were jolted awake in a manner that definitely went against Tufted Duck policy.

An age later, she still hadn't settled. Every time

she dozed off, and Daniel placed her back in the cot, she woke up, squawking in outrage.

'Okay, so there is something else I can try,' he whispered, after she'd nodded against his shoulder for the fourth time.

'I could squeeze into the cot, and she could have my space in the bed?' I suggested, only half joking.

'If I tuck something that smells of me in there, that usually settles her.'

Good plan. I could imagine the gloriously sweet dreams I'd have surrounded by Daniel's reassuring scent.

'The only trouble is, if I put my T-shirt from today in her cot, and then wear another one now, I won't have a clean one for tomorrow.'

I squinted through the shadows, my brain failing to decipher his point.

He shrugged awkwardly. 'I'm asking if you mind me sleeping without a T-shirt.'

Okay, so *now* I couldn't breathe.

I grabbed my phone and skedaddled out of there.

24

Grabbing my phone wasn't some automatic millennial addictive response. I needed to set an alarm to ensure I got up before my parents, which on a Tuesday morning in March would be somewhere around five-thirty. After all, the Weighbridge Walkers would be setting off with the sunrise, and a whole lot of eggs needed cracking and sausages needed sizzling before then.

Unfortunately, due to my disturbed emotional state when setting my alarm before collapsing on the biggest sofa in the lounge room, I failed to actually switch the alarm on.

Fortunately, Grandma was up, about and on the

prowl well before her son, and while being woken up to find her wrinkled, bloodshot eyes an inch from my own was not the best start to the day, it beat a poke with an umbrella or a lecture from my mother, so I forgave her even before she'd made me a coffee.

By the time my parents emerged, I was showered, changed and already sprinkling the first pot of porridge with cinnamon and brown sugar.

Daniel and Hope arrived towards the end of the breakfast sitting. I left my apron in the kitchen and went to join them with a platter of eggs, smoked salmon and home-grown tomato salsa.

Daniel busied himself loading up his plate and making sure Hope had her toast under control before squinting at me. 'I'm so sorry about last night. If it makes you feel any better, I spent several hours reflecting on my disgustingly creepy, white male privileged behaviour and putting strategies in place to ensure it never happens again.'

I sat back in surprise. For someone so attuned to, well, everything, Daniel had seriously misread the situation.

'I also kept my T-shirt on.'

I ducked my head, sure that my cheeks must be on the brink of bursting into flames.

Daniel lowered his voice even further. 'I really am sorry. I honestly meant nothing by it beyond trying to get Hope to settle and keeping a clean T-shirt so I didn't stink in front of your family.'

I took a sip of coffee. Not that I needed any chemical stimulus adding to my jitters. Daniel looked devastated. I couldn't let him go on thinking I'd taken what he said the wrong way.

'I didn't run away because I thought you were being creepy.'

He gave me a sharp look, a forkful of egg halfway to his mouth.

'I left because I didn't trust myself not to act creepy when in the same bed as you, in the dark, with no top on.'

Then I picked up my empty plate and mug and ran away.

* * *

Having put away the last glass and wiped every stray crumb I could find off the kitchen surfaces, I couldn't keep hiding any longer. I met Daniel coming down the main stairs, jacket and boots on, Hope in the sling. We both automatically paused when we saw each other coming, but Daniel was the first to start moving again, affecting what I think he considered to be a nice, normal expression.

'Are you going out?' I asked, my freewheeling thoughts not being able to grasp anything beyond stating the obvious.

'Yeah, I thought we'd go on a walk, see the lake. Give you some space to catch up with your parents.'

'Oh, we did that, last night. Dad already asked if there'd been an emergency and I said no. Nothing more to catch up on.'

'Right. Okay. Do you... want to come with us?'

While I appreciated the invitation, and under different circumstances I might have been tempted to say yes, the look on his face was enough to have me making my excuses about wanting to go over the booking system before I scuttled into the office.

'Ah, Eleanor, there you are!' Dad came in a few minutes later, his solid stomach leading the way. 'Gadwall, Pintail and Goosander all need a changeover.'

We had ten rooms in total, most named after a bird that normal people had never heard of.

'I'm just going over some of your admin processes, if that's okay.' I shuffled the office chair an inch or two closer to the desk, to prove my point.

He frowned, baffled. 'Room changes are done before admin, you know that.'

'Dad, I'm here visiting, not as a temp staff member. I've already helped with breakfast.'

'You're either here as family, and all family pitch in on changeovers, or you're here as a guest, in which case that'll be ninety pounds a night. You can have Pintail, as of this morning it's unoccupied.'

'Are you serious?'

I pulled my eyes away from the numbers dancing across the cranky old desktop screen. Dad stared back at me. Of course he was serious. I supposed that if I helped change the beds and clean the bathrooms I might be able to wangle some information as we went.

One sparkling, spanking clean Gadwall, Pintail and Goosander later, I had garnered the following.

The systems and processes employed by the Tufted Duck were in place because they'd always been that way, and why change something that worked? With that attitude, I was impressed they'd progressed to a computer. I did manage to gather some dribs and drabs on how they managed accounts and budgets, but honestly there was nothing I couldn't have found in half the time by looking on the internet. Mum did, however, reveal something of genuine significance.

'Did that person manage to get hold of you?'

'What person?' I focused very hard on smoothing down the fresh sheet on Pintail's bed as my heart began tap-dancing in my chest.

'They called asking to speak to you.'

'What did you say?' *Could have been an old friend. Someone from the town... one of the staff at the* Cumbrian Chronicle.

'Well, I told them you weren't here, of course.'

'And?'

Mum flicked on a duvet covered in frolicking forest animals with expert speed. 'And what?'

'What else did they say?'

'They asked where you were.'

'*And?*' I tried to keep my voice below a screech, despite my throat having seized up.

'Well, I asked who was asking. They said an old friend from school. I don't know who they were but with an accent like that they weren't from round here. I'm not about to give away any details to some stranger. I know all about stalkers and super-fans and things. I'm not an idiot, Eleanor. I told them to try your online whatsit. They could have been a tabloid journalist looking for a dirty scoop.' She bent over to start damp-dusting the skirting boards.

'Was it a man or a woman?'

'A woman. I think.'

'Anything else about her you remember?'

Mum stood up and went to shake the duster out the window. 'No.'

'When did she call?'

'A few weeks ago I suppose. Please don't stand there staring at me. That mirror won't clean itself.'

'After I'd called to tell you I'd left London?'

'Well, it must have been, or else I'd have mentioned it then.'

'Okay. Thanks for letting me know.' I gave the mirror a squirt of cleaner.

She was the one to stop then. 'Is everything all

right? Because you've just sprayed bathroom cleaner on a glass surface.'

'Yes.' I used the duster to wipe off most of the fluid. 'It's fine.'

'And you've no idea who it is?'

'Like you say, probably a fan of my writing. They can always get in touch with me online. Thanks for letting me know.'

My mother was about as convinced by that theory as I was.

I ducked into the bathroom and started scrubbing before she could see my hands trembling.

* * *

Daniel messaged to say that he'd not be back for lunch. I shoved down the immediate thoughts of panic that I'd scared him away forever, and made a cheese and tomato toastie.

Dad and Grandma joined me with locally bred ham and mustard rolls left over from the Weighbridge Walkers' picnic choices. Not a squeak of halloumi anywhere.

Ah, home sweet home. I took a happy bite of toastie and sat back in my chair.

'Did the woman find you?' Grandma asked, around a mouthful of white bread.

The toastie formed a solid lump halfway down my throat. 'What woman?'

I was torn between being relieved I hadn't decided to come home, and terrified that someone from the Alami family might come looking for me while I wasn't here to deal with it.

'She phoned. Asking for you.'

'Did you get her name?'

'I did!' Grandma nodded eagerly, before pausing to think. 'I can't remember it.'

'Okay, it doesn't matter.' *And if it's who I think it is, they won't have given a real name, anyway.*

'She sounded posh. Like that woman off the telly.' That made Grandma smile. 'Perhaps it was her! Maybe she wants to invite you onto her show.'

'Maybe.' I smiled as brightly as possible considering a heart-in-a-box-posting stalker was quite possibly still on my trail.

'Did you tell her where I was?'

'I don't know where you are!' Grandma shook her

head. 'I said that you live with a friend now and to try there.'

'Did they ask what friend?'

'Yes. I told them your friend who had died.' She frowned. 'She hung up then.'

'Okay. If she calls again, please don't tell her I'm staying with Daniel. She might be a deranged fan.'

'Who's Daniel?'

I felt pretty confident that my secret was safe with Grandma, even if I did feel sick to my stomach at the thought of this person contacting my family.

Worst of all, I realised with a jolt of horror, this meant they had definitely figured out my true identity.

I waited for Grandma to shuffle off to the lounge room to watch 'that lovely man' and made sure I caught Dad's attention before he rushed off to the next job.

'Dad, I'm a tiny bit concerned about that call. If it is an obsessive fan, they might come here.'

Dad beetled his brows. 'Why would they do that if they know you aren't here?'

I shrugged. 'They might think Grandma's lying.'

'Oh no, they've spoken to me and your mother, too. We were very clear.'

Him too?

'Okay. Thank you. But if they are really obsessed, they might come here anyway. To find out more information, or see the place where I was raised and used to work. They could book in and then try to trick you in pleasant conversation into giving more information about where I am. Or, I don't know, poke about until they find a phone number or something.' *Sheesh, Eleanor, stop!* I was really scaring myself now!

'This is quite a big jump from a couple of phone calls, to someone sneaking in here and stealing information.' Dad's look conveyed that he knew full well I was hiding something.

'Dad, I've had a lot of nasty trolling – messages and threats online. It's part and parcel of being a woman in the media these days, but it's one of the reasons I decided to stop. Some of it was vicious. I don't know what someone who could make those kinds of threats might do. I don't want you to be scared...'

'Good, because we aren't!'

'... but I do want you to be careful.'

Dad rolled his eyes. 'Eleanor, when have you ever known your mother and me to be anything else?'

I managed a real smile, then. 'That's true. Okay. And if they call again, will you let me know, please?'

He got up to carry our plates into the kitchen. 'Of course.'

I knew he wouldn't let me know, but at least I'd asked.

While half-heartedly going through more of the Tufted Duck files that afternoon, I tried to process the information that felt far more pressing. Grandma had told the caller that I was staying with a friend who had died. Could that lead anyone to Charlie, and then Damson Farm, and then Daniel, Hope and me?

I'd never written about Charlie, and even if I had, I hadn't mentioned that she'd died, because I hadn't known. I hadn't told Lucy or Miles, so they couldn't inadvertently mention it to anyone. There had been nothing on social media about Charlie's death, because she had closed down her account, and Daniel stayed well away from all of that. Plus, the Perrys had worked hard to keep the whole thing quiet because of Billie's issues around the way that she died.

After going round and round, prodding at every argument, trying to figure out if I'd missed anything, I had to conclude that Grandma's clue wouldn't have helped anyone. I ached to talk it through with someone, a person who didn't have most of their brain frozen solid in fear and so could think half-straight, but who could that be?

There was no way I could tell anyone this, without telling them everything. It may have been twisted priorities, but that was what scared me most of all.

* * *

Daniel arrived back at the same time as the walkers, who tramped through the door in a flurry of muddy boots and rosy cheeks just after four. The Tufted Duck being a B & B, they had all booked dinner at the nearest pub, about a quarter of a mile along the lake.

'We need to think about food,' I said to Daniel, once Hope had been settled with a bottle on Grandma's knee in the lounge room, their presence nicely avoiding the post-creepy comment awkwardness. 'I think I saw some pasta bake in the fridge.'

'Is that a joke?' Grandma said. 'Whatever your parents might think, you three are meant to be on holiday!'

'She's got a fair point,' Daniel replied, cradling his mug of tea. 'I'm sure the pasta is lovely, but how about going out to eat?'

'A good idea!' Grandma said. 'Somewhere swanky that even a big, fancy pants famous restaurant reviewer would approve of!'

'Grandma,' I chided. 'I'm not that famous or fancy pants. And we can hardly take Hope somewhere like that.'

'Well, of course not. Leave her with us. We'll watch her.'

'Um.' I glanced at Daniel. While Hope was having a lovely time playing with Grandma's beaded necklace, I wasn't sure she was quite up to babysitting duties.

'I've actually already booked us a table at the Red House.'

'What?' The Red House was about as swanky, fancy pants as Windermere got.

Daniel shrugged, and behind his mug he appeared to be *blushing*. 'We were driving past and it looked nice. It's ages since I've eaten at a restaurant. And like Grandma said, you might be on a work trip but I'm on holiday.'

Oh my goodness.

He had booked us a meal in a restaurant.

While one part of my brain knew this could be in order to relocate to a neutral venue to tell me that due to my inappropriate feelings I would need to move out of Damson Farm, a larger part was jumping up and down in a mixture of ecstasy, excitement and full-blown nerves.

Surely this was a date?

A man asking a woman, who strongly indicated that she found him attractive only hours earlier, to eat out with him in a fine dining restaurant? If it wasn't a date, it was downright cruel not to be clear about it.

My heart was flapping like a demented chicken.

'Are you sure?' I asked, my voice humiliatingly hoarse.

'Well, why wouldn't he be sure?' Grandma exclaimed. 'It's only a meal out, isn't it? Although...'

She leant towards Daniel's chair. 'You are paying, aren't you?'

'Well, given that I'm staying here for free, I think I'd better pay.'

'Very good. I wholeheartedly approve. Eleanor?' Grandma nodded, satisfied. 'Go and do all the things I've not done since your Grandad was here, God bless him.'

25

On my first 'first date' since Marcus, back in June, I would have ideally had something nicer to wear than jeans and a baggy brown jumper. In a perfect scenario, I would have worn some make-up, and gone to the hairdresser for the first time in forever.

I might have even worn shoes that didn't have a rubber sole and laces.

I tried to remind myself that Daniel had seen me looking far worse on many occasions, and at least I'd showered and brushed my hair this time, but still. No one wants to go to a Michelin-starred restaurant and look like they'd just rolled in off the sofa, even if it wasn't a date.

I eyed myself in the Pintail full-length mirror, thought about all my designer clothes left behind in London, and reminded myself how much happier I was to have left that shallow, fake life behind, too.

Just then, my phone beeped with a message. It was Becky:

There's another bag in the car. Might be useful this evening xx

What??

For your date! XX

WHAT?!?

Did I guess right that you failed to pack anything other than jeans and jumpers?

Before I could think of a reply, she sent one more message:

Yes, I asked Daniel if he was planning on taking you out. He dodged the question but the dreamy look in his eyes gave the answer away. ENJOY!! And make sure you tell me EVERYTHING when you get back xx

Wow.

He'd thought about this even before the creepy comment.

Even if he hadn't thought about it himself, Becky had made him think about it.

I checked the time, grabbed Daniel's car keys from the bedside table and raced to the car.

* * *

Half an hour later, looking pretty darn fine if I do say so myself in a black midi dress with mesh sleeves and a swishy skirt, my hair pinned up and wearing a pair of heeled ankle boots that had survived the trip from London, I went to find Daniel.

He was standing awkwardly by the reception desk, facing the lounge room. As I reached the bottom of the stairs, the sound of Hope shrieking with laughter burst through the open door.

'Hi,' I managed.

He spun to face me. 'Oh. Hi!'

For a long moment, we stood there, the air so still that I heard Daniel swallow.

'Here.' He managed a smile then, thrusting a bunch of pale pink tulips towards me.

'These are lovely!' They were. Simple, beautiful. Not a hint of showmanship. I hurried into the kitchen to put them in water, my heart pounding.

'You look lovely,' Daniel said, once I'd returned, nodding a little stiffly.

'Thank you. So do you.' He wore a moss-coloured shirt that made his eyes look green, and trousers that were smart without looking like he'd just left a work meeting.

Wow. This was really happening. I was on a date with Daniel. I hoped we weren't walking because I wasn't sure how long my legs could hold me up.

'Is Hope okay?' I asked, remembering how unsettled she'd been the night before.

'Your grandma is planning on letting her fall asleep while being cuddled. She's got a bottle, a banana and unwavering attention. Plus the T-shirt I wore today. Oh, and your mum and dad have promised to Grandma-sit while she babysits. Hope's more than okay.'

A perfectly timed wave of giggles wafted through the door.

Daniel checked his phone.

'Come on then, the taxi's here. My plan is to slip out without her noticing.'

It was a clear evening, but not a cold one. The air carried a definite hint of spring, and the fading twilight shimmered on the lake. I pointed out the odd random landmark as we wound out of the town and to where the Red House nestled against the edge of the water. Its lights twinkled through the glass-enclosed deck that wrapped around the building so that patrons could enjoy the view whatever the weather.

The restaurant was quiet, as expected on a Tuesday night in the middle of March, and our table was right up against the water's edge. The sun had already sunk behind the mountains, but I could have watched the moon glimmering on the gentle waves all night.

'Do you miss the lake?' Daniel asked.

I turned to see him watching me, grateful that the candlelight would probably hide my blush.

'Sometimes.' I shrugged. 'I've not lived near

water for six years, so having the Maddon nearby is brilliant.'

'What about the mountains?'

I took a sip of water. 'Again, I've grown used to concrete and tarmac. While Nottinghamshire farmland is completely different to here, I'm simply enjoying being surrounded by fresh air and green spaces again.'

'Good.' He smiled and nodded. We both took a sip of water, and did some napkin straightening, menu inspecting and glancing about while we tried to remember how to make conversation at a dinner table. Something that had felt like the easiest, most natural thing in the world until we dressed it up with a smart shirt and lipstick.

'This trip is the first time we've been off the farm together since you found me in the ditch,' I said, with a spark of realisation.

Daniel looked up at me through lowered eyelashes. 'That's the main reason why I came.'

Before he could say anything else, or I could remember how to breathe, the waiter arrived to take our order, and by the time he'd left I'd thankfully regained the ability to look in Daniel's general direction and open my mouth at the same time.

'So, what did you get up to today?' I asked, at the exact same time he said, 'Did you have a useful day?'

Cue awkward laugh, which only made me feel even more awkward, until thankfully Daniel plunged in and answered the question.

'I visited an orchard.'

'Oh?'

We paused while another waiter produced our wine with a flourish, inviting Daniel to taste it while completely ignoring me until he'd had the go ahead to pour a proper glass.

'They have apples for cider, pears, and beehives.'

I could see where this was leading. 'It sounds great.'

We talked about it right through our starters and main course. No more first date tension, simply me and Daniel dreaming and debating about another idea over dinner, only with a white tablecloth and classier tableware.

By the time we ordered passionfruit cheesecake and rhubarb caramel tart, we had dreamed up a fully-fledged venture, carefully integrating the orchard year into the retreat events. Another member of Daniel's team at work was looking to reduce their hours to part-time, and having totted up the figures, he had already spoken to his manager about a potential job share.

'I've been saving money, investing in a fund for Hope's future. I don't know, uni costs, a nice wedding, enough to be able to hand what's left of the farm over to her in a decent state. But all these plans for the retreat business got me thinking. The farm means so much to me, meant so much to Charlie, not because it's been our family home for generations, but because it was *our* family home. Nearly every memory I have is of us being together. Grandad sitting me on his knee while he drove the tractor. Dad showing me how to mend a fence. Helping Mum collect the eggs. Every single type of weather you could think of, every season and time of day, I have a memory for. And while I loved roaming the fields alone, I knew that at some point I'd spot Dad or one of the farmhands in the distance, that Grandma would be in the kitchen or with Mum in the garden. Charlie would be out looking for me as soon as she got bored, which was all the time. It was always about family and then all that got lost. First when Dad died, and we sold most of the land and let go of the animals, but then after Charlie, it was like our family died with her. Especially since Mum doesn't want to even talk about it, let alone visit.'

'And burying your head in work meant you didn't have to think about it.'

Daniel sighed. 'It's almost like a part of me wanted to pretend the rest of the farm had gone, too. It was less painful than trying to keep it going by myself. Even if it did mean feeling guilty about letting the Perry ancestors down and being the family failure. But the family hasn't died. My family is learning to crawl and hold a spoon and wave goodbye. And what are her memories going to be? Of a dad too tired and busy and miserable to even show her how to pick the apples that are right outside her garden gate? Will her memories of the farm be of a rundown mess?' He shook his head. 'I can't let that happen. I'm going to cut down my work days and introduce Hope to her orchard.'

Daniel's eyes sparkled as he shared out the last of the wine. I flashed back to the exhausted, lifeless man who I had met two months ago, and decided that if getting the Damson Farm orchard up and running would help keep this transformation, then I was with him all the way.

'Right, I've done your question. Time for you to answer mine,' he said.

I broke off a forkful of tart, trying to work out what he was talking about.

'Did you have a productive day?'

'Oh! Okay. Um. Well. Productive in that I've confirmed the secret to the Tufted Duck's success.' Daniel waited while I ate the chunk of tart, the sharpness biting against the caramelised sweetness in a way that made me decide to ask for the recipe. 'Mum and Dad know what their customers want, and they stick to it. Face to face contact, minimal online anything. No frills, no fuss, no faffing about. Just plain, simple, exactly the same as every other time they've been here, even if that is since 1972. Cheap, and if not quite cheerful, at least it's clean and excellent quality.'

'Useful, then?'

'Useful in that it's made me realise that the most important thing about what we're doing isn't trying to please everyone, but in making sure we decide what we want to be, being clear about that, and then sticking to it, so the people who do find us aren't disappointed.'

'So who are these people, and how do you know what they want?'

I thought carefully about that, even as I felt a stab of shame at my cowardly censoring of the answer. 'I've met a lot of people through work in the past few years. People like Stephe and Saskia, who have worked so hard to get where they are, whether that's a job, or a look, a social media following. The right postcode, the right partner, all the right hashtags. Even being on holiday has to be the most fabulous experience. It's exhausting trying to appear so chilled out and relaxed. I think maybe our target market is people who just want to not care about what other people think for once. To be a total mess, scrabbling in the dirt for potatoes, while possibly crying about how they'd love to feel this way all of the time, not just while on some quirky retreat. To imagine that if it was completely up to them, which at the end of the day it usually is, who would they be and what would they do.'

I shrugged, finishing off my dessert. 'Those sorts of people.'

Daniel screwed up his forehead. 'Ugh. You don't get many of those in Ferrington.'

I gave a pointed look. 'It could be argued that *you* fit into that category.'

His eyebrows shot up in horror. 'What? I'm the complete opposite of that category. I don't even go on social media.'

'Working yourself half to death, refusing to accept any help in order to prove some sort of point. No time for friends, no energy for fun, not once asking yourself if you might actually prefer to give it all up and grow fruit or teach your daughter how to drive a tractor instead.'

He ran a hand over his mouth, but it didn't hide his grin. 'Fair enough. There is one clear difference, though, between me and *those sorts of people*.'

'Just one?'

'I've figured out that things need to change without spending £2,000 on a life-regeneration retreat.'

'No.' I risked a smirk as Daniel paid the bill. I was tipsy, and happy, and so stuffed with delicious feelings for Daniel that I was having trouble keeping them from tumbling out. 'It took picking up a random stranger in a ditch to get you there.'

'Best random stranger I ever found in a ditch, that's for sure.'

'*Only* random stranger. I hope.'

He held the door open for me, pointing to the taxi waiting by the roadside.

'Could've been a thousand random strangers stinking of ditchwater, you'd still be the best.'

Then he turned, face bright in the night air, and bent his head close to mine, eyes burning right into the deepest heart of me. 'It was the second-best decision I've ever made.'

'Second best?' I whispered, because the question begged to be asked, even if it was taking things slightly off-track.

His eyes crinkled, and he answered at the same instant I realised. 'Hope,' we said together, smiling. I could be second best to Hope.

'We should probably get back to her,' I breathed. Daniel ignored me, instead he slowly reached one hand up and stroked my hair back from my face, keeping it caught in his hand as it rested against the side of my head. As every nerve in my body hummed with anticipation, he bent even closer, not once breaking my gaze, and then, so gently I might be able to convince myself later I'd imagined it, he closed his eyes at the very last millisecond and pressed his lips against mine.

The taxi horn beeped. 'Meter's running!'

Daniel pulled back, waving in acknowledgement while somehow keeping his eyes fixed on mine, and wrapped my hand in his as though he'd done it a hundred times before. We hurried to the car, climbed in and rode the brief journey back to the Tufted Duck in silence. Whether Daniel's was regretful, embarrassed or contented I hadn't a clue. Mine was a mix of the last two. Potentially the first one, depending upon what happened next.

What happened was that Daniel kept my trembling hand tucked safely in his right up until we reached the kitchen door. He paused to smile at me – and by smile, I mean an expression of delight that I'd only seen him direct at his daughter prior to this moment – then he carefully smoothed back a loose strand of my hair, as if that one small kiss had been enough to dishevel my appearance as well as my heart. He cleared his throat, straightened his shirt and stepped inside.

Mum was in the kitchen, boiling the kettle for her evening herbal tea.

'Hi, Mum.'

'Did you have a nice meal?'

'It was amazing, thanks,' Daniel replied.

'Adequate cleanliness?'

'Faultless,' I said.

'Right then. Goodnight.'

After that grilling, she headed upstairs, leaving us to find Dad, Grandma and Hope in the lounge room, watching the end of the ten o'clock news.

Hope was fast asleep, curled up on a cushion beside Grandma and swaddled in Daniel's T-shirt.

'She's been perfect,' Grandma cooed.

Dad nodded in agreement, clicking off the television. 'Right then, we'll leave you to it. Come on, Mother.'

'I haven't asked Eleanor and her friend about their evening, yet,' she protested.

'Well, go on then,' he said, pointedly checking his watch.

'How was your evening? Did you have a lovely meal?'

'Yes, it was incredible,' I said.

'The company or the food?' Grandma asked, throwing an exaggerated wink at Daniel.

'Both were lovely,' he smiled back.

'Hygiene?' Dad asked.

'Five stars.' I rolled my eyes.

'One to add to the guest folder then.'

'Not one to write one of your horrible reviews about,' Grandma chortled, as Dad stood by the door, impatiently rocking on his heels. 'Can you remember, she used to say such mean things about places! What a good job you moved to London, Eleanor, and started that nice blog instead before anyone found out!'

My heart, as if it hadn't been through enough excitement for one evening, shrivelled to a stop. I would have interrupted her, or changed the subject, but I was too blindsided to think, let alone speak.

'We'd have been shunned throughout the whole town, wouldn't we, Colin?' she asked, gripping his arm as she shuffled through the doorway into the foyer. 'I mean, I know all those things you wrote were true, but you didn't have to tell everybody, did you? Our customers have the decency to complain to our faces, not spread it all over the paper.'

Her words faded away as Dad led her upstairs, but they still hung in the air like a giant neon cloud, swirling in front of us.

'Horrible reviews?' Daniel had picked up Hope and now cradled her against his chest. 'Your reviews are so positive I needed sunglasses to read them.'

I shrugged, ignoring the nausea splashing about in my stomach. This was it. I'd been on a date with Daniel. We'd kissed and held hands. He thought inviting me to stay was the second-best decision he'd ever made. He liked me. He liked who I was now. Surely now was the time to tell him who I'd been, before things got more complicated? If this was going to become something worth building on, surely I had to be honest. I'd spent so many years with this double life, pretending to the world that Nora Sharp was a strong, confident, kick-ass woman, while the truth was I daren't even admit to my own parents that I was her. The thought of laying it all out, having Daniel know, so I could finally talk about it, and more to the point, stop having to worry about whether he'd still like me if he knew, was almost irresistible.

Almost.

Because, at the same time... I'd been on a date with Daniel. We'd kissed and held hands, and it had been the best date I'd ever been on. If not the best night ever, full stop. For the first time in far, far too long, I thought I might have someone on my side.

How could I tell him that I was that person who'd said such horrible things that businesses – maybe even *lives* – had collapsed as a direct consequence? That I'd been her right up until he found me in that ditch? And I couldn't even pretend that it was a courageous decision to stop, given that it had taken a gruesome threat to push me into finally resigning.

I couldn't risk it.

I couldn't risk him.

I was weak, and stupid, and so, so scared.

'When I worked for the *Cumbria Chronicle* they wanted more balanced reviews. Some of the places I went to were terrible, and I was honest about it.'

Ugh. I almost choked on my own hypocrisy.

'Right. That's fair enough, I suppose.'

'Mmhmm.' I nodded.

'Do you want a hot drink? It's still fairly early. I could put Hope down and we could... well. We could talk a bit more? Whisper so we don't wake her up? Or maybe we could...'

'I've had the most amazing evening, thank you so much but I'm honestly exhausted and a little bit tipsy, and Mum and Dad are going to be expecting me to help with breakfast service again. So if you don't mind I think I really need to go to bed. Sleep. In the Pintail room. Sorry.'

For the second time that day I ran away from Daniel Perry.

26

I spent a long, unpleasant night going over and over how much I hated myself before tumbling into dreams where I was Nora Sharp, writing the worst review ever about the Tufted Duck, and Damson Farm, my words spewing out in a torrent of hate until I realised, with a mixture of relief and disgust, that the reviews were actually all about me.

An hour flipping hash browns and frying mushrooms before the sun had even come up was a good way to find some perspective. Throw in a mild hangover, my mother's pragmatic instructions and a mix-up with the baked beans, and by the time Daniel and

Hope emerged I was as ready as I was ever going to be to face him.

'Sorry about last night. Again.' I placed a stack of pancakes and various toppings on the table, and went back to fetch a pot of coffee.

'No, I'm sorry. Again.' Daniel squinted. 'Did I totally misread things?'

'No.' I shook my head, my heart so confused it hurt. 'I meant it about having an amazing time.' I dared to peep at him from under my eyelashes. 'Every time I have with you is amazing.'

Oh, Eleanor, you are playing with fire. Where are you hoping to go with this?

Maybe I was hoping to have some more amazing times, with a wonderful man, and see how it goes without overthinking it all! Maybe normal people don't feel obliged to confess their worst secrets to a potential boyfriend on their first date?

Maybe.

Daniel was trying to play it cool, but a flush of pale pink had crept up the side of his neck.

'So, what now?' he asked, handing Hope a chunk of pancake.

'Um, well, check-out is by eleven, but we don't

have to head straight home, we could go for a walk, or take a boat out on the lake? It's probably warm enough for a picnic.'

Daniel smiled. 'Yes to all of those things. But what now for you and me?'

To my relief, I managed not to splurt out my mouthful of coffee.

'Um?'

'I know it's not cool to be applying labels after one date, but we have been living together for two months. I got virtually no sleep last night thinking about you. About us. About whether there was any chance of there being an us.' He paused to smile at my mum as she strode past, flicking seamlessly back to me the second she'd moved out of earshot. 'I'm not sure I can bear to go back home not knowing whether there's at least a chance of being able to kiss you good morning, or stare at you across the dinner table, or ask if you want to stay up late and talk without you running away again.'

Okay, so I had planned to be strong, play it cool, keep things casual. But come on! How could anyone fail to melt in response to that?

'Yes.'

'Yes, there's a chance?' Daniel quirked up one side of his mouth. 'Can you give me a percentage?'

'Um... one hundred?'

'I'll take those odds.' He ducked his head, concentrating on helping Hope with her breakfast, but I'd seen the joy shining in his eyes, and it perfectly matched the delight in mine.

I shoved the twinge of unease deep down beneath my fluttering stomach, and finished my breakfast.

It was a movie montage of a day. The sparkling lake reflected a sky the colour of forget-me-nots as we cycled into the town on bikes borrowed from the Tufted Duck's tourist stash. Stopping for coffee by the shore in the spring sunshine, Hope's eyes grew round with delight as she jabbered at the ducks quacking around our table. Afterwards, we caught the ferry over to the western side of the Lake, where I knew every trail and bike track, only stopping for lunch once Hope was nodding off in her toddler seat. We ate sandwiches pilfered from the kitchen sitting in a clearing, our coats a makeshift blanket. The air was fresh and sweet, spiced with the scent of earth and trees. The sound of birds and boats drifted across like a long-forgotten mix tape from my youth. Being here with Daniel sent pure joy fizzing through my veins.

And knowing he felt the same? The way he caught my eye and held it in the warmth of his gaze? The way that his hand kept brushing mine, how the spot he settled down on to eat meant that our shoulders were only millimetres apart... it was like an all-day internal firework display.

If it hadn't been for Hope cooing beside us on the coats, I'm certain that a lot more would have happened. But that was fine, the anticipation and gentle flirting was delicious.

After dropping the bikes back, we loaded up the car and left for home. Even sitting beside Daniel in the car had my skin tingling. At one point, while waiting at a traffic light, he took hold of my hand and rested it in the space between the seats, and those endless seconds before he needed to let go and change gears felt like I was already home.

We stopped at a roadside café styled as an American diner, sharing steaming bowls of chilli with a mountain of nachos while Hope methodically spread jacket potato and cheese all over her face and hair.

Night had fallen by the time we arrived back at the farm, and returning to a cold, dark house gave the impression that we had been away far longer than two nights. I did an expert job of tucking a still sleeping Hope into her cot, praying the whole time that she wouldn't wake up, and ducked into the bathroom to brush my hair, give my teeth a surreptitious clean and try to get my jangling neurones under control.

The recent sleep-deprived nights and busy days had exhausted me, but there was enough adrenaline whizzing through my bloodstream to keep my senses wide awake.

Daniel had lit a fire in the living room and switched on the artfully placed table-lamps rather than the main overhead light.

'I wasn't sure if you'd prefer wine or tea?' he asked, rising to his feet as I walked in.

I checked the time on the clock above the fireplace. Just after eight. 'Wine?'

'Perfect.' He picked up a full glass from the sideboard and handed it to me.

'Sure enough, then?'

Daniel smiled. 'I lied. I was completely sure, I just thought you might be offended if I told you.'

'Well, now I'm doubly offended that you must think there's something wrong with me wanting a glass of wine to end a virtually perfect day.'

'I'm going to assume you mean, "thank you for being so thoughtful and anticipating how much I would appreciate a glass of much-nicer-than-our-usual-supermarket wine, you are *virtually* the most incredible, considerate man I've ever met".'

'Assume away.' I took a sip. It was indeed nicer than usual, so I took another one.

'A *virtually* perfect day?' Daniel's voice had dropped to that soft rumble that caused my stomach to flip over. Instead of picking up his own glass, he took mine and placed it back on the sideboard, then stepped right up close to me and took hold of my hand. 'Where did I mess up?'

I managed to stifle my nervous giggle into a smile. 'I cooked breakfast for a full house before you even got up. And as much as I'm used to it, a cursory two second goodbye from my parents still brings back painful memories.' I lifted our clasped hands and gently bumped them on his chest. 'The rest of it was perfect.'

'So there's nothing I can do to make it any better?' His mouth was so close to mine I could practically taste the trace of wine on his breath.

'How about you stop talking, and we'll see if we can figure it out?'

* * *

Being curled up on the sofa with Daniel was virtually perfect. All the times I'd imagined how well I would fit tucked up against his chest were now proven to be right. We sipped our sophisticated wine and kissed and chatted, and it was lovelier than I could have dreamed of.

I say *virtually* perfect, because as beautiful as all this felt, my traitorous brain couldn't stop thinking. It kept rewinding to the conversations I'd had with my family about the mystery caller. I knew it was one of the Alamis. Who else would call the Tufted Duck, several times, pretending to be a school friend?

Now I was home, awareness of the phone hidden in my bedroom above, unchecked for a whole three days, loomed like a sinister shadow over my head. The more I tried to ignore it, and enjoy the rest of the evening – it wasn't as though checking it now or later on was going to change anything – the greater the shadow grew.

In the end, I fudged an excuse about wanting to get changed into something more comfortable. 'Literally more comfortable,' I warned Daniel with as light-hearted a smile as I could summon. 'It's not a euphemism for "something sexier that is in actuality far more *uncomfortable*". I'm thinking a pair of leggings and a jumper.'

'Okay. Thanks for the clarification. But having lived with you for two months, I was expecting your fluffy pyjamas and that ugly green sweatshirt.' He tugged on a strand of hair. 'It was when I started to find even the sweatshirt sexy that I knew I was in trouble.'

How on earth was I supposed to resist falling head over heels for this man?

'I'll put the kettle on.' He followed me out,

pulling me closer to snatch another kiss before I scampered upstairs.

My shame expanded with every loving gesture Daniel gave me. The better things got, the worse I felt and I had no idea what to do about it.

I opened the drawer and waited anxiously for the phone to warm up, heart thudding for entirely different reasons than it had a couple of hours ago.

Two new messages. One sent on Monday, the day we left:

Time we talked in person.

Another this morning, at 4.30 a.m. It somehow felt worse that this had slithered into my phone when I was sleeping, even if it had been miles away from me, and switched off:

See you soon.

It was a threat. Meant to cause every hair to stand on end.

A threat, no more real or present than the hundreds of promises to mutilate and murder Nora

Sharp. No one who knew I was Nora had the faintest idea where I was.

Unless they'd been staking out the Tufted Duck, and then followed me home.

No! *No.* I flung off that preposterous notion with the contempt it deserved. No one would be that crazily obsessed with finding me. Nora Sharp had made one comment about the quality of restaurant entertainment. She had not been responsible for what happened to Layla Alami. Even if one grief-stricken woman thought it was worth giving up months of her life staking out a tiny B & B in Windermere for, the rest of the family would have intervened.

I was pretty sure of it.

Being sure of something in your rational head and getting the message through to your quivering, jellified limbs is another matter. I hastily swapped my muddy jeans and lightweight top for a pair of soft leggings and an oversized jumper, and did my best to stick on a suitable expression for one of the best nights of my life.

I found Daniel poking another log onto the fire.

'Hey!' he smiled, nodding to where he'd laid out a pot of tea and a plate of cheese and crackers.

'I know we had a massive dinner, but we skipped dessert. This was the closest I could find.'

'It's perfect.'

He grinned.

I waited until we'd settled down with plates and mugs before I spoke again.

'These past few days have been fantastic. Genuinely. And I was serious about wanting to... be more than friends.'

'That's good, considering the number of times you've kissed me since we got back.'

'But, well. You don't have to try so hard.'

He sat back, frowning. 'What?'

Oh crap. How was I going to do this?

'What I'm trying to say is... this is still very new. There's this whole added layer of complications because we share a house, and I sort of work for you and you're a Director of Damson Farm Retreats. A lot of people would say it's disastrous to even think about adding the hassle of a relationship on top of that.'

'I don't consider being in a relationship with you a hassle. Is that how you see it?'

'No! No. But I don't expect us to seamlessly transition into being a romantic couple without any issues, either. Even normal couples have stuff to work out as they go.'

'So why is me trying hard a problem?' Daniel shook his head, as if baffled.

It took a moment to try to come up with the right words.

'I don't want us to add any unnecessary pressure, that's all.' I paused to rub my face. It would be a lot easier to convince Daniel of this nonsense if I believed it myself. 'I guess I'm concerned we might rush this into being more serious than it is.'

'So, what is it?' Daniel's voice was steady, but his eyes flashed with hurt. 'Because from where I'm sitting, it was dinner, followed by a day out and a plate of cheese and crackers.'

'And kissing.'

'Are you saying you don't want us to keep kissing?'

I want us to keep kissing so much my face aches. I want to keep kissing you for the rest of my life.

'No! No. I love this. I love kissing you. I loved dinner and our day out and the cheese. I think I'm saying that I'm scared by how much I love it, I'm scared that I don't know how to do this properly, and so can we please stick with this while I take some time to catch my breath.'

Daniel picked up his mug of what must by now be freezing cold tea. 'Are you talking about sex? Because the leggings and jumper were enough of a hint.' He gazed at me over the rim of his mug, and I was very tempted to peel off my comfortable clothes right there and then.

'Um. Partly? I'm also talking about how we are and what we say to other people.' I took a deep breath. The look in Daniel's eyes coupled with the notion of sex floating about between us had rendered me more than a little flustered. 'If we didn't live or work together, we'd be at the casual dating stage about now. Can we keep it there for the moment?'

The truth was, Daniel and I were way beyond casual dating. I was fairly sure I was in love with him. I already knew what he looked like first thing in the morning after a night pacing the floor with a fretful baby. I'd seen him grieving, learnt how to handle him grumpy, knew instinctively what would make him laugh or cause his hazel eyes to spark with pleasure.

I wanted to be with him.

And now, this sham of keeping things casual and being nervous about committing too soon, concealing the truth about how committed I was whether I liked it or not, was just one more secret to hide.

How could loving someone be so wonderful and yet so heart-wrenching at the same time?

'Of course.' Daniel waited until I'd plucked up the courage to look him in the eye, so he could show me that he meant it. 'We'll take this slow. Do it right.'

'Thank you.'

On that note, having successfully tainted the evening with my poisonous past, I called it a night and went to bed.

27

The next few days continued on much the same note. Becky was ecstatic to hear all about the trip while we added the finishing touches to Hope's bedroom. She was unsurprisingly bewildered about my insistence on taking things slowly.

'You are clearly potty about each other. Why hold back?'

I stood back to check that the photograph of Charlie I'd hung on the wall was straight. 'Why not? If it's meant to be, we've got plenty of time to settle into it. Besides, my track record with men is unanimously dismal. It's wise to take things slowly, given the potential fallout if things go wrong.'

'The only thing that could go wrong is you being so feeble and cowardly that things fizzle out and one of you moves on before it gets anywhere good!' Becky retorted through a mouthful of curtain hooks.

'It's already good, thank you very much. I'm not going to let you bully me into rushing it. Especially not when there's a baby involved.'

'Oh, but...' she started to protest.

'And I will remind you, as if there was any chance of you forgetting, that Luke starts on the bathrooms on Monday. Until then, you get to decide where the line goes when it comes to embarrassing interference in friends' love-lives.'

Becky turned bright red at the mere mention of Luke. She had it even worse than me. 'I'll behave. I promise! Please don't say anything, Eleanor. It's different with me and Luke.'

'Like I said, you get to draw the line.'

'The line is very, *very* far back!'

'Excellent.'

* * *

By Friday evening, we were ready for the grand reveal. I didn't go so far as to move any of Daniel's personal possessions upstairs, but Becky and I had done what we could to make it feel homely. The main attic room was now painted a soft white, with a dark grey accent wall behind the bed. We'd added photographs of the farm and the family, along with a selection of Charlie's old postcards set in a mahogany frame.

We'd reused the original shelving, sanding it down and painting it a lighter grey to match a rug that we'd relocated from another bedroom. Geometrically patterned blinds hung at the huge windows, and a few touches like bedside lamps made out of a tree-trunk and a stash of books and his 'player of the year' football trophy finished it off. It was a mix of cosy warmth and practicality, and it suited Daniel perfectly. I had even framed an old spreadsheet of farm accounts and hung it on one wall as a joke. He said that he loved it. Then he draped an arm around my neck, pulled me close and planted a smacker on my lips, right in front of Becky, so I supposed he meant what he said.

I would have been embarrassed at the show of

affection, but seeing Becky wrestling with the temptation to make a comment was worth it.

Hope was less bothered about her room, but I knew in years to come she'd appreciate the cornflower walls and life-sized stencil of an apple tree. Her soft furnishings were a stripy mix of buttercup yellow, red and navy, and above the changing table we had hung an enlarged copy of the picture of her on the day she was born that Charlie had kept in her room. We had re-covered an armchair in vibrant yellow fabric scattered with tiny red chickens, and placed it next to a bookshelf crammed with stories. Everything was orderly and bright, and I was optimistic Hope would sleep long, sweet dreams in here compared to the dingy junk-room she was used to.

Daniel cried. Actual tears. Which made me cry, too.

'I don't know how you ended up here, or where you came from, but I'm growing more and more convinced you must be an angel,' he whispered, burying his face in my hair.

I allowed myself to enjoy the rush of pleasure for a lingering moment until the age-old stab of guilt wormed its way between us.

Becky beamed at me, eyes brimming. I ducked my head and turned away.

Having barely spent any proper time together since arriving back home due to Daniel slaving away at his work backlog, and me alternating between working on the top floor and avoiding him, while grabbing a quick bowl of pasta that evening, he asked if I wanted to walk into Ferrington on Saturday to have lunch.

'I would love to. On one condition.'

Daniel eyed me expectantly.

'We go to the Water Boatman.'

He put down his fork so quickly it clattered against the bowl. 'That's on the New Side.'

'I know. I've been there before.'

'We can't walk there.'

'Yes, we can. It will take longer, that's all.' I carried on eating, all easy-breezy as if no one sensible would consider it a big deal.

'It's miles along a dual carriageway. You can't walk it!'

I pulled out my phone and opened the maps app. 'Here. You can follow the footpaths along the Maddon, turn off through this farm, past this wood. And look, here. There's a footbridge over the river that leads to another footpath. It's three and a half miles from the farm to the pub, and not a main road in sight.'

'The Old Boat House has a really good lunch menu. Do they even allow kids in the Boatman? I've heard it isn't the most... family friendly clientele.'

I rolled my eyes. 'Luke goes there every Friday night, according to you.'

'He's the one who told me.' Daniel resumed eating.

'They have a whole family dining area in a separate room. And Alice is working there on Saturday. I've not seen her in ages.'

Daniel raised an eyebrow. 'Do you want to show me off?'

I shuffled in my seat. I didn't *not* want to show my friend that Daniel and I were exploring being more than friends. Maybe partly because I wanted to remind her what a decent boyfriend looked like.

* * *

We set off after a fortifying breakfast of eggs on rye toast, relieved to see the good weather was continuing. We spotted a smattering of new buds on the apple trees as we weaved through the orchard, the ground awash with a sea of daffodils and speckled with the first of the bluebells.

'Excited about reviving it again?'

Daniel nodded, his head tipped up to inspect the straggling boughs overhead. 'I'm thinking about Apple Day. It was a much smaller thing when we used to celebrate it, but they're all over the place now.'

'Apple Day?'

'It's held in October.' We began moving on towards the other side of the orchard. 'Everywhere does it differently, but there's usually cooking demonstrations and cider tasting, games and village fete stuff like music and craft stalls. Loads of apple related produce on sale. We used to serve cups of apple and parsnip soup and masses of pies and cakes. In the evening we'd have a bonfire, and get some of the old miners' band to play. It was Charlie's favourite day of the year, when her orchard became one big party.'

'Sounds fantastic. Are you thinking of doing one this year?'

He shrugged as he opened the gate to the meadow beyond. 'I spoke to Ziva about it. But we've both reached the point where a community day involving only the Old Side feels wrong.'

'Were only the Old Side invited before?'

'Only the Old Siders ever came.'

'You never know what could happen between now and October.'

Daniel winked at me. 'Up until somewhere around the middle of January I would have rebuffed that comment. These days, I'm inclined to believe anything is possible.'

As usual, time in Daniel's company soon dissolved any resolve to keep an element of distance between us. Walking and talking together, Hope joining in over his shoulder with her happy nonsense chatter, felt a mixture of thrilling and at the same time blissfully comfortable. He listened to everything I had to say, asking interested questions and following up with his own stories and observations that were rele-vant and in no way constructed to boost his ego.

We talked more about the orchard, and potential plans, how we could incorporate pruning and fruit picking into the retreat programme. We shared more anecdotes from our childhoods, Daniel now able to fully appreciate how my parents had shaped my younger years, and both of us swapping notes about the blessings and frustrations of growing up in a home that doubled up as the family business.

By the time we'd moved on to modern conserva-tion issues and the environmental impact of intensive farming versus the economic trials of more sustainable methods, we had braved crossing the tiny, crumbling footbridge and had officially entered the New Side.

Another mile or so, and we reached the row of red-brick terraced cottages that preceded the Water Boatman. As we wound back towards the water, tired and hot from the walk, the riverside pub garden ap-peared idyllic.

'A table in the sunshine or the shade?' I asked, already eyeing up an empty picnic bench sitting in a pool of sunlight.

'I was thinking table inside.' Daniel glanced warily across the water towards the Old Boat House, where every table appeared packed with a mix of families and couples out enjoying the warmer weather.

'Seriously?' I looked at him, surprised. 'Are you ashamed to be seen at the Boatman?' And then another realisation struck. 'Or ashamed to be seen with *me*? The incomer who swaggered in with her grandiose saviour complex and attempted to rectify decades of devastation with a cheese and wine evening?'

'Either that or I've been mates with the manager of the Old Boat House since I was four, and two days ago I met with him to pitch Damson Farm Cider. I promised him first dibs.'

'Okay, I can see how you now turning up here could be misconstrued.'

A man around Daniel's age, who looked as though he had sampled more than a bellyful of beer in his time, currently stood on the far side of the river, hands on hips, a knowing tilt to his head.

'Gavin,' Daniel called, with a half-hearted wave.

'Danny.' Gavin nodded back, folding his arms, bar towel dangling from one elbow.

'Just calling in to see Eleanor's friend. She works here.'

'Alice Munroe.' He sneered Alice's name as though it was a euphemism for a pub toilet.

'Right. Great to see you.' Daniel turned to me, jaw set. 'Let's eat at that table in the sunshine. If he's got that much of a problem with it, I'll take the cider I haven't even grown the apples for yet elsewhere.'

'Okay.' I gave an internal sigh of relief that he'd seen sense.

I fetched us drinks and menus from inside, saying a quick hello to Alice, who was busy serving plates of sandwiches to the Ferrington Foxes football club. Luke gave me a brief nod, which I guessed was his equivalent of someone else running over and throwing their arms around me.

A few minutes later Alice came to find me in the garden.

'Well, this is cosy.' She bent down to give Hope a kiss. 'Nice to see you venturing over to the dark side, Daniel.'

'Your words, not mine.'

'Becky told me the news.' She threw me a wink.

'What news is that?' Daniel asked.

'Dating, kissing... For what it's worth, I agree with Becks that if you're going to take a man like Daniel off the market, the least you can do is make the most of it. Men like him are all too rare.'

Daniel looked momentarily surprised, before burying a grin behind his bottle of cider.

'They aren't that rare,' I replied, pointedly. 'Amazing women, like, ooh, I don't know, *you* for instance, have no reason to be settling for a man who is any less than equally as amazing.'

Alice pursed her lips. 'Right, what'll it be?'

Halfway through our decidedly average burgers, there was a sudden shout from the other side of the garden. A crowd quickly gathered around the figure of a woman who had collapsed onto the grass beside her table.

'Is anyone here a doctor?' a younger man called out, stepping away from the huddle. His face was scrunched in distress. 'She's not breathing. I don't think the ambulance will get here on time.'

'She's allergic to nuts,' a woman said through floods of tears. 'I can't find her epi-pen anywhere.

She's always leaving it at home. Does anyone have one?'

'Does anyone have an epi-pen?' the man repeated, shouting loudly to catch everyone's attention. 'Sylvia's allergic to nuts!'

The rest of us in the garden answered a collective no. Alice ran back out from the pub with a regretful shake of her head on behalf of the customers inside.

'Can somebody please do something?' the woman cried in panic. 'There must be something at the doctor's surgery!'

Everyone whipped their heads around in response to a shout from the other side of the river. Dr Ziva was craning her neck from the footpath beside the Old Boat House. 'Somebody needs a doctor?'

Ziva's face turned grim as she was offered a brief explanation. 'I'll fetch my bag. But keep looking for a pen. By the time I've driven round...'

Luke suddenly appeared from somewhere behind us, sprinting across the garden and disappearing over the river's edge in one smooth manoeuvre.

'Is he going to swim across?' somebody gasped. 'The water's freezing!'

Before anyone could answer, a little boat came into view as he rowed furiously to where a gaggle of onlookers were waiting at the dock that gave the Old Boat House its name.

In the endless minutes it took him to reach the far side, Ziva was waiting. Ably assisted by one man on the dock and Luke in the boat, she clambered in and they set off back to where the woman on the grass was turning a terrifying shade of purple.

Daniel rushed forwards to help Ziva up, and she immediately got to work.

It felt like forever.

Sylvia's daughter sobbed into a napkin while her son stood, white-faced and trembling, and waited to see if his mother was going to make it.

Eventually, Ziva moved back, gesturing to Sylvia's son to help his mother into a sitting position.

There was a spontaneous smattering of applause and cheers from both sides of the river. People looked at each other as the clapping built in volume, with expressions a mixture of uncertainty, defiance and tentative joy.

Sylvia was assisted inside the pub and out of the

sun's glare and the ambulance arrived a few minutes later, but the twin crowds lingered.

After a swift assessment of the situation, Alice disappeared into the Boatman and reappeared with a microphone.

'Right, then, Ferrington,' she called, clambering up onto a picnic bench. 'I think this is it. Enough. Sylvia Jackson has lived in this village her whole life, she raised her kids here. Taught most of yours, as did her grandparents, her mum and dad, and now her daughter Kerry. None of them took sides. None of them said a bad word about any of you, New or Old. Everything they did has been for the good of this village and our children. And now she nearly died, because one, she ordered a slice of cake without checking whether it contained almonds, and two, the only person who could help her was stuck twenty metres away because the bridge that should have got her here lies in ruins.

'If it wasn't for Luke Winters' quick thinking, Sylvia would have been yet one more needless life lost, on the back of decades of pig-headedness.'

A ripple of indignation rumbled through both sides. Some shook their heads angrily.

'It's true!' Alice waved her free arm in frustration. 'I'm not talking about what happened back then. I know I can't speak on the hardship that you older ones went through. I only need to look in my nan's eyes to know I can't ever understand. But for each one of you who share in that suffering, surely you should be the first to stand up and say enough! A good woman nearly died in my garden today. Who here thinks that Sylvia's life would have been worth it?'

Alice let the microphone drop to her side, her chest heaving as the adrenaline started to take hold. The only sound was ducks quacking as they zipped through the water between us, indifferent to the momentous developments unfolding either side of them.

There was a stirring in the crowd by the far side of the river as it parted to allow someone to pass. An older woman wearing a buttoned-up beige raincoat shuffled to the water's edge. Stooped over, her face depicting a wrinkled map of tribulation, she took a moment to survey the crowd.

'That's Caris Smith,' Daniel whispered in my ear. 'Her husband drowned after the New Siders knocked him into the river when he barred their way during the strike. She had five small children, and one of them died of an overdose at nineteen.'

Caris Smith waited a moment longer. The tension grew, forming a tangible bridge of its own.

'You all know what I been through. Who I lost.' Despite her frail stature, the words breached the gap with piercing clarity. 'I got every reason to hate. To demand that bridge stays as destroyed as my life has been, that you ain't got no right to set one foot over here. But it won't bring my William back. It won't save my son. But it might save our village if we decide to stop this, now! Ferrington is withering away all around us and we don't even see it any more, how weak and rotten it's got. But this stranger – her – she saw it. She was brave enough to say it.

'For goodness' sake. For all our sakes. For the sake of William and Richie and wee Janey Thomson. The Wright twins, Trevor Brown and everyone else who can't be here to say it – we need to say *enough*. It's time to start again. To let go of this damn feud. To build a bloody bridge. Here.' She pulled a small brown purse from her coat pocket, opening it up with trembling hands and taking out a note, which she held aloft. 'Here's my contribution to the new bridge fund.'

Gavin from the Old Boat House ducked forwards and held out a beer tankard for her to drop it into.

Caris Smith gave one slow, determined nod of her head, stiffly turned around and began hobbling back into the crowd.

Alice was the first to start clapping. Becky, who had appeared on the other side at some point, was second, swiftly followed by Luke.

By the time the cheers had subsided, Alice had come up with a plan.

'Right. The first meeting of the Rebuilding Committee will be next Sunday evening at seven. At the Damson Farm barn, so none of you can gripe about sides before we've even got started. Ziva Solomon and me'll be co-chairs. There'll be a zero-tolerance policy for anyone who turns up with any goal in mind that isn't saving this village.'

'Will you start a Facebook group?' someone called out.

'No, I bloody won't!' Alice shouted back. 'I've got a pub to run, I ain't got time to waste policing the cesspit of social media.'

'Free drinks on the house to celebrate?' someone else cried.

'Free drinks all round!' Alice grinned. 'Once the bridge is officially open and you can walk across to the Old Boat House to fetch them!'

28

On Monday, Luke arrived to start renovating the bathrooms while Becky and I worked on research and costings for various garden designs in the living room. It wasn't the most productive of days, given that one half of Team Damson was in charge of a baby who'd just learnt how to pull herself up using the furniture, and the other half spent most of it staring into space, jumping out of her seat every time a particularly loud thud came through the ceiling.

Tuesday we spent trawling through local garden centres, Hope safely in her pushchair, and Wednesday Daniel took the afternoon off while Becky and I redrafted the plans to fit with the various sale items that we couldn't resist buying, despite not being on the list.

Becky managed a whole two-minute conversation with Luke without spilling the tea she'd brought him or tripping over anything. Unfortunately, that resulted in even more swoony staring at the ceiling, and even less work done. I almost went upstairs and asked him out on her behalf, but I suspected that would make her worse.

Thursday, Becky messaged to say that something had come up and she wouldn't be in that day. I didn't ask what, but it had to be a big something if it meant missing her daily dose of Luke. That made me feel slightly less peeved that she wouldn't be there today of all days. I hadn't said anything, but it was my birthday. My thirtieth. And while I hadn't wanted to make a big deal out of it, I had planned us a nice lunch to celebrate, and had even invited Alice to join us.

She sent me another message a minute later:

Alice said to tell you she can't come either.

What? How did Becky even know Alice was invited? The thought that they'd been having cosy conversations without me somehow made my disappointment even worse.

Before I could muster a fake reply along the lines of 'That's fine! No probs!' another message pinged through:

Get your sparkle on later though, we'll pick you up 7.30 xxx

I had no idea how to reply to that. It made no sense. Did they know it was my birthday, and if so, how? And if they did, then why had they cancelled lunch at the last minute?

I clocked your DOB when we registered Damson Farm as a business xxx

Oh. Okay. So what about lunch? I had no answer to that until Daniel found me mooching around the garden with a pad and pencil later on that morning. He'd had an early conference call, so had already been holed up with Hope in the study when I got up that morning, and I hadn't seen him since.

'Hey.' He came up behind me, wrapping his arms around my waist and planting a kiss on the side of my neck that sent tingles shooting right up to the top of my scalp. 'Making plans?'

I shrugged. 'Pretending to, at least. I can't really concentrate.'

He rested his head gently on top of mine. 'You should probably take the rest of the day off, then.'

'Really?'

'Yeah. Come and have a stroll in the orchard. The damson trees are starting to blossom. Let's take a look.'

'Okay...' I hadn't told Daniel that it was my birthday, either. I'd meant to, at some point. I knew that when he eventually found out he'd feel awful that he'd missed it, but I wasn't sure how to bring it up without sounding like I was angling for a present, or a meal out or something, so I'd taken the path of least resistance and said nothing.

'Where's Hope?'

'At Mum's. I'm picking her up later.' Daniel kept one arm around my waist as he propelled me around and started walking towards the orchard.

'Oh?' I couldn't help a smile creeping over my

face as we crossed the garden and through the gate. The sun was shining in a vivid blue sky, the air was mild and fresh and the orchard was thrumming with the springtime revival. Butterflies danced with the bees, pheasants clucked among the under-growth and the floor was a carpet of bluebells and yellow primroses. Daniel led me through the shade of the trees to a far corner I'd not ventured into before.

'What's this?' I said gesturing at a bright blue wooden arbour I'd only just spotted.

Daniel's whole face was beaming. 'Happy birthday.'

'What?'

He led me around to see that the arbour over-looked the meadow as it ran down to the river below. Beneath the roof were two benches angled at ninety degrees around a circular table, all painted in the same azure blue. The benches were covered in pink and yellow cushions, and on the table was a picnic basket.

I love you.

I bit my lip to prevent the words spilling out, but I'm sure they must have beamed from my eyes, the watery blinks spelling it out loud and clear in some sort of lovesick morse code.

'This is for you.'

'You mean the picnic?'

'I mean the whole thing.' He laughed then, and I couldn't help laughing with him as the sheer joy bubbled up and out along with a tear.

'You built me an arbour?'

'I paid a guy in the village to build it. But yes, it's for you. I hope the tears and laughter mean you like it?'

'Are you joking? I *love* it! This is the best gift anyone has ever given me. Even better than when Mum and Dad gave me a Powermop.'

'There's also this.' He reached into the basket and handed me a rectangular package. Removing the wrapping, I found a framed photograph of Charlie and me, from the first time she'd come to work at the Tufted Duck. We were both wearing aprons and brandishing wooden spoons in a Charlie's Angels pose. Charlie had a streak of flour in her hair. Beneath the dramatic expressions, we were clearly about to burst into laughter.

'Where the dream began,' Daniel said, slipping his arm around my shoulders.

'Okay, so I changed my mind.' I turned my head to bury my face in his neck. 'This is the best gift.'

We stood there for a long moment, and as my memories settled, only one thought replaced them: *I love you!*

Could I say it? Should I? I had never said those words to a man I wasn't related to before. Let alone one I'd been dating for less than three weeks.

Before I could make up my mind, Daniel pulled back, tugging me over to the nearest bench. 'Come on, Charlie wouldn't want us moping about on your birthday. Let's eat.'

* * *

Lunch was delicious in every sense of the word. An entrancing view, picnic food from an upmarket farm shop that even Nora would approve of, including a rich, gooey birthday cake, and the best possible company.

Once we'd finished eating, and Daniel had waited politely for me to finish waffling on about the garden plans, we snuggled closer and lost ourselves in long, indulgent kisses.

I couldn't say the words out loud, but with every touch my body declared the undeniable truth:

I love you.

No offence to my new friends, but I wasn't sorry that they'd bailed on my birthday lunch.

It was late in the afternoon by the time we packed everything up and ambled back through the trees, arms entwined, hair mussed, wearing matching stupid smiles as we floated along in a romantic haze.

Luke met us in the farmyard, having just finished up for the day. 'You missed a parcel delivery.' He nodded back towards the house. 'It's on the kitchen table.'

He swung up into his van with a nod and the barest hint of a knowing smile, and left us to it.

'It's for you,' Daniel said, handing me a box about eight inches square.

'Oh?'

'Did you order something for the house?'

'No.' I shook my head, puzzled. 'Maybe Becky did.'

I carefully ripped off the parcel tape and opened the top of the box. Peering in to catch a glimpse of the contents, I instinctively jumped back, gasping in alarm. I dropped the box onto the table, my adrenaline revving into overdrive.

The box fell on its side, causing some of the contents to spill out onto the table.

It was jam-packed full of bees.

Dozens and dozens of dead bees.

My stomach contracted in horror and revulsion.

'Do you think they were supposed to still be alive?' I stammered, trying to cling on to any possibility that this was not what I thought it was.

'It's a sealed box. I can't imagine anyone being stupid enough to think bees could survive being sent through the post in these conditions.' Daniel picked up the box and gently tipped a few more out onto the table. 'And if you'd opened a box of live bees, wouldn't that be worse?'

I allowed a moment to imagine quite how much worse that scenario would be, before shutting it down as best as I could. Releasing a swarm of bees into the kitchen while Hope was here didn't bear thinking about.

'There's a note,' Daniel said, taking a card out from the bottom of the box.

'I'll read it,' I blurted, reaching to take it off him, but he'd already scanned the message.

'Happy birthday. Hope you get everything you deserve.' Daniel scrunched up his face in disgust. 'What? Do you know what this means? Who's this from?'

I sank into a chair, feeling as though all the blood in my body had pooled around my feet. My head collapsed into quaking hands. 'They won't be from Ziva's hives, will they?' I managed to rasp the words through my seized-up throat.

Daniel pulled a chair up close to mine and took hold of my hand. 'I hope not. But I'll ask her to check.'

We stared at the pile of desiccated insects.

'I can't believe you've annoyed someone enough to go to this much trouble. If it was to do with Ferrington, surely they'd have done something weeks ago? Though it might be worth asking Alice if she's had any unexpected packages.'

'Did you tell anyone it was my birthday?'

Daniel shook his head. 'No. I didn't even mention it to Mum.'

After hasty messages to Becky and Alice, I quickly established that no one else in Ferrington knew it was my birthday.

'I think we can safely rule those two out,' Daniel said, grimly. 'Who else knows you're here?'

'No one,' I whispered, lost in a whirlwind of dread and disbelief. And the list of people who knew my birthday was not a long one.

'So, who the hell sent this?' Daniel's face was set, all hard lines and clenched jaw. His scar stood out stark against his cheek. 'What's it supposed to mean, "I hope you get what you deserve"?'

I took a deep breath. Now was the time. I had to be brave, and honest, and if it meant the best birthday ever became the worst, then so be it. I steeled my spine in preparation.

'I don't understand why anyone would want to do this to you of all people.' He pulled me close into a hug, and as my face sank against his chest, my steely spine dissolved into mush.

'I was a writer.' I pulled myself upright again, heart splintering at the swirl of compassion and anger in his eyes. 'Every journalist gets hate mail. I've had plenty of nasty comments on social media over the years, people taking an irrational dislike to me, or offended by something I've said.'

'Eleanor, someone packaged up a load of bees into a box. This is way beyond a snarky tweet. And if someone went to the trouble to find out both your birthday and your current address, that's not a passing dislike. It's a stalker.'

I blew out a shaky sigh. 'You're not really making me feel any better, here.'

'I'm sorry, but I'd rather you took this seriously and ensured you were safe than tried to cheer you up by dismissing something potentially dangerous as nothing to worry about.'

'I *am* taking it seriously.'

'We need to call the police.'

I shook my head frantically, trying to come up with a good reason why not. 'It's just a parcel of bees. I don't think we need to do anything drastic. Like I said, this is par for the course for a journalist. Especially a reviewer. And I'm not sure they can do anything, even if they had the time and resources to bother.'

'They could start by scouring the area for people covered in unexplained bee stings.'

'Look, it's my birthday, we've had a lovely day up until this. If we call the police now I might have to stay in and talk to them, miss my birthday night out with Becky and Alice. They've told me to put on my sparkle. I can't remember the last time I did that. Please can we leave it for today, see how we feel in the morning once the shock's settled? I'll have a proper think about who it might be. Go over my old social media accounts, see if there's any helpful clues there. And you can talk to Ziva, give her a chance to check out the hives.'

He huffed, rubbing at his scar. 'I need to pick up Hope now anyway.' Looking at me, he narrowed his eyes. 'But we're calling them tomorrow. This needs dealing with properly.'

He grabbed his keys and left, leaving me to sweep the tiny corpses back into the box before changing into the closest item I had in my wardrobe that resembled sparkle.

Needless to say, I was not feeling sparkly.

29

It was beyond late by the time I tumbled out of the taxi, waving a groggy farewell to Becky and Alice as they hooted and hollered their happy birthdays at me one final time.

We'd had a night full of food, fun and utterly fabulous friendship, and while deciding to drown my rampant terror with cocktails was probably not a sensible idea, it had been a successful one.

I did ask whether either of them knew if anyone was still mad at me for the wine and cheese fiasco, or whether Alice had noticed any animosity since her table-top announcement at the weekend. They waved off that suggestion with flapping hands and insistent cries that I was being paranoid.

I'd of course checked my old phone at least every two minutes before I'd left that evening. There'd been nothing. But at the end of the night, once I'd stumbled up the stairs, tugged off my velvet trousers and glittery top, I couldn't resist checking it again.

Did you like your present?

And a second one, sent a few minutes later:

Would you like to thank me in person?

The threat hit me like a fist in my guts.

They knew where I lived. Were they coming for me?

I made it to the toilet just in time to spew up my birthday celebrations.

Sweating, shaking, head spinning with panic, I crawled back into bed and clutched the duvet for dear life, as if a mound of stuffing could save me.

My past was about to catch up with me. In more ways than one.

* * *

The following day, I dragged myself out of bed just after eight. I needed at least four days' more sleep, but that wasn't happening any time soon, and I desperately needed water and painkillers for my pounding head.

Daniel arrived back from dropping Hope off at Billie's while I was boiling the kettle.

'Ouch!' He winced at my bleary state.

'Thanks,' I croaked.

'A good night, or a bad one?'

I shrugged. 'Both.'

He vanished into his study, magically reappearing the second I'd finished my tea.

'Right, are you ready to do this?' He nodded at my phone.

I slid the phone closer with a frail hand. 'Don't feel the need to hang about. You've already taken yesterday afternoon off.'

He leaned against the worktop, arms folded. His expression was grim, but when he spoke the words were gentle. I wasn't the focus of his carefully suppressed fury. I wondered how long it would be before that changed. 'I'm not going anywhere.'

'Okay.'

I made the call, giving the briefest of details and being reassured that someone from the local police department would be in touch. This was followed up with a return call and appointment made for later that day. By that point I needed a second cup of tea, and Luke had arrived with new bathroom doors for the recently made doorways leading to the smaller bedrooms.

Becky joined us soon after. 'I was going to take it easy this morning, but then Mum called and said about the bees. Bloody hell, Eleanor. Why didn't you mention it last night?'

I mumbled something along the lines of it really not being that big a deal, but then a wayward tear slipped out, and Becky wasn't buying it anyway, instead wrapping me in a hug before plying me with yet more tea and leftover birthday cake.

Ziva called in ten minutes later, her face scarlet, hair bristling, hands wringing with distress. 'The H boys are gone.'

It felt as though a trapdoor had opened in the

kitchen floor right where I stood. To my relief, at that point the police officer arrived, a woman in her fifties who firstly insisted we called her Brenda and secondly took charge with a brisk efficiency that was simultaneously reassuring and intimidating in equal measure.

Having relayed why we had called her, and gone over the little we knew, she then asked the question I had been dreading.

'Has anything like this happened before?'

I took a deep breath, kept my eyes firmly in Brenda's direction and away from Daniel, Becky and Ziva. 'Yes.'

Brenda's eyes flicked to Daniel, sitting beside me, who had gone rigid.

'Can you tell me about it, please?'

'Um. Before moving here, I was a journalist. I wrote food reviews, and a few other things, and sometimes... people sent me... messages...'

Brenda, sensing I was on the brink of choking on my own witness statement, carefully put down her pen and notepad.

'Dr Solomon, Becky, I think I've got all I need from you, for now. Please don't let me take up any more of your day.'

Taking the hint, they made their excuses and left.

'Okay, Eleanor. Take your time. You were telling me about your previous messages?'

I nodded. Daniel was gripping his coffee mug so hard his knuckles were white.

'I had the usual trolling on social media. Letters to the paper I worked for, comments on my blog. It was nothing unusual, never anything extreme enough to worry about.'

'And then...?'

'And then...'

And then I told her about the messages to my phone, the heart in the box, and the middle of the night phone messages, and with every word Daniel grew even more still.

'And have you heard anything since?'

Oh boy.

'Yes.' My voice broke. I swallowed, taking a moment to breathe in some much-needed air before I continued. 'I bought a new phone, but I've had a couple of messages to my old one.'

'Can I see them?'

As I pulled my old phone out of my hoodie

pocket and handed it to Brenda, to my enormous relief Daniel's own phone rang. He glanced at it before pushing back his chair, swearing under his breath.

'I have to take this.'

'Of course, no problem.' Brenda smiled. She waited for him to leave before looking me straight in the eye. 'Now, are you going to tell me what's really going on?'

So, with many more choked back tears, my head hung in shame, I told her precisely that.

An hour or so later, Brenda left, taking my old phone with her. She'd said that the obvious place to start was trying to locate the Alamis, but she would also look into the other restaurants that the stalker had messaged me about on the night I left London. She'd call Miles Greenbank at the newspaper, as well as seeing if she could get any more information from my parents. Another priority, of course, was to speak to Lucy. Although it seemed clear the animosity was aimed at me, and the chilling discovery about the missing H boys suggested their focus was now here, not in London, Lucy needed to know what was happening. She also had all the new passwords for Nora's social media accounts, so we needed that information from her, too.

However, while Brenda reassured me that a crime had been committed, and she was proceeding accordingly, I couldn't help thinking that surely underneath the calm professionalism Brenda and I shared the same opinion: I had brought this on myself. A box of bees and a lamb's heart were insignificant compared to the upset and damage I had caused over the past few years, and I should feel ashamed at wasting valuable police resources.

I wouldn't have involved the police at all, would have packed up my stuff and run away again if it was only me involved. But I wouldn't even consider risking a grief-stricken maniac turning up at Daniel and Hope's home.

So, I would stay, and cooperate as best I could, and follow Brenda's advice about keeping an eye out for anything out of the ordinary, keeping the doors and windows locked, and not going for any long rambles around the countryside alone.

I would hope, and pray, and do anything I could to make sure that I wasn't responsible for ruining any more innocent lives.

* * *

I couldn't call Lucy myself, as Brenda now had my old phone. I did, however, look her up on every online platform I could think of that didn't require me to set up a profile, as well as reading through as many of the comments as I could stomach.

Nora Sharp was riding high. I had no idea what was happening with her venue or event reviews, but she had clearly been having fun reviewing her own life, and the seemingly endless free items that now accessorised it.

And while I would generally baulk at the idea of any human being degraded to the level of 'accessory', that was clearly how Nora viewed the man currently featuring in around half of her pictures. Nameless, consistently relegated to the back of the frame, or used as a prop to drape herself over, her new boyfriend clearly wasn't choosy about which version of Nora Sharp he hung out with.

Marcus.

I was distracted from my stalker-search enough to scroll through the pictures until I found one that stopped me in my tracks. Nora was staring into the lens, lips pursed in defiance. She wore a tiny white crop-top, across which was written in red lettering, 'FireStarter'.

FireStarter was the name Marcus had used for the woman he'd been seeing behind my back.

Lucy had ended up with my job, my pen name, the opportunities and the attention that came with them. Had she started with my boyfriend?

Had she planned the whole thing?

She certainly didn't look like a woman being tormented by creepy and disgusting packages.

* * *

Daniel finished his call in time for lunch, not that either of us managed to eat more than a few token bites of a sandwich. My whole body felt seized up with tension as frenzied thoughts raced through all the potential ways he might react to the interview with Brenda. Pushing his plate away, he finally put me out of my misery.

'You should have told me.'

I gave a wretched nod. 'I know. I'm so sorry. I genuinely didn't think this was anything more than nuisance messages. I never would have knowingly put you and Hope at risk. I never would have stayed here if I'd known. Like I said—'

'I can't believe you were dealing with this by yourself,' he reached across the table and took my ice-cold hand. 'Why didn't you tell me?'

I shrugged. 'I thought I'd left that awfulness behind. I was trying to start again. I didn't want to contaminate this lovely place with the disgusting dregs of my life in London.' The one millionth tear of the past two days dribbled out, and I swiped it away with a frustrated hand. 'I was ashamed.'

'Eleanor, you did nothing wrong. Why would you be ashamed? And can I remind you that this entire village has been at war for the past thirty-six years? Can you imagine the nasty, petty, ugly things that people have said and done around here? I'm not living in some naïve idyllic countryside bubble. And I know that sometimes people hate for reasons that are completely irrational and unjustified.'

I knew I should tell him quite how much I deserved the hate, but I was so tired, and so scared, and needed him not to hate me too.

'I'm a little insulted, to be honest, that you

thought so little of me – of what we're building here, together – that you wouldn't share this.' He let go of my hand, then, and the pain in his eyes made my throat ache.

'It was a couple of messages... this kind of thing was an everyday part of my job. You don't tell me every time someone at work has a go at you, or sends an arsey email...' My voice fizzled out, unable to deliver such a feeble argument with any conviction.

'Or sends me a heart in the post?' He shook his head, frustrated. 'Don't downplay this. They sent messages to your personal phone. You left your home in the middle of the night.' He paused, waiting for me to find the courage to look at him. 'You should have told me.'

My whole body drooped. 'I know. I can't tell you how sorry I am for embroiling you in my problems. Do you want me to go?'

He sat back, then, eyes wide with shock. 'No! I want you to trust me enough to let your problems be our problems. This is your home, Eleanor. I want you to stop thinking like I'm *allowing* you to stay. Like there's any doubt about whether you belong here. I want you to not even think about that as an option.'

He paused, mouth curling in the hint of a smile. 'Team Damson.'

I managed a rueful smile in return. 'Team Damson.'

'Most of all, I want us to stop dithering about pretending to play it cool and officially admit that we're a serious, committed, exclusive, head-over-heels-for-each-other couple.'

Wow.

'Okay.' I ducked my head, suddenly overcome.

'Okay? That's it?' Daniel leant forwards across the table so that his face was looking right into mine. When that failed, he gently reached under my chin and tipped my head up so my eyes met his.

I took a deep breath. This man, his gorgeous smile, his tenderness. He was downright irresistible.

'That would be lovely, thank you very much.'

I would tell him. I just needed a little more time to pull myself together first.

30

By Friday, my heart rate had almost returned to normal. Brenda had spoken to my parents, my old boss and to Lucy, currently safe and sound in a resort in the Alps. She had apparently been appalled and concerned, promising to be vigilant and immediately inform Brenda if she spotted anything that might be related to what had happened.

'She said that since taking Nora in a new direction, the trolls have largely lost interest, so it will be a lot easier to spot if the Bee Murderer tries to make contact.'

'Okay.' I pressed my phone tight to my ear, just in

case Daniel could hear the other end of the phone from the study.

'She also said to tell you that she hopes you're keeping safe, and to send her love.'

'Thank you.' Despite our awkward ending, I felt a rush of relief that Lucy was safe, and even more so that she seemed to have veered away from the Even Nastier Nora.

Brenda had not much else to add. 'I'm following up with the Alamis, but it seems Layla's parents have left the country, and it'll take a while to locate the wider family. I've got another officer looking into the bee theft, and contacting the parcel delivery company, but again there's not a lot to go on. Be reassured, though, that I've dealt with plenty worse in Ferrington over the years, and none of it came to anything. Try not to worry, leave it to the experts.'

Her calm demeanour helped settle my nerves down another notch. I spent an afternoon tidying up the garden with Becky, and even managed to stop looking over my shoulder every two minutes, instead allowing myself to enjoy the spring flowers peeping out from amongst the weeds. We saw rabbits hopping through the meadow beyond the fence, and a family of ducks sailed along our stretch of the river.

Recent events had dragged my mind back to my life in London, to the constant nag of inadequacy and discomfort and the never-ending need to cram my life so full it would smother the self-loathing.

My world had been filled with the illusion of glamour. I'd had parties and clothes, notoriety and enough money to enjoy it, but it had all counted for nothing, because this was what I had needed all along: to sit with a friend and share a pot of tea, the birds singing, sheep bleating in the distance, and to savour the satisfaction of taking something neglected and shambolic and setting about restoring it to something beautiful.

I didn't know if it would ever be enough, these small attempts to counteract the damage I'd caused but I would pledge myself to keep trying, and that was the best I could do.

It was five o'clock, and a distinct nip had settled in the air when we decided to down tools for the week.

Luke was also finishing up. We went to inspect the progress and found him packing up the last of his equipment. We now had the bare bones of a bathroom and two single bedrooms. On Monday, the shower and other fittings would arrive, and we would be able to start painting the bedrooms.

'Wow, you've done loads!' Becky said from where she stood by the window. Given that she was contained in a small room with Luke, her voice was impressively close to normal frequency. 'You must be ready for the weekend.'

'Yep.' Luke nodded as he checked through his toolbox.

'Any plans?'

'Heading to the Boatman.'

'I've always wanted to try the pie at the Boatman. Alice says they're amazing.'

'They're not bad.' Luke clicked the toolbox shut.

'Like, with a pint.'

Luke did one last visual sweep of the bathroom. It was a good job he scanned straight past Becky because she looked about ready to melt in a pile of molten mortification.

'They probably go really well together.'

'It's a classic combination.' Luke picked up his toolbox and walked the three steps to the doorway, where I stepped back to allow him past.

'I heard they do an offer. On Fridays?'

He twisted back to face Becky, one eyebrow raised, the hint of a smile at the corner of his mouth. 'I'll save you a seat.'

And then Luke Winter swung down the stairs and into his van before Becky had time to collapse into the space where the toilet was supposed to be.

* * *

In between jumping at every sudden noise, thrashing about in my duvet all night and going over increasingly disturbing scenarios involving the bee killer's return, I did my best to spend the weekend immersed in weeding, and talking to Alice about her plans for the Rebuilding Committee meeting on Sunday evening. Daniel was trying to pretend he was totally chilled out about his girlfriend being on the receiving end of multiple sinister messages from someone who had broken into his orchard and stolen a hive of bees, but he always seemed to coincidentally be drifting about wherever I found myself to be. At one point I had to turn around and tell him that I was going to the toilet and really didn't need a chaperone.

On Sunday, once Alice arrived, we spent an hour sorting out the barn before the meeting was due to start. This meant dragging in whatever makeshift seating we could find – a few garden chairs, followed by some crates, boxes and a couple of logs. We had no idea who – if anyone – would come, but both Alice and Ziva had been working hard at promoting the message on each side, and we were buzzing with anticipation that we were on the brink of seeing Ferrington history in the making.

A few minutes before seven the first few people began to arrive, with a fairly even mix of wariness and enthusiasm, and by five past it was standing room only. As expected, the Old and New Sides had naturally drifted to different halves of the barn, and so the first thing Alice did was instruct everyone to find someone from the opposite side to them and say hello.

'That'll wheedle out the troublemakers,' she

whispered, eyes scrutinising the stilted interactions now taking place.

Once she'd called everyone to order and gone through some ground rules, most of which involved trying to prevent violence from breaking out, the first item on the agenda was to agree the purpose of the committee.

Alice nodded at the manager from the Old Side off-licence, who was waving his hand in the air.

'Can you state your name and then make your point, please?'

'DJ Vapes.' He paused, glancing around to absorb the room's admiration for his cool name before realising that it didn't exist, and hastily carrying on. 'Er, isn't the purpose to rebuild the bridge? I thought that was obvious,' he said, revealing a remarkable change of heart since he'd thrown Alice out of his shop.

'Surely that's only part of it?' Ziva replied. 'There's no point rebuilding the bridge if the village is still divided.'

This elicited a murmur of approval.

'Well, yeah, but we have to start somewhere,' DJ Vapes said. 'You can't just tell people to get over it, forgive and forget and that's that. We need a project like the bridge to get people working together again.'

'We aren't planning on building the bridge with our own bare hands!' another man said.

'Why not?' an older teenager called, huddled at the back with a small group of similar aged boys. 'Save us some money.'

'Raising the money, applying for planning permission or whatever else needs doing, that'll be where we work together,' Ziva said.

'How about a massive party on the bridge once it's finished?' a younger woman suggested, bouncing a baby on her hip.

Lots of people liked that idea, throwing out suggestions for local businesses to provide food and drink, and entertainment, maybe even to make it an annual event.

'Okay, that's all fantastic, just what we're looking for,' Alice yelled above the growing enthusiasm. 'But we've got a long way to go before we can start thinking about that. I'd like to invite Malcolm Blackthorn, chair of the Ferrington Parish Council, to come and fill us in on some details.'

'The Parish Council?' several people asked, faces

scrunched up in confusion. 'Since when did we have one of those?'

'Since the 1894 Local Government Act!' Malcolm retorted, coming to stand beside Alice at the front of the barn.

'Well, of course we wouldn't know anything about it, if it's run by Old Siders!' a man who had ambled in ten minutes late snarked.

'Jase!' Alice warned. Jase opened his mouth and raised his hands in a 'who, me?' gesture. Despite the straggly nondescript hair and slouchy tracksuit bottoms, he oozed the kind of cocky charm that some women seem to find irresistible, and I could understand why Alice had been drawn to him.

'It is run by a democratically elected council consisting of an equal number of members from each side!' Malcolm stuffed his hands in his tweed jacket pockets, his pointy white beard bristling.

'Elected? I don't remember any Parish Council elections,' DJ Vapes said, glancing around to see if he was the only one.

Malcolm coloured slightly. 'We only have an election if the number of people standing is greater than the number of positions. So we haven't had an actual election for a while.'

'How long's a while?' Ziva asked, incredulous.

'Nineteen seventy-one.' Malcolm coughed. 'All the details of minutes and meetings are on our website.'

'How come nobody knows anything about you?' another one of the teenagers asked. 'You can't have been doing much.'

'The Parish Council is responsible for maintaining parks, footpaths, community buildings and bus shelters! Amongst other things,' a heavy-set woman with stringy grey hair barked back. 'We serve this village tirelessly. And if it's been undercover for the past three decades, then you can hardly blame us! You lot might all think that no one in this village works together, or even wants to, but the FPC have been sneaking about like secret agents and improving things right under your noses the whole time!'

'Awesome!' The teenagers nodded. 'Can anyone join?'

'Can we please get back to the matter in hand!' Alice called. 'As Malcolm said, the Parish Council has a website, which I'm sure is easy enough to find if you want more details. Now, Malcolm, what can you tell us about getting the bridge rebuilt?'

'Right. Well...' Malcolm then proceeded to take the audience on a meandering tour of local council policies and proceedings, with many a detour to examine various by-laws along the way, until eventually Alice, who by that point may have been the only person not lulled into a parish stupor, had to stop him.

'Okay, so, bearing in mind that most of us have no knowledge, experience or interest in the intricacies of local government, would it be fair to say that the bridge is going to cost at least three million pounds?'

Malcolm nodded, opening his mouth to start talking again before Alice stepped in.

'Thank you, we can save the details for another time.'

'Well, that's that, then, isn't it?' said Sylvia, whose nut allergy had kick-started the whole thing.

'There's a thousand-odd people in this village, if you add both sides together. If we all chip in, that's three grand each!' Ziva exclaimed.

'And that includes every man, woman and child!' Gavin, the Old Boat House landlord said. 'How are those of us with kids meant to do it?'

'Hang on,' Becky said, moving towards the front. 'No one agreed that we'd all be chipping in an equal amount. Times have been hard for a lot of us in recent years, and there are a lot more ways to raise money.'

'Yeah, but even if it's cake sales and raffles and that, it's still got to come from us,' Jase said.

'Or sponsorship from businesses. Or grants like the National Lottery. Or organisations willing to donate to the regeneration of a historical landmark. We haven't even investigated whether the government would pay. The whole point of setting up a committee is to find solutions to these problems. All Malcolm is doing is managing expectations, and letting us know that it won't be easy. But we can handle a challenge, can't we?'

She scanned the crowd, expectantly. 'We don't back down or give up because the answers don't come strolling in straightaway? I've met a lot of vastly different people while working in five different continents, and if there's one thing I know about Ferrings,

Old and New, we are strong and tenacious and we know how to make it happen.'

The room broke out into spontaneous applause, causing Alice to give her forehead a relieved wipe.

'Right. Next item on the agenda, we need to form a proper committee. After everything we've heard, I hope some of you are up for committing to the challenge. We'll need a chairperson, secretary, treasurer, events officer, publicity...'

'But that's only a handful of people,' Ziva interjected. 'You can't send most of us home kicking our heels for the next however many years until we can have the bridge party.'

'Well, I was kind of presuming you'd be joining the committee,' Alice replied.

'Well maybe so, but what about the rest of us? You've got everyone all worked up and raring to go. We need a project. Something to keep momentum going in the meantime, so we can see that progress is being made.'

'She's right.' Caris Smith spoke up for the first time. 'Otherwise everyone'll just find something else to bicker about.'

'Okay.' Alice looked at the agenda in her hand, as

if that would be able to provide an answer. 'Like what?'

While everyone stood there trying to come up with precisely what, Daniel cleared his throat loudly enough to have all heads swivel over to where he leant against the wall.

'I have a suggestion.'

Alice's face lit up.

'Well, come on up to the front then so we can all hear you!' Caris Smith said, sitting up straighter in her garden chair.

Daniel went to join Alice. 'We need a project that the whole village can get involved with. Preferably something on neutral territory that can start right away, and ideally help raise funds for the bridge.'

'Well, yes, we all knew that already!' a woman at the back tutted. 'What we need to know is what that's going to be.'

'A community orchard,' Daniel announced.

'Yes!' Ziva hollered.

'For far too long the Damson Farm orchard has lain abandoned. If it wasn't for Ziva's stealth attacks with her pruning shears it would be totally re-claimed by the wild by now. I don't have the time to restore it to a working orchard, but if we work together, the possibilities are fantastic. It isn't just fruit trees, we could build raised beds for vegetables, and have a go at woodworking projects like picnic benches and compost bins.'

'Eh, we could do a bit of that,' an older man sitting on a crate nudged the man squeezed on next to him. 'Couldn't we, Frank?'

'Aye,' Frank nodded vigorously. 'Could rope in some of you youngsters an' all. Teach you how to use a hammer and a chisel.'

'Awesome!' The teenagers did a complicated high-five thing that Frank and his friend reciprocated faultlessly.

'We have a cider press on the farm already,' Daniel continued. 'I've been talking to Gavin at the Old Boat House, and Miranda who owns the Boatman. We can look at other produce like pies and cakes, depending upon what we decide to grow. Plus, we could create an outdoor classroom for school visits, and other groups. And most of all, there's the chance to hold whole community events. Lots of orchards get involved with Apple Day, in October. We can celebrate Bonfire Night, do something at Christmas, May Day. If everyone gets involved we can raise money, bring the community together and have fun at the same time.'

'Awesome!' someone cheered, and I don't think it was even one of the teenagers.

'That's bloody brilliant!' Alice exclaimed.

It was. It was brilliant.

'Are you sure?' Becky asked, her business head whirring. 'We had plans for that orchard.'

Daniel shrugged. 'I'm sure the retreat guests can still join in. It might prove inspiring to them, hearing the story of how the Feud of Ferrington came to an end. Some of them might even be moved to contribute to the bridge fund.'

'We should include a memorial.' This was the first thing I'd said all meeting, having promised myself that I wouldn't be the interfering Out-Sider this time, but the idea popped into my head and it was too good not to share. 'We can have a competition – get the school involved, maybe – to design a memorial to all those who died or who for whatever reason suffered because of what happened.'

'That's perfect,' Caris Smith said, eyes filling with tears.

'Maybe you could be one of the judges?'

'Or maybe the kids could design something to-gether, have each of them contribute, so for the first time ever in this village everyone wins instead of everyone losing,' she replied.

'Well, an orchard will need an entirely different committee,' Alice said. 'And a whole load of time and effort. How do you see this working, Daniel?'

'I see me dropping my work hours, and spending a couple of days a week heading it up. I see us forming a charity, with a board of trustees. I see the Parish Council donating some funds to help us get going, and I see Damson Day to kick-start us off in a few weeks' time: food and produce stalls, local crafts, a band put together with musicians from both sides, a duck race down the river, some games.'

'Damsons aren't ready to be harvested until Au-gust,' someone helpfully pointed out. 'How can we have a Damson Day in April?'

'I really don't think anyone will care about that.' Ziva rolled her eyes.

It wasn't long before we had agreed that May Day would be the very first Damson Day, put a volunteer team in place and left the whole room buzzing with

anticipation after they had agreed one last suggestion from Caris Smith.

We would start the evening festivities with a funeral pyre. The deceased? Why, the Feud of Ferrington.

I was so excited I almost forgot to worry about
the stalker.

I did not, however, forget to grab Becky and drag
her into a quiet corner as soon as the meeting was
over. I'd not missed her doe-eyed glances over at
where Luke hovered near the back of the room, or
how he wove through the clusters of people chatting
and leaned in close to say goodbye before he left.

'So?' I asked eagerly, pleased to be on the other
end of the romantic interrogation for once. 'How did
it go?' I'd obviously messaged her on Saturday, but
the answers had been about as descriptive as if I'd
asked Luke.

'The pie was... not too bad!' She squinted. 'The
pint was better.'

I jabbed her in the ribs hard enough to make her
squeak.

'Okay! We had a lovely time. We stayed until last
orders and even managed some decent conversation.

Not the whole time, but when we were quiet that was fine, too. Like, a companionable silence.'

'A dreamy, transfixed-by-Luke's-gaze silence?'

'Well. That, too,' she giggled.

'Everything you've imagined it would be when mooning at him in year nine Geography lessons?'

She hugged herself, letting out a heartfelt sigh. 'Better.'

Alice sauntered over. 'All right, Becky? Survived your evening on the New Side?'

'Yes, thanks.'

'Only when I was locking up, I thought I saw Luke giving you the kiss of life.'

'He kissed you?' I grabbed her arm in delight.

'Nope.' Becky looked strangely happy about that. Before Alice could protest, she declared, 'I kissed him!'

'What?'

'I've waited twenty years for a chance with Luke Winter. It might have been my one and only date, I wasn't about to waste it.'

I grinned. 'Sounds like he kissed you back?'

'With all the passion and attention to detail that he put into grouting my kitchen,' Alice chipped in.

Becky's pink cheeks said it all.

'Did he take your breath away?' I asked.

'On the contrary, I feel as though for the first time in forever I've stopped holding my breath.' She looked it, as well. 'He called me on Saturday. Not even a text, a *call*. To say that he'd had a great time and would I like to go out on his boat next weekend. I'm so happy I could pop.'

'I could pop I'm so happy *for* you. Look at us, all loved up.' I glanced at Alice. 'Speaking of which, it was good to see Jase here.'

Alice shrugged. 'I hid the controller to his Xbox. Said I'd help him look for it if he came.'

'Alice.' Becky screwed up her nose. 'He's not being supportive if you've tricked him into it.'

'I know.' She shook her head, morose. 'Where do you draw the line, though? If I was going through a bad patch, I wouldn't want him to just bail on me because I needed some time to sort myself out. That's not how relationships work.'

'If you were going through a bad patch, would he even notice?' I couldn't help asking.

'He bought me a box of chocolates when our cat

died.' She sniffed. 'But then he did eat all the white ones and he knows they're my favourites.'

She burst out laughing at the memory, the kind of laugh that is on the brink of a sob. 'Don't worry. I'm not going to keep giving him endless chances. But I need a plan before I decide whether this is a phase, or if it's just him. However crappy things have got, it's still better than going back to sharing a bedroom with Nan.'

'You could come here,' I said. 'Only £200 a night, breakfast included.'

'Make it two a night and I'll pack my bags.'

I nearly accepted her offer, only we had guests booked in and a business to run and I was still a bit scared of Alice so wasn't quite ready to share a house with her.

'You could stay with me?' Becky said.

Alice frowned. 'That would mean a really long commute.'

'Unless you borrowed Luke's boat? He keeps it at the Old Boat House dock anyway.'

She looked at Becky, a long, open stare, and although I couldn't ever really understand what it meant, how significant the invitation was to cross this metaphorical bridge between their communities, I knew that this was how it started. Two individuals, prepared to lay the past behind and take a step forward.

'I'll think about it. But, well, thanks. That means a lot.'

Ain't that the truth.

31

'A community orchard?' I asked Daniel an hour later, lying on the sofa with a hot chocolate, my feet in his lap. 'When did you decide that?'

'About two minutes before I said it,' he smiled. 'While I've been doing research for the orchard, the idea kept cropping up. There are plenty of places where it seems to work.' He shrugged. 'I think Dad would have liked the idea.'

'Charlie would have loved it.'

He rested his mug on my knee. 'What do you think? Will you mind having the whole community hanging about just over the garden fence? Helping themselves to our apples?'

I pursed my lips. 'I have one major problem with it.'

'Oh?'

'What about my arbour?' I poked him in the stomach with my foot, causing his drink to wobble precariously.

'I will personally see your arbour relocated to the garden. Around the side of the house where the retreat guests won't spot it, either.'

'Hmm...'

'There's a corner where the hedge is low enough to see over if you're sitting down, with a view right across the valley.'

'Sounds perfect. I give my wholehearted endorsement and support to the Damson Farm community orchard.'

He grabbed my hand, pulling it up to kiss the palm. 'You did realise the date of the launch?'

'I know! Our first proper guests arrive two days before Damson Day.'

'It'll be a busy month.'

'Right now, keeping busy might be the only thing that keeps me sane.'

And there it was again, the shadow from my past life leering over us, forever hanging there ominously.

* * *

The next few weeks were indeed jam-packed with our joint ventures. For the first two weeks Daniel was still working full-time while trying to get things started with the orchard, and with Becky and I getting everything ready for the upcoming retreat, we had little time or energy to do much more than share the odd meal, and hand over Hope with a quick kiss and a catch-up. However, as the days rolled by, things were gradually taking shape, transforming before our eyes, and the joy of seeing the finishing touches, final programmes printed and the pantry overflowing with ingredients ready for both events was exhilarating.

An army of locals had been pruning, planting and constructing in the orchard, like some amateur farming version of *DIY SOS*. There were now sturdy fences and a beautiful new gate opening onto the footpath that led through the meadow and along the river into the village. By the second week, there were raised beds and a pagoda with benches and tables for the educational area. It turned out that Ziva's husband, John, was an admin whizz, and he spent hours looking into charity applications and setting up a board of trustees. Various staff from the pubs and takeaways made regular trips bearing drinks and trays of sandwiches or pizza. There was a clear sense of rivalry between the different eateries, but it was gradually becoming a friendly one, and if it meant the food grew better by the day, no one was about to intervene.

One of the teenagers bashed out a basic website, and where she'd created a bookings page for carpentry workshops, a range of gardening and horticultural classes and Ziva's beekeeping for beginners, the places were getting filled quicker than she could organise them.

Daniel was reborn. His face shone, he laughed with new vigour and strode about the farm as if he finally owned the place, and loved every inch. Hope was, if possible, even more delighted. She spent hours outside, transfixed by the sawing and sowing, charming everyone who stopped to say hello when she was confined to her pushchair, and inspecting every leaf and ladybird in the times she was free to explore. She grew more like her mother every day.

Becky and I had to reluctantly miss out on this stage of the community reformation, although Becky minded a lot less during the first week, when Luke was still finishing off the work inside, than she did once he'd joined the orchard volunteer crew. The first day he was out there, she spent a whole afternoon cleaning the windows on the orchard side of the house, and found every excuse going to 'nip outside'. Despite this, we were making fantastic progress, and as each room was signed off and various plans were finalised, our excitement blossomed.

We had opened the website for further bookings, and Becky was putting together a marketing plan. While Charlie's brilliant but ridiculous notion of 'exclusivity' had enabled us to charge a fortune to those who could afford it, it also went against her original dream, that anyone who needed a Damson Farm Retreat was welcome, and for that to happen they needed to be able to find us. We decided to try offering a range of events that balanced a viable profit with being able to look our customers in the eye while handing them the bill. The ultra-exclusive breaks that offered extra 'luxuries', a full programme of jargon-soaked activities and unlimited everything, through to a simple stay where guests could enjoy good, nourishing food in beautiful surroundings, and then join in with group sessions or laze in the hammock with a cold drink.

After holding our breath for a couple of days while Becky bombarded her contacts with promotional links, we had our next booking. And then the next, and by the time we were ready to open our doors we had at least one booking every month until the end of the year.

The weekend before the first guests arrived, Daniel and I celebrated with leftovers from the Pepper's Pizza lunch run.

'I know you've spent hours crafting perfectly planned menus, but nothing beats a Pepper's Pizza.' Daniel breathed a sigh of pleasure, leaning back against the newly positioned arbour.

I pointed my half-eaten slice at him. 'That's because food is intrinsically emotional. Pizza to you is all about relaxing at the end of a busy week, it's like an automatic trigger to chill out.'

He shook his head. 'No. That's not it. Pizza is all

those evenings when instead of eating alone, sat at my desk, praying my baby didn't start screaming so I could get some work done before I collapsed face-down into my laptop, I got to spend my evening in the company of an astoundingly beautiful and interesting woman.' He paused. 'I mean beautiful on the inside.'

'Oh, what, and interesting on the outside?'

He laughed. 'You *are* interesting on the outside. I could watch you all day. You're both those things, inside and out. And you make me laugh. You give me hope... You are quite possibly the loveliest woman I know, and I love Pepper's Pizza because it reminds me of you.'

'Wow.' It wasn't possible to hide behind a tiny chunk of pizza crust, but I tried anyway.

'You've changed everything, for the better.'

'You're one to talk. You've given me a whole new life.'

Daniel frowned. 'You gave yourself that life. I just offered a stuffy old box room and free rein of my kitchen.'

'No.' I shook my head. 'You gave me hope.'

'Well, sounds like we're even then. Do you think we should have pizza at our wedding reception?'

He winked, but it didn't stop the flood of elation and guilt and panic all the same. I didn't know how to feel about this horrible shadow that still hovered two steps behind me. Wandering through a sunny orchard packed with cheerfully hardworking people, the threat seemed a silly, distant memory from another lifetime. When Daniel was shut up in his study working all evening, or out on orchard business past sunset, every creak was approaching doom.

I lay awake at night, and in the early hours of the morning, repeating Brenda's reassurances like a mantra: *It was a harmless stunt. Try not to worry.*

Until, two days before the guests were due to arrive, four days before Damson Day, as I sat down at the kitchen table with a mug of tea and a slice of rye bread with Damson Farm honey, a new message arrived through the website contact page:

Your 'about us' page on the website appears to be missing some important information. Like who you really are and what you've done.

Needless to say, my tea went cold.

Daniel was down by the river with Luke and some of the older men who'd been helping out. He called and waved when he saw me coming, his face glowing, body barely able to contain his energy.

'You'll never guess what Frank and Eddie found!' he grinned, bursting with glee.

I eyed the enormous piles of lopped off branches. 'Loads of brambles and undergrowth?'

'*Underneath* the brambles and undergrowth. Take a look!'

I waited for Luke to drop another huge branch on the pile, and then peered around it, my head in no state to start guessing what might be there.

Oh, now that was worth getting excited about. It was a *bridge*.

A narrow stone strip, no rails or other features, about ten feet from one bank to the other, and wide enough for one large man or a couple of children to walk across without risk of toppling into the water.

'This bridge has been here all along? Did you know?'

'I had no idea! This has been a thick mess of weeds for as long as I can remember. The brambles made it impossible to get near to it, even if we'd have wanted to. It was these guys who found it.'

Frank pulled off his cap and scratched his bald head before putting it back again. 'We got to talking, me and Eddie. Remembered that back in the day some of the New Side lads had used a different way to get over the river to the mine. Alec Perry let the bushes grow so that folks who didn't need to know wouldn't. We kept the smallest gap through the middle, had to crawl on hands and knees with every inch of skin covered to avoid getting half-scratched to death. We didn't know if it would still be here, let alone be safe to carry any weight, but thought it worth a look, save us New Siders taking the long way round.'

'It looks all right though, doesn't it?' Eddie added, with a smug smile. 'James Perry knew how to build things to last.'

'James?' I glanced at Daniel.

'My great-grandfather.'

'Wow. This is incredible.'

'Means we'll need to get them young lads back, to get a path sorted, save us churning the meadow into a mud-pit,' Frank said, rocking back on his boot heels.

'I'll put something on the Facebook page.' Luke wiped a smear of dirt off his forehead with his wrist.

'Tell them Damson Farm will pay good wages if they put the work in.'

'Aye.' Eddie nodded his approval. 'We know the Perrys'll do us right.'

As I turned to go, Daniel took hold of my hand. 'Did you need to ask me something, or did you just come to have a nosy?'

I looked at my boyfriend, how his face shone, a Perry farmer in his element. I swallowed back the terror and dismay and offered them all a cup of tea.

For the rest of the day, I sat at the laptop and scrutinised all those who had booked a stay so far, racking my brains as I scrolled through online images and LinkedIn profiles for any hint of a restaurant connection.

I don't know why I deleted the email as soon as I'd copied it into a new folder on my laptop. I don't know why I didn't call Brenda or alert Becky, who I knew would make me stop being an idiot and tell Daniel. I didn't want it to be real.

I told myself that I didn't want to contaminate something as brilliant as Damson Day. I also didn't want our first proper retreat to be riddled with fear and anxiety.

I didn't want to ruin everything.

I made a promise, in order to prove to myself that I wasn't always going to be a coward and a liar, that I would tell Daniel everything, including that I had invented Nora Sharp, as soon as Damson Day was over. I even put it in the calendar on my phone: *confess*.

Did the thought enter my mind that in four days' time it might be too late?

If it did, I soon chased it out again.

32

Friday, the day before the retreat, Becky and I were flat out cooking and prepping and adding the last-minute touches. The garden was still on the wild side, the exterior of the farmhouse needed a lick of paint, but we were embracing nature, and as long as the house was clean and in good order, we were happy that we'd done enough for now. Alice was due to join us on Saturday, as all day Friday she was on shift at the pub, but to our surprise she skidded up the farmhouse drive while we were grabbing a quick lunch on the freshly weeded patio.

Flinging open her car door, she tumbled out and

hurried over to join us, face glowing, hair curled on one side, still straight on the other.

'What's happened?' Becky asked as soon as she'd swallowed her mouthful of feta salad. 'Is it Jase?'

Alice, gasping for breath, could initially only shake her head and flap her hands about, while trying to smile. Once I'd pushed out a chair for her to collapse into, she managed to gasp out her news.

'I only might have bagged us a celebrity event reviewer for Damson Day.'

'What?' Becky was ecstatic. I felt a prickle of horror at the back of my neck.

'I sent her a few messages, but I never thought for one second she'd even read them, let alone consider accepting. Not that she's confirmed it as a definite.'

'She doesn't confirm unless she has to, waits to see if she gets a better offer,' I mumbled, with a certainty that I knew who she was talking about.

'What? Who?' Becky asked, bouncing on her chair.

'Nora Sharp might be coming to Damson Day!'

I gripped the arms of my chair with both hands and tried not to swear out loud.

'*What*?'

'I know!'

While Alice and Becky watched a clip of a video on Alice's phone, drowning out the audio with their increasingly overdramatic exclamations, I held on tight and waited for the world to stop spinning.

'You don't look thrilled, Eleanor. Why aren't you excited about this?'

'Um. She's just a person... Damson Day is about Ferrington. And I can't see her bothering to come all this way for what to anyone outside the village is a glorified country fete.'

'Er, hello?' Becky was baffled by my response. 'It's also about raising money for the bridge, which means raising the profile of the events. If millions of people hear about us, then loads of them will come to other events. Who knows what it might lead to? Never mind the boost to Damson Farm Retreats. This could be exactly what we need to get the business off the ground!'

'Plus, she's posted about it in advance, so even if she doesn't come, we'll probably end up packed out on the day,' Alice said, eyes round with animation.

'Do we want to be packed out with strangers on the day?' I asked.

'If they're spending money, then yes!' Alice grabbed Becky's sleeve. 'Maybe we should start selling tickets. Or limit numbers somehow? Can we do that at this late stage? I should probably speak to Daniel and see what he thinks. Check out the guidelines on crowd control.'

'Daniel hates Nora Sharp.'

They looked at me, faces full of hurt and bewilderment that I wasn't jumping for joy.

'Have you seen her reviews? Nora Sharp turning up is probably the worst thing that could happen. Daniel will be furious. Everyone will be fawning over her, taking all the focus off what the day is meant to be about – building something wonderful for this community. She'd hijack Damson Day and with one careless comment destroy our business before it's even started.'

I pushed back my chair and, heart stuttering, on the brink of hysteria, I fled.

I was in my bedroom rewatching Lucy/Nora's video for about the dozenth time. She'd been pretending to scroll through invitations, listing her 'options for the week'. It had included new restaurants, an album launch and a bespoke cruise around the coast of Ireland. Then, right at the end, she'd added one more.

'Now, what's this? Damson Day. Oh my goodness, it's like some retro country fair! I've half a mind to go simply because they had the guts to invite me. And come to think of it, it might be a nice change from nine-course tasting menus and small talk with impossibly rich people...'

There was a tap on the door. 'Can I come in?' Daniel asked.

'Yes.' I shuffled into a sitting position and pushed the straggles of hair off my face while Daniel took a seat on my bed, depositing a mug of tea and a raisin scone on the bedside table.

'Becky told me what happened.'

I sighed. 'What, that I ruined their celebratory moment by freaking out and then ran away?'

'That you shared some understandable concerns about a horrendous D-list celebrity derailing the day.' He shuddered. 'The thought of her flouncing about insulting everything we've worked so hard on – it makes me seethe, and she's not even here yet.'

I plastered on a watery smile. 'She wouldn't criticise while she was here. It'd be all fake smiles and mock politeness. But it only takes one wrong sentence from her and people will end up feeling crushed.'

'I'm not so bothered about what she writes. People know what she's about. I'm more annoyed that she'll be stressing out the people who've been working so hard to make it a success.'

'Well, if she was rude then it might unite the sides with a common enemy for once, help them forget how much they're meant to hate each other.' I sighed. 'She isn't going to come, anyway. I just hope Alice and Becky aren't too disappointed.'

Daniel gently took hold of my hand, looking carefully into my eyes. 'Why did you hide up here, instead of talking it out with them?'

My heart began to pound, and not because his eyes were so soft and kind.

'I think I got overwhelmed by everything. This is your family farm. If the retreat doesn't work out, then I can find another way to earn a living. But I've turned your home upside down. I guess the thought of Nora Sharp tainting it with her toxic opinions felt like one pressure too many.'

'I wondered if it might have triggered some panic about the stalker. Given that you and Nora are both reviewers, your subconscious could have made a link.' He tugged gently on my hands. 'Not that I see you and Nora Sharp as having *anything* in common beyond both having been food writers.'

I shrugged, my vocal cords too clogged up with sadness and shame to speak.

He leant forwards and kissed me on the forehead. 'You know, I might appear to be chilled and unbothered about this stalker freak, but don't be fooled. I'm like an undercover bodyguard, alert at all times. I don't believe they'll show up – if I did, I'd have found us somewhere safe to stay weeks ago – but in the none in a million chance that they do, I'm here, and I'm on it, and I'll defend you with my very life.' He smiled, to show how preposterous the whole idea of it was.

I forced myself to smile back. 'I know. It's last-minute nerves.' I nodded to the bedside table. 'A mug of tea and a scone and I'll be fine. Can you tell Becky I'll be down to help in a minute?'

He kissed me again and left me to pull myself together.

I scrolled through my phone to Tuesday, 6th May: *confess*.

I had a sickening feeling that Nora Sharp might end up forcing a confession a day early.

* * *

The next forty-eight hours flew past in a blur. Friday evening started with a confused and concerned apology from Alice on the phone, followed by an embarrassed apology from me, and went on to become a tornado of baking, prepping and final touches. After the expected next-to-no sleep, on Saturday morning I lugged myself downstairs to start again. The four guests, all female, arrived in a spray of gravel and overblown enthusiasm, declaring everything 'totally perfect!' and 'super-cute!' before devouring lunch on the patio.

'I can't believe how great this is, Tammers!' Felicia, who had made the initial booking, shrieked as Alice and I cleared their empty plates. 'I *swear* that gluten-free bread is a certified miracle.'

'I *know!*' Tammers hollered. 'And when was the last time we ate *cheese?*' She broke off into snort-laughs.

'And it's like, I *don't even care!*' another guest, who they called Dinky but whose credit card said Bethany Brown, tittered. 'Bring on the cheese! Extra dairy, extra cheesy, please!'

'This place is like a cross between Narnia, heaven and my Grandma's house,' the fourth guest said, tossing a mane of silver hair over her perfectly tanned shoulder. 'It's like *anything is possible.* They could totally bring out some cake and I would even eat some?'

'Yes! It's like my grandmother's house!' Tammers agreed. 'Not Granny Rose, she lived in a haunted hovel. But Grandma Camelia, oh, I *loved* going to her house! And it was *just like this*, only with a pool and tennis courts.'

'I think we can see a theme emerging for your sessions,' Alice said to Becky as she loaded the dishwasher.

'Oh?' Becky was arranging cocktail ingredients on a tray. 'Should I be worried?'

'No.' I scraped the smear of leftovers into the

compost bin. 'Underneath all the supers and per-
fects, they're actually pretty super themselves. I've
spent a lot of time eating in places stuffed with posh
people, and I've never heard so much gratitude for a
two-course lunch.'

'She's right,' Alice grudgingly agreed. 'Not a hint
of snark between them. They're like you two. Genuinely, nauseatingly nice.'

'Sounds like it's going to be a good weekend,'
Becky stuck her tongue out at Alice as she went to
see for herself.

I smiled as I carried on clearing up. I couldn't see
the resemblance to me, but almost everything about
them reminded me of Charlie.

* * *

In retreat terms, it was as good as we'd hoped. Our
guests continued to bounce from one activity to another, enchanted by our tiny taste of country life. In
response to their gentle begging, we even diverted
the sunrise hike to visit some newborn calves.

'Is he spoken for?' Tammers asked Becky out of
the corner of her mouth, her gaze transfixed on

Luke, hefting trellis tables out of his van and over to the orchard in readiness for the stallholders on Monday.

'Um...' Becky turned a startling shade of damson.

'Oh, okay!' Tammers gave her arm a sympathetic squeeze. 'Say no more, I totally get it!' She lent a little closer, electric blue eyelashes fluttering. 'Though I must say, you have outstanding taste!'

Seeing all the preparations going on, the foursome insisted on helping out on Sunday afternoon once the retreat was officially over, stringing up bunting and fairy lights between the trees, arranging tables and artfully stacking wood on the bonfire. They spent another hour in the kitchen cutting out apple scones and decanting jams into individual portions. Tammers would probably have stayed a week if we'd let her.

'I'm on a total mission to find myself a yummy farmer!' she trilled, wiping floury hands on her apron. 'I feel like I was born to wear wellies!'

'We're so glad you've enjoyed it,' I said, trying to politely usher them in the direction of the door. 'If you could write a review, it'd be greatly appreciated.'

'Oh, we already have!' Dinky smiled. 'We've been posting non-stop since we got here. See?'

She flicked through a stream of images of them smiling, posing and looking genuinely relaxed and happy. I wasn't aware so many different emojis existed, but she'd made good use of them.

The number of likes made my head spin. I'd had a lot of followers, but this was a whole other level.

'Are you an influencer?' I asked, feeling awkward for not realising it earlier.

'Totally!' Dinky beamed. 'Tammers is, too. Felicia and Bo are along for the ride.'

Our website crashed. Damson Farm Retreats was in business.

* * *

It was another back-achingly late night. We left the retreat clear-up for another day, moving straight on to Damson Day prep. I felt like I must be sweating apple juice by now, and my hair would probably smell of honey for days.

Daniel came to find us once it was too dark to carry on outside. We feasted on the broken scones and leftover cheese and fruit from the retreat. We chinked the one small glass of cider we allowed ourselves the night before a day that would be taught about in Ferrington schools for generations and toasted great food, even better friends – including those no longer with us, of course – and crazy ideas that somehow seemed to have turned into something fantastic.

I scurried up to bed before Becky and Alice had left, avoiding any risk of the conversation drifting over to our unlikely special guest, and my reaction to her earlier in the week.

I woke up just after seven on Monday morning to a soft beam of sunlight peeping through the crack in my curtains. It had been a muggy night, and it was only thanks to my extreme sleep deprivation over the weekend that I managed to doze as much as I did. Throwing on some denim shorts and a stripy T-shirt, I went downstairs to find an empty coffee mug on the side and smears of toast crumbs on Hope's highchair. Following the clues, I slipped on my flip-flops and found them in the orchard, surrounded by a hive of activity (not one of Ziva's hives, which were safely cordoned off for the day). Stallholders were already unpacking their goods – cakes and cookies, pickles and preserves, arts and crafts including all things knitted, carved and framed. Traditional games were being set up – hoopla, hook-a-duck and a coconut shy – alongside more modern touches like an electronic penalty shoot-out and a rodeo sheep.

The cider press was set up in one corner, although we had only a few crates of apples, none of which had been grown in the orchard, but it was a start. In the meadow, a couple of people were setting out markers for a rounders game. Six teams had entered the tournament, the only rule being that at least two people from each side had to be on every team.

The staff from Pepper's Pizza and Ferrington Fish and Chippy had set up a giant barbeque with accompanying side-dishes, next to which was the gazebo where Becky and I would serve cream teas and other light refreshments.

The atmosphere was electric, and we still had over two hours to go. I shoved thoughts of Nora

Sharp to one side, vague fears about the crazy stalker to another, and got stuck in.

By the time the gates opened at eleven, there was a line of people snaking halfway down the lane. Shortly before that, I'd found Daniel down by the newly discovered footbridge, which would be officially opened when we held the duck race that afternoon. He was sitting on the riverbank, arms resting on his knees, so lost in thought that he didn't hear me coming.

'Hey.' I sat down, gently bumping his arm.

'Hi.' He nodded in acknowledgement, but kept his eyes on the far shore of the river. The air was ripe with the scent of newly cut grass, where a path had been mowed through the meadow, and enough undergrowth cut back to allow a clear route into the New Side of the village. Someone had added a safety rope either side of the concrete bridge, and this was now covered in brightly coloured ribbons which fluttered gently in the breeze.

'It's a big day.'

'Yeah.'

'Thinking about your great-grandad?'

His mouth flickered up in a brief smile. 'Great-grandad, Grandad. Dad...' He paused, his voice breaking.

'Charlie,' I said, softly.

He nodded, closing his eyes for a long moment.

'They'd be so pleased.' I tucked my arm through his, leaning up closely against him. 'Not to mention proud. It's incredible what you're doing. For the farm, and for Ferrington.'

He didn't reply, but found my fingers, tucked up against his chest, and clutched them tightly. A brown mallard drifted past, a brood of black and yellow striped ducklings following closely behind.

'I got you something.' I unwound my arm from his and opened the bag that I'd brought with me. Daniel waited while I drew out a glass bottle and handed it to him.

'Damson Farm Cider.' He read the label, face creasing into a grin. 'A commemorative bottle, marking the very first Damson Day.' He inspected it closer. 'Empty?'

I laughed. 'It's a prototype only. A promise, of great things to come.'

'Thank you.' Daniel's gaze was soft. 'I love it.' He stopped then, his eyes flickering down before meeting mine again. He took a deep breath in, and carefully took hold of my hand. 'Speaking of which.' He swallowed. My heart started thumping in response. 'Of... love...'

'Oy!' Alice's bellow caused us both to jerk back in surprise. We turned to see her standing where the orchard gate opened onto the meadow, frantically waving her arms. 'Have you seen the time? They're going to break those lovely new gates down if you aren't here to open them in the next thirty seconds!'

Daniel checked his watch. 'Whoops. We'd better go.' He jumped to his feet, pulling me with him. We both started jogging up the meadow towards the orchard, when he suddenly stopped, still holding onto my hand, and pulled me up against his chest. 'Stuff it. They can wait another ten seconds. I'm not sure this can.' He tipped his head towards mine. 'What I was going to say, before being so rudely interrupted, was that... I love you, Eleanor. I have fallen completely, utterly, head-over-heels for you. I love everything about you, and the things I don't know yet, I can't wait to find out because I'm so certain I'll love them, too. I can't imagine life without you. And I've been waiting for weeks to say that.'

I stood there, speechless, every inch of me aglow.

'It would help my blood pressure if you said something...' He squinted, smile faltering.

Should I say it? Could I? Would it be wrong to tell him how I feel, when I was still holding back so much?

'Daniel!' Alice again.

'I love you, too,' I whispered, stretching up to kiss him soundly on the lips before dragging us both into the orchard and through the trees. My heart was floating along about three metres above us, but my conscience was dragging through the dirt.

33

The next few hours were a whirlwind of scones and jam, pouring teas and coffees and handing out soft drinks. It seemed as though the whole village had turned out to, at the very least, have a nosy and check out how the other side were behaving. However, to my enormous relief, there was no sign of any celebrity guests, and as the day wore on I began to relax, even more sure that Nora wouldn't be showing up.

One surprise guest, however, was Daniel's mother, Billie. She ordered two cream teas, sitting with her husband, Rob, in the shade of the gazebo, glancing around in amazement the whole time.

'Everything okay?' I asked, ducking over to collect their plates and mugs.

'It's incredible,' Billie replied, shaking her head. 'I thought... I thought it would be odd. Seeing the orchard full of people, some of them who never knew Daniel's dad, who don't understand or care what this place is. I haven't been in here since... since we lost Charlie. I wasn't sure I could do it. But seeing what you've done, the beautiful decorations, the laughter.' A gaggle of small children ran past us, squealing with joy, as if to prove her point. 'I keep seeing their faces, how much they'd have loved this. It's perfect.' She used a paper napkin to blot both eyes. 'I don't suppose you have any space on this orchard committee you're setting up?'

'You'll have to speak to Daniel about that.' I wiped my own eyes on the sleeve of my dress. 'But I'm sure you'd be very welcome.'

Later that afternoon, we gathered the crowds to unveil two brand new, very special features in the orchard. The first, a sculpture of a bridge, designed by the children of Ferrington Primary. It was a bit of a jumbled mess, if I was being honest, but from what I could tell, the various shapes carved into the wood included some boats, ducks, apples and bees, various people holding hands and I think what might have been a tableau of Sylvia Jackson collapsed with anaphylactic shock while Ziva stuck a needle about the size of her own arm in her chest.

Of course, nobody cared that the standard wasn't quite what we'd hoped for. When the new, youthful recruits to the Ferrington Carpentry Club pulled off the sheet, you could have heard the whistles and cheers all the way across the river.

After the requisite speeches, everyone moved a few feet across to where a large hole had been dug near the orchard fence. Daniel stood, holding onto a tree sapling, his face a blend of sorrow and pride.

'It's a cherry tree,' he told the onlookers. 'My sister Charlie's favourite. Although I think she loved the blossom more than the fruit. Either way, I know she'd be so happy to see the orchard coming back to life. This was her favourite place, so I wanted to include something beautiful, in her memory.'

'She was a wonderful young woman,' Sylvia Jackson called out. 'I was honoured to have her in my class.'

While some onlookers rumbled in assent, Daniel

beckoned for his mum to come forwards. With trembling hands, Billie held the sapling while Daniel filled the hole with soil, and together they patted it down and gave it a good watering. Hope was invited to help with her own little watering can, although most of it ended up down her playsuit rather than anywhere near the tree.

It was as the spontaneous applause began to die down that another wave of interest rippled through the crowd.

My heart plummeted.

I knew that reaction. I'd witnessed it far too many times before.

Someone famous had entered the vicinity.

Thankfully, before I could do anything other than try to remember how to breathe, Alice spotted it too. Grabbing Becky with a look of unbridled glee, she stopped, smoothed her hair into place, took a deep breath in and out and then weaved around the outside of the now transfixed group of onlookers to where the new arrival stood, fanning her face with one hand, taking rapid fire selfies with the other.

Lucy – *Nora* – had changed. While she'd purposely adopted a similar look and hairstyle to mine for the time she'd been working as my stand-in, she now wore her hair in a waist-length tumble of auburn extensions. Most of her face was covered in huge, round sunglasses, emphasising pursed, fuchsia lips. She wore black denim shorts that were smaller than most of my underwear, and a white shirt knotted above her belly button, snakeskin wedge-heeled sandals on the end of her toned legs. I could see why Lucy hadn't had as much time to write reviews lately. That stomach had looked quite different a few months ago. She'd been working hard.

'Hi!' Alice breathed, coming to a stop in front of her. 'Welcome to the first ever Damson Day. I'm Alice, part of the organising committee.'

Lucy flashed a quick smile, phone still aloft.

'We can't quite believe you're here!' Alice gushed, in a most un-Alice-like fashion. I wanted to give her a shake to bring her back to her senses.

'Well, please just pretend I'm *not* here,' Lucy said. 'I'd rather be treated as a normal paying customer like everyone else.' She accompanied this by vigorously tossing her hair over one shoulder, in a way that suggested she actually wanted people to very much know that she was there.

'Right, of course!' Alice said, her smile wavering. 'We're about to start the duck race, but, you know, do feel free to wander round, or sample the barbeque. Eleanor and Becky have made some fabulous cakes.'

'Well, thank you for giving me permission to walk about and buy some food like everyone else. Much appreciated.' Lucy – or I really should start calling her Nora if she was going to keep this attitude up – swung around, nearly smacking Alice in the face with a giant bag that matched her sandals, and strode over to where a young woman stood trembling with nerves and excitement from behind her fudge stand.

I daren't move. If I did, there was a risk Nora would spot me. I also didn't trust my legs to carry me anywhere. A thousand mixed-up thoughts were jumbling and tumbling through my head.

I can't believe she's here. Why is she here? Has she come because somehow she knows I'm here? But how could she know that? Not even my own parents know I'm here. Did Alice mention me? Either way, what will she do when she sees me? I'm her old boss, her friend – will she want to hug or to slap me across the face? She was mad that I'd fired her via an answerphone message, but it did

mean she ended up with an outstanding promotion...
Hang on a second, what about Marcus? She cheated on
me with my boyfriend! Maybe I should slap her?

So, yes, I was somewhat discombobulated.

To my relief, Becky snapped me out of it.

'Coming to the race?' she asked, linking her arm through mine.

I nodded, distractedly, eyes still unable to tear themselves away from Nora, now peering at a jar of pickle.

'Hang on, did you used to know her?' Becky's eyes narrowed suspiciously as she followed my gaze. 'Or have you met in a professional capacity or something? Ooh, did she beat you to the job writing the column?'

I shook my head, steering us around in the direction of the river. 'I used to sort of know her, but things didn't end well so I don't know how she'll react to seeing me here. I really don't want to be the cause of any Damson Day drama, so please don't tell anyone. Even better, if you could stand between us and shield me from her for the rest of the day, that'd be perfect.'

'Best friend's honour.' Becky nodded gravely. 'On

the condition that you tell me all the details some-time. Oh, and by "sometime" I mean either this evening or tomorrow morning.'

'How about tomorrow afternoon?' I said, as we started winding our way through the meadow to where several dozen people were clustered by the new bridge. 'I need to speak to Daniel in the morning.'

'Oh?' she asked. 'Everything going okay?'

'I think so.' *I hoped so!* I watched Daniel hand the ceremonial scissors to Frank and Eddie. As they officially reopened the footbridge, to resounding cheers, I felt grateful that Nora was sneering over the stalls back in the orchard, and not ruining this special moment.

By the time the hundreds of rubber ducks were bumbling their way downstream towards the village, however, she'd tottered her way down towards the bank.

'What is this?' she asked, loud enough for most people to pause their conversations to stare at her.

'It's a duck race,' Ziva replied, with an eye roll that suggested she didn't know who was asking, or if she did, she wasn't impressed.

'But they aren't even real ducks!'

'No, because that would be cruel. Not to mention pandemonium,' Luke said, after giving Becky a quick wink and a nod.

'Well, thousands of plastic ducks—'

'Three-hundred and sixty-one rubber ducks.'

'A stupid number of whatever they are is hardly environmentally friendly!' Nora retorted. 'I imagine real ducks are considerably more biodegradable.'

'These ducks are years old, borrowed from other duck races,' Ziva cried, her face wrinkled in disgust.

To everyone's relief, especially mine, Nora said nothing, instead waltzing off in the direction of the finish line.

'What an odious woman.' Ziva shuddered.

'Ugh. I can see why you didn't want her here,' Becky said, lip curled in distaste in a startling imitation of her mother. 'How could anyone bear to live like that. Making a career out of being horrible?'

'I don't know.'

I really didn't. I couldn't bear it, and at least I'd been polite and pleasant in person, saving my negativity for the page.

Becky looked over at Luke, her offended expression instantly replaced with a shy wave that Luke responded to with a secretive smile and a wink.

'Are you able to man the cream teas for the last half hour?' I asked. It was nearly four, and soon the Bridge Band would kick-off the evening festivities before we lit the feud funeral pyre.

'No worries.' Becky dragged her eyes away from Luke, and put her arm around my shoulders for a quick side-hug. 'You look like you could do with taking five minutes.'

I hurried back up and through the orchard, making my way around the farmhouse to the arbour. Planning on collapsing onto one of the yellow cushions, I came to a stuttering stop.

Of course. Because Nora Sharp turning up here isn't enough for one day.

One hand pressed against the top of my chest, the other one fumbling for the edge of the table. It felt as though every muscle was rendered numb, like an all-body pins and needles. My vision blurred, but I could still see the photograph, pinned to the back of the arbour by my favourite chopping knife.

It was me. Walking along the footpath to the village. A tiny curve of Hope's downy head poked over my shoulder, from where she rode in the sling on my back.

I staggered the few metres to the hedge and was violently sick all over the pale pink hawthorn blossom.

They were here.

They were here.

Wiping my mouth on a tissue I'd used earlier to clean Hope's nose, I span around, as best I could given that my nervous system was in chaos. Scouring the horizon, before zooming in on every nook and cranny in this corner of the garden, I willed myself to get a grip and focus.

They might not be here. They might have simply *been* here. Again.

As well as in my kitchen, to steal the knife.

I tried to remember the last time I'd sat in the arbour. Yesterday morning. Enough time to have been and gone. Recently enough to still be here, hiding in plain sight of the crowd.

With flailing fingers, I managed to summon up enough presence of mind to take photos of the picture. I then clicked through to the Damson Farm Retreat email account, and hastily scrolled through the most recent messages.

I didn't have to scroll far.

It had been sent at eleven o'clock that morning:

Hello Eleanor. Looking forward to the big day? I am.

Oh, crap.

I stumbled out of there.

'Daniel?' I managed to ask Luke, manning the sheep rodeo. He glanced at me, forehead creasing as he took in my distraught appearance.

'Over by the barbeque last time I saw him.' He paused. 'Eleanor, are you all right?'

I didn't bother answering, instead veering over towards the food stands, my eyes frantically searching the crowds for any sign of an Alami. Once close enough to spot Daniel through the trees, I skidded to a stop. Nora was standing right next to him. She threw back her head, shaking her red mane, and rested a hand on his forearm as if sharing the funniest of jokes. Daniel at least had the decency to look puzzled rather than join in. Even through my distress, I felt a surge of love for that man.

But I wasn't about to approach while Nora Sharp

had her talons on him. Let alone while I was on the brink of hysteria.

Instead, I changed course for the refreshments gazebo, where Becky was sorting the remaining few scones.

'I'd ask if you're feeling better, but your face is *green*.' She looked at me, concerned. 'Have you had a run-in with her?'

'I think the bee man is back,' I managed to blurt. Becky grabbed my arm and manoeuvred me into a folding chair, before grabbing a bottle of water and crouching down next to me, unscrewing the top as she spoke. 'What's happened?'

'I found a photo of me, stuck to my arbour with a kitchen knife.'

Becky went as pale as I felt.

I told her about the email.

'You've called Brenda?'

'Not yet. I came straight here.'

'Give me your phone.'

'Becky, wait.' I put a hand out. 'The band is about to start. And then the bonfire. We can wait three hours and not ruin the day.'

'We can call Brenda, have a discreet chat in the

farmhouse and that won't ruin the day either, but it might save you from being impaled by your own kitchen knife!'

'And then what – she calls a load of back-up uniformed policemen, who whizz up the drive in their police cars, before stampeding through the orchard, hunting through the crowd and accosting anyone looking suspicious? The whole village would know in seconds. Let alone the Nora Sharp factor. Can you imagine how she'd spin that chain of events? No super-cute posts from Dinky and Tammers could counteract that.'

Becky thought for a moment. 'Okay.' She checked the time on her phone. 'It's just after five. We light the fire at half past, and then the band starts at six. We give people an hour to enjoy the music, and call the police at seven.'

I nodded. Surely two hours wouldn't make that much difference?

Becky hadn't finished, though. 'On one condition. No, actually two. We ask Mum and Luke to keep an eye out for anyone they don't recognise. Between them they must know just about everyone in Ferrington. And...' She took hold of my hand. 'This is how close you're sticking to me until I can hand you over to a police officer. Seriously. This close.' She waved her other hand between us to confirm the distance, which I estimated as about sixteen inches.

'Okay.' I attempted a smile, but before I knew it I was bawling.

'Oh, sweetheart.' Becky wrapped her arms around me. 'It's going to be fine. I'm being overly cautious because that's my job as your friend.' She rubbed my back as she spoke. 'Honestly, it's fine.'

'I know,' I sobbed, leaning into her shoulder. 'I know it'll more than likely be nothing. I'm not even crying because I'm upset, or I'm scared.' Though I was, of course, both those things, my overwhelmingly predominant emotion was something different altogether.

'I can't remember the last time someone had my back. That you'd insist on sticking this close to me...'

'Well, maybe not *this* close.'

'That you'd stay anywhere near me at all... the only person who I could ever rely on like that was Charlie. And to be honest, she meant well, but in practice, being reliable wasn't really her forte.' I did a big sniff to avoid getting snot on her top, which under the circumstances was the least I could do. 'Thank you.'

Becky squeezed me even tighter for a second before pulling back and handing me a tissue. 'You're very welcome.'

'I think I love you, Becky Adams.'

She winked. 'That's good, because I *know* I love you. Now, a funeral pyre awaits. I'll message Luke and my mum once we're safely surrounded.'

34

I tried not to think about how easy it would be to slip a knife into someone's back while hidden in a crowd. If this stalker was here, I knew they would want to confront me rather than remaining anonymous. As we made our way over to where the bonfire was safely cordoned off in one corner of the meadow, my eyes continually scanned the remaining few people wandering up to join the crowd. The villagers were waiting solemnly in an arc around the pile of wood about six feet high, and we deliberately positioned ourselves well away from Nora, typing away on her phone. Daniel, standing on the far side of the rope fence, waited for the last few stragglers before calling everyone to attention.

'Good evening, good people of Ferrington!'

Everyone hooted and cheered.

'I'd like to start by thanking you wholeheartedly for joining us on this historic day. I know how much it means for some of you to have come, given our history. For most of us, this is the first time we've attended a village event where all of us are welcome. I know that for those of you who remember the days before the feud, this is even harder. I'm so grateful that you've made the difficult choice to start healing the rift that's blighted us for so long. I know this won't be simple, or something that happens quickly, but together we took a step of faith in saying that it's valuable enough to try.'

He walked over and took Hope from Billie's arms, carrying her back to his original position. 'We take this step in letting go of the past, not to diminish the hurt and the hardship that so many of us faced, but so that our children can have a better future.'

He might have had more to say, but there was no chance anyone would hear it. The roar of support and affirmation from the crowd was spontaneous, and heartfelt.

While the cheers continued, three men stepped forwards and set the bonfire alight. Daniel called Caris Smith and her four adult children forwards. They were each carrying a stick. Caris turned to face the onlookers, reading the word she'd written on her stick in a loud voice: 'Loneliness.' She threw the stick onto the flames.

Each of her children called out what they'd written on their branches:

'Grief.'

'Anger.'

'Being broke.'

Into the flames they went.

One by one, various others stepped forwards with their sticks. They burned bitterness, hate and hunger. Sickness and sadness. Violence and vandalism. Hardship and loss. One person had written 'self-service checkouts', but we cheered them anyway.

When the last stick was ablaze, Frank and Eddie declared in a loud voice that the Ferrington Feud was officially dead. Some of the villagers embraced their neighbours from the other side of the river. Many of the men who had once pickaxed together deep below the ground held each other as they wept. Women who had once worried about their men together, shared gossip and advice and childrearing, until turning their backs on one another, gripped hands and began catching up on thirty-six missed years.

Not all of them. Some kept their distance, frowned and shifted uncomfortably but they were here, and that was an enormous step, to be celebrated not judged.

Daniel then called Becky forwards.

'Crap!' She glanced at me, holding tight to my hand. 'I'm doing a speech.'

'I'm not coming up there,' I whispered, glancing over to where Nora was still engrossed in her phone.

Becky looked torn.

'I'll stand right here where you can see me. Look, Alice is just there. Go! I'll be fine for two minutes.'

'Three minutes and forty-five seconds.'

'Go!'

It was Becky's role to move our focus from the past onto the future. She spoke about the plans for the orchard, and the retreat, the opportunities to develop skills and forge relationships. She mentioned all those businesses and individuals who had helped get things off the ground, or promised their support in the future. She even floated an idea about converting the barn into a wedding and events venue, which had Daniel raising his eyebrows in my direction. I shrugged and managed a sort of smile. Maybe we would hold our wedding there one day.

As Becky ran through the list of people she wanted to thank, she then took a deep breath, lifted her chin and said, 'I would like to finish by thanking Nora Sharp, the well-known food and event reviewer, for taking the time and trouble to come and visit our little festival. I do hope that having seen what Damson Day is all about, you'll be able to write one of your inspirational, positive reviews!' She paused then, thrown by the sneer on Nora's face, before pressing on, voice now wavering. 'Well. Either way, all publicity is good publicity, right?'

'Let's put it this way – it'll be an honest write-up.'

Nora, to my surprise, stepped out of the crowd and went to stand by Becky. She allowed the stunned silence to linger, sharp eyes roaming over the shocked faces, until they stopped dead. On me.

'Eleanor.' She smiled. It felt as though the temperature suddenly plummeted about twenty degrees. 'Finally decided to stop hiding from me?' She waited for me to reply, but I couldn't breathe, let alone speak. 'I'm sure you're all wondering why I bothered travelling over a hundred miles into the backside of nowhere, for a – and I'm being polite here because children are present – bog-standard little fete. I had a backstage pass for Take That at the O2 tonight. Why on earth would I come here? Well. I'm sure Elea*nor Sharp*ley could explain perfectly.'

She thrust one pointed finger in my direction, which felt a little overdramatic, but that was Lucy for you. There was a collective hiss from the people around me. I think I swayed a little, but my head was numb so it was hard to tell.

'Yes, up until January this year, I was Nora Sharp's assistant. *That* Nora Sharp. I spent two years devoted to building her profile, curating her image, *standing in for her* at events and in the videos. Painstakingly planning her diary. Editing her reviews so that they are actually readable. Basically, doing it all while getting paid in a few cast-off clothes and leftovers.

'And then, the moment my videos started out-shining her sad little columns, she fired me. *Via answerphone message.* Oh, don't look so surprised – what else would you expect from Nora? A generous redundancy package and a goodbye hug? She didn't even write me a reference. Although I ended up not needing one, because the moment her editor knew I'd been dumped, he fired her and gave the real Nora the job.'

'That still doesn't explain why you're here, or what that has to do with Damson Day!' Alice, God bless her, called out. 'This is about the Ferrington Feud, not whatever issues you happen to have going on with Eleanor.'

Nora went deathly still. I could feel the animosity of her stare boring through my head into the back of my skull. 'I thought it only right that you knew what you were getting yourselves into. Eleanor Sharpley, Nora Sharp, whoever she's pretending to be these days, didn't just try to ruin my life, she's destroyed countless others over the past few years. Don't be fooled like I was. Once a lying, secretive, callous bitch who enjoys profiteering from other people's misery... always the kind of woman who turns up on the doorstep of a supposed best friend – such great friends she hadn't even realised she's passed away! – and decides to profiteer from hijacking that friend's dream! She'll do anything for attention.'

'That's utter crap!' Becky yelled, voice trembling as she turned to look at me, her expression pleading with me to deny the whole thing.

'I think you'd better go,' Luke said to Nora. I could barely hear him. It felt as though the bees had come back to life and burrowed into my brain.

I forced myself to drag my head up and find Daniel, standing off to one side with Hope, staring at me with a look of utter horror.

'No.' I don't know how I managed to speak, but instantly everyone whipped their heads around to focus on me. 'I'll go.'

Before anyone could try to stop me – not that anyone did – I turned and ran.

35

Stumbling, wheezing, I found myself in the farm-yard. My first instinct was to head inside, and bury myself under my duvet until I was in a fit state to start packing. But it would be the first place Becky or whoever else came looking would expect me to be.

Instead, spying the barn, I lurched over to it, before veering off around the corner to where I remembered there being a smaller, ramshackle outbuilding that as far as I knew was in disuse. It took a few moments of working at the rusted latch before I could push the rotting door wide enough to slip inside. In the muted evening light I could still pick out several old farm implements and shelves lined with huge cider jars thick with cobwebs. I pushed past a wooden sledge, a ride on lawnmower with only one wheel, and stacks of splintered pallets. Spiders scurried into the shadows, and I heard a scuffling that could definitely have been a rat. I squeezed into a gap behind a large crate and the back wall, and sank to a squat, hoping that I could stay undetected long enough to unscramble my thoughts and collect my breath. Dropping my head onto quaking hands, I tried to piece myself back together so that I could begin to figure out what I was going to do next.

Despite every effort to the contrary, I had now become the tawdry talking point of Damson Day, contaminating the best moment of the day – *of over thirty years* – with my disgusting secret.

Crap.

I squeezed my eyes shut, but it failed to dam the torrent of tears.

It must have been twilight, judging by how the light had dimmed through the cracks in the roof, when I finally made my decision. As tempting as it was to sneak inside, pack up my bags and flee before anyone noticed I'd gone, that was not how this was going to go down.

Whatever anyone might think of me, thanks to Nora's revelations, I was done with running away. Daniel and Hope meant far too much for that. *I* was worth more than that. It was time to own up to who I was, who I'd been and what I'd done. Daniel would either still love me, or he'd find me utterly repugnant, but at least it would be the real me.

I was flexing my toes, trying to ease agonising leg cramps before I made a move, when I heard footsteps approaching the outhouse door.

My heart automatically panicked, the blood accelerating through my veins. Trying to quieten my rasping breath, I waited as whoever it was performed the same wrestle with the latch as I had, and then wrenched the door open so hard it smacked into the outside wall. The beam of a phone torch darted across the walls, but unless they stepped right inside and through the clutter, I was still concealed. I would wait for them to say my name, before deciding whether or not to reveal myself.

But instead of asking for me, they instead tugged

the door closed, and took a step further into the shadows.

Twin snakes of dread and alarm unfurled in my stomach, as the terrifying thought slithered through my brain that my friends might not be the only ones looking for me.

I hadn't called Brenda.

I'd completely forgotten.

Would Becky have called?

Surely if she had, she'd have called me. Only I realised with a jolt that my phone was in my bag, over in the gazebo.

I pressed both hands against my mouth to smother my whimpers.

There began a steady rustling and scraping as the prowler started to search through the junk.

They might not be looking for me.

Maybe it's Daniel looking for a tool, or a box.

Maybe it's an opportunistic thief...

Maybe...

There was a startling clatter as they picked up a wrench and hurled it against the back wall. The clanging hid my panicked gasp.

As the phone light now strobed across the wall in

front of me, I saw the clear outline of my fresh foot-prints in the dirt and dust. The beam froze, hovering on one footprint, before slowly following the trail to where they disappeared behind a box, a couple of feet in front of me.

A muffled giggle.

The stomach snakes writhed in terror.

I was sure I knew that giggle. So I didn't know why I felt so afraid.

It's not them.

It's not the Bee Murderer.

I'm okay! I'm okay!

Slowly, painfully, my limbs stiff and sore from squatting for so long, I shuffled out before Lucy could get any closer.

She stopped, squinting through the dust motes lit up in the torch beam. I could just about make out the smirk slowly emerging as she confirmed it was me.

'Well, well. Haven't you come down in the world?' she sang.

My arms instinctively rose to shield my eyes from the light, now pointed at my face. 'What are you doing here?'

'Hunting you,' she snarled, and in an instant her expression transformed from cool superiority to raw, rampant hatred. 'I did promise, after all.'

'What?' Call me slow and stupid, but until a few months ago, Lucy had been my close colleague and my friend. She'd seen me in my underwear, tweezered my stray hairs, and last summer we'd sat on a Cornwall cliff-top, chatting and laughing and sharing stories until the sun rose. She'd encouraged me when I felt overwhelmed and out of my depth. Celebrated when our followers multiplied. Protected me from the worst of the trolls, while offering reassurance that I was not completely unlovable.

'So. Where were we?' She mused, one finger pressed against her lips as if pondering. 'Ah yes! We were coming up with a suitable way for you to pay for what you've done.'

I stood there, dumbstruck, and tried to process what the hell was happening.

'We could continue the funeral pyre theme – people seem to like a good blaze around here. How about setting this little wood-filled shack alight, and then I'll stand at a safe distance and listen to you scream?'

She paused, forehead creasing. 'Oh, except someone might spot the flames and come to investigate. Hmmm... What else? Oh – I could impale you with that fork over there. Pin you to the wall while I remind you of the names of every business you've closed, every last waiter who ended up out of work, every life you've trashed. I have a list here, ready on my phone. That might be fun. Or – how about I tie you up and drag you to the river, watch the bubbles rise to the surface as you drown? A fitting tribute to your so-called friend, don't you think? Your boyfriend will appreciate the gesture.'

'You're insane,' I croaked.

'Probably,' Lucy shrugged, before her voice hardened again. 'But you drove me to it.'

'The police will know it was you. Everyone heard how much you hate me.'

'Hundreds of people hate you! Not to mention the Alami family, who after their little attempt at intimidation last year, provided the perfect cover. And so what if the police do figure it out? My life is over, anyway.'

'You have an amazing life!' I tried to jumpstart my brain again, to keep her talking until maybe someone got worried and came looking for me, or I could think up some other way to get out of this. 'You've got a glamorous career, money, fame, a fabulous social life. Marcus. Why would you risk all that?'

'Why would I give a crap about that, compared to what you did to my family!' She shrieked. My panic jolted up another level. She genuinely was insane.

'Well? Don't you have anything at all to say about it?'

'I... I'm sorry. Whatever happened to your family...'

'Don't pretend you can't even remember!' Tears and spittle flew as she shook her head, enraged. 'We were just another column to you, another cheap laugh. After your review my dad had to sell the restaurant! We lost our house. Had to move into a two bedroom flat! *A two bedroom flat*! I was fifteen years old! Can you imagine what that felt like? *You ruined my life!*'

'Lucy, I get that it must have been hard, but moving house is not worth going to prison for murder for.'

'What would you know about it?' she screeched.

'I shared a bunk bed with my grandma until I

was twenty-six. That's why I couldn't turn down being Nora Sharp. I needed a job. A chance to get away. A life! But you have that now – you stole my life. My job, my reputation. My boyfriend. Please don't throw that all away on some fleeting revenge. I'm not worth it.'

'You didn't want them any more! Don't pretend that by scaring you off, I wasn't doing you a favour. And I don't have those things. Miles fired me. Marcus got bored. Turns out no one liked the new Nora. Now I have nothing. And you've ended up, yet again, with everything. So there's no point trying to ruin your life, you'll just get yourself a new one. I'm ending it.'

'Lucy, please...'

'Stop talking!' She sized up the nearest farm im-plements to her, before taking hold of the huge garden fork.

'No, wait...'

'Shut up!' Lucy dropped her phone, and in the dim light cast from where it lay on the floor, I saw her shove a pallet out of her path, clamber over the lawnmower and launch herself across the short dis-tance still between us.

Along with freaking out and bracing myself for

the prongs, I somehow found the presence of mind to dodge to one side and grab something to block her follow-up thrust.

I'd seized a soggy, rotten cardboard box. I might as well have plucked a fistful of cobwebs from the shelf. The fork instantly tore through the sagging card, and Lucy flicked it away.

I took an automatic few steps back, before my back smacked against another shelving unit, causing the glass contents to rattle dangerously. A couple of bottles toppled off and smashed, tiny shards catching in the glow of the phone.

Glancing either side, I realised how stupid I'd been. I could just about make out a huge, menacing-looking metal contraption on my right. On my left were the pallets, stacked haphazardly about waist high, two deep and at least five long. Scrambling across them would be slow and clumsy, and I'd be an easy target for my attacker.

For a millisecond, I wondered about using one of the pallets as a shield, at least until I could reconsider my escape route, but before I could reach down to haul one off the pile, Lucy, grunting with effort, held her weapon aloft and jabbed it straight towards my head.

Adrenaline powering my reflexes, I twisted to one side, and as the fork thrust past, I somehow managed to grab the wooden handle. Holding on for dear life, we wrestled and thrashed for control. In the confined space it was inevitable that the more we fought to get the larger portion of the handle, the closer to each other we got. Within what must have been seconds, but felt like hours, we were right up against each other. Lucy's breath was hot against my neck, and I inhaled the reek of her sweat and fury. She wasn't the only one sweating – my hands were starting to slip precariously down the handle, until they hit against the prongs.

I took a moment to focus on my breathing, sucking in as much air as my heaving lungs could manage before releasing it in a scream that bounced off the bottles and echoed through the darkness. No one would hear me – unless they happened to be walking around this side of the farm. But it was loud enough to rattle Lucy, and she momentarily relaxed her grip enough for me to wrest the fork out of her hands.

Unfortunately, I'd not quite believed in my own strength, so hadn't braced my stance for the sudden decrease in tension when Lucy let go. I stumbled back, scraping my shoulder blades against something sharp, and jabbing the back of my knee into a metal spike.

I automatically bent double to clutch my leg, the fork clattering to the ground. If I was some kick-ass heroine from a film I'd have ignored the agonising pain now shooting up my leg like flames. But I wasn't, I was a clueless, frightened wimp, and I was too exhausted and too traumatised to think any more.

Ignoring the fork, Lucy simply threw herself at me, and we both toppled over, smacking onto the floor side by side with groans and grunts. Hands clawed for my neck, my eyes, ripping out a chunk of my hair. Her feet scrabbled for purchase, those stupid sandals scraping down my shins.

And then a powerful beam of light suddenly appeared from the direction of the door.

A cry of horror, in a voice that instantly made me feel safe.

Lucy jerked, momentarily startled by the intruder.

Darkness.

Shattering pain.

Nothing.

36

I woke up in a hospital bed.

My first thought was, 'Ow!'

I must have said it out loud, because Becky jerked awake from where she'd clearly been snoozing in the chair beside me. Taking a moment to orientate herself, she spotted that I was also awake, and quickly shuffled the chair up close enough to take hold of my hand.

'Eleanor. How are you feeling?'

I tried to answer, not that I knew what to say, but my throat was hoarse and dry, so instead what came out was an ugly croak.

'Here.' She offered me a sip of water from a paper

straw, smoothing my hair back from my face after I plopped back onto the pillow, finding that lifting my head up an inch for three seconds was about as much as I could manage.

'Okay?' She peered at me, her expression a mixture of concern, compassion and relief.

I nodded. Clearly I was not okay, but I thought she probably knew more about that than I did.

'What happened?' I rasped.

'It was Lucy. Do you remember? You were in the old cider store.'

'How?' I flicked my eyes around the room, hoping she'd understand my question.

'How did you get here?' Becky gave the barest of smiles. 'Daniel heard you scream. After you left, there was a whole big kerfuffle with Nora. She was ranting on about the retreat. Daniel told her to leave, and eventually while the band got going, he and Alice called a taxi to drive her to her hotel. It was pretty clear that she'd lost it, though.

'And then I remembered about the knife in the arbour, so I called Brenda and left a message, and tried to find Daniel to tell him, but he was putting Hope to bed, so that took me a while, and people kept wanting to stop and talk to me, ask if I was okay, if *you* were okay. I ended up yelling at DJ Vapes to leave me alone so I could try to find out. So,' she paused to take a deep breath, 'I eventually found Daniel, once Hope was in bed and Billie and Rob were babysitting. Once I'd managed to get him alone and explain, and then we'd found Luke and a couple of other guys to help search for you, Brenda had called back and said she was on her way. But we couldn't find you anywhere. You weren't answering your phone. The band were winding down, so we asked more people to help, but a lot of them assumed you'd simply gone off on your own. To be honest, we did too. If we'd seriously thought... maybe we would have looked faster.'

She stopped, wiped a stream of tears from both eyes, blew her nose and wiped her eyes again. 'I'm so sorry, Eleanor. This is totally my fault.'

'Er, excuse me?' I said, trying to heave myself up into a sitting position, and ending up sliding several inches further down the bed. 'You didn't do this. You didn't even make *her* do this. The two Noras are completely to blame.'

'Yes, but...'

'Yes, but I'm going to get really angry if you even hint at being in any way responsible for that woman's crazed campaign of revenge. And that will make my head hurt even more, which will be your fault. Now, please carry on.'

'Okay.' She rubbed her face, gave her head a brisk shake and carried on. 'We'd all spread out, looking for you. Other people were busy tidying up and sorting everything out. Daniel had stayed by the farmhouse, in case you came back – and because he wanted to be near Hope. Then he heard you scream, and got there just as Nora was about to... well. Do something horrible. She was startled and you fell backwards. Your head smashed into the concrete floor.'

'So that explains the thumping headache.'

'You've also hurt your knee, and are covered in bruises and cuts. Oh...' Her eyes filled with tears again, as she gently stroked my hair. 'That monster pulled out a chunk of your hair.'

'What happened to her?'

'She's been arrested. Daniel restrained her while he waited for the police.'

'It was all her?'

'Looks like it. The Bee Murderer is vanquished. The queens and their boys can rest in peace, and so can you.'

Not likely. Becky was ushered out soon after that, but the last thing I felt was peaceful.

I hadn't asked her where Daniel was, why he wasn't here. I had a fairly good idea every time I re-membered the look of revulsion on his face.

I tried to start thinking up a plan, but my thoughts were a jumbled mess, and before I could process more than a few disjointed phrases about 'sort business,' 'new place to live,' 'pack,' 'car,' I had forgotten what I was trying to think about.

Later that afternoon a nurse came to give me a thorough inspection, and straight after they'd brought me a plate of flavourless mush and a tub of ice cream, my phone – thoughtfully left on the scruffy bedside table – rang.

I snatched it up, my anxious, hopeful heart plummeting back into disappointment when I saw it was my parents. Not that I was sorry to hear from them – their brusque, matter-of-fact manner was as comforting as a cosy blanket and a mug of cocoa.

'Your friend said you've been in an accident, but you're okay.'

'Yes,' I whispered, my throat contracting with unshed tears.

'Nothing broken, no permanent damage, just plenty of rest and as much time as it takes.'

'I think so.'

'Sounds like you'd better come home. We've made up Goosander, and don't worry about getting here, we'll book a taxi.'

'Thanks, Mum.'

'Grandma's paying, you can thank her. Try to get some sleep.'

She hung up before I could say goodbye.

I slept about as well as is to be expected when in a strange bed, an elderly woman wheezing on one side of me, another groaning and muttering all night on the other, the weight of my guilt and shame pressing down on my skull, the pain of my heartache sharper than my injuries. By the time the doctor did his rounds the following morning, I was ready to lie through my teeth while performing a tap-dance if it meant I could be discharged.

Alice had popped in for a few minutes the evening before. Ziva had stayed a while longer, chattering about nothing, answering my questions about the rest of Damson Day with brief, bland answers before directing the conversation back to something else. In the end, I couldn't help asking her where Daniel was.

She stilled, face a careful blank, hands clasped in front of her in a pose I imagined she had adopted when delivering bad news to thousands of patients over the years. 'He's taking care of Hope. She's spent a lot of time being passed between babysitters in the past couple of days, and after everything it's only natural he'd want to keep her close.'

'He's not called. Or messaged.' I tried not to choke on the words. 'He hates me.'

'Of course he doesn't! It's been a hectic day. Can you imagine how busy he is trying to get the farm straight?'

'I can't imagine being so busy he can't take ten seconds to send a text.' *To the woman he had said 'I love you' to only a day earlier.*

My heart was so heavy it pulled my gaze down to the sheet, unable to look Ziva in the eye.

'He's probably giving you time to rest...'

'Right.'

Ziva was quiet for a moment.

'I'm so very sorry.'

I shook my head, feebly. 'I was going to tell him.'

'You'll get a chance to explain. For now, you need to concentrate on resting up and getting better. Daniel will be ready to talk in time.'

It was late afternoon by the time I left, clutching a bag of prescriptions as I hobbled to Becky's car on my injured leg, which was refusing to bend more than about two millimetres. She'd brought me a clean pair of yoga pants and a hoodie, but there was still blood encrusted in my hair, and I both looked, smelled and felt like I'd been sleeping under a bush. We'd agreed that she would take me back to the farm to help me pack what I could fit in the boot of a car – fortunately I'd not added much to the items I'd brought from London. A taxi would then collect me. I'd sort out what to do with the hunk-of-junk car later on.

Arriving at Damson Farm in about the same state

as the first time, I saw Luke's van and another couple of cars parked near the orchard entrance, and as Becky helped me limp inside, the sound of voices drifted over the gate.

'Does he know?' I asked, my voice close to a whisper.

'I told him you were on your way,' Becky said.

So, he was deliberately avoiding me.

I nodded, ignoring the tear that dribbled out as I levered my stiff leg over the doorstep. Ignoring that there was no strong, caring man here to help me.

It was a long, laborious ordeal to get up to my bedroom. My head throbbed in time with every broken heartbeat, and the wound in my knee felt as though it had been shredded open all over again. Still the tears streamed constantly, like a faulty tap. I mutely started opening drawers while Becky beavered beside me, packing several bags by the time I'd weakly stuffed three tops into a holdall.

Noticing my pathetic progress, she stopped and handed me a towel that had been draped over the chair. 'I'll sort this, you go and have a shower. Even better, run a bath.'

I glanced towards the window. 'I think I'm best just getting out of here as soon as possible.'

'Eleanor, do you really want your parents to see you like this?' She gently turned me towards the mirror, and I watched my face crumpling.

Hair looking like a bad wig, face and arms flecked with dark red scrapes and purple bruises, an ugly crimson slash across my chin, haggard eyes ringed with black. I was almost relieved that Daniel hadn't seen me. Becky was right. Never mind my parents, no respectable taxi driver would allow me in their cab looking like this.

Once in the shower, it was almost impossible to drag myself back out again. The sensation of the near-scalding spray, how the sound muffled both the world outside and within my ravaged head, the frail hope that if I let the water wash over me for long enough, I would feel clean.

Eventually I had to come out, or else risk passing out into the shower tray. I gingerly got dried and dressed, every wincing movement a vivid recollection of the last time I had stood in this bathroom battered and bruised. A lifetime ago. Back then, I had been mourning the loss of Charlie. Now, the grief at having to leave her family engulfed me.

And yet.

Beneath the shroud of bleak despair, I still had a tiny spark of hope.

Maybe Daniel was busy.

He needed some time, like Ziva said.

He wouldn't leave the others to clear up the orchard without him, he wasn't that type of person.

He loved me... he would listen because he loved me...

He would see that the woman he'd fallen in love with was the real me, after all...

He would surely ask me to stay, at least until we'd talked about it, until he'd let me explain...

* * *

He was waiting in the kitchen.

Face grim, arms folded. It was only when he looked at me that I saw hiding behind the defensive stance was pain.

Becky helped lower me into a chair. 'Right. We're all packed up. Taxi should be here in about half an hour. I'll leave you two to talk.' She bent down to envelop me in a hug, her face pressed against my now not-quite-so-terrible hair. 'I'll speak to you soon. Don't worry about the retreats, I'll keep things going until you're ready.'

I nodded, meekly, not having the strength to argue. She turned to Daniel. 'You'll make her a drink and something to eat before she goes?'

Daniel gave one sharp nod, before Becky gave me a squeeze goodbye and left us to it.

For a long moment, the silence hung between us, dripping with unspoken questions and the unwelcome answers. Eventually, Daniel flicked the kettle on, fetching two mugs from the dresser. I felt another flicker of hope when I saw he'd used my favourite mug.

'I don't really know where to start,' I said, voice trembling.

'You don't need to say anything. The internet told me plenty. Brenda filled me in on the rest.'

'I was going to tell you,' I gabbled. 'Yesterday. After Damson Day.'

'Tell me what?' he asked, placing my drink on the table. 'That you've been concealing from me who you really are? That you weren't an honest, hard-working, uplifting food critic, but one who got famous through being vile? Or that you knew a potentially violent stalker was here, on my farm, where me, my daughter and hundreds of innocent people were gathered, and you didn't even tell me, let alone call the police, because you were afraid that we might all find out that you're not a nice person?'

'Tell you that I'd worked as Nora Sharp, and why I did it, and why I left, and how I hadn't told you because I hated who Nora had become, which was largely out of my control and not what I wanted. I loathed myself, and the only way I could bear to keep on existing was to stop being her, and go back to being the person I really am. If I'd told you, you'd not have let me stay. You'd not have given me time to show you that I'm not her. If you read her actual reviews, you'll see they're mostly constructive, positive ones.'

Daniel shook his head, scoffing in disgust.

'You must know that if I genuinely thought staying here would have put you, or anyone else – let alone Hope – in danger, I would have left. I'd told Brenda everything, and she didn't think there was anything to worry about. We thought we knew who it was, and the police were tracing them. I'm so sorry! I'm so, *so* sorry. If I could undo any of it, I would. I was scared, and lost, and alone. Then you gave me a bed, and a place to stay... A home. You gave me a second chance, a new start. I didn't want to blow it.'

'But you have blown it.' Daniel blew out an exasperated sigh. 'I feel like a total fool. I trusted you, with everything that means anything to me. My farm. My child... my heart. And you took that trust and smashed it to smithereens. You're not who I thought you were.'

'I am!' I was trying not to cry because how dare I feel sorry for myself? 'I have never been more myself than when I was here, with you. This farm, the retreat, being your girlfriend. Baking and cleaning and walking through the fields with Charlie's daughter on my back. This is who I really am.'

He looked away, shaking his head. It was then that I knew I'd lost him.

'Daniel. Please...'

His face was like a castle. Drawbridge up, portcullis slammed shut.

'You can't believe what Lucy said about me. You have to let me explain.'

'Don't you see, it doesn't matter?' He ran a hand through his hair, the anger rippling through his bicep. 'It doesn't matter if you spent every day saving lives instead of wrecking them. You lied to me.'

'I never lied...'

He simply stared at the floor.

'So that's it?'

One nod.

'Can I say goodbye to Hope?'

'She's with Mum. I thought it best for her not to be around.'

I couldn't reply, my throat too swollen with regret and self-loathing.

'I'll take your bags out to the taxi when it gets here.'

He left the room, unable to even look at me. I didn't blame him.

By the time I'd shuffled outside to the taxi my bags were already in the boot.

'That everything?' the taxi driver asked, clearly wondering why a man had dumped my bags and left me to limp to the car myself, but knowing better than to ask. It was all I could do to nod in response. Yes. That was everything. My heart. My home. This place, these people, they were everything. But it was my own idiotic fault I'd lost it all. No more than I deserved. No less than the hurt I had done to countless others.

37

I have to confess, there were fleeting, desolate, dark moments in the days that followed when I wished that I hadn't screamed that night. That Daniel had been a few seconds too slow, or Lucy that bit stronger. Waking up each day and having to face myself, I couldn't help wondering if it would have been easier not to have to bother.

I had lost everything except the one thing I had tried to get rid of – myself.

Thank goodness for practical, straight-talking, no-nonsense parents. That, and my wonderful, on-the-brink-of-bonkers grandma.

Together, over the next few weeks, they got me

up and gave me something else to think about. Wholesome, nurturing food that was impossible to resist no matter how scrunched up and tender my stomach. Simple, satisfying tasks that were impossible not to take a teensy bit of pleasure from accomplishing – scouring the grill, ironing sweet-scented sheets or snipping sprigs of flowers from the garden and arranging them in pretty vases.

Even better, they only ever asked me once, that first evening, what on earth had happened and they never asked me how long I would be staying, or whether I would be going back to Ferrington.

It was the beginning of June, nearly a month since I'd arrived back home when I found out they were even more remarkable than I'd given them credit for. My knee was still stiff, the scar red and gnarly, although the other abrasions had faded, and when I looked in the mirror, I was starting to appear slightly less like a bedraggled zombie. I'd had a call from Brenda, filling me in on what was happening with the case against Lucy (not a great deal yet, these things took time). I'd spoken to Becky the day before about the business, and was painfully aware that she was running retreats without me, and the next few months were jam-packed with guests.

Even worse, she'd told me that my old editor had been trying to get in touch with me about something important. When I called Miles, he'd warned me that the story of Lucy's arrest was about to break in the tabloids. It was inevitable that my name would be printed along with it. My dad found me, sitting at the kitchen table where I'd been peeling potatoes for hash browns, head in my hands.

'Eleanor, is there something wrong?' He stopped by the table, and even went so far as to put one hand on my shoulder.

'Yes. Yes, there is.' I took a deep breath. 'Dad, there's something I need to tell you.'

'Oh?' He took a seat opposite me.

'It's about my previous job. Writing the reviews. I wasn't... it wasn't quite... I mean... have you heard of Nora Sharp?'

Dad looked at me steadily. He let out a little huff and tapped his fingers on the table a few times. 'We know.'

'What?' I sat back, genuinely stunned.

'We've always known.'

'But... *how?* And why didn't you say anything?'

'We knew you'd tell us when you were ready.'

'Yes, but *how?*'

'Eleanor, we've read everything you've written since you could pick up a pencil. We know you. We know your voice. And didn't you think we'd put two and two together when suddenly a mystery restaurant reviewer appears in town, coincidentally the exact same time you suddenly develop a social life and start eating out all the time?' He raised his eyebrows, but his face was kind.

'But then I moved to London.'

'And could afford to rent a flat in the capital on the income you made from that little blog? Don't get me wrong, the blog was wonderful. But not big city apartment wonderful.'

'Didn't you think it was horrendous?'

His brow creased, adding even more wrinkles. 'We thought the reviews were balanced and fair. Anyone working in hospitality would agree. We also of course found the memes and the click-bait headlines awful. But we knew they weren't you. That image wasn't you, and we believed you would find your way back in due course. You were miserable, and in a perverse way, the more miserable you got, the more we felt sure you would give it up.'

He reached across the table and took my hand. His calloused palm was as familiar to me as the sunlight on the lake, but I could not remember the last time he had wrapped his fingers around mine.

'We know you, Eleanor. We love you.'

I held on tightly to my father's hand, even as we cried together. Even when my mum came in to find out why no one had set the tables, we didn't let go, and so she made us a cup of tea with not one but two biscuits each. Even as Grandma then joined us, chuckling at the early reviews I'd written in Windermere, and how I'd called out their arch-rivals, the snooty, overpriced establishment a mile down the road, for 'ironically' serving Heinz tomato soup still in the tin, as that justified charging eight pounds for it.

I had a weird family. We didn't do big heart-to-hearts or emotional outbursts. We rarely said, 'I love you,' and barely ever showed it. But here, sat at the table where I'd chopped ten zillion onions and cracked a squillion eggs, I remembered again the reason why people kept coming back to this strange little B & B year after year. Why they put up with the rigid rules and archaic systems. It was because absolutely everyone was welcome here. Welcomed, and accepted, and treated with dignity and uncommon kindness. No matter who they were, or what they might have done.

Right down to the newest member of staff.

For a fleeting moment, I made a mental note to never lose sight of that when running Damson Farm Retreats. Until I remembered that I didn't do that any more. I would mention it next time I spoke to Becky. She might find it useful.

'Right. We're twelve minutes late starting the linen. Eleanor, if you don't mind?' Mum said, whipping away my mug and plate.

I didn't mind, at all.

Well. Only a tiny bit.

I booked the rest of the week off. My parents, of course, insisted I pay for my room if I wasn't there to work, but then later on both Mum and Dad refunded me the money separately, on top of the basic wages they'd been paying me.

I was there to work, but that week it wouldn't be for the Tufted Duck. For four days I wrote, deleted, rewrote, cut and pasted and deleted most of it again. I had moments where I nearly cracked under the pressure, and others where the words flowed like the Maddon river. Eventually, what emerged was the article of my life. It wouldn't make or break me – no words would have the power to do that to me again. But it did at least express the most honest apology that I could offer, and I hoped a stark warning and a useful insight to others who may have been temporarily dazzled by the bright lights of fame and fortune, as well as my lessons learnt on the crushing impact of living a lie, rather than facing up to being true to yourself, however tough that might be.

I sent it to Miles, with a clear stipulation that my fee would go to the Ferrington Bridge Fund. I would not be filming any YouTube videos or commenting on social media. He replied within an hour to inform me that it would be the main feature in the Saturday supplement.

He also asked if I would write a follow-up on the

Ferrington Feud. I said that I would think about it, which I did, for most of that night and several more that followed. Wondering if I would ever be brave enough to turn up in Ferrington with a notepad, my phone set to record.

Then, one week exactly after the article was published, the Tufted Duck had a new booking.

'A walk-in?' I asked Mum, incredulous. The Tufted Duck had no room for walk-ins at the best of times, let alone mid-June.

'Can you handle it? I need to... do something else.'

'You want me to stop cleaning this room, and handle a walk-in? But Dad's on check-in today.' I was talking to an empty doorway, she'd disappeared as quickly as she arrived.

Putting down my cloth with a sigh, gathering the bucket of spray bottles and dumping my gloves in a bin bag, I made my way down to the reception area.

When I glanced up to see who was waiting in the foyer, I nearly tripped down the remaining few stairs.

Giving myself a mental slap for still being so pathetically obsessed with Daniel that I saw him everywhere I went, I quickly yanked myself together, swallowed back the lump in my throat and carried on.

Then he turned around.

The man smiled, hazel eyes crinkling, one hand automatically reaching up to rub at his scar.

Daniel.

Here.

In the Tufted Duck reception, holding an overnight bag and *smiling.*

'I'm sorry.' He shook his head. He didn't look sorry. His grin was growing by the second. 'I shouldn't be smiling. That's not what I had planned.'

'What did you have planned?' I stammered, coming to a stuttering stop a few metres away.

He shrugged, trying and failing to tug down the corners of his mouth. 'An appropriate level of contrition to show you how completely sorry I am, and that I am fully aware of what a total arse I was.' He took a hesitant step towards me. 'Miserably lost and utterly heartbroken. Because that's how I've been since you left.'

I don't know how I did it, but despite my thumping heart and wild thoughts running around inside my head, I managed to reply in a manner that was just about on the right side of composed.

'So why are you smiling?' I don't know why that was the question that popped out. Seeing the state the rest of me was in, my mouth appeared to have gone rogue.

He looked at me for a long moment. When he blinked, it was like someone flicked the lights off and then on again.

'I'm happy to see you.'

'Okay.' I didn't ask why he was happy to see me, let alone why he was here. I wanted this moment to drag out forever. Before the hard questions came, and the heart-breaking answers and then Daniel went away again. 'Do you want to check in?'

'Yes, please. If you've room.'

I moved over to the check-in desk and flicked through the reservations book, Mum and Dad still not having upgraded this aspect of the system to a computer. My movements were robotically calm, but beneath the surface I was a gibbering wreck. 'Yes, the Mallard room is free again.'

'Perfect.'

'Will you be needing a cot?'

'No.' Daniel was still grinning like a loon, but I felt a stab of disappointment that I wouldn't get to see Hope. It was probably for the best, though. She was too young to understand any of this. I was thirty, and I could barely get my head around it.

'Same address and phone number as last time?'

'Yes.'

I added all the details and then paused, hand trembling, lips horribly dry. 'Do you have any plans for the rest of the day?'

'You.'

'Excuse me?' I nearly choked on my own breath.

'Um. I mean, would you like to go for a walk, or find somewhere to get a drink or something?'

It was my turn to blink, about 300 times in quick succession.

'Because, obviously, I'm here to see you.'

Up until this moment, if Daniel had asked to meet up, or phoned wanting to talk to me, *my* plan had been to say no. It had been a long, hard slog, trying to deal with the trauma of what had happened with Lucy, on top of my whole life tumbling upside down for the second time in six months. Let alone losing the man I loved, and the child I'd begun to care for like my own daughter.

I didn't want to go over it again, to have to try to explain myself, or beg for forgiveness. I couldn't bear to ever see that look of revulsion on his face again.

I had reached a point where I was starting to be able to live with being me, but it was so tenuous and fragile that I daren't risk slipping back again.

But now he was here. Now he was *smiling* and his arms were stuck in his pockets, not folded angrily forming a barrier between us. Now he was looking at me like he had in the moment he told me he loved me...

'I have three more rooms to clean. But I could go for a walk after that?'

If anything, Daniel's smile grew even wider. 'I'll help you.'

'No, you won't!' Grandma called from where she was clearly hiding round the corner. 'Me and your dad'll sort the rooms. You go off and kiss and make up or whatever it is you need to do. We won't expect you back until nightfall.'

'Well,' Mum retorted, from where she must have been lurking right beside Grandma. 'There is a mountain of breakfast prep still to do, and the back stairs need a proper vacuum...'

'Hi, Wendy, hi, Grandma, nice to... hear you,' Daniel called.

'She's joking!' Grandma called back. 'You go on, now, off you go!'

'I am not joking!'

They were still arguing when we slipped out of the door.

We walked the whole hundred yards or so to the far end of the garden, where I led Daniel to a bench hidden behind a wall of clambering roses.

'I think we should talk before we do anything else,' I said, eyes firmly fixed on the roses.

'Right.' Daniel took in a deep breath. He wasn't smiling any more. 'I have a speech planned, if that's okay?'

I nodded, unable to do anything else.

'I can't really remember it any more, but I'll try to give you the gist... I'm so, massively, overwhelmingly sorry for how I handled everything. I have regretted it every second since you left. I *can't believe* I let you go. You'd been beaten up and scared half to death, and instead of being there for you, I... froze. I can't ever undo not racing to the hospital, I can't ever be there for you when you needed me then, but I can promise to always be there if you ever need me again.'

'Daniel... I think you had every right...'

'No.' He shook his head, vehemently. 'No. What you said was true, I *knew* you. I know you. I was hurt and shocked that you'd hidden all that from me. I'll admit that I was angry, and I felt betrayed. But once you'd gone, and I stopped being such an idiot and actually took a few minutes to think about it, I re-alised that I was angry you'd not told me. That you were going through this huge deal, and hadn't felt able to trust me with it. You didn't tell me because you thought I'd judge you, I'd think less of you and reject you for it. And I proved your fears right, didn't I? I was a terrible boyfriend. I totally let you down in the worst possible way. I'm so sorry.'

'I put you and Hope in danger. You should have been angry.'

'No. Lucy was the danger. I put *you* in danger be-cause you didn't feel like you could tell me.'

'But I was Nora Sharp. I wrote nasty things about people for money.'

'I also read the beautiful, uplifting things that Eleanor Sharpley wrote, remember? And I also read a whole load of Nora's reviews. The ones that people didn't bother to mention, because they're decent and written with integrity. I also read the article you wrote last Saturday.'

'Is that what made you come?'

'It's what made me brave enough to come. If you could do that, admit you'd done some awful things that you regretted, refuse to make excuses for it, and only say that from now on you were determined to do things better, it made me hope that maybe you'd allow me to do the same.'

'I still don't understand why you think you did anything wrong... Daniel, I need to know that you're not trying to shove what I did to one side or sweep it under the carpet. I'm not a perfect person. I'm a long, long way from that. Not least, I have borderline approval addiction. The compulsion to make people like me has caused me to be dishonest with myself, and other people, and while I'm working on it, I can't promise it won't ever happen again. I'm really bad at getting up in the morning and I have a hideous, lumpy scar on the back of my leg.'

Daniel nodded, thoughtfully. 'Okay. You may have noticed that I'm not the most emotionally intelligent of men. I am woefully bad at recognising and dealing with my own feelings, which means I can hurt the people I care about most. I also still push about a wheelbarrow of guilt and shame, and the need to somehow make things up to people who aren't even alive any more. I have a frustrating tendency to try to do everything alone, in some warped need to prove myself to no one who even cares. I bury myself in work to avoid facing up to my problems, and I think that you are the most incredible, wonderful woman I have ever met.' He paused. 'I love you, flaws and failings and all.'

'I love you, too.'

Daniel's eyes sparkled. 'So, perhaps for now we just need to agree that we forgive each other, and accept each other, as we are?'

'That sounds like a good plan,' I replied, my voice so soft I could barely hear it over the buzzing of the motorboats in the distance.

He coughed, scratched the back of his head, and looked up at me from under his brow. 'I don't want to suggest starting again, because we aren't going to gloss over what happened, as if it didn't matter. But I, for one, would very much like to restart what we had. I've had weeks to think about it, though. I understand if you need some time.'

'I don't need any time,' I blurted, in one rush of breath. 'I forgive you for behaving like a perfectly normal, rational person, and if you can honestly forgive me for all the crap I put you through, and for being a famous bitch, then yes please, I would really like to try again.'

The grin was back. He hadn't stopped looking at me, and it sent a flutter of joy through my body that only intensified when he slowly reached out and took hold of my hand. Once he'd wrapped his hand around mine, he gently tugged me across the bench, closer and closer until our lips met. It was a challenging kiss, given the smiling and the laughing and the crying, but still managed to be the loveliest kiss ever.

It wasn't, of course, a simple case of forgive and forget. We talked well into the night, while walking and drinking ice-cold cider and eating fish and chips on the shoreline. We curled up on the sofa in the living room and laid out the whole truth.

We talked about how Hope had grown in the past few weeks. It was her birthday in a few days, and it looked as though she might even be walking by then. Becky had been working flat out running the retreat, absolutely convinced that her business partner simply needed a bit of time.

'How's Alice getting on as Operations Manager?' I asked.

'Good. The Boatman threw her one hell of a leaving do. They got the Bridge Band to play, and the two pubs ended up having a skinny-dipping relay race across the river and back.'

'Who won?'

'Nobody knows. An argument broke out about whether Caris Smith was cheating for using a rubber ring, and next thing we knew the swimmers were being attacked by a flock of geese.'

'Becky said Alice is still with Jase.'

He nodded. 'But Luke said she had a look at Becky's spare room the other day, eyeing it up for size.'

'Maybe I'll give her a ring, tell her how putting off making the right choice only leads to regrets later on.'

'Maybe you should tell her in person.'

'Maybe I should.'

He described how the orchard was now bursting into life, with tomatoes, courgettes and spinach nearly ready for harvesting, and plans taking shape for its first wedding – childhood sweethearts from separate sides who broke off their engagement thirty-four years ago, but never had eyes for anyone else since.

'Well, if they can forgive and forget and go as far as getting married, I'm not sure we have any excuse.' I sat back on the sofa, horrified at my own words. 'Not that I'm... I didn't mean to imply...'

'Was that a proposal?' Daniel pretended to be horrified, but his eyes were dancing.

'No! Oh my goodness, no!' Every inch of my skin had flushed with mortification.

'Good.'

'Yes! Yes, very good. Not to be suggesting that we...'

'I'd quite like to do that myself, if you don't mind. And without Grandma earwigging from the corridor.'

'I'm not earwigging, I was on my way to get a mug

of cocoa!' a croaky voice retorted from the other side of the door.

'Shall we take this conversation somewhere more private?' Daniel lent closer to murmur in my ear, the heat of his proximity doing nothing to ease my blushes.

'Okay,' I whispered back.

'And then, tomorrow, Eleanor Sharpley, will you come home with me?'

A surge of warmth exploded inside me. I think it was joy. Joy, and hope, and the freedom of being known, and loved all the same, while understanding that there is always more to know – some good, some bad – but the one thing that will remain is love.

'I will.'

I was going home.

AUTHOR'S NOTE

I first moved to a Nottinghamshire 'ex-mining village' fifteen years ago, where the proud mining heritage remains an inherent part of the community.

However, it was only when researching this book that I discovered the ongoing impact of the national miners' strike in 1984–5. During the strike, whole towns and villages were split into strikers and the 'scabs' who crossed the picket line.

For some, this divide has never been bridged, and they still avoid certain pubs or shops because 'that's where the scabs went'. At the time, people travelled miles to avoid meeting someone from the 'wrong side' in the supermarket.

Those who went on strike weren't entitled to benefits. Many relied on handouts. Others were reduced to burning shoes in an attempt to heat their houses once all the furniture had gone. Tensions often ran high on the picket lines, resulting in violence and destruction of property. Across the country, 20,000 were injured or taken to hospital, three men died and over 11,000 were arrested.

While the village of Ferrington and all that happened there is a work of fiction, it was inspired by the true story of a mining village in Nottinghamshire that is divided in two by a river. Here, one side went on strike while the other side remained working. In recent years, an award-winning community orchard was established to help bring local people together in creating a place of beauty and peace that will help heal the wounds of the past.

ACKNOWLEDGMENTS

Thanks again to the fabulous team Boldwood for their unfailing support – especially Sarah Ritherdon, who is simply everything I could have asked for in an editor. My wonderful agent, Kiran Kataria continues to consistently go above and beyond in providing timely help and encouragement.

Thanks to Matt Arnold who was willing to chat to a stranger about a range of unexpected and interesting topics, but most importantly community orchards and ex-mining communities. That conversation significantly shaped the whole book.

As always, to everyone who has read my books, taken the time to write a review or get in touch – I'm so very grateful. Knowing you are out there reading and loving my books means more than I can say.

For Ciara, Joseph and Dominic – who never failed to provide my dinners with an honest review. May our home always be the place where you can find peace, love, laughter and an endless supply of food.

And for George – without a doubt, we belong together.

MORE FROM BETH MORAN

We hope you enjoyed reading *We Belong Together*. If you did, please leave a review.

If you'd like to gift a copy, this book is also available as an ebook, digital audio download and audiobook CD.

Sign up to Beth Moran's mailing list for news, competitions and updates on future books.

http://bit.ly/BethMoranNewsletter

Explore more uplifting novels from Beth Moran.

ABOUT THE AUTHOR

Beth Moran is the author of four novels, including the bestselling *Christmas Every Day*. She regularly features on BBC Radio Nottingham and is a trustee of the national women's network Free Range Chicks. She lives on the outskirts of Sherwood Forest.

Visit Beth's website: https://bethmoranauthor.com/

Follow Beth on social media:

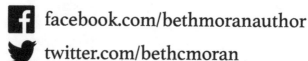

facebook.com/bethmoranauthor

twitter.com/bethcmoran

bookbub.com/authors/beth-moran

ABOUT BOLDWOOD BOOKS

Boldwood Books is a fiction publishing company seeking out the best stories from around the world.

Find out more at www.boldwoodbooks.com

Sign up to the Book and Tonic newsletter for news, offers and competitions from Boldwood Books!

http://www.bit.ly/bookandtonic

We'd love to hear from you, follow us on social media:

facebook.com/BookandTonic

twitter.com/BoldwoodBooks

instagram.com/BookandTonic

9 781802 803457